Send Me Safely Back Again

Adrian Goldsworthy

W F HOWES LTD

This large print edition published in 2012 by
W F Howes Ltd
Unit 4, Rearsby Business Park, Gaddesby Lane,
Rearsby, Leicester LE7 4YH

1 3 5 7 9 10 8 6 4 2

First published in the United Kingdom in 2012
by Weidenfeld & Nicolson

A CIP catalogue record for this book is available
from the British Library

ISBN 978 1 47120 657 3

Typeset by Palimpsest Book Production Limited,
Falkirk, Stirlingshire
Printed and bound in Great Britain
by MPG Books Ltd, Bodmin, Cornwall

MIX
Paper from
responsible sources
FSC
www.fsc.org   FSC® C018575

For Siân

CHAPTER 1

Lieutenant William Hanley of His Britannic Majesty's 106th Regiment of Foot looked down at the great battle unfolding before him and knew that he was not wanted. Far more soldiers than he had ever seen in one place were stretched in a long crescent across the wide plain. There were Spanish regiments in white and brown and blue, and half a mile beyond them the darker masses of the French cavalry and foot. There were far more Spanish soldiers.

Hanley decided to draw. A tall man, he perched on the low stump of a shrivelled vine tree and crossed one leg over the other to rest his sketch pad. Soon his right hand was moving quickly across the page, caressing the paper as he shaded to give depth to the tiny lines of soldiers. The limits of his skill no longer frustrated him as once they had done. Hanley had lived in Madrid for years, studying art in the company of other passionate young men who believed themselves to be creative and despised those who were not. In those days his constant failure to capture on canvas the images in his mind enraged him. Now, he

1

could sketch or paint for the sheer pleasure of the act, the old dream of artistic greatness long gone.

The death of Hanley's father merely confirmed the end of that episode in his life, since his half-brothers had immediately cut the allowance paid to their bastard sibling. Hanley fled the French occupation of Madrid and returned to England with barely a penny to his name. Many years before, when he was just an infant, his father had bought him a commission in the army as a source of income, before such abuses were stamped out. Left with no alternative, Hanley found that he had to become a real soldier. He still found it difficult to see himself as especially martial, and struggled to understand many of his duties, but at least he no longer tortured himself because he was not a great artist. Indeed, his new life made him surprisingly content.

A thought struck him, and he wrote, 'The plains before Medellín, 28th March, 1809' at the top of the page. The picture would be a true record, if nothing else.

A groom glanced at the Englishman and paused as he brushed down a horse with an ornate saddle and lavishly decorated saddlecloth. The man had the very dark skin of an Andalusian, and although he was still young his black hair was streaked with grey and currently covered with dust and loose hair from the white horse. He shook his head in bafflement at the eccentricity of the foreigner.

Hanley nodded amicably to the man and then

turned to look behind him at the redcoat standing watching over their own three mules.

'How is he, Dob?'

'Sleeping like a baby, sir,' replied Corporal Dobson, his battered face creased into a smile.

The loud snore that followed lacked any infant-like quality, but confirmed that Hanley's friend and fellow officer, Ensign Williams, was indeed still asleep. Dobson had fixed his bayonet on to his musket and driven the point into the hard earth. Then he had stretched the shoulders of his greatcoat between its upturned butt and the branch of another stunted vine, giving some shade from the noon sun to the officer as he lay in a shallow hollow to rest. Williams' wide-brimmed straw hat covered his face.

Hanley felt pleasantly warm, for he revelled in the heat and found it hard to remember the snow and bitter cold of three months ago, when the 106th and the rest of the British Army had retreated through the mountains, pursued by Napoleon's army. Their Spanish allies beaten, Sir John Moore's British had run to the sea to take ship and escape. Already the horrors of that march seemed unreal to Hanley.

'Think he's over the worst of it now,' Dobson concluded, snapping Hanley's thoughts back to the present. 'Still tired and weak, but he should be himself again soon. God help us,' he added out of habit, but his expression betrayed his deep fondness for the dozing officer.

Williams was shy, rather pious, and seemed a natural soldier. Hanley was unlike him in almost every respect, and yet they were close friends, although he had to admit that the man had not been congenial company in the last few weeks. With a Welsh father and a Scottish mother, Hamish Williams had cast a profound and most definitely Celtic gloom over all those around him. His mood had not been helped by an attack of dysentery, and the ensign was still weak. The ride to get here had been long and exhausting, bouncing on the uncomfortable saddles of the mules which the alcalde of the small town had sworn were the only available mounts.

Hanley, Williams and Dobson were part of a detachment of their regiment whose ship had been blown back to Portugal instead of returning to England with the rest of the army. The commander in Lisbon had happily employed these additional soldiers, and two weeks ago had sent them into Spain again to secure some supplies left behind in Moore's campaign. Hanley and the others had ridden ahead to the headquarters of the Army of Estremadura to seek assistance in their task.

They arrived to find their Spanish allies advancing to attack Marshal Victor's French Corps, and with a battle to fight the three redcoats had so far not found anyone with time or inclination to deal with them. Hanley did not mind, for he rather suspected that he was witnessing a miracle, for the French were being beaten.

Last summer the Spanish had forced a French army to surrender at Bailen, and the British had beaten the French in Portugal. In the autumn, Napoleon himself crossed the Pyrenees with a quarter of a million of his veterans. One after another the Spanish armies were shattered in ruin, and the British chased away. There were no more victories, even after the Emperor himself went back to France and left the mopping up to his generals. A few months ago it looked as if nothing could stop the French from overrunning all of Spain and Portugal.

Somehow the Spanish armies had recovered, and now one of them was attacking and the outnumbered Marshal Victor was retreating. Hanley could sense the excitement in the men around him. They were mostly grooms, servants and a few junior officers from General Cuesta's staff. The general himself, and everyone of real importance, was off inspecting the battle line. He was expected back soon, and so Hanley and the others waited for him, instead of chasing him around the field on their weary mules.

A group of grooms cheered suddenly as a squadron of French cavalry wheeled about and retreated, throwing up great clouds of dust. The Andalusian noticed Hanley once again, and clearly disapproved of this phlegmatic Englishman who sat and drew pictures when he should have been cheering on the victory. He removed his cheroot to spit on the grass, and then shook his head again.

'*Jesús, María y . . .*'

Hanley could not help smiling when the man stopped halfway through the oath. Patriotic Spaniards were no longer so willing to invoke the name of Joseph, ever since the French Emperor had placed his brother Joseph-Napoleon on the throne of Spain.

The groom thought for a moment. Hanley's Spanish was fluent enough to catch the muttered words. 'And the one who was the father of our Lord on earth. Not the hunchback usurper.' The man spat again, and crossed himself. Pamphleteers depicted the new king as a one-eyed hunchback of monstrous appetite for food, wine and women.

'Looks like their general's coming, sir,' said Dobson. Hanley followed his gaze and noticed a colourful cavalcade of horsemen trotting briskly across the fields towards them, although still a few minutes away.

'Our allies are doing well today. The French are going back everywhere.'

'Aye, sir, they are. But no quicker than they choose to.' The veteran was knocking out the embers from his clay pipe, evidently deciding that the arrival of senior officers of whatever nation required a degree of formality.

It was obviously a common instinct, for there was a bustle of activity among the grooms and servants. Fresh horses were brushed down and their tack quickly inspected. Other men prepared jugs of lemon juice or wine to quench the thirst of the approaching officers. Hanley paid little attention, and instead set down his pad and stood up, pulling at the front of his cocked hat to better shade his eyes. Out on the plain, some French cavalry were advancing.

The British officer extended a heavy telescope. A present from Williams' mother to her son when he enlisted, it was intended to be mounted on a tripod, and it took Hanley a moment to steady the heavy glass. The effort was worthwhile, for the magnification was excellent. He could see the French cavalry in dark uniforms, and when one of the leading squadrons wheeled to alter its line of advance, a row of flickering dots shone off brass helmets. That meant that the cavalry were dragoons. Hanley smiled to himself, for part of him had come to take a delight in the colourful uniforms worn by the different armies, although personally he struggled with the military obsession for neatness.

There was another twinkle of light, repeated by each of the three squadrons behind the first as the men drew their long, straight swords. It suggested a considerable complacency and confidence that the French officers were only at this late stage ordering their men to ready their weapons. The leading squadron began to go faster.

Hanley shifted his gaze a little. A Spanish battery of six cannon was deployed between two regiments of infantry in drab-coats. The French cavalry came closer, going from trot to canter.

Then the guns fired. Hanley was sure he saw tongues of red flame spit from the distant muzzles before all was lost in thick clouds of dirty smoke. The lines of infantry fired a moment later, adding to the dense bank of powder smoke and blotting the French from sight. The range seemed long for muskets, but the drab-coated battalions were not moving and looked steady. Then he saw French dragoons retreating, no longer in neat ranks, but as little knots of individuals.

At that moment the noise of the firing came like the rumbling of an approaching storm. Williams sprang up, suddenly awake, his hat falling to the ground, but then he wrapped his head in Dobson's greatcoat, pulling its sleeves off the branch and musket, and plunging himself into darkness. Muffled cries of alarm and rage came as the ensign fought with the coat, and succeeded only in more tightly entangling himself.

Hanley watched in amusement as his friend struggled. There was chuckling from some of the grooms and servants, and the lieutenant found it infectious until he dropped the telescope and doubled up with laughter. Several of the closest horsemen from the general's staff were watching aghast, but he paid them no attention.

'*Jesús, Maria y Joseph*,' said the Andalusian, too astonished to stop himself from saying the last name.

Williams finally won the battle and flung the coat down. He was breathing heavily, his gaze wild eyed. Then he realised where he was and began to recover. A brief flash of anger at his friend's almost hysterical amusement quickly subsided and he found himself smiling ruefully. He tried to ignore the expressions of amused contempt from the surrounding Spanish, who had only been confirmed in their low opinion of the heretic English.

The ensign cleared his throat. 'Any water, Dob?' he asked.

The veteran proffered his canteen. 'Bad dreams, Mr Williams,' he said softly.

Williams nodded, and then gulped down a good third of the warm, brackish liquid. He cupped his hand, poured in some water and then splashed it on to his face. Handing back the canteen, the ensign ran his hands through his fair hair, smoothing it into some sort of order.

Wrenched from sleep, he had mistaken the cannon fire for thunder and in his mind returned to the horror of the storm almost six weeks earlier. He, Hanley and the others had seen little, entombed below decks in their tiny cabin. They had felt the pitching and rolling of the transport ship growing greater and greater, seen the white flashes, and heard the peals of thunder and the dreadful crack when part of the mainmast was shattered, and suddenly the deck was lurching as if giant hands were flinging the *Corbridge* like a child's toy. It had seemed an age before the violence began to subside. Several soldiers had been injured and one man was dead, his uniform and skin badly scorched, and his bayonet melted just like lead. The smell of cooked meat was sickening.

Williams shook his head to clear the memory. 'I think I shall learn to swim,' he told Hanley, who had at last recovered from his hysteria.

'This seems hardly the place or the time. Although there are the rivers, I suppose.' The plain was flanked on one side by the wide Guadiana and on the other by a tributary. 'However, Billy tells me that many naval men consider that learning to swim is profoundly unlucky.' Their friend Billy Pringle commanded the Grenadier Company of the 106th in which Hanley, Williams and Dobson all served. Pringle's poor eyesight had kept him from following the family tradition of serving in the Royal Navy. Hanley still found it more than a little odd that the army had no objection to such a weakness.

'Easier for him to be complacent. After all, some of us are more naturally buoyant than others.' Williams gave a grin, and that was good to see for it had been rare enough these last weeks. Pringle was a little less tall than Hanley, who in turn lacked an inch or so on Williams, but Billy was a large man, whose girth remained undiminished by the rigours of two campaigns.

'Damn me, if it isn't Mr Williams! We witnessed your dance just now, old fellow. Some local fandango, I presume! And Hanley too. This is a delightful surprise.'

The voice was immediately familiar, if wholly unexpected, and none of them had noticed the approach of the three horsemen from the wider mass of General Cuesta's entourage. Wickham was beaming with every show of sincerity, and clear enjoyment of Williams' recent embarrassing display. Another officer from the 106th, George Wickham, was mounted on a nervous chestnut whose every line proclaimed it to be a thoroughbred. The other horses looked tired, and sweat stained, whereas his gelding seemed barely warmed up. Wickham's cocked hat was high and obviously new, his uniform jacket was bright scarlet and beautifully cut, his tight grey overalls were trimmed with a row of gleaming silver buttons, and his boots were polished to a high sheen. George Wickham looked every inch the fashionable military gentleman. His back was straight, and although not too much beyond average height, he looked taller. His thick brown hair and luxuriant side whiskers only added to his strikingly handsome face and utterly confident demeanour.

Williams loathed the man. He knew Wickham to be a scoundrel and strongly believed that he was a coward. Hartley's feelings were less intense, and he found Wickham pleasant enough company although wholly self-interested. Both of them had assumed that he was in England.

'This is indeed a great surprise, Mr Wickham,' said Hanley.

'Good day to you, Captain Wickham,' added

Williams, who genuinely believed that there was no excuse for discourtesy. Part of him was desperate to ask Wickham for news. They had received no word of the rest of the regiment since they were swept back to the Portuguese coast, and indeed it was more than likely that their own survival was unknown. As far as they could tell the bulk of the fleet had reached Portsmouth without loss, but Williams longed for certain news that the 106th had got home – most of all that their commander, and his wife and daughter, were safe. He loved Miss MacAndrews with a passion that had only grown as the months passed. All his hopes for happiness rested on her, although their last meeting had ended in an angry refusal of his proposal, and he did not know whether those hopes were forever dashed.

'Ah, actually it's Major now,' drawled Wickham complacently. 'My brevet came through at the start of the month, before I left England.' The newly minted major dismissed their automatic congratulations with becoming modesty. 'Gentlemen, may I present some members of my old corps . . .'

One of his companions cut in. 'I am well acquainted with Mr Hanley already, and it is a great pleasure to see you again,' said Ezekiel Baynes, a round-faced, portly civilian, who looked like a cartoon John Bull sprung to life. Ostensibly he was in the wine trade, but many years of commerce in Spain and Portugal had allowed him to be of service to the government. Hanley had met him in the autumn, when army officers able to speak Spanish were in great demand. 'Do you recollect that I mentioned Hanley to you not long ago, Colonel D'Urban?' This was to the third rider, an officer with the laced blue jacket and fur-trimmed pelisse of the light cavalry. The colonel was in his early thirties, with a slim face, long nose and bright eyes that suggested a quick intelligence.

'I am glad to see you, Mr Baynes,' said Hanley with a smile. The merchant was good company, although he suspected that his bluff exterior veiled a mind which was both sharp and probably ruthless.

'This is Ensign Williams, also of our Grenadiers.' Wickham was somewhat put out to have lost his control of the conversation, but made the most of what little was left to him. He considered Williams to be a rather dull lump of a man, lacking accomplishments or notable friends. 'This time last year he was a volunteer in the 106th.' A Gentleman Volunteer was a man who lacked the money to buy an officer's commission or the friends to secure one for him. He served in the ranks, wore the uniform of the ordinary soldiers, but lived with the officers, waiting for battle to create a vacancy. If Wickham had intended to inform his companions that the fair-haired officer was a man of little standing, he failed.

'Promoted for gallantry, no doubt,' said D'Urban enthusiastically. 'Yes, of course, your regiment did splendidly in Portugal. Let me shake your hand,

Mr Williams.' He reached down and took the ensign's hand in a hearty grip.

'You must tell us all about your exploits,' added the genial Baynes, his red face once again radiating honest joy. 'And what brings you to us now?'

There was no chance to answer, as a Spanish officer urged his fine Andalusian mount alongside the three Englishmen. 'Excuse me, your excellencies, but the general is to address his officers. Would you care to follow . . .' He stopped, obviously astonished. 'Guillermo! It is you, isn't it? Holy Mother of God, I'd never have believed it.'

The recognition was not instant. It took Hanley some time to see past the heavily braided white coat, the gold sash and the round hat with its brass plate proclaiming 'Long live Ferdinand VII – Victory or Death!' to recognise Luiz Velarde, one of the circle of artists he had known in Madrid. It was hard to detect much trace of the loose-limbed, shabbily dressed dressed sculptor in this dashing officer. Yet the eyes were the same, and immediately confirmed his recognition, for there was the same mix of quick humour and passion, and yet all the while the sense that the soul behind them was impenetrably veiled.

'Luiz,' he began, but then their mutual surprise and reunion had to wait, for a voice called for silence and all who were able turned to see the general.

It was the first real glimpse Hanley had had of Lieutenant General Don Gregorio García de la

14

Cuesta, and the first thought that struck him was how old the man looked. He wore a powdered wig, which reinforced the impression of a relic of a bygone age. Yet he sat his horse well, and his gorgeously laced and gilt uniform graced a body still straight. For all his years – Hanley guessed that the general was nearer to seventy than sixty – there was the vigour and determination of a much younger man. Advancing years looked to have made the Spanish commander tough rather than frail. His words were positive, delivered in that rapid, deep tone that was so characteristically Spanish. Hanley translated quietly for Williams' benefit, for his friend still understood little of the language. He noticed that Wickham was also paying attention to his explanations.

'Marshal Victor is trapped with his back to the river. There is only the single bridge in Medellín and it will take time for all his guns and men to file across that narrow crossing. So he must fight, and when we beat him his army will have nowhere to go and will be destroyed. The only advantage the French have is in their horsemen. We have a river on either side of us, and they cannot sweep round our flanks. They can only come at us head on and meet our shot and steel.'

The general swept his audience with a fierce, determined glance.

'Honoured gentlemen,' Hanley continued to translate. 'The whole army will continue to attack.' There were enthusiastic murmurs from the senior officers. 'Urge your men on and lead them to victory. God is with us!' A tall priest sat astride a donkey just behind the general, backed by a row of friars. All now bowed their heads in prayer. Many of the officers crossed themselves.

'This is the beginning. When we smash Marshal Victor the road to Madrid will lie open. The atheists will be driven from the sacred soil of Spain and His Most Catholic Majesty Ferdinand VII restored to his rightful throne. The days of revolution and the rule of the mob are over. Spain will be restored. Let us take back what is ours.

'Follow me to victory! For God, Spain and Ferdinand VII!'

'For God, Spain and Ferdinand VII!' The shout resounded as the officers, and even the grooms and servants, cheered. Hanley could not help joining in as the cry was repeated. 'For God, Spain and Ferdinand VII!' The other British officers cheered in their native fashion, although Williams' enthusiasm was muted.

'It is a little peculiar for a commander to explain his intentions at so late a juncture,' he said quietly.

'Perhaps for your army,' said Velarde. Hanley had forgotten – if he had ever known – that he spoke good English. In Madrid they had always spoken in Spanish. 'Not so peculiar for us, and especially for the lieutenant general.'

Neither Williams nor Hanley showed any sign of understanding. Velarde lowered his voice so that they could barely hear him. 'In the last year

Don Gregorio has faced an angry crowd determined to hang him if he did not do what they
wanted, and since then he has led a revolution,
failed, and been a prisoner.

'The cry of "Treason" is a common one these
days, and often fatal.' That at least they knew.
Spanish generals whose untrained and badly
equipped armies had fled from the French had
more than once been lynched by their own men.
'These are dangerous days,' Velarde continued
unnecessarily. 'But today we should win!' His
enthusiastic smile was back.

'I trust your task is not urgent?' asked Colonel
D'Urban, leaning down to speak to Hanley.

'No, sir, we are tasked with recovering stores.'
There was activity all around them. Spanish
officers were changing to fresh mounts and some
were already heading off bearing orders to the
divisions.

'Just the two of you?' said Baynes archly. 'Oh,
and your man, of course,' he added, and Williams
could not help finding a little disturbing the ease
with which everyone had ignored Dobson.

'There are two companies of our battalion
under the command of Captain Pringle, three days'
ride to the north. He sent us down to Badajoz in
case the Spanish authorities there could help us.
Instead they sent us here,' explained Hanley, and
then lowered his voice. 'There was a particular
concern that a magazine of shrapnel shells should
not fall into the wrong hands.' Colonel Shrapnel's

new explosive shell was a secret of the British artillery, used for the first time and with great effect last summer.

D'Urban nodded, and then gave an impish grin. 'Of course, but there will be plenty of time to deal with the matter after we have run Marshal Victor to ground. And in the meantime you fellows can make yourselves useful.

'Wickham, you are the best mounted of all of us on that hunter of yours. Hanley speaks Spanish, so take him with you and go over to the far right. The Duke of Alburquerque's division holds that part of the line. Report to him and observe the fighting. Obviously, do anything you can to assist our gallant allies.'

Major Wickham had arrived the day before, newly attached to the British mission to General Cuesta's army. It baffled D'Urban that a man unable to comprehend more than a few words of Spanish had been chosen for the task. Wickham's French was good, but many senior Spanish officers could not speak the language. Others, like Don Gregorio himself, refused to do so. Wickham's usefulness in other respects was yet to become apparent. He was certainly a personable fellow, and perhaps this was seen as sufficient qualification for his task. More probably, he had powerful friends advancing his career – or perhaps just eager to have him outside the country.

D'Urban tried without much success to dismiss that uncharitable thought. At the least, the man ought to be capable of taking a look at the performance of the Spanish. It was important to judge the mettle of their allies, and see best how Britain could aid their cause.

'Perhaps Major Velarde would accompany you?'

The Spaniard nodded. 'An honour, your excellency.'

'Splendid. Now, Mr Williams, I would like you to go with Mr Baynes and take a look at the left wing, over there, near the River Hortiga. He is only a civilian, and they are rarely safe to be let out on their own, so look after him as if he were a child. Restrain him if he gets any dangerous urges – such as peering down the muzzle of a loaded cannon! Take your man with you. What is your name, Corporal?'

'Dobson, sir.' The veteran had stiffened to attention and barked out the reply.

'You look like you have seen plenty of service.'

'Aye, sir, a good deal.'

'Wonderful. In that case you keep an eye on them both and stop either from doing anything foolish!

'Time to go, gentlemen. I shall remain with the general's staff and go where he goes. I wish you all the joy of the day.' With the slightest flick of his heels, D'Urban set his sturdy cob moving.

Dobson unhitched the reins of their mules from a vine branch and brought the animals over. Hanley's mount bucked and snapped in protest at being forced to stir from rest so soon. The others simply stared mutely, chewing at mouthfuls of thin grass.

The three men were grenadiers, the tallest soldiers in the battalion, and their feet reached almost to the ground when they sat in the rudimentary saddles, legs dangling as there were no stirrups. Their uniforms failed to create a better impression. Both officers wore the same jacket in which they had landed in Portugal last August. Faded by sun and drenched in snow, rain and storm, they were badly frayed and heavily patched. Williams had cut off the long tails of his coat so that at least the patches were red. Purchased in an auction of a dead officer's effects, the coat had never fitted him well, even before his recent illness. The sleeves of Hanley's jacket were sewn up with brown Portuguese cloth. His hat was at least military, but now rose to a low, misshapen crown. Williams' broad-brimmed straw hat shaded his eyes and protected his fair skin from the sun, but little more could be said for it, other than that it was marginally more respectable than his ruined forage cap. His cocked hat had long since been lost. As he sat astride his mule, his bent legs accentuated the almost transparent cotton on the knees of his trousers, showing the skin beneath.

Dobson wore the poorer-quality, duller red coat of the ordinary soldiers, now faded by the sun to a deep brick red. His shako was battered and lacked the white plume marking him as a grenadier. His issue trousers had decayed beyond salvation and been replaced with a pair in dark blue that he had foraged from an unknown source. These were already ragged and sewn up with patches of brown and black cloth. Only his boots were fairly new, well polished, and worn no more than enough to be comfortable. Cut off from the main body of the regiment, and their pay months in arrears, the companies of the 106th stranded by the storm had been unable to re-equip and reclothe themselves fittingly. Only boots had been issued, and they were glad enough to get them, for their existing ones had been worn to destruction in the winter's campaign.

In spite of his worn uniform, the veteran at least cut a proud martial figure. A country lad in his distant youth, he rode the mule comfortably, his well-cleaned and maintained firelock slung over his shoulder. Williams also carried a long arm, but had to keep grabbing at the stock to stop the musket from slipping off as he sat far less confidently on his own mount. He had no sash, and only his sword – a very fine, slightly curved Russian blade – confirmed that he was an officer.

'It makes you proud to be British,' said Ezekiel Baynes, gazing at this reinforcement to the British mission.

CHAPTER 2

Wickham gave the tall horse its head, racing off across the hard earth, hoofs brushing aside the long grass. Hanley guessed that the elegant officer was none too keen on being seen with so inelegant a figure as himself. Velarde barely kept up with the chestnut hunter, and his own mule refused to move any faster than a walk, in spite of repeated efforts to kick or slap it onwards. The two horsemen quickly grew distant. The Spanish officer turned, called an apology and gestured in the direction they were going.

Hanley was sure that he knew the way, until a troop of hussars in sky blue and green thundered past in front of him. They had tall, tapering shakos hung with scarlet sashes to complete a most striking uniform. His mule protested at the noise and movement, and bucked so badly that Hanley almost fell off. One boot touched the ground and he pushed hard on it to shift his weight back up into balance. By the time the cavalry had passed and their dust had cleared, he could no longer see the others. The fields, so flat from the modest height from which he had sketched, rolled more than he expected. He knew that they were to go to the far right of the army, and presumed that the duke and his staff would readily stand out as soon as he was closer.

He headed a little to the left, until he was no more than a couple of hundred yards behind the main line of Spanish infantry. The closest battalion wore white uniforms with red facings. Most had bicorne hats, worn crosswise just like Napoleon himself. They were halted for a moment, but then the drums beat furiously and shouted orders sent the battalion moving forward again. A cannon boomed, and then came a smattering of shots as skirmishers fought their private battles ahead of the main lines. A few men came back, some limping and leaning on their muskets as if they were crutches. Others clutched at roughly bandaged arms or heads. A few men carried others, and he knew that in the 106th they were always ordered to leave the wounded to the aid of the bandsmen assigned to the task. Helping others offered too easy an escape to the timid. Perhaps the Spanish did things differently, he thought, but it was clear that the casualties and their helpers were so far few in number.

As Hanley rode along behind the line, he could see that the Spanish were still going forward at all points. Sometimes there were pauses, but always the men would begin to advance again after a few minutes. The infantrymen cheered as they marched on, and he heard cries of 'Victory or death!', 'Viva Ferdinand VII' and the grimmer 'No quarter!' The Army of Estremadura was advancing. The plan still seemed to be working.

It was the same all along the line, although the colours of the uniforms changed, and he passed regiments still in civilian clothes, and another where there were uniform coats of half a dozen colours. The Spanish infantry fired, cheered and moved forward.

Hanley found the Duke of Alburquerque farther forward than he had expected, attended by a gaggle of colourful staff officers and with an escort formed by another troop of hussars like the ones who had passed him. He heard a call, 'Guillermo!', and spotted Velarde beckoning to him.

'Glad you made it,' came the cheerful greeting. Wickham acknowledged him with a nod, and then they were immediately ushered up to be presented to the duke. Alburquerque was a slim, handsome man with jet-black hair and a ready smile. He clearly liked the English, and via Velarde's translation displayed great admiration for Wickham's thoroughbred.

'Please express my fullest gratitude to His Grace, and say that I believe much is to be admired in Andalusians, preserving as they do the Arabian bloodlines,' said Wickham, visibly relishing his reception by the aristocrat.

The duke was even more delighted to be told that Hanley spoke Spanish, and Wickham enjoyed being associated with this enthusiasm

and for the moment disregarded his fellow officer's attire.

'That is wonderful,' enthused the duke. 'I wish
I had time to learn the language of our allies, but
for the moment there is no time for anything not
needed for the field of Mars. I fear that I am
unable to pay many compliments to your steed.'

'Yes, I fear it is not even worth the name
Rocinante!'

The duke laughed. 'Well, of course, we are close
to La Mancha today, although sadly it is mainly
held by the French. Do you know this country?'

'I travelled a little hereabouts, but for almost two
years I lived in Madrid.'

'Well,' said the duke, 'it is greatly to be hoped
that soon we will all march back there. It is good
to have the English here to watch. Together, we
will drive the invaders forever from Spain. Then
it is up to us to build a better country.' The last
words were added as a low afterthought, and
Hanley could not be sure that he had heard them
precisely.

A cannonball skipped over the infantry battalion
some fifty yards ahead of them and bounced just
short of the group of staff officers. It flicked up a
plume of dust and shattered the front legs of
Hanley's mule. The beast gave a scream of agony
that was almost human as it dropped forward, its
rider sliding over its head to fall against its neck.
Horses whinnied as the other officers managed
somehow to drag them back out of the path of

the shot. The escort troop split like a shoal of minnows frightened by a pike, but no one else was hurt. There was much urging and cursing as the ranks reformed.

Hanley pushed himself up. The poor mule thrashed in agony, and its snapping teeth caught his right sleeve and ripped the patch off the elbow. He tried to spring away, stumbled and rolled into the grass, but at least he was out of reach of the mule's head. His trousers were moist, and he glanced down to see them covered in blood and flecks of shattered bone and flesh.

'Poor Rocinante,' he said, breathing hard.

The duke said something to Velarde and then spurred his horse forward to the infantry line. His staff followed, but the Spanish major beckoned to one of the escort and had the hussar dismount. The man drew a pistol, and efficiently dispatched the crippled mule, before handing the reins of his mount to Hanley.

'Much obliged to you,' said the Englishman, who was still a little shaken. He had forgotten how sudden and appalling the violence of battle could be. The horse was small, no more than fourteen and a half hands, and it was easy to put one foot in the stirrup and swing himself up.

'Now you look more like a gentleman,' suggested Wickham. 'Although not perhaps a gentleman at his very best!' The mule's bite had ripped off a fair chunk of the original scarlet wool of the sleeve to show the white of Hanley's shirt.

A rolling surge of musketry rippled along the front of the Spanish infantry. Hanley and Wickham both turned at the moment another cannonball whipped through the cloud of smoke and this time struck squarely, smashing muskets into matchwood and flesh and bone into bloody ruin. The battalion was six deep, and debris flew and blood sprayed high as one file of six men was cut through by the shot, grazing at waist height. The gunners were getting the range.

'Remember, Hanley, that we are merely observers. This is not our battle, and so duty dictates that we should not get too closely involved. We are to watch and report.' Wickham's speech was steady enough, although he looked a little flushed.

'That is most proper,' said Velarde, and then added in Spanish for Hanley's benefit, 'and I rather think our own officers will manage without your assistance!' The major's face betrayed no trace of sarcasm. Reverting to English once again, he continued, 'You must judge your own position as is fitting, Major Wickham. However, I ought to rejoin the duke and his staff.'

'We shall accompany you.' Wickham's response was automatic, prompted by the fascination of nobility – even foreign nobility – and especially a senior officer and aristocrat who had received him so cordially. Hanley was pleased. Some men were reassuring to be near in battle, and the duke struck him as just such a man. Pringle was another, as was Williams, and indeed Corporal Dobson.

Before they reached the duke, he had bellowed the order to cease fire, and after much repetition by the officers and some blows by the sergeants the battalion had obeyed. With a cheer they charged. There were similar cheers from the regiments on either side as they joined in the attack. They had gone a good quarter of a mile before Hanley and the others caught up with the duke's staff. The commander himself was shouting orders as the battalion's leaders halted and reformed the line.

Hanley saw French guns, limbered up to their teams of four horses, the drivers on the left of each pair whipping the animals to speed them as they retreated. Gunners jogged along on foot beside the carriages. To the left was a battalion column of infantry in very dark blue coats. They did not look much like the French he had seen before, and as he looked more closely he could see that they were wearing tall black helmets.

'Who are they?' he asked.

'The enemy,' said Velarde with a shrug. 'It is good to see you, by the way. There was not the chance to say so earlier.'

'It is a pleasure to see you again.' The two men had known each other tolerably well during his time in Madrid, and had many mutual acquaintances. He would not have described Velarde as a friend. Indeed, he wondered whether any of the self-absorbed, driven young men of his circle had been capable of making true friends with anyone.

Certainly, he had never become as close to any of them as he had so quickly done with Pringle and Williams.

In Madrid they had all argued with each other. He remembered Velarde as an even more fervent and vocal admirer of France's Revolution than he was himself, and as willing to adopt deliberately provocative arguments. The sculptor had never struck him as a likely soldier. Still, he had no doubt that everyone – himself included – had once thought the same about William Hanley.

If Velarde chose to remember a close bond then there seemed no harm in it. 'So, a major?'

'Yes,' replied the Spaniard. 'And after more than six months with the army. I really ought to be at least a colonel by now!' The conversation was in Spanish, and the excluded Wickham quickly preferred to edge his horse closer to the duke, doing his best to exude the ardent enthusiasm of a true ally. There was never any harm in being noticed.

'Obviously a great hero,' said Velarde. 'What would we do without the English?'

The French had withdrawn well beyond musket range. The Spanish batteries were moving forward, but this took time because the heavy gun carriages were drawn by plodding oxen, which had to be goaded into life by their drivers. The infantry lines reformed, and men loaded their muskets. The lucky ones had some water in a bottle or canteen and took the chance to quench their thirst.

Skirmishers on each side kept up a desultory squibbing of charges, but for the moment there was a lull.

'I think they may be Germans,' said Velarde suddenly, nodding in the direction of the dark-coated enemy column when Hanley looked puzzled. 'From Baden, I would guess. We believe that some of General Leval's division has joined Marshal Victor. Leval has Germans and Dutch.' He paused and then gave a grim laugh. 'The whole world seems to have come to Estremadura! Well, they do breed pretty women in these parts.'

'I bow to your greater experience.'

'Not much greater, from what I remember of you, Guillermo. Although one caught you in the end.'

Hanley presumed that he meant Maria Pilar, the dancer he had taken as a lover in Madrid. He had abandoned her when he fled back to England, a decision which still caused him shame, even though he had no longer loved her. Perhaps one day he would confront that guilt, and maybe even meet the girl again, assuming that she had survived the brutal French suppression of the May uprising. For the moment, he did not want to be reminded of his actions, still less to discuss Mapi with Velarde.

He was also intrigued by the Spaniard's remarkably precise knowledge of the French Army, surprising in someone so recently turned soldier, whose manner otherwise conveyed a cavalier approach to his duties.

Hanley looked over to the far right of the Spanish line, where the cavalry secured the flank. In the lead was a straggle of riders on lean, quick horses. Most had green jackets, and all broad-brimmed hats and tall lances, whose points sparkled with light.

'Are those the famous Garrochistas?' he asked. 'The ones whose charge broke the French at Bailén?' In June a French army had been trapped in Andalusia and forced to surrender. It was the first serious check suffered by Napoleon's men for many years. It was also the only major battle won by the Spanish in almost a year of war. Since then there had been only defeat.

'Yes. Their fame spreads as quickly as they can boast. The generous ones concede that there were others at Bailén as well, and that perhaps they helped a little.' Velarde's expression was wooden, reinforcing the heavy sarcasm. 'It is a story people want to believe. Simple cattle herders rushing off to war, and herding the French soldiers as easily as they tamed their bulls. No need for training, no need for proper armies, no need for leaders and governments, no need for money.'

'You have become serious, my friend.' Hanley felt that there was nothing to be lost by behaving as if their companionship was as deep as Velarde believed or pretended.

'My country has been invaded. Is that not a time to be serious?' The Spanish officer spoke quite openly, his tone light, and his conversation attracted no particular attention from those near by. Only Hanley could see the hardness in his eyes. 'We have had three kings in as many months, and more governments and leaders than a man can easily count. Now there is one Central Junta led by "Rey chico" doing its best to control the juntas in each region. That best is not very good.

'The French hang and shoot those who oppose them. Our patriots hang those who do not. Bandits rob and kill whoever they please, and there is no one to stop them. Armies are everywhere, stealing and burning. There are the French, and their German and Italian lackeys. There are Portuguese soldiers on the borders of Leon. And now you British are back, after running away in the winter.'

'We are allies, are we not?' Hanley felt obliged to defend his countrymen.

'Is that why you try to steal Cadiz?'

'I understood that a force was sent to provide a strong garrison so that the city would be secure against any French attack.' Soon after they had reached Lisbon, many of the regiments there had embarked on transport ships bound for Cadiz. It was felt that southern Spain would provide a more defensible base for operations than Portugal. 'Is that not natural assistance from one ally to another?'

'The French came first as allies. Now they have taken our country. Should we trust you?'

'We are not Bonaparte.'

'And he does not hold Gibraltar.' Velarde's quick retort was loud enough to draw attention.

Wickham caught the name, and even if he missed the sense he could not help wondering at his fellow officer's lack of tact in raising such a delicate subject. He held his reins tight, and made his chestnut step back until he was closer to Hanley.

Before he could speak, there was a burst of heavy firing from over on the far left. The French held a low hill – the only feature of any note on the whole wide plain. They had a battery of guns there, backed by infantry, and the challenge of the salvoes was answered by guns and volleys from the Spanish line. From this distance it was hard to see what was happening, but it seemed that they were still making progress, because all the Spanish regiments in sight began to move forward once again. The Duke of Alburquerque ordered his own division to press on, and followed them with his staff. On their flank the lancers led the Spanish horsemen forward to keep pace.

A single squadron of hussars was ahead of the French cavalry. Hanley could see their brown jackets and sky-blue trousers clearly.

'They are the Chamborant Hussars,' said Velarde, noticing the direction of his gaze. 'Is it not curious that they call themselves by their old royalist name, preferring that to the plain number given to them under the Revolution?' The confident assertion was no longer quite so surprising, and yet Hanley remained unsure of its purpose. For all Velarde's vices – and he believed that they were many – he had never suspected the Spaniard of parading his accomplishments or knowledge merely for the sake of it. Presumably, he was hoping to gain something, but the Englishman could not guess at his goal. For the moment, he contented himself with observing the battle, since the other mystery showed no ready solution.

For all his continuing bafflement at so much of the military way, Hanley was now just enough of a soldier to see that the enemy hussars were withdrawing skilfully. The same was true of the rest of the regiment, which lay in support, some two or three hundred yards behind. What was it Dobson had said – 'not going back any quicker than they choose to'. They threw up so much dust that it was hard to see much behind the hussars, but Hanley thought that he glimpsed more cavalry.

One rider stood out from the rest, and even from the gaudily uniformed ADCs surrounding him. Hanley wished that he had Williams' telescope to study the man. Wickham had his own glass to his eye, and his attention was clearly drawn to the same man.

'Wonder who that plucky fellow is?' asked Wickham, in the same tone that he might use to remark on an elegant gentleman or lady promenading. 'Cocked hat and green jacket, and great moustaches. And yes, I do believe that he is smoking a long pipe.'

'That is Lasalle,' said Velarde, in a voice of so little animation or feeling that it was all the more striking.

34

'Can you be sure at this distance?' asked Hanley. The Spanish officer was not even using a telescope.

'No man who was at Medina de Rio Seco will fail to recognise Lasalle.' That battle was one of many Spanish defeats, followed by a brutal pursuit when the French horsemen ruthlessly slaughtered fleeing men.

'Looks a fine, dashing gentleman,' said Wickham, oblivious to the Spaniard's tone and perhaps ignorant of the disastrous battle.

'His family were aristocrats,' said Velarde flatly.

'Ah, you can always tell.' Wickham spoke with the utter conviction of a man who dearly wished that his own blood was noble.

The firing from the far left was even heavier now, audible over the sporadic shots of the skirmishers in this part of the field. Hanley saw few men fall as a result of this, but several riderless horses wandered between the lines, one of them dragging a rider whose foot was trapped in a stirrup, bumping across the ground. There were a few corpses – little bundles of brightly coloured clothes dumped untidily in the grass.

'They're going back again!' said Wickham approvingly. A trumpet sounded, its brass call clear over the bickering of the skirmishers, and the leading squadron of French hussars wheeled about and went back, just as they had done so many times. 'I must congratulate the duke, for I believe that we are about to witness a great victory.'

Hanley felt that the pronouncement was a little premature, but even he sensed that momentum was with the Spanish. They really were winning, the miracle happening before their eyes.

Ahead of them, the Spanish lancers trotted gently forward to occupy the ground abandoned by the enemy. A Spanish battery had just arrived, but the duke ordered his battalions to march without waiting for the guns to deploy. The gunners were told to wait until the line formed again, a little farther forward.

Firing slackened, and they heard cheering from over on the left.

The brown-and-blue hussars halted at another trumpet signal, and wheeled back towards the enemy. Then the trumpeter blew another command and the squadron did not halt, but sent their horses into a trot. Almost as one, the two ranks of sky blue and brown hussars drew their curved sabres.

The Garrochistas seemed to ripple like a sheet in the wind. Some stopped, some clustered together, a few went forward, but more were turning their little horses to the rear.

'The French are fools,' said Wickham. 'They're outnumbered five to one!'

The trumpet sounded again and the French spurred into a canter. Barely four or five strides later they went into a gallop, without waiting for the order. Sabres were held high, points arced forward ready to thrust.

'*Vive l'Empereur!*' The shout came from a hundred parched throats.

The lancers scattered and fled, their horses plunging back into the supporting regiments behind them.

'*Vive l'Empereur!*' The shout was more distant, but powerful, as Lasalle led the remainder of the hussar regiment to join the charge.

The miracle died as the Spanish cavalry collapsed and fled.

CHAPTER 3

Williams was more than two miles away across the great plain and he knew before Hanley that the Army of Estremadura was beaten. For a long time the Spanish made good progress, and he almost began to doubt the instincts which told him that the real battle had scarcely begun. His past experience of the French assured him that they were never so easy to beat. Yet Baynes was a most genial companion, asking a stream of questions and listening with great enthusiasm to the explanations, professing an egregious ignorance of all things military.

'Is that a usual deployment?' the red-faced merchant had asked, as they rode behind a battalion of infantry. The French had given a good deal of ground, falling back to a gentle ridge, and it was taking time for the Spanish line to close with them again. They could see an enemy artillery battery deploying on the higher ground, with infantry forming to protect each flank. Green-coated dragoons were farther back, covering the whole position.

'Not common, perhaps,' replied Williams, 'although a similar formation is included in our drills and no doubt also in the Spanish. In most circumstances the Spanish form in a line of three ranks. It is solid, and allows the first and second ranks to fire their muskets. I am not certain whether the Spanish practice is for the third rank to fire as well. In some armies this is the custom, but in others it is not, and the men either wait to fill casualties or pass forward their loaded muskets to the men ahead of them.'

Baynes was nodding and smiling encouragingly, although it was hard to believe that he did not already know these things. 'And yet I perceive this line to be deeper. There are five – no, six – ranks at least.'

'Yes, it is a line of double the normal thickness, and so six rather than three deep.'

'To what end?' The merchant guided his horse around the corpse of a man dressed in green jacket and grey trousers. His collar and cuffs were black and his belts were buff. His face had the familiar waxy pallor that left them in no doubt that he was dead. Williams had not seen anyone dressed in such a uniform in the Spanish Army, and guessed that the corpse was one of the enemy skirmishers.

'It makes the formation more solid,' he explained. 'In addition the line is less wide, and so it is easier to maintain good dressing – I mean a certain neatness and order about the ranks and files – as it advances. The chief disadvantage is to reduce the number of men able to employ their muskets against the enemy.'

'I see, I see.' Ezekiel Baynes was beaming. 'Yes, that is most clear. And in the circumstances of today, does this strike you as an appropriate formation? I hope I have used the military word correctly.'

'Most exactly,' said Williams, returning the warm smile. 'Yes, I believe it may serve handsomely enough. The French have many cavalry, and young soldiers have a better chance of facing a cavalry charge if they are in deep formation.'

The men of the closest Spanish battalion looked very young indeed, some no more than boys. A few men – mainly the older ones – had white uniform jackets with green front and facings. The rest had no more than white waistcoats.

'And as an old campaigner, what do you think of our allies, Corporal Dobson?' asked Baynes, readily including an ordinary soldier in their conversation.

'They've plenty of pluck, your honour. Good lads, by the look of it, but most of them are still children.' Williams saw the same ungainly movements in many of the Spanish infantry, who held their muskets in a way that looked awkward. 'Could do with a few months of training to make 'em ready.'

'Alas, I am sure that you are right,' conceded Baynes. 'Yet needs must at times like this.'

'Oh, aye, sir, probably can't be helped. Mistake to put everything in the shop window, though,' added Dobson, who had also taken to the friendly merchant. Williams had seen the same thing, but was reluctant to voice open criticism of any general, even one of another nationality.

'Well, I hope I understand selling goods, but confess I am at a loss,' said Baynes, although his look was intent, and Williams half wondered whether his ignorance was feigned.

'There is no reserve,' explained the officer, emboldened to speak by the veteran's frankness. 'If one regiment fails then there are no fresh troops to plug the gap.'

'Then we must pray that none fails.' Baynes was clearly listening, and Williams was sure also comprehending, but nevertheless preserved his infectious optimism.

The French battery opened fire in a rolling salvo. Williams guessed that there were around a dozen guns. The sound was less deep than the full boom of heavy cannon, which suggested lighter pieces, probably those used by the fast-moving horse artillery, and so most likely four-pounders.

'Well, we had better see what is happening,' said Baynes in a jolly tone, and immediately set his horse off at a trot towards the noise. Williams and Dobson followed and the merchant took care not to outstrip their mules. They were heading farther left, towards the higher ground held by the French.

A battalion was advancing at a steady, controlled pace, the soldiers still with their muskets resting on their shoulders in the march position. All wore white jackets, but the facings were a mix of blue, green, red and black. Each man had a tall fur cap, with a richly decorated bag at the back matching the colours of their facings.

'Are these not grenadiers like yourselves?' asked Baynes, betraying the military knowledge Williams had always suspected he possessed. 'The bravest of the brave.'

The Spanish practice was to take the elite companies from their individual regiments and combine them into temporary battalions well suited to leading a charge. The grenadiers' fur caps made them stand out from the rest of the army, but it was their pride that truly set them apart. The men were capable and confident, and simply their bearing marked them out from the raw soldiers in almost all other battalions.

'Good lads,' muttered Dobson.

The French guns fired again. With the range little more than two hundred yards, the gunners were using canister. Each metal tin burst as it left the muzzle, spraying dozens of musket-sized balls in a cone stabbing towards the enemy. At this distance the balls were spreading widely and each shot was lucky to claim two or three victims. Williams watched as a pair of grenadiers were pitched back. The line closed around them and marched on. There was a tall officer at the rear, directing the sergeants, who kept the line steady. He turned for a moment, glancing at the flanking units, and Williams noticed that he wore spectacles. In fact, even from this distance he reminded him of a slimmer version of Pringle, with the same quiet competence.

The battalions on either side of the elite unit wavered as men dropped. The one closest on the left stopped. A man brought his musket down to aim vaguely at the enemy and fired. Another followed, then two more, and in a moment flame and smoke ran along the front of the line. One or two men fell, and Williams suspected they had been hit by balls fired by the rear ranks of their own formation.

A gentle breeze washed over them, bringing smoke and the stink of powder. Williams' eyes smarted and he blinked to clear them. The grenadiers pressed forward, marching steadily.

'Good lads,' said Dobson again.

The battalion to the right of the grenadiers checked, and Williams could see that some men were lowering their muskets. Then General Cuesta and his staff galloped up behind them. Don Gregorio's voice was loud, his manner commanding as he bellowed at the infantry. The battalion started going forward again, although by now it was some way behind the grenadiers.

Again the battery fired. One gun commander must have adjusted for the range badly, because there was a strange whirring noise as a small cloud of balls passed a few feet over Williams' head. Baynes looked up like an excited schoolboy having the time of his life.

'Glad I'm not taller!' he declared happily.

The grenadiers marched on. Most of the gun commanders had aimed well and as the Spanish soldiers went forward they left behind clusters of dead and moaning men, fur caps strewn on the grass and their white uniforms torn and stained red.

Three horsemen sped forward from the general's staff to urge the grenadiers on.

'There he goes, the silly fellow,' said Baynes fondly, for Colonel D'Urban was one of them, charging with his sabre held high and view hallooing in a voice that carried over the noise of battle. General Cuesta led more of his staff over to the battalion on the left, yelling at the soldiers to stop firing and press on.

Williams felt useless. The Spanish officers seemed to have everything under control but it would almost have been better to march forward musket in hand beside the grenadiers than to be a mere spectator.

Baynes obviously sensed his mood and reached over to touch his arm gently. 'You stay with me. Colonels are allowed to play the fool, but the same licence does not extend to ensigns, Mr Williams.'

The French battery fired again and the range was now murderous. Holes were torn all along the front of the battalion, as men were plucked backwards in the first, second and sometimes even third rank. The line seemed to stagger as if it were a live thing.

'Poor sods,' said Dobson.

One of the Spanish staff officers was down, but the man quickly kicked himself free of his dead horse and jogged forward. D'Urban was unscathed. Sergeants yelled at the grenadiers to close ranks. Their officers urged them on, their swords pointing at the enemy, who were now so very close. The battalion recovered as men closed to fill the gaps left by the fallen. At an order muskets dropped down to the charge. The men cheered and the cheer turned into a scream of rage as the grenadiers charged, bayonets reaching out for the gunners who had hurt them so badly.

Perhaps it was instinct, a sudden blur of movement glimpsed out of the corner of the eye, or just blind chance, but Williams turned and saw that the French dragoons were moving forward to threaten the right of the attack. A glance in the other direction showed that the green-coated horsemen were also advancing against the left. Squadron followed squadron and he judged that there were four or five regiments aiming to counter the Spanish attack.

The general realised the threat and, leaving much of his staff to steady the infantry, the old man galloped over to the brigade of cavalry which formed the far left of his own line.

'That's where it will be decided,' said Williams, and without fully knowing why he urged his mule to follow the Spanish commander. Baynes was surprised, for he was still watching the grenadiers surging forward to reach the French guns, D'Urban riding among the leaders.

'Come on, sir,' said Dobson, and he and the merchant went after the ensign.

'Not too close, Mr Williams!' called Baynes. 'You have no duty there.' The three of them halted some hundred yards or so to the side and watched as Cuesta went to inspire his cavalry. Unlike the infantry they were formed in two lines of squadrons. One regiment wore bright yellow jackets and tight yellow breeches with cocked hats worn squarely east-west. Other dragoons were in dark blue. It was the closest Williams had been to the Spanish cavalry, and for all the bright colours there was much to prompt concern. Horses were of all sizes and shapes, and many looked scarcely broken, stirring in the formation, and snapping or kicking at their neighbours. Some of the riders seemed just as inexperienced. A few had no stirrups, or old bridles where the leather was tied together. There were dragoons without high black boots, wearing simple civilian shoes or even barefoot.

The French dragoons were walking their horses forward, their lines silently immaculate. Spanish officers urged their men on, but the commands were often lost in the noise as many of their troopers shouted praise of the king or hurled abuse at the French. The front line of squadrons went forward at a walk, and instantly the lines were ragged as the untrained horses refused to stay in place. Officers raised their swords and then swept them down as the trumpet sounded for the trot.

Their men abruptly halted. Then some began to turn, while others yelled encouragement and tried to persuade their comrades to go forward together. Officers joined in the shouting. The French dragoons kept on at a walk, their straight swords resting on their shoulders.

General Cuesta rode between the two lines of his cavalry, calling out in his deep voice for the men to remember their country and drive the enemy back. Williams could not understand the words, but the force of the man's determination was obvious and for a moment infectious. The leading squadrons began to walk forward again.

Trumpeters, riding grey horses and keeping station just behind the colonel of each French regiment, sounded a new call. The dragoons went faster and the Spanish resurgence died as nervous riders and horses panicked.

Both lines of Spanish horsemen fled. Williams saw the general bawling at them to stop, and then the old man was surrounded by a mass of his own troopers, barging and pushing as the herd ran from danger. The general fell and was lost from sight. Then Williams thought he caught a glimpse of him lying on the ground, beneath the scrimmage of horses.

'Take Mr Baynes to the rear, Dob, and look after him,' said Williams, and swung down from the mule, unslinging his musket. He did not look back, but ran straight towards the spot where the Spanish commander had fallen. Sprinting to a pair of unkempt vine trees, he crouched down behind one and began to load his firelock. Most of the Spanish cavalry were streaming straight back along the river-bank, but some veered to pass near him. The men stared blankly ahead, hunched down in the saddles.

Baynes saw the expression on the veteran's face. 'I can take care of myself, Corporal Dobson.'

'Thank you, sir,' said Dobson with a nod. 'Would you please take care of this for Mr Williams?' He unhooked the long telescope from the mule's harness and handed it across. 'Obliged to you, sir.'

The veteran jumped down and ran after his officer. Baynes shook his head, and then turned his horse and spurred into a canter away from the battle. French dragoons were already among the stragglers of the Spanish cavalry, stabbing at the backs of the fleeing riders.

Williams crouched down, still not quite sure what to do, but happier now that he had a loaded musket. Dobson was expertly charging his own piece as he knelt beside him. The little vines were not enough to conceal them, but as the French dragoons swept past none of them was inclined to trouble much over the huddled redcoats when there were so many mounted enemies to chase. There was too much noise to speak and little need for it. Dobson strongly suspected that the officer had no real idea of what he planned to do and had simply felt an impulse to help.

A yellow-coated cavalryman dropped from his horse, arms flung out to either side, and tumbled on to the ground beside them. Williams dragged the Spanish trooper behind their modest shelter so that he would not be trampled. Blood pooled underneath the wounded man. Dobson looked at the wounded soldier, and then glanced at Williams, and there was no need to say that there was no hope.

They could see little, but then the press of horsemen rushing past and around their sanctuary began to thin, and a little after that the dust started to disperse. Williams guessed that most of the French cavalry would be wheeling to take the Spanish battalions in the flank and roll up the whole line. There was nothing to stop them.

He peered out from behind the branches of the stunted vines. Trumpets sounded as the general's escort squadron arrived at last and charged the French. A whirling melee broke out as they threaded in among the enemy cavalry, blades clattering against blades, and men grunting with effort and screaming in pain as the blue-coated cavalrymen mingled with the dragoons in green. A few riders managed to force their way through the French and headed towards the spot where the general had fallen. Bodies were scattered there and almost all were in Spanish uniform. One was in dark blue, and Williams glimpsed heavy gold lace on the sleeve when it stirred.

The officer tapped the corporal on the arm and the two redcoats emerged from their cover and went cautiously forward. One of the Spanish horsemen fell, a dragoon's sword thrust between his ribs, but the French trooper struggled to free the blade and was quickly hacked from his saddle by another of the Spanish officers. A shot – clearly audible over the cries and metallic clashing of swords – and the Spaniard was staring blankly forward with a neat hole above his right eye. He slumped to the side, hands lifeless, but sword still suspended from the strap around his wrist.

There were some ten skirmishers in the same deep green jacket and buff equipment Williams had seen on the corpse. Tall green plumes with yellow tips decorated their shakos and they had the epaulettes of an elite company.

There were more shots, but the two remaining Spanish officers rode on unscathed. Three French dragoons were walking their horses through the debris of the routed Spanish wing. A sergeant with a red stripe on his sleeves carried a captured standard, its crimson flag hanging lifeless in the still air. It was a trophy that would guarantee praise, reward and promotion, and the dragoon assumed the officers were riding to recapture the symbol of their pride and turned to carry it to safety. The other two Frenchmen stood to cover his escape, their swords ready. By chance their horses were just a yard or two ahead of the fallen Spanish general, who had not stirred again. The skirmishers came on, lured by the prospect of fresh corpses with full pockets, and Williams was relieved that the men who had fired did not bother to reload. No one paid any attention to the two scruffy redcoats, walking slowly on.

There was heavy firing away in the direction of the main line of Spanish infantry, followed by a great, almost unearthly moan unlike anything Williams had ever heard. Then there were screams, individual voices lost, but together joining one long, extended cry. The two Spanish officers reached the French horsemen and now the noise of steel on steel was closer.

Several of the green-uniformed skirmishers knelt down to rifle bodies. One of the fallen Spaniards moved and cried out in pain, but the infantryman ignored his complaints and lifted him so that he could pull off the man's tunic. He laid the man down again with some tenderness, but ignored his scream of agony, and started to run one hand along the seams of the coat, feeling for any coins sewn into the lining.

The NCO leading the skirmishers noticed the two British soldiers. He called out in a language Williams did not understand, but knew was not French.

'Amis!' called Dobson, before the officer could think what to say.

The NCO looked suspicious. He reached back to draw his bayonet from its scabbard and said something to his men. It was awkward to load and aim a musket when the bayonet was fixed, and so most skirmishers preferred not to attach the blade until absolutely necessary. Several of the closest men also drew their own blades. One slung his musket and instead reached for the short sword carried by the French elite companies and known as the *sabre-briquet.*

Dobson stopped, raising his musket so the butt was snug against his shoulder. Then he fired, the noise appallingly loud just beside Williams' ears, and shot the NCO through the throat. The man's unfixed bayonet and musket dropped to the ground and he clutched at his collar as his knees gave way and he slumped forward.

Williams followed the veteran's example. He saw one of the skirmishers pulling back the flint to cock his musket and guessed that the man was loaded and so aimed at him. He made himself wait, hoping to steady the weapon, but then pulled the trigger more strongly than he should have. The powder flared in the pan and an instant later set off the main charge, but by the time the musket slammed back against his shoulder the muzzle was pointing a little down. The ball slapped into the skirmisher's left thigh and the man gasped in pain as he was knocked from his feet.

Dobson was screaming out a challenge as he charged, musket down and bayonet reaching hungrily forward. Williams followed a moment later and wished he had time to draw his sword as he no longer carried a bayonet.

There was a shot, and Williams felt a ball pluck at his sleeve, but there was no pain and he ran on. One of the French dragoons had vivid red blood spreading over the pink front of his green jacket from a great cross-bodied slash. His companion cut suddenly, slicing the fingers off the left hand of one of the Spanish officers. The man hissed in pain, and his horse reared, thrashing its hoofs and forcing the group apart, as he let go of his sabre and grabbed the reins with his right hand. There was time and space for the dragoons to turn and break away, following their sergeant, who could now be sure that his trophy was safe.

Dobson beat aside the thrust of one of the skirmishers and then flicked his bayonet back to jab under the man's ribs, twisting the blade to free it as the man yelled and fell. Williams came against the greenjacket with the short sabre, and brought his musket across his body to parry the slash which carved a notch in the wood. The officer's instincts took over and he kicked the man in the groin before the skirmisher could raise his short sword for another attack. Then Williams reversed his firelock and slammed the butt into the face of the doubled-up greencoat.

Williams ran on. The uninjured Spanish officer cut down at one of the green-uniformed men, but the blow was stopped by his shako and the man simply sagged before pushing away from the ground to run off. Dobson was standing over the general, his bayonet ready, and none of the enemy chose to challenge the large, grim-faced man. The skirmishers retreated, for there would be other bodies to loot. Two of them took the arms of the man wounded in the leg and supported him as they went back.

The man Williams had knocked down rose up on all fours. Blood was streaming from his nose, broken by the blow to his face. The officer slung his musket and lifted the man, giving him a shove in the direction of his friends. 'Clear off,' he said, and then felt a fool for saying such a ridiculous thing.

Thankfully none of the enemy was still loaded and they seemed willing to escape. There were no other enemy infantrymen near by, and he guessed that this file of men had gone far from their supports.

The wounded Spanish officer walked his horse to stand guard facing the French. He hid his pain, and from a distance no one would know that he was incapable of fighting. The other Spaniard dismounted and was crouched down beside the general. Williams joined him as Dobson began reloading.

Don Gregorio de la Cuesta was conscious, but he said nothing and his eyes stared blankly. He was badly bruised, and his almost bald head shone, as his wig had fallen to the ground, but as the Spanish officer gently ran his hand over the general's limbs it seemed that no bones were broken.

'Canteen, Dob,' said Williams, and the veteran looped the strap of his wooden canteen off his shoulder and passed it down. The general managed to swallow a little of the water.

There was a drumming of hoofs and Williams looked up, fearing a new threat, but instead it was a handful of Spanish officers and three troopers from the general's escort. Colonel D'Urban was with them and nodded cheerfully when he saw the redcoats.

'Well done, Williams, well done indeed. And you too, Corporal Dobson. Now we must get him away.'

'What about the French?' asked Williams.

D'Urban's face became grim. 'They are fully occupied killing an army.'

There was one spare horse, and the general was lifted into the saddle, one of the troopers holding him around the waist. Dobson and Williams jogged either side to help support him.

They saw no French for five minutes as they followed the riverbank and the low hollow cutting on the side of the ridge where Hanley had sketched and Williams had slept a few hours ago. A couple of hussars joined them, and as they climbed on to the hill they were amazed to see a few grooms and servants still waiting in place for their masters. The two redcoats were given horses.

Williams turned to look back across the plain before following the others as they began to move off. Three months ago he had watched as a Spanish brigade was caught in a hopeless position and massacred by French cavalry. Now the same thing was happening to an army ten or twenty times the size. Many regiments had dissolved into hordes of fugitives streaming to the rear. Hussars in brown and blue and dragoons and chasseurs in green rode among them, hacking down without mercy.

A few battalions held together. Williams shaded

his eyes to stare at two well-formed squares of men in dark blue.

'The Royal Guard,' said D'Urban, who had come to fetch the ensign. 'Good soldiers, but there is little they can do.' The French were moving up artillery to shatter the squares at close range while the cavalry kept them in the tight, vulnerable formation. 'We must go.'

They saw few French, and as their numbers grew, the enemy pursuers were reluctant to close and went off in search of easier victims. A body of some fifty or so dragoons threatened to do more, but then a line of white-uniformed grenadiers marched up from a hollow and levelled their muskets at the enemy. They were led by the tall, bespectacled officer, who had lost his bearskin cap and had a bloodstained bandage around his forehead.

The French dragoons withdrew. After two miles they saw no enemies at all, and had gathered hundreds of stragglers. No French reached the army's camp, but Baynes was waiting there to greet them. With him was Wickham, sitting on a camp stool, but with the reins of a Spanish trooper's horse looped over his elbow. The man looked pale, and ready to retreat again, but was otherwise unscathed.

Baynes was not his usual genial self. 'I fear there is bad news.' He looked at Wickham, who looked more weary than sad.

'Hanley has fallen,' he said flatly.

CHAPTER 4

Whenever the carriage slowed, Williams felt the heat of the sun and longed for them to be moving quickly again. At speed the wind kept them cool and he was willing to put up with the lurches and jolts as they raced along the better stretches of the rutted track. He clung tightly on to the brim of his straw hat, but could not risk removing the long brown coat and refused to take off his uniform jacket and so wore it underneath. Neither he nor Dobson would be mistaken for spies and risk being hanged or put in front of a firing squad and shot. That was prudence, but Williams also felt an instinctive distaste at the thought of the slightest association with so dishonourable a role.

Wickham was immediately swayed by the sentiment, regretting that he had not expressed it first, and so wore his red coat and overall trousers underneath his black priest's robes. D'Urban did not try to dissuade them. Baynes was obviously amused, and yet showed no sign of offence.

'As you wish,' he had said. Williams now believed that the round-faced merchant was himself partly the spy. 'I suspect it will be most uncomfortable, but I have no wish to tarnish your reputations in any way.'

'Your hope must be in concealment,' added Colonel D'Urban, as the plan was explained in the camp where Cuesta was rallying the broken remnants of his army. A day had passed since the battle and as evening fell they were on the edge of the mountains to the south.

'The French are between us and your detachment under Mr Pringle,' he continued, his slim face keen and earnest. 'Marshal Victor has led most of his regiments down towards Merida, and only a few squadrons of cavalry have followed us. He does not have enough men to occupy the whole area, but there are bound to be patrols and foraging parties. He will not find it easy to feed his men and horses. God knows, General Cuesta has had enough trouble. This was a poor region, even before armies started marching through it and eating everything in sight.'

Baynes took over, feeling that his military colleague was wandering from the main point. 'If you try to go straight to Badajoz and north from there, you will be moving through the heart of the French army. Major Velarde has gone to take a message to your Mr Pringle, telling him to take his men even farther north beyond the Tagus, where you will join him.'

'And what of the stores we were sent to find?' asked Williams.

D'Urban could not decide whether the man was desperately unimaginative or trying to assert a stubborn independence. 'As far as we can tell they were taken on the road to Madrid. Velarde will make more detailed enquiries at Badajoz, and assist in any other way.'

'It is quite possible that the local authorities have already taken or destroyed them,' added Baynes. 'Or the French may have them. That would be regrettable, but you all have an opportunity to perform a great service to our allies and ourselves.'

'Of course, we understand our duty,' said Wickham. 'Although I will regret being unable to assist you here.'

'We shall miss you, of course.' Privately Baynes could see little sign that Wickham had been or could be useful as part of their delegation. 'But this is a task requiring a man of experience and rank.'

Williams loathed the thought of being placed under Wickham's command, but the army never gave a man choice over such things. The latter's account of his flight from the battle and the loss of Hanley sounded plausible enough. In the confusion, there was every chance that a man might fall behind and could not be rescued. His instincts told him that Wickham was hiding something. Williams had hoped to gain a clearer account from Velarde, but the Spanish officer had ridden for Badajoz before there was a chance to see him privately.

'Travelling as part of the household of the Doña Margarita you should be able to pass unmolested by the enemy,' continued Baynes. 'Her late husband was the younger son of the Conde de Madrigal de las Altas Torres, one of the great families of old Castile. The war had already taken both of his two older brothers and made him the heir to the title and the estates.'

Wickham's interest became all the more evident, and he sat straight and eager on the folding camp stool he occupied.

Williams was sceptical. 'Does wealth bring safety even in the middle of a war?'

'It never does any harm,' chuckled Baynes. 'At any time.'

'Doña Margarita's father-in-law is a very old man, as well as a wealthy and influential one,' explained D'Urban. 'His political inclinations remain unclear, but you can be sure that they will carry great weight. So he is courted by all sides, and his family treated well. Doña Margarita carries letters of protection signed by Joseph-Napoleon himself, as well as others bearing the seal of the Duke of Astorga, of General Palafox, and many other men of note in Spain. She can move almost at will throughout the country. A few weeks ago she resided in a family house in Toledo, in spite of the French occupation.'

'Is she safe from marauders?' asked Williams. 'They may not trouble themselves to read any letters.'

'She has her servant, who was an hussar in her husband's regiment,' replied Baynes, pleased at this sign of intelligence amid the suspicion. 'But that is why you will be performing such a service by protecting the lady and that which she carries.'

'The child?' Williams had glimpsed the heavily veiled Spanish aristocrat only from a distance as she climbed down from her carriage and was ushered to a tent. It was clear that she was heavy with child, and that brought back memories of the terrifying hours back in the winter when Dobson's daughter Jenny had given birth in a tumbledown shack. Williams, Jenny and Miss MacAndrews had been cut off when the army retreated. For that night Jane MacAndrews had taken charge, and ordered the nervously clumsy officer outside. To his immense relief the boy was born sound in limb and voice, and the mother survived the ordeal in robust health – so robust, indeed, that she absconded and left the child in the care of the other two. Williams had no idea what had become of Jenny.

'If it proves to be a boy, then the child will be the grandfather's heir,' said Baynes. 'In the case of a girl, then I believe the legal situation is less straightforward. But I did not speak of the babe, for all the joy of new life. In addition the lady's confinement is not expected for several months.'

Williams was relieved. He was also a little puzzled, since the lady looked very large for someone still in the earlier stages of pregnancy.

Yet the relief was by far the stronger emotion, for the suggestion of another delivery terrified him, especially without Miss MacAndrews' reassuringly capable presence. The thought of the girl brought the usual pang. Wickham had confirmed that the rest of the regiment had reached Portsmouth without incident and that Major MacAndrews and his family were safe. He was reluctant to ask more closely, since he strongly suspected that the married Wickham had displayed an unhealthy interest in Jane.

'The Doña Margarita carries something of far greater value for the course of the war,' said Colonel D'Urban. Wickham's arms pressed against the frame of the stool as he listened intently. Baynes and D'Urban exchanged glances.

'She carries news,' said the merchant after a long pause. 'And that can be beyond price.' Wickham's grip slackened and he sagged slightly, sitting again more comfortably.

'The Iberian peninsula is extensive, and much of it mountainous,' D'Urban explained. 'Bonaparte has sent more than two hundred thousand men to occupy it and they operate in half a dozen armies. Much of the time we have little idea of where these are. We may watch those closest to us, although even then mistakes are made. It was believed that Marshal Victor had fewer troops than proved the case.'

Williams doubted that numbers had been the cause of the previous day's disaster. In the end, raw youngsters were sent against hardened veterans and that was all there was to it. Numbers would not have made enough difference unless truly overwhelming. The French were simply better led and better trained.

'We do not know where King Joseph's reserve is stationed and whether he moves to support Victor. Ney is in Galicia – we think – and Mortier perhaps in Leon. Marshal Soult is somewhere in the north, but whether in Spain or Portugal no one knows.'

'Except the poor devils fighting him,' added D'Urban after a moment.

Baynes ignored him, once again feeling his military colleague was wandering from the main point. 'Nor do we know much more about our own side. Many of the local juntas and generals are unable to communicate quickly with the Central Junta at Seville. Some choose not to. As far as we are concerned Aragon and Catalonia might as well be on the moon for all we know of events there.

'How much were you told, my dear Wickham, of the situation in Spain before you left London?'

The elegant officer looked surprised, and took a moment before giving his reply. 'Well, I had been on General Paget's staff and so saw a good deal of the last campaign.'

Yes, but from as safe a distance as you could manage, thought Williams to himself.

'Yet I would say that more recent information was vague,' continued Wickham, speaking the truth, but also aware that the colonel expected him to reply in this way, and he had never been one knowingly to disappoint a superior. 'Indeed, I was told very little. The plans of the Ministry seemed unformed, with a definite desire to assist in the liberation of Spain, but uncertainty over how to achieve this, or whether indeed it was practical at all. Our army will take time to recover from the rigours of the winter. The cavalry in particular.' He added this last comment knowing that the colonel was a light cavalryman himself. 'Very few horses were embarked. However, there are confident hopes that Austria will declare war on Bonaparte.'

Williams had heard such rumours before. He hoped that this time it was true, as a new threat would prevent the French from focusing all their attention on Spain.

Wickham gave an easy smile. 'It was also understood that events might change during my journey, so from the beginning they were wise enough to trust that the members of the British mission to General Cuesta's army were likely to be best informed about the current situation.'

D'Urban snorted at the idea of wisdom in his country's government. 'Well, as you now know, our best is by no means satisfactory. The Spanish are unaware of much that happens, and tell us less than they know.'

'In fairness, Colonel D'Urban,' said Baynes, 'the Spanish often do not tell each other all that they know. And it is not as if we hold no secrets back from them. Your magical shrapnel shells, for instance, Mr Williams.' He stared at the ensign. 'You have come from Lisbon not long ago?' Williams nodded. 'How large a force does General Craddock dispose?'

Williams thought, and Wickham noticed that he had the uncouth habit of pressing his tongue against the inside of his cheek as he did so. 'Well, the bulk of his force was at sea on the expedition to the south. I would guess at some three or four thousand. Perhaps double that if the expedition is included.'

D'Urban nodded. 'A good guess. Yet perhaps it would surprise you to learn that many Spaniards, including a good few of their senior generals and politicians, fervently believe that we have ten times as many in Portugal. And they cannot understand why so strong a force has not marched to the aid of their beleaguered armies.'

Baynes took a deep breath. 'It makes them believe that we have ambitions of our own, and are willing to let Spain's armies bleed to boost our own power. The recent offer of installing the expeditionary force as a garrison of Cadiz was both naively concocted and clumsily made.'

'Many of the Spanish do not trust the British,' concluded D'Urban.

Baynes shrugged. 'Which given our government's habit of fomenting dissent in their American colonies and the enthusiasm of our men of commerce for bullying their way into the most profitable of Spain's markets seems unduly suspicious of them.'

D'Urban ignored his companion's cheerful sarcasm. 'Certain information of what is happening is vital. Much of it will concern the little things – numbers and names of regiments, the quality of roads and bridges or the availability of forage. We need to learn about everything to understand the war and wage it better. Both we and our allies must understand the true strength of the other, and we must be doubly sure of the enemy's dispositions and their intentions.

'The Dona Margarita became caught up in the fight against the French at Saragossa last year. Now she travels speedily and often, in spite of her condition. She carries such knowledge and helps to gather more. Others do the same, and in time they may help us to pierce through the mists and see clearly what on earth is going on. After that, we might stop making such a hash of everything and start winning.'

Williams was a good soldier and Colonel D'Urban a man in authority. When given orders Williams obeyed, but tried to do so shrewdly rather than blindly. That was something he had learnt from Dobson, back when he was still a volunteer and served as the veteran's 'rear rank man' in the company's formation. He was glad that D'Urban and Baynes had explained something of the wider situation, and as they travelled the next day Williams took Dobson into his confidence. The corporal had not been included in the previous night's conference.

The veteran listened without betraying any opinion until the ensign had finished.

'So are we supposed to pass as dagoes, sir?' he asked sceptically. Williams was blond, and both men bigger and thicker set than was common in Spain.

The coach was moving quickly again, bringing its cooling wind at the price of making the two seats on the rear of the carriage far too precarious for safety. Instead Williams and Dobson stood, so that their heads and shoulders looked to the front over the top of the car, and they held on to the rails designed for that purpose. Wickham in his priest's garb travelled inside the carriage as the lady's confessor.

'No, thankfully.' Williams laughed and then coughed as dust from the road caught in his throat. 'The Doña Margarita returned from Mexico last year after many years in the country,' he continued after he had recovered. 'So we are her American servants. What Frenchman is likely to recognise the differences of speech?'

'Yes, sir, very good, sir,' replied Dobson, a master of the old soldier's art of expressing contemptuous disbelief while avoiding punishment. 'And do you reckon any Crapaud with eyes in his head won't spot himself as a soldier?' The veteran jabbed his thumb towards Ramón, the former hussar who drove the carriage. 'Or us for that matter?' Dobson had replaced his shako with a brown felt hat in the broad-brimmed, Spanish style. Their muskets, equipment and Williams' and Wickham's swords were hidden in a box under the carriage. A wide-mouthed blunderbuss was clipped to a notched bar on the roof within Dobson's easy reach and another lay beside the driver. Williams and Dobson each had a heavy horse pistol tucked through their belts, and the officer had another to hand.

'No law against being an old soldier,' said Williams blithely, although without much conviction. It was true, there was simply something about the way a soldier stood that got into the blood.

'No law against getting killed either, sir. That's if the buggers don't try to recruit us.'

'Good promotion prospects in the French Army,' Williams grinned. 'No flogging either.'

'Too much garlic in the food.'

'Then let us hope that we do not meet them.' If he had permitted himself to believe in superstition, Williams would have regretted saying that thought aloud as making it inevitable that it would come true.

An hour before sunset half a dozen chasseurs in green jackets and dust-covered shakos stood their horses on the road ahead of them. Two more closed in on the carriage from each side. Such a fine vehicle was a rare sight. Even more unusual were the six well-matched grey horses drawing the coach. Only the very wealthy could afford horses rather than mules.

Ramón halted the team impeccably, looped the reins over a hook and raised his hands. Williams and Dobson did the same. The grey-haired sergeant in charge of the piquet had a scar running from his right ear to his mouth, gold rings in his ears and looked capable of any villainy.

Wickham leaned out of the window, and in French so rapid that Williams struggled to follow introduced himself as Father O'Hara, priest of the daughter-in-law of the Conde de Madrigal de las Altas Torres, and demanded that they be escorted to his superior officer.

'He's plausible, I'll give him that,' whispered Dobson, who grasped the sense if not the precise meaning of the little speech.

The sergeant was not a man to take unnecessary responsibility if there was an officer close enough to take any blame. Four chasseurs took them down a side track to a walled farm where the main body of the chasseur company was settling for the night. A lieutenant, whose furious desire to grow a bushier moustache continued to be frustrated, at first looked with suspicion at the priest, and at Dobson and Williams with downright hostility.

'They're Americans,' said Wickham, as if that explained everything. 'Ugly, aren't they, although of course all God's children.'

The lieutenant laughed, and began to warm to the charming priest, and was suitably impressed when he saw the pass signed by King Joseph. When the carriage door was opened again and he was

69

presented to the Doña Margarita, he bowed low. She gave him a smile which won his heart. Her mantilla had slipped back a little to show her round, pretty face and the coils of her long black hair fastened up in braids. Although the black dress of mourning was modest, it nevertheless betrayed the line of a full bosom.

Her French was also excellent and completed her overwhelming conquest of the light cavalry officer's admiration. She spoke lightly of the savages of the new world, and presented him with a little leather pouch, decorated with beadwork.

'The women of the tribes make them for the bravest warriors to carry their musket balls,' she explained.

After twenty minutes they left, and were escorted by a dozen chasseurs until they reached the inn two leagues away.

'That lady's a cool one,' said Dobson as the carriage sped along at a good trot. 'Pretty too.'

'And you a newly married man!' joked Williams, who suspected that the veteran was right, although he had yet to enjoy a very clear view of La Doña Margarita. At least her condition ought to prevent any misbehaviour by Wickham.

'Don't mean you stop looking.' Dobson's wife of many years had died at Christmas, crushed underneath the wheels of a wagon during the retreat. For a while the veteran had been shattered. Williams did not see it, but Hanley and Pringle had a haunted look when they told him of what had happened. Yet he recovered, and in the army way had taken a new bride when they were on board ship sailing away from Spain. The new Mrs Dobson was herself the widow of a sergeant, and a very religious and proper woman. It was an unlikely combination, and yet they seemed happy. The veteran had quit drinking on his new wife's insistence. In the past, he had been repeatedly promoted and broken for drunkenness. Pringle had risked raising him to corporal immediately, and Williams suspected that sergeant's rank would soon follow. No man was more capable when sober.

'No, she's a good lass.' Williams assumed Dobson still meant the Spanish aristocrat. 'Wouldn't trust her an inch,' he added. 'Nor our major, of course, or them other two that sent us off.'

'I see no reason to doubt Colonel D'Urban as anything other than a gallant officer,' said the shocked Williams.

'They can be the worst, sir.' The veteran laughed. 'But if this cart is carrying only news then I'm a Dutchman. Look how low it hangs on the springs.'

Williams did not know what to say or think, but experience taught him that the old soldier's suspicions were usually sound.

Dobson looked around at the French cavalrymen riding as escort. He glanced at Williams and then smiled happily. 'Still, I will say it makes a change from marching!'

CHAPTER 5

Hanley had never seen so much death. For as far as he could see in any direction there were bodies. Last May he had fled the massacre in Madrid. In August he fought at Roliça and Vimeiro and had been spattered with the blood, brains and flesh of men ripped to pieces by cannonballs. During the winter's retreat he had seen the frozen corpses lying in the snow, many with trickles of wine still dribbling from their lips from when they had drunk themselves senseless and let the cold claim them.

He had seen nothing on this scale.

'There's Jacques,' said a lean-faced hussar with pigtails on either side of his forehead and his dirty brown hair tied back with a black ribbon. 'He'll not have to worry about finding wine any more.' Four troopers in the brown and sky blue of the Chamborant Hussars escorted the thirty prisoners back across the plains of Medellín. A man in the same uniform lay stretched on the ground with a great stain of almost black blood on his chest. His eyes stared blankly up at the evening sky.

The vultures were the worst. Scruffy, thin, and

more grey than black, they had come from nowhere and now there seemed to be at least one for every corpse. He had never seen so many birds in one place.

A shot rang out as a French infantryman put a ball into the head of a Spaniard whose innards were spilled on the ground by a great slash across his stomach. The man had been moaning softly, and Hanley thought he could see scars on the pinkish intestines where a vulture had pecked and ripped. The Frenchman jabbed at the bird with his bayonet and screamed in rage. The vulture flapped its wings and hopped back a few paces until the man lost interest. The birds were already getting fat. Soon they would be fatter. Half an hour ago a sudden musket shot sent clouds of the carrion fowl into the air. They were no longer so easily frightened.

'Poor Robert. Well, he won't have to flog that dog of a horse any more.' They were passing another man in brown and blue, this one with half his face carried away. His horse stood dutifully beside him, cropping the thin grass as if nothing had happened.

'Take the reins and lead him off,' ordered the corporal of the hussars.

They passed other Frenchmen. 'Looks like Philippe has had his last woman.'

There were far, far more Spanish. The dead lay in every posture. Hanley passed men whose faces remained fixed in a rictus of appalling horror, cut down as they fled. Others lay in clusters, shot or hacked down as they stood in a knot and fought to the end. They passed a battery, whose crews had all died around their four guns. There were the shattered corpses of French infantrymen in a swathe of blue ahead of the position to testify to their stubbornness. French gunners were lifting the dead off barrels and carriages, as they prepared to tow the trophies away.

Blades had done most of the work. Half the prisoners marching with him had wounds to the head and shoulders from the French sabres. So had most of the dead. Severed hands and arms were dotted over the ground. So were heads. They passed half a dozen neatly decapitated men whose necks had been sliced evenly through above the collar.

'That'll be Sergeant Blanchard of the Tenth Chasseurs,' said the lean-faced hussar in a matter-of-fact tone. 'Saw him do the same to the Russians at Friedland. He's a wicked bastard.'

Another trooper looked down approvingly. 'Knows how to use a sabre, though.'

'Use the point, lads, not the edge,' said the corporal out of habit. 'Always the point.'

They moved on, and still there were more corpses in white, brown, grey and blue coats. In Portugal the peasants and the camp followers had stripped the dead within hours. This did not seem to be happening here, and Hanley wondered whether there were simply too many dead or whether the nearest villagers were too terrified to scavenge. Most of the corpses had their pockets turned out. Papers wafted on the air as the breeze scattered precious letters from mothers, and from wives who were now widows, but did not know it.

Hanley felt alone. There were no officers with the group and the Spanish soldiers treated the foreigner with suspicion. They said little to each other, and nothing to him. It made it worse that as an officer he was permitted to keep his sword according to the usual conventions of war. The Spanish soldiers were unsure which side this tall man was on, with his ragged and unfamiliar uniform.

The hussars took them to a much larger group of two hundred or so prisoners, and left them for the infantry to escort. They waited while other parties were brought in. Hanley tried to talk to the dozen or so officers in charge of the captives, but none of the Spaniards had seen him before.

'Long live Napoleon and his invincible troops!' More than half of the prisoners raised the shout when a French colonel trotted past with his escort of a few dragoons. None of the officers joined in the cry, and several looked bitter. The captives were afraid, standing within sight of thousands of dead or dying men dressed in uniforms like their own. They did not know what fate lay in store and were pathetically eager to please their captors.

There were far more dead than prisoners, for in

the first hour the French had not been inclined to accept surrenders. Their doctors did their best to help the wounded, but their own men came first and there were not enough surgeons to cope. Sporadic shots continued to echo across the fields as the suffering were killed quickly. Better that than wait for the vultures.

'I am an English officer. My name is Lieutenant Hanley.' A new party of prisoners straggled in to join the main group and Hanley tried to talk to a man in a light blue coat with a yellow front and the gold epaulettes of an officer.

'My name is O'Donnell and I'm the Pope,' was all the reply he got before the man barged past him. The man had spoken in Spanish and showed no trace of being Irish.

Hanley needed to talk. He was not a man who thrived on solitude, unlike Williams, who seemed to be quite content in a private world of silence when none of his close friends was near. Hanley wished the ensign were here, and then told himself that such a desire was selfish since that would mean that his friend would be a prisoner as well. Pringle would have cheered him up. Billy was always lively company, apart from those occasions when he was paying the price of a night's drinking that was heavy even by his standards.

The English officer stood on the edge of the great huddle of prisoners, and wondered whether he should try to speak to one of the French guards. The folly of confirming the Spaniards' suspicion of him was all that stopped him, and then the guards were shouting at them to move, clubbing with the butts of their muskets at anyone who did not go quickly enough.

'Long live Napoleon and his invincible troops!' Another mounted officer rode past and almost all of the Spanish rank and file took up the cry.

Hanley tried to work out how he had got here, but the memories of the rout were confused. He remembered the lancers and other cavalry fleeing, and the infantry battalions collapsing as the French hussars came from their front and at the same time swept round their flank. Men panicked and fled, and some shouted out 'Treason!' The duke also was shouting, trying to stem the flow, but then all the horses were running back in a wild stampede.

He could remember that Wickham was there beside him, and in the press of horsemen the man's big hunter could not speed away. Velarde disappeared. There were screams and shots all around them, the thunder of so many hoofs pounding across the fields, and the dull, wet thuds of steel sinking into flesh.

Then the press began to thin, but all was confusion, French mixed in with the Spanish and every rider galloping as fast as he could in flight or pursuit. A French hussar was ahead and to his left and he watched helplessly as the man drove the point of his curved sabre into the back of a Spanish officer in a heavily laced blue coat.

Wickham gave the chestnut its head and was streaming away, flicking up clods of earth as he went. Hanley had lost his hat and his horse stumbled, sinking down at the shoulder, but somehow he kept his balance and the beast recovered and was running again. A Spanish dragoon was galloping ahead of him, and the man turned back, aiming a pistol straight at him. There was noise and the creak of leather close behind him, and the dragoon fired, a small cloud of smoke following the flash of flint which flared the powder. The Englishman felt the wind of the ball and heard a cry behind him and glanced back to see a French trooper clutching at his arm.

His horse tightened its muscles and then sprang to clear a fallen animal, and he noticed that it was Wickham's chestnut and that the red-coated officer was sprawled in the grass, pushing himself up on all fours.

Hanley wrenched hard on the reins. His horse protested, snapping at its bit, but turned and came to a halt.

'Come on, old fellow!' he called, and was amazed that his voice sounded so calm and that his choice of words was so banal. He reached out his hand to pull the major up behind him.

Wickham saw him and sprang up, running fast to grasp the offered hand.

Something hit Hanley hard from behind and he was pitched down from the saddle, the wind knocked out of him as he landed badly on his face. There was movement all round him, boots on the ground, and horses rushing. He felt rather than saw his own mount spurred away.

Hanley pushed himself up. His left arm hurt where he had fallen, and he reached with the right to feel his shoulder. There was no wound, no sign of blood, but he was sure a bruise was swelling. Turning, he saw Wickham riding hard to the rear on his horse, and beside him was Velarde in his round hat.

The Englishman winced as he turned back and it was almost too late because a French hussar was bearing down, his arm raised across his body preparing to cut.

'I am an English officer!' he bellowed in fluent French, and just at the last instant the man checked his blow, and the sabre merely flicked across an inch or two above Hanley's dark hair. An officer was following, his wounded horse making it hard for him to keep up the pace. The battle flowed on past them and Hanley was a prisoner.

Hours later he was still a prisoner and feeling lonely and isolated. He guessed that it was his own fault. If he had not stopped for Wickham then no doubt he would have escaped. Williams would be sure to tell him that the major was a scoundrel and not worth such a sacrifice. The thought made him smile, for he knew with absolute certainty that Williams himself would have gone back, for the man was as devout a worshipper of honour as he was of God.

'Long live Napoleon and his invincible troops!'
The cry went up again.

This time the officer was less pleased. 'No, no,'
he cried. 'Long live King Joseph!' The rider was
dressed in a deep blue jacket smothered in gold
decoration at the cuffs, collar and down the front.
Beside him was a man dressed in a brown uniform,
only a little less ornate, and Hanley suspected this
man was Spanish.

'Long live Napoleon and his invincible troops!'
The cry was taken up by more of the prisoners,
including a few of the officers. This time it was a
challenge.

'No, I tell you, long live His Most Catholic
Majesty King Joseph!'

'Long live hunchbacks!' came a muffled cry from
somewhere in the column.

'You, my man.' The rider in brown pointed to
one of the nearest prisoners, a boy of scarcely
sixteen who wore a military waistcoat as his only
uniform. 'I'll give you a silver dollar if you praise
your king.' Listening to his speech, Hanley was
now sure that the rider was Spanish.

'And I'll have you shot if you don't!' said the other
officer, angrily twisting his brown moustache.

'Long live King Joseph,' said the soldier without
any enthusiasm or real understanding. Until two
weeks ago he had never strayed more than a few
miles from a tiny village where no king ever visited.

'Good fellow,' said the man in brown. 'Here is
your dollar.' He tossed the coin down.

The man who called himself O'Donnell whipped out his sword in an instant. 'And here's the true payment of a traitor.' He lunged from beside the young soldier, skewering his throat so that blood jetted down on to the front of his off-white waistcoat.

A French grenadier marching on the edge of the column raised his musket and cocked the weapon, aiming at O'Donnell. The two riders shouted at him to hold his fire.

'That was murder,' said the man in blue. 'If I give the word then the private will shoot you.'

O'Donnell shrugged, but after freeing his sword he lowered it. 'That was discipline,' he said.

'Barbarian.' The Spaniard in brown was shaking his head. 'So speaks the old Spain.'

'Lower your musket, grenadier,' ordered the Frenchman in blue, his gaze never leaving the captured officer. 'Who are you, Sir?'

'Major O'Donnell of the Irlanda Regiment.' Several regiments of men descended from Catholic refugees from Ireland fought in the Spanish Army.

'Be grateful that your king is merciful.' The Spaniard raised his voice. 'His Most Catholic Majesty King Joseph comes to sweep away the corruption and savagery of the old Bourbons and their creatures. Have you forgotten the Prince of Peace and how he lowered Spain to the dust? The King brings the light of justice as well as the sword of retribution.

'I tell you that one day you will all shout his

praises. And on that day you will be free men living in a glorious and strong Spain!'

'Who the hell is this?' The French officer had noticed Hanley in his torn red jacket and the *GR* plate on his sword belt. Before the grenadier could answer Hanley stepped forward.

'My name is William Hanley and I am a British officer, and demand to be treated as such.' After coming back to Spain it was an effort to find the French rather than Spanish words. He suspected Pringle or Williams would have made the speech more confidently.

'Are you indeed? Well, you don't look much.' The French officer seemed more amused than anything else. His Spanish colleague saw an opportunity.

'Is that why you fight?' he almost screamed at the prisoners. 'For the gold of Protestant England? For the heretics who steal our lands? Tell me, where are the dead Englishmen today? They spend the blood of Spain for their own ends, and you are fools enough to let them.'

His rage seemed to be sated for the moment, and his tone became one of gentle reason. 'Join the army of King Joseph. Fight as free men for yourselves, your families and a better Spain. Any officer or man who wishes to enlist may speak to one of the guards. You could soon be free, earning pay and serving your country.'

There was no flood of volunteers, but the man did not seem especially disappointed. As he resumed his pleading, the French officer ordered the sergeant in charge of the guards to find a horse for Hanley. 'The marshal will want to see you,' he explained.

As Hanley rode his third mount of the day the whole situation felt bizarrely unreal. It was almost amusing to think that his being taken off no doubt confirmed the suspicions of his fellow prisoners.

They saw a group of staff officers up ahead, but before they reached them came a clatter of hoofs and harness and they were joined by Lasalle and his ADCs. The staff officers were gaudy, but outshone by their leader. Up close Hanley saw the gold lace on the green pelisse, and the immense baggy red trousers. The hussar general was not an especially big man, but he was an extremely handsome one and exuded a raw power and restless energy. He seemed delighted to meet the captive Englishman, especially since the man was civilised enough to speak French. Again Hanley was oddly reminded of their meetings with Spanish officers earlier in the day.

'Well, my friend, it has been our day rather than yours, I think,' said the hussar. 'Even so it is a joy to meet a brave enemy. I'd offer you my hand, but I am still carrying my sabre.' He winked. 'It never does any harm to show a marshal a bit of blood and gore!'

Hanley liked him instantly, and that seemed absurd, for the same man had only a few hours before led a charge which slaughtered thousands of his allies. As he puzzled with the thought, they reached the marshal and his staff. A succession of French soldiers tossed captured standards at the commander's feet. Most were the big white flags with the royal crest or ragged red cross carried by Spanish infantry, but a few were odd creations of the volunteer units, their dramatic slogans of victory or death now having an ironic touch.

'Thirteen!' he called in cheerful greeting to his light cavalry general. 'And they tell me over a score of cannon!'

'Himself will be pleased, then,' said Lasalle with great nonchalance, and raised his bloody sabre in salute, prompting just the surprise and admiration he had anticipated.

'Orders have arrived, my dear Antoine, from Himself no less. He wants you with him in Austria.'

'Good, there is little glory in this damned country.'

'Except today.' The marshal obviously liked his general.

'Yes, and a few others. I'll be happier giving the kaiserliks a good kicking. That's a clean war.'

Marshal Victor, the Duke of Belluno, wished that he too was going back to the great battles fought under the Emperor's eye, but could not confess such a sentiment. 'Have we a count of prisoners?' he asked an aide instead.

'One thousand at least, probably two thousand when they have all come in.'

'We killed four or five times as many,' said

Lasalle as if speaking of a day's hunting. 'My boys were in a right mood because of that ambush at Miajadas. Oh, by the way, you can add one Englishman to the tally of prisoners. He's tall, so you can count him as two if you like!'

Hanley was ushered forward.

'This is Lieutenant Hanley,' said Lasalle.

'Well, even though enemies there is no reason we cannot be courteous. It is good to meet you, and even better surrounded by the spoils of victory.' The marshal had traces of a once strong accent, which Hanley could not quite place. 'I am sorry if that appears discourteous. Haven't fought you English since Toulon back in '93. Chased you away then as well.'

'We keep coming back, though,' Hanley replied, surprised at his own nerve, but it was difficult not to like these men. For many years he had admired all things French and thrilled at the thought of the Revolution and the new society it brought. The marshal was obviously a man of humble origins, and yet here he was a duke and the leader of a great army. Lasalle was a nobleman, but in the Revolutionary days that was a hindrance – sometimes a death sentence – rather than a blessing. These men had got where they were through talent, and that seemed just. It was a pity those talents were for war and destruction, but Hanley, the penniless, unwanted bastard son of a banker, wanted a world where merit counted for more than anything else.

There was much for the marshal and senior officers to do, and Hanley quickly found himself on the fringes of things, waiting for someone to remember his existence. A wild thought of grabbing one of the horses and galloping to freedom came and went almost as swiftly. He did not even know in which direction the Spanish Army had gone. It was odd to think that he was so warmly received by his enemies and obviously distrusted by his allies.

Then there was Velarde. Hanley was still trying to understand what the man wanted. He was almost sure that it had been the Spanish major who tipped him from his horse, but that made no sense. Why would the Spaniard want him dead? Or did he want him captured?

'Ah, Hanley, I thought it was you as soon as you were brought in, and then they said your name. How are you, my friend?' The speaker was a short and plump man who nevertheless looked elegant in his French-style white jacket with its green front, collar and cuffs. He wore a cocked hat with a tall white and red plume, but then he plucked it off his head in greeting and the setting sun shone off his almost bald head.

'Espinosa!' said Hanley, and for some reason was less astonished than he felt he ought to be. For the second time in the same day, his old life in Madrid reached out once more to claim him.

CHAPTER 6

'Your shading is too heavy, as ever.'

Hanley did not bother to turn around. 'You always mix your colours too brightly. And your nymphs look fat and drunk.'

'The best kind,' said José-Maria Espinosa. 'Bacchus would approve.' He leaned closer, looking over Hanley's shoulder as the Englishman sat cross-legged beside the wall of the bridge and sketched.

'Did no one ever tell you that it is the height of bad manners to watch an artist at work?' Hanley still did not look back.

'Genius grants considerable licence.'

'You must remember this day, Chasseur Lebeque,' said Hanley to the French light infantryman who was acting as his guard this afternoon. 'For it seems we are in the presence of genius.'

'Very good, sir. I'll write and tell my mother all about it.' Lebeque had taken off his shoes and gaiters and was sitting on the parapet, with his legs dangling over the swollen waters of the Guadiana. He had bent a piece of wire into a hook, tied it to a string and lowered the line into the river.

'Caught anything yet?' asked Hanley.

'No, thank God. I hate fish.' Lebeque was a conscript, making his best of the army. This afternoon was dull, but at least that meant no one was making him work. The lad had told Hanley that he was eighteen. With his small body and smooth, olive-skinned face he looked much younger. 'That's why I like to catch the little sods, just to teach 'em.'

Espinosa's French was as good or better than Hanley's, but he ignored the exchange and continued to speak in Spanish. He gestured at the sketch of the marching regiments. 'I am surprised you haven't turned them into legionaries.'

Hanley was sketching the columns of French soldiers marching across the long Roman bridge into Merida. As they came on to the crossing sergeants bellowed at the men to straighten their shoulders and march to the beat of the drums and look like the Emperor's finest when they stepped into the town. In truth he had wondered about turning the billowing greatcoats the men wore into the cloaks of Augustus's soldiers.

'Might just as well record the new conqueror as the old,' said Hanley, and for the first time he turned to look at Espinosa. It was three days after the battle and the Spaniard no longer wore uniform. Instead he was all in black, save for the white silk stockings and the brass buckles on his shoes. There had always been something very neat and controlled about José-Maria Espinosa.

'You look like a lawyer,' said the Englishman. 'I was not aware that such a profession encouraged genius.' Espinosa had dabbled in many things in the years in Madrid. He painted a little, wrote verse and satirical plays, but always talked more than he produced. Hanley mainly remembered the man's acidic wit.

'Genius flourishes by its very nature, wherever it chooses,' the Spaniard replied airily. 'But no, Sotero is the lawyer. He goes around telling everyone of the wonders of our new king.' Hanley wondered whether Sotero was the man he had seen trying to persuade the prisoners to join King Joseph's army.

'And you?'

'I spread enlightenment in a dark world.'

'That must keep you busy,' replied Hanley, going back to his sketch. The infantry regiment had passed and a long line of artillery caissons was following. He worked in silence for five minutes, knowing that every stroke he made had become clumsy because he was being observed.

'I believe your calculations are wrong,' said Espinosa at last.

Hanley had written several columns of numbers on the open top right corner of the page, beginning with '60 arches'. Then, after a few rough guesses on the length of the bridge, he had begun noting down the number of each French regiment to pass by, their strength, and the number of cannon following them. He was not sure whether he would ever find such information useful, but it had made him feel as if he was doing something. His French captors had shown no interest in him during the last few days, and he had not seen Espinosa since their brief meeting on the evening of the battle. Hanley was given a good deal of freedom, but had the strange sense of waiting for something without knowing what it was.

'I believe the three arches near the centre are medieval,' he said.

Espinosa took off his round hat and passed a hand over the smooth top of his head. 'Crude work,' he said. 'So very obvious.'

'Well, I am not a genius.'

'You hear him, soldier?' said Espinosa, switching for the first time to French. 'It seems our friend is not a great artist after all.'

'Sorry to hear that, sir,' replied Lebeque, staring fixedly down at the river. A month ago he had seen the body of a friend sawn in half by peasants and was not inclined to like any Spaniard. Nor was he that keen on civilians, much as he longed to be one himself.

'You spoke of enlightenment?' Hanley sensed the discomfort of the light infantryman, and liked the cheery young fellow enough to continue speaking Spanish.

'Indeed, yes,' said Espinosa. 'The knowledge of science and the wisdom of philosophy. Joseph-Napoleon brings all of these things to a new and better Spain. He is a learned and intelligent man, gentler of soul than his brother. I am sure that you will like him.'

'Well, should he care to call on me when I am returned to my prison cell . . .' In truth Hanley was billeted in a modest and clean room near the ruins of the old Moorish citadel in the town.

'No need. You are coming with me to Madrid.'

Hanley said nothing, although he could not conceal his surprise.

'Are you not going to ask why?' asked Espinosa.

'A prisoner is not entitled to such questions.'

'Asking questions is the beginning of wisdom. Have you really become so much the soldier to forget that and merely submit to orders?'

Hanley shrugged.

'Perhaps you are confident that the King simply wants a mediocre artist brought to him?' Espinosa laughed at his own joke. 'This really is a compliment. We have need of clever men, men of reason and letters to build a new Spain and a new world.'

'We?'

'The forces of progress. Or did you think I mocked Godoy and the Bourbons, and yet had nothing better to offer?'

'You prefer the invaders?' Hanley stared at Espinosa's face, struggling to know how much the man genuinely believed.

'I prefer what is right. I prefer a state when knowledge triumphs over ignorance, and where ability counts for more than family or inherited wealth. And I can remember you speaking of such things with fire in your eye.'

'And no doubt wine in my belly,' said Hanley a little wearily. 'I said many things.' Ideas had always thrilled him, but had rarely imposed any fixed beliefs or great consistency. 'But then I had not just seen thousands of my countrymen cut down.'

'More than once I have heard you say that the truly enlightened man knows no country, only the truth and the lust for making a better world.' The words sounded treacherously familiar, and Hanley still liked the sound of them, even if he had never worried too much about their meaning.

'Look at that,' Espinosa continued, and he waved his arm at the walls of Merida. 'Eighteen hundred years ago the Emperor Augustus settled his veteran soldiers here as farmers and they took local women as their wives. They built a bridge that we still walk on today and which will no doubt still be here when all the ones made in the last fifty years have crumbled into ruin.

'What was here before the Romans? Would you prefer Viriathus to the Caesars? Yes, the Romans came as conquerors and killed many. Many more Spaniards joined them. They became Romans, they lived in fine houses and read Virgil and Homer. There were senators from Spain, and eventually even emperors!'

'Both of whom showed a marked preference for boys rather than women,' said Hanley. He was used to the immense pride so many Spaniards took in the great and 'Spanish' emperors Trajan and Hadrian. The pair's embarrassing homosexuality was rarely mentioned.

Espinosa ignored the provocation, and the way he continued made Hanley wonder whether the speech was rehearsed rather than genuine. The Englishman felt like a student listening to one of his duller teachers drone on.

'Bonaparte is making a new Rome,' declared Espinosa. 'You cannot win when you fight him, any more than you could resist the consuls of Rome or the Caesars. The French have beaten the world. Can Spain hope to hold out against the power of the united world? Can Portugal? The English will make peace or watch as their power dwindles. To fight against the French is hopeless.'

Espinosa's enthusiasm had raised the pitch of his voice until he was almost shouting over the trundling wheels, creaking harness and echoing hoofs of the passing artillery. 'Yet you can join them and share in the great new civilisation being built. That is the path of progress. That is the chance for a man to be judged and rewarded according to his merit!'

For a moment Espinosa switched back to French. 'Return to your fishing, soldier.' Lebeque had been staring open mouthed.

'Very good, sir.' The light infantryman turned back to the river, for he had been long enough a soldier to know when to mind his own business.

'Do you honestly believe all that?' asked Hanley, genuinely curious, and as always unsure what to say after someone had made so passionate an outburst.

'I believe the truth, and I do my best to see it,' said Espinosa. 'But tell me, now that you are a soldier, do you risk your life for King George and all the milords in London? Men you have so often scorned?'

Hanley did not really know. He had become a soldier because there seemed no alternative apart from utter penury. Once a soldier there did not seem any choice other than to fight whenever he was told to fight.

'I fight to free Spain.' That was true enough, although he guessed that he would have behaved no differently if the 106th had been sent some-where else. He suspected that what mattered most to him now was his friends.

Espinosa was pleased with the answer. 'So do I, as a true liberal.'

'Oh,' said Hanley, pretending the thought had just occurred to him. 'I saw Velarde with the Army of Estremadura.'

'Luiz?' Espinosa's tone suggested mild surprise, but no great interest. 'That would be like him. The man was always a fool and a pig. It seemed so very fitting that he had so little skill as an artist. Any more would have been offensive in so ordinary a man.'

Hanley felt that the contempt was only half

sincere. Espinosa was still acting, playing the part of the pompous convert to the new regime. The only puzzle was why.

They left the next morning, riding back across the same long bridge in the hour just before dawn, escorted by a squadron of German cavalry from Westphalia, dressed in green like the French chasseurs, but with a black leather helmet with a tall crest and decorations in dull brass. Now and again Espinosa would ride beside Hanley, holding forth on the glories of the new regime. 'Look how these Germans fight for Bonaparte and receive their reward.'

On the second day the Westphalians returned to Merida and Hanley and Espinosa joined a column made up from detachments of all of the cavalry in Marshal Victor's army – dragoons, chasseurs and hussars in their colourful uniforms. They were going back to their depots to form new squadrons to reinforce their regiments. Their mood was light, for the prospect of leaving Spain even for a while lifted their hearts. Spirits soared even higher on the next day when Lasalle and his staff joined them.

'Ah, my Englishman, it is a joy to see you again.' The hussar general took Hanley by the hand and appeared genuinely delighted to encounter him. 'Come, you must dine with my officers tonight.'

Espinosa was not invited, and Lasalle barely acknowledged the man. 'No soldier,' he said quietly to Hanley. At the start of the evening the general was in high spirits. Entertainment was prepared for his ADCs and officers in what was clearly a well-practised drill for him. By the time they arrived at the inn the food was almost ready, long tables laid in the main room, and the serried ranks of wine, brandy and champagne awaiting their onslaught. So were half a dozen women, better dressed and more polished than the whores normally to be expected in a coaching inn.

'The general likes his officers to live in a proper style,' explained an ADC with sabre scars on his cheek and forehead and a carefully waxed moustache. 'I made arrangements with an establishment in Madrid for the women and they were sent here to wait for us. One is French and a couple are Italians so we are assured of civilised company. I'm not sure about the blonde, as I haven't seen her before.' A woman in a pale pink dress with a plunging neckline had a mound of dyed golden hair piled high on top of her head. 'Pretty, though, if you like them pale.'

Lasalle placed Hanley beside him at the table. The wine flowed freely, and Hanley found his glass refilled almost as soon as he set it down. The general drank much less than his officers, but even so remained in the highest of spirits.

'I'm going to Paris to see my family and give my wife another baby. Then off to Vienna to a decent war against the Austrians. They are brave men who fight cleanly. Best of all we always beat them! Now drink with me a toast to the women of Vienna!'

Hanley found the spirit infectious. It was like being surrounded by a horde of bounding puppies, brimming over with excitement and joy.

'Who has my heart?' called out the general as the main courses were complete.

'Your wife!' chorused his officers in what was obviously a familiar ritual.

'My blood?'

'The Emperor!'

'My life.'

'Honour!'

Officers began to disappear in turn upstairs, taking one of the women with them. Others began to drink even more heavily, or lit their pipes and smoked. Lasalle stayed with Hanley, a captain of the 2^{ieme} Hussars and the scarred ADC sitting around the table. They played cards, gambling with piles of dollars the general had generously provided.

'Go and have fun, Robert,' Lasalle said to his ADC. 'You're having no luck tonight.' The general had just won again.

'I'll try another hand, sir. Plenty of time for the battlefield of Venus later on.'

'How old are you, Mr Hanley?' asked the hussar captain.

'Twenty-four.'

'You should be more than a lieutenant by now,' said the hussar. 'You should have been born a Frenchman!'

'Everyone should have been born a Frenchman,' said Lasalle. 'Although then we would have no one to fight and life would scarcely be worth living. How could you enjoy peace without war?'

'But do we need hate to know love?' Hanley suggested. He had already drunk far more wine than was his habit and thought was beginning to become an effort.

One of the girls came past, supporting a chasseur lieutenant who was struggling to walk. It was the blonde in the pink dress. She let the man slump into a chair, bending down to lower him with her back to the scarred ADC. The temptation proved too much.

'I know love!' he yelled, and both hands grabbed the woman's bottom through her flimsy dress.

She screamed, turning round in outrage that was more than half serious.

'Saucy bugger!' she yelled, and Hanley wondered why she spoke in English. There was something vaguely familiar about the girl's face as she glared at the ADC and slapped him with just enough vigour to arouse him even more by joining the game.

'Go, Robert,' said the general, and the ADC almost sprang to his feet, and then grabbed the blonde and lifted her in his arms. She stared at Hanley for a moment as she was borne away, and his fuzzy thoughts tried to pierce the heavy powder and dyed hair, but could not.

'I wish I was so young,' said the general. 'To be

twenty-four again like you, Englishman – or younger still like Robert.'

'I have always wanted to be older,' said Hanley. 'To be experienced and wise.'

'Hussars need to be clever, not wise,' said the captain, and the general nodded.

'Winning the experience is a greater joy than having it,' he said with an overwhelming melancholy. Hanley did not think that the general had drunk enough for this to be the brandy talking.

'I should be dead,' said Lasalle. 'So many times I should be dead. A man should not live as I live and survive so long.'

'A hussar who isn't dead by thirty is a *jean-foutre*,' said the captain in a tone that suggested a quote. Seeing Hanley's puzzlement, he added, 'A nothing, a scoundrel, a pile of horse dung, but worse than all of those.'

Lasalle drew deeply on his immense pipe. 'Yes, I said that, and have tried to live up to it.'

'I am twenty-nine.' The captain's words were solemn.

Lasalle blew out a cloud of smoke. 'And I shall be thirty-four come summer. My luck should already have run out.'

'A man makes his own luck,' suggested Hanley, his mind too clouded to come up with anything original. In truth he was finding the sombre tone deeply oppressive. Penniless, he was now a prisoner too, cut off from his friends and facing what might be years of captivity. Then there was the strange purpose of Espinosa. He drank from his refilled brandy glass.

They were sitting in silence when the ADC returned.

'You need to learn patience, my boy,' said the general with just a hint of his earlier liveliness.

'I knew I shouldn't have left,' muttered Robert under his breath so that Hanley barely caught the words. 'Go with her, Englishmen,' he said loudly. 'You may disappoint after a Frenchman, but she knows her business. Take him, *cherie*.' His hand darted back and pinched the blonde again. She yelped, hissed a string of Spanish, French and English oaths at him, but then dutifully put her arm around Hanley's shoulder and began to lift him. He stood unsteadily. As they climbed slowly up the stairs, he glanced back over his shoulder and saw the ADC with the landlord, supervising a couple of the inn's staff who were hanging a big mirror back up on the wall.

'General!' shouted the ADC. 'You must show us again!' The officers bellowed their approval.

Lasalle's face changed, the desire to entertain his officers wrenching him from his own thoughts. 'Gaston, my pistols,' he called, and turned to find his orderly holding the weapons ready. 'Robert, set up the glasses.'

Hanley stopped the girl, and made her wait. One of her hands began to smooth his chest in a way that was soon taking more and more of his attention, but he was still curious to see what was about to happen.

Empty glasses were lined up on a bench lifted on top of one of the tables. Lasalle stood with his back to them at the far end of the room, looking into the mirror. He raised a pistol in his left hand and then rested the barrel pointing back over his shoulder and took aim.

The bang resounded through the room as the pistol sparked and the first glass shattered into fragments.

The officers cheered, and the general was handed his second pistol.

'He's a mad 'un,' said the girl, and Hanley was no longer capable of puzzling that she spoke English.

They walked on up the stairs and came to a door that lay ajar. Another shot rang out and there were more cheers. Hanley's body now demanded that he give attention to the girl and he began a clumsy fumble.

'Wait a minute, Mr Hanley,' she said. 'We're nearly there.'

They went into the room, and he sank down on to the bed. His energy was fading, but he grabbed the blonde around the waist and tried to wrestle her down.

She slipped from his grasp and took a glass from the table. 'Here, have this. It'll do you good.' He did as he was told. It tasted bitter, and then he flung the glass down and pulled the girl on top of him in spite of a squeal of protest.

In moments he was asleep, snoring loudly, and one arm flopped out of the bed on to the floor. The blonde disentangled herself, pulled at her dress to cover her bosom once again and refastened the buttons his eager hands had undone. She got up and stared down at him for a while, a thoughtful expression on her face.

'Pity,' said Jenny Dobson, and then managed to shift his dead weight enough so that there was sufficient of the bed for her to sleep. Half an hour would be about right before she should reappear and meet her next client.

CHAPTER 7

By the fourth day, Williams' frame ached from the jolting of the carriage and his skin itched from the bites of the lice infesting his clothing. Apart from one night at Cáceres, they stayed at rustic coaching inns. There was always a good room for the Doña Margarita, and a smaller but decent one for Wickham the confessor. The aristocrat brought her own linen with her to ensure a clean bed and Ramón strictly supervised the inn's maids to ensure the lady's bed was decently made.

He and the other 'servants' found space in the stables on dirty straw alive with vermin, and surrounded by the horses, mules and the other folk unable to afford or demand a room. Williams and Dobson slept in their clothes, both because it was still cold during the nights and to keep their red jackets concealed. Apart from that, it would, as Dobson said, 'Stop any thieving hound from making off with them.'

They made good progress, and the Doña Margarita's fine name and even finer letters of recommendation carried them through every check. Each French officer they met was treated to a warm smile, elegant flattery and the gift of another Indian purse.

'A man in the market at Seville makes them,' the lady replied when Williams heard Wickham express surprise that she carried so many mementoes of her years in the New World.

'Smart girl, as I said,' whispered Dobson to the ensign.

They overheard little conversation from the inside of the carriage. Sometimes this was because the noise of the wheels and creaks of the springs and harness muffled the sound, but more often it was simply that there was no talk. La Doña Margarita appeared to prefer silence. At the beginning Wickham had constantly attempted to strike up a conversation, but his persistence met with little encouragement and no real success. Williams had no opportunity at all to converse with the lady, and indeed rarely saw her, since he was on the far side of the carriage. At night, the Doña Margarita pulled her thickly laced mantilla down over her face before leaving the carriage. After all these days, Williams doubted that he could have picked her face out in a crowd. There was a distinctive badge sewn on to the sleeve of her black travelling dress, which had an embroidered figure of the Madonna surrounded by a wreath.

'Saragossa,' said Ramón the driver, as if that explained everything. 'We were there in the siege.' He spoke slowly and haltingly in English, although

Williams suspected that he concealed a better knowledge of the language. 'A big fire in the hospital. My lady go in. She pull out *tres*. All alive, but she burn her arms. My poor lady. Very brave.'

They got no more from him, and the servant was otherwise as resolutely silent as the mistress. Williams had heard a little of the heroines of Saragossa, who had helped the city repel the French last year. The most famous was Augustina, whose lover had fallen, but who nevertheless fired the cannon he had loaded and so shattered a French attack. Ramón's story made Williams regret all the more the lack of opportunity to converse with so brave a lady.

At dawn on the fifth day they crossed the Tagus by ferry – the signature and seal of King Joseph once again speeding their way. Then they went north-west along a good road, which ate up the miles.

Williams struggled to maintain his sense of where they were. He wondered about Pringle and the detachment of the 106th and whether or not they would be waiting at the rendezvous. It was hard to believe that men could march as fast as the carriage, even if their route was more direct. On this, at least, he was willing to share some of Dobson's doubts about the hearty assurances of the colonel and Baynes.

He missed Pringle and the familiar faces of the grenadiers. Even more he missed Hanley, and wondered where he was. Wickham had admitted that he saw the lieutenant fall, but did not see him wounded or killed. Williams wanted to believe that his friend was alive, although that increased his sense of guilt that he had done nothing to find him. The explanations readily came to mind. The Spanish had lost the field to the French and it was impossible to return. As importantly, he had almost immediately been ordered away as escort to the Doña Margarita. Reason might be satisfied, but in his heart he wondered whether the affair would have happened differently if he had been with Hanley instead of escorting Baynes.

The carriage rolled on. Another night was spent in the outhouse of an inn, heavily populated with vermin of all kinds, stinking of decaying meat and resonating to the snores of a dozen pedlars on their way south.

The next morning they turned off the main road and struggled along a track where the mud was deep and sucked at the wheels. Ramón, who seemed to have excellent eyesight, spotted movement in the trees edging the road and called a warning. The former hussar pulled the blanket away to uncover his loaded blunderbuss. Dobson brandished his own heavy firelock and Williams very obviously readied his pistol. They caught a glimpse of a villainous face with a red headscarf lurking behind a low wall, but no one dared to challenge them. Ramón drove the team on as fast as the mud permitted. The horses were tired, since they had had no opportunity to change them and this meant that they had to rest the team more and more often.

The country was rugged and empty, the track winding through valleys where rows of olive trees clung to the slopes. They crossed little bridges and went through long stretches of forest without seeing any other travellers.

Once again it was Ramón who spotted the rider at the moment when they were ready to begin after a rest of an hour, during which Wickham had dismounted and done his best to be genial and draw a somewhat sullen Williams into light conversation.

'I see 'im,' said Dobson. 'On the crest to the right of those pines.'

Williams searched the slope, caught the movement and saw the silhouette of a cloaked horseman slip behind the trees.

'Looks like a soldier,' said the veteran.

Williams nodded. He had even thought he glimpsed the shape of a helmet.

'Could be a deserter, or a wandering Spaniard,' said Wickham dismissively. 'Even if they're French the Doña Margarita's pass will surely get us through. Nothing to worry about.'

Williams' instincts made him doubt such a sanguine assessment, and he sensed Dobson felt the same. So too did Ramón, and the driver used his long whip mercilessly to push the team hard and get quickly through the series of defiles they saw up ahead. He was good at his job, and if the carriage rocked on its springs as it took the tighter corners, he never lost control. Wickham yelled in protest, but then came the higher, sharper tone of La Doña Margarita ordering the driver to keep going.

A sharp corner led to a bridge, and Ramón braked for a moment as the horses' hoofs threw sparks off the cobbles as they swung to turn in time. The left wheels brushed against the parapet, their iron rims sending up more sparks and squealing as they scraped past in a dark flurry of old mortar, but the carriage was still moving on. Williams looked back to see several stones tumble from the wall and splash into the brook.

They were going uphill now, and the horses naturally raced up the rise. Williams was still looking back, and on the longest stretch saw a horseman following them, with two more behind him. Then the man reined in hard and his horse reared up as he stopped sharply. He was bare headed, and wearing a long cloak.

A musket ball flicked a long splinter from the wood of the carriage roof just beside the rail he held. The report was almost instant, and as Dobson yelled a warning and pointed to the left, Williams spotted a French dragoon struggling to control his mount, frightened by the noise and smoke. Beside him, two more dragoons steadied their own horses and drew their long swords. Each had a cloth cover over his helmet to prevent the brass from glinting in the sun and betraying their position. On the right four more dragoons appeared from the trees and followed them, the carriage throwing up a great spray of muddy water as Ramón flogged the horses to pelt down the track.

Wickham heard the Frenchmen crying and leaned from the window of the carriage, calling at the driver to halt.

'Don't shoot!' he screamed in French at the pursuing cavalry. 'We are friends of King Joseph!'

Ramón did not stop and the Frenchmen splashed down the trail after them. Another man fired, this time with a pistol, and the ball snapped through the window above Wickham's head, ripping a neat hole in the leather curtain. The major's head shot back inside, and Williams was sure he caught a burst of clear, feminine laughter.

'Don't shoot! We are friends!' This time the shout came from inside the carriage.

'These lads mean business,' called Dobson, clinging desperately on to the handrail as the carriage lurched and swung. He had his blunderbuss cocked, but knew that one-handed he would not be able to aim and feared wasting his charge when it seemed unlikely they would get the chance to reload.

Williams leaned back, pointing his heavy pistol at the closest dragoon. The carriage bounced, and the muzzle leapt from its aim squarely at the yellow front at the centre of the Frenchman's dark green jacket. Thankfully he had not pulled the trigger, but the threat of the gun was enough to make the dragoons rein back a little. Another fired a pistol, but the ball must have gone high or wide, because neither Dobson nor Williams felt it pass near.

The carriage lurched again as Ramón skilfully took another bend in the road. Williams almost lost his footing as he leaned back, and for a moment his left foot was in the air, his balance going, and then another jolt pitched him back against the back of the car.

There were more dragoons waiting, this time six men on foot and two more holding their horses. The dismounted men fired a ragged volley. One shot cut a groove in the roof of the carriage, and another twitched at the heavy curtain on the left-hand window and slapped into the far side of the car, prompting a cry of alarm that sounded more male than female.

The right lead horse was pumping blood from a wound in its neck. Ramón knew the animal was dying, but wanted to get as far as he could, and so he whipped the poor beast and the team ran on. Gouts of blood sprayed back red from the wound.

After a hundred yards the team began to slow perceptibly. Then more dragoons appeared, weaving through the trees beside the road, four on either side. The green-coated riders had their swords out, and an officer was bellowing orders. Two men raced along beside the team. Dobson aimed as best he could, one arm looped through the hand-rail so that both hands could try to steady the blunderbuss. He anticipated the bump, waited for the moment when the carriage sank back down on its springs and pulled the trigger.

The detonation seemed huge and the cloud of filthy smoke blew back around the two men on the rear of the carriage, but the explosion of the nails and scrap metal struck the dragoon on the right from behind, punching through the cloth cover and the brass of his helmet and shattering the rear of the man's skull. His head flopped to one side, but some nervous reaction kept the man's knees in their high boots firmly astride the horse, and the animal ran on with its dead rider.

Williams aimed at the man on the other side, but then another dragoon closed with him, sword lunging, and the ensign swung his arm back and fired with the muzzle of his pistol no more than a yard away. He pulled the trigger and the flint snapped down and sparked. Nothing happened; perhaps the powder in the pan had been shaken out in their jolting drive. The dragoon was closing, and almost by reflex Williams flung the pistol at him, striking him in the mouth and making him yank with his left hand at the reins and swing away. He blocked the path of the men that followed, and for the moment they opened up some distance.

Williams reached for the other pistol and hoped desperately that this would fire. The carriage was starting to slow, and then the right lead horse died and the left's collar was grabbed by the French dragoon who had sped up on that side. The trees fell back from the road as they came to a cross-roads marked by a little shrine to a local saint. Ramón fumbled for a pistol just as the right lead slumped down. The team swung to the side, tugging the Frenchman from his saddle, and then the front wheel sank into a shallow ditch. There were screams from inside the carriage as the whole car rocked violently and the occupants were flung about. Dobson lost his balance and fell, rolling on the grass. Williams somehow stayed on.

Half a dozen French dragoons were closing, led by a slim officer whose uncovered helmet had a leopard-skin band and a tall white plume as well as the black horsehair crest. Farther back down the road, more dragoons cantered up in support. Williams jumped to the ground, and levelled the pistol at them, using his free hand to unbutton his greatcoat.

'Jackets, Dob,' he said. He was not sure the French would be inclined to take prisoners. With one man killed he could not blame them, but at least he would make the effort and show the enemy that they were British soldiers.

'View halloo!' The cry came as clear and purposeful as the brass call of a trumpet. 'Tally ho! Come on the Twentieth!' Williams could not see who was shouting, for the cries came from behind the carriage and the road off to the right. Then there were the thuds of a heavy-footed horse pounding through the mud and an immaculately dressed light dragoon officer shot past. His cloak billowed behind him, his trim-waisted tunic had rows of white lace widening at the shoulders, and he had the distinctively British Tarleton helmet with its comb of a crest. Behind him rode a corporal in the regulation place for a cover man. Both officer and NCO had their heavy curved sabres raised high.

'Charge, my lads!' the officer called, and behind him another rider appeared, this one a trumpeter in a green uniform Williams did not recognise. The man raised his trumpet and blew the intoxicating notes of the charge.

Williams fired, and had the satisfaction of seeing the shot strike home on the chest of a dragoon's horse.

The French fled. Their horses were tired and they were spread out, and that was the worst condition in which to meet a cavalry charge. The officer yelled the order and the men wheeled sharply, and then kicked their spurred boots to send the horses racing as fast as they could back the way they had come. The dragoons coming up in support joined the prudent withdrawal.

None of the French looked back to share Williams' surprise when he realised that the three horsemen were alone and that no squadron followed them.

'Mad bugger,' said Dobson admiringly.

The Frenchman with the wounded horse lagged behind, and the light dragoon corporal kept after him even after his officer had reined back. He closed steadily, and with a well-aimed and heavy swing the stockily built man cut the French dragoon from his saddle. His cry of pain hastened the flight of the others.

The light dragoon officer nodded approvingly, and then walked his horse back towards the foundered carriage. He had thick side whiskers framing his open, handsome face.

'Well, that was all rather thrilling,' he said happily. A couple of shots echoed up the valley. 'Ah, that must be the excellent Charles, and the admirable Corporal Evans. They should keep Johnny Crapaud amused for a few hours. Corporal Evans displays a natural talent for banditry. Well, he is Welsh. Those fellows will be lucky to get away with their boots by the time he has finished.'

Williams dropped his long coat and revealed a red jacket which, for all its failings, still showed him to be an ensign in the British Army.

The light dragoon officer noticed and gave an easy smile. He wore a number of decorations Williams did not recognise. 'I hope you will not take offence, my dear fellow, but if I were you I would have strong words with your tailor. A horse whip would seem the ideal way to start.

'By the way, my name is Wilson.'

CHAPTER 8

'My lady,' said Colonel Wilson with an impeccable bow. 'It is good to see you again. I hope you were not in any way incommoded during the chase?' Wickham took the Doña Margarita's hand to help her step down from the carriage. In spite of her condition she did so with graceful ease.

'I am perfectly recovered, Sir Robert. And must thank you for such a timely and heroic arrival.' Her voice was deep, the English perfect with the barest trace of an accent, and her speech less formal than before. With her mantilla now around her shoulders, Williams for the first time saw her face clearly. Her long black hair was coiled on top of her head and braided down to her shoulders. Her eyes were such a deep brown as to seem almost black, and she looked boldly at each of them in turn, her gaze strong and unblinking. They were set in a round, almost heart-shaped face, with lips that were wide and a little fleshy. If her features were not perhaps wholly perfect, there was an animation in her expression and movements which leant them a lively beauty. As much as her appearance, Williams admired the coolness she had displayed in the recent chase, confirming what Ramón had told them of the lady's courage.

She was taller than he had guessed, or perhaps for the first time was standing straight, so that she was only a few inches shorter than Wickham. Her skin was a dark cream, at the moment still somewhat flushed with excitement. 'You are the perfect caballeros, appearing at the moment when all seemed lost,' and after the compliment, she made the slightest motion of a curtsy, hardly bending her knees and yet conveying a considerable elegance.

'I am most delighted to hear it, although I dare say your fellows would have fought the enemy off without our aid.'

It was a generous, if absurd, compliment. 'We are most glad you arrived,' said Williams.

'Indeed, for we were most surely outmatched,' added Wickham.

'A happy chance,' replied Sir Robert, 'and we are pleased to have been of service. Now, we ought to get your carriage ready to move again in case any more of those fellows turn up.' They were surprised to see the colonel undo his helmet's chinstrap, take it off, and then peel off his cloak and jacket. 'Come, Dobson, is it not? Let us see if we can shift this wheel, while the Doña Margarita's man attends to the team.'

Williams was surprised to see a senior officer so readily submitting to manual work. Wickham was aghast, but immediately reprieved from copying the example when the lady asked him to help carry her travelling case over to the shade of a tree so that she could sit down. He was all attention.

The ensign happily joined Wilson, his corporal and Dobson as they clambered down into the shallow ditch. The wheel was undamaged, but the slope of the little trench almost vertical, although no more than eighteen inches deep. Without tools, they could not dig out a gentler slope.

'Well, brute force it is,' declared the colonel. The dead horse had been taken from the traces and dragged away by the rest of the team. Then the remaining lead was moved back to replace the animal behind, and Ramón led them forward while the four others heaved at the axle to raise the coach. The horses strained, were whipped on, and with a sudden surge the rim of the wheel gripped the top of the bank, crumbling the edge, until the carriage was rolling on. All four of them quickly let go to save themselves from being dragged forward as the team raced a few yards before the driver restrained them.

'I must thank you again, sir, for your most timely appearance,' said Williams, brushing the dirt and grease from his hands.

'Don't mention it. Happy to be of service, and simply good luck that we were here.'

Williams doubted that it was luck, and suspected that the colonel had been looking for them. So had the French dragoons, for there seemed no other reason for such an immediate and determined attack. The other enemy soldiers they had encountered had always behaved with considerable caution. There was, after all, no obvious threat posed by a single carriage.

The French must have wanted either the lady herself or something she carried. Perhaps they were after the messages she bore, but Williams could not help thinking of Dobson's suspicion that the carriage concealed something heavy. It had certainly been a bigger effort than he expected for the four of them to lift the wheel of so lightly constructed a vehicle.

'I must say, sir, that it was a bold and gallant stroke to attack so many.'

'Capital sport!' After a moment Colonel Wilson chuckled to himself. 'Reminds me of the time back in Flanders when a couple of squadrons of their chasseurs tried to snaffle a battery while most of our fellows were dismounted and resting their horses. Lord Paget, Willy Erskine, myself and a few other officers were the only ones on horseback so we flung ourselves at the Frenchies and laid about for all we were worth. Gave our light dragoons the chance to saddle up and we put the whole lot into the bag. Capital sport, Mr Williams, capital sport!

'Audacity is the key. Never give them time to think or count how many you are. Just go bald-headed at the enemy and he will spring back "as one who has tread on an unseen snake amid the briars, when stepping firmly on the earth."'

Williams felt the quote was familiar, and suddenly the rest of it came to him. '"And in sudden terror pulls back as it rises in anger and puffs out its purple neck."'

'"And so we charge and with serried arms flow around them",' added Sir Robert, delighting in the exchange. 'I shall not claim the prowess of a son of Venus and his warriors for myself and Corporal Gorman, but the outcome was just as satisfactory.'

Wickham and the lady were close enough to hear the conversation and now the major joined them, confident that any unbecoming labour was at an end. 'Mr Williams and I had the honour of serving under Lord Paget at Sahagun last winter,' he said, seizing the opportunity of parading any acquaintance with such a great man, and resenting his subordinate's ready knowledge of the classics. 'I was on General Paget's staff. Mr Williams was there to act in the capacity of a translator.' Wickham's tone indicated the unimportance of such an unmilitary task. 'Although in the event Lord Paget was too busy setting about the French to give much thought to communication!'

'Ah, so you are familiar with modern languages as well as ancient, Mr Williams?' asked the colonel with evident enthusiasm. 'That is an excellent practice for a young officer.'

Williams' honesty surfaced immediately. 'I fear there was a wholly mistaken esteem for my skills. Since returning to Portugal, I have attempted some small study of the language, but confess that my success is limited.'

'Your diligence does you credit, as does your modesty. Vanity and promotion of one's own deeds are the most terrible of vices, and ensure that all too often the higher commands go to the braggarts rather than the men of true worth. Such is the world we live in.'

'The Doña Margarita wonders when we shall be recommencing our journey, Sir Robert,' said Wickham, relishing such a level of intimacy with two persons of title.

'Of course, of course, we shall leave immediately. Mr Charles and Corporal Evans will be able to catch up with us as soon as their business is complete. We ought to move, just in case another stray patrol chances upon us. We will take you on and guide you to a far stronger escort waiting to take the lady the rest of the way.'

'Escort, Sir Robert?' asked Wickham.

'Two companies of your own corps, under the command of the estimable Captain Pringle. I spoke with him last night and suggested that he wait for you in a little village lying on the old coach route.'

That was splendid news, and Williams saw no point in commenting that Sir Robert had obviously been aware of their coming – and indeed a good deal more than he was choosing to tell.

'Wickham my dear fellow, I feel it is best if you continue to travel in the carriage and attend to the comforts of La Doña Margarita. She is a fine and spirited lady, but given her situation the journey itself must be fatiguing, apart from the threat of the enemy.'

'Of course, Sir Robert.' Williams noticed something new in Wickham's expression, which went beyond mere satisfaction at so comfortable an assignment. The Spanish aristocrat seemed more inclined to conversation than in the past, and perhaps this encouraged the major.

'Mr Williams, we have saddled the spare horse with the Frenchman's tack, so would you do me the honour of riding with us. An additional pair of eyes would not go amiss. I doubt that we shall have more trouble with the French, but one can never be sure.'

The carriage horses were tired, and now reduced to a team of four, but they kept to as fast a pace as possible, helped that the trend in the road was downwards. After two hours, they were joined by Captain Charles, a gunner officer with a boyish face and a nose left crooked by some childhood misadventure. He was followed a few minutes later by a ginger-haired rogue who proved to be Corporal Evans. He had an infantryman's jacket with yellow facings and yet looked as comfortable on horseback as any cavalryman. He confirmed that no French were following. The two men seemed exhilarated by the recent skirmish, reflecting Sir Robert's own light-hearted enthusiasm.

'Charles is my adjutant,' said the colonel, after

the gunner and Williams were introduced to each other. 'He helps me to run the Legion. Without him I would no doubt forget to issue the men with musket balls to shoot or breeches to wear!'

'I am sure you would manage, sir.'

'Well, I do let you have some sport as well as making you slave away. Eh, James, better than manning some godforsaken fort on the windswept cliffs of Sussex?'

'Undoubtedly, sir,' replied Captain James Charles. 'That was such a dull existence, without the slightest chance of action. With the Legion there is always such capital sport.'

Williams could not help noticing the officer using the same expression as his commander. When Sir Robert took a turn riding ahead to scout, the gunner was even more effusive.

'The chief is a wonder. Do you know that with just one battalion of ours, a few dozen horsemen and the support of the local Spanish, we have kept General Lapisse and a whole French corps busy. We move fast, you see, and the chief will attack at any opportunity. Sometimes it's just a handful of us, a troop of cavalry, a howitzer and a company of infantry, and we'll pounce on their outposts. There's usually more of them, but then they don't know that, do they? So we charge in and overrun the piquets, and usually take every man. The shock of that is sufficient to make their regiment think thousands are attacking. Nine times out of ten they pull back, and we nibble at their heels like terriers. If they do choose to fight, then we will not give them the chance. It's easier for our small numbers to escape.

'For the last month we have led Lapisse a merry dance. Convinced him he had no chance of capturing Ciudad Rodrigo up north, and so the French broke the siege. The way things are going we may chase him out of the whole country. If only those damned fools in London and Lisbon would realise it and give the chief more men, we could keep the border secure and liberate half of Spain.'

'I understand your corps is principally recruited from the Portuguese,' asked Williams when the flow slackened.

'The Legion? Have you heard of us?'

'I confess little more than the name. The Lusitanian Legion is it not?'

'The *Loyal* Lusitanian Legion,' said Charles with heavy emphasis. 'Show him your hat, lad.' This was to the trumpeter, who dutifully took off his helmet and showed the plate to Williams. It bore the crest of Portugal and the letters L L L. 'I suspect Bonaparte has one as well so we need the full title! Yes, like young Arturo here, almost all of the Legion is Portuguese.

'When the French invaded, a number of officers and patriotic gentlemen found their way to London. As you might expect, they were without exception adventurous men, and they all wanted to fight against the invader.'

Williams wondered cynically whether it might have been easier to fight the invader if they had stayed in Portugal, but quickly dismissed the thought as unworthy. He knew that the Portuguese army had been in no state to mount a long resistance. 'And Sir Robert was appointed to lead them?' he said, lest his silence seem rude.

'Quite so,' continued the artillery officer happily. 'Not sure whether he or the Portuguese ambassador came up with the splendid title of legion.'

'It does have a ring to it, and such a marvellous heritage.' Williams' love of the classics ensured his enthusiasm was now wholly sincere.

'The chief wants a well-balanced light corps of foot, horse and guns to move quickly, but strike with great precision and force. From the beginning there were a few British officers like myself to assist in the task, but most of the commissioned ranks and all of the soldiers are Portuguese. The recruits flooded in as soon as we arrived and with all the usual bloody-minded selfishness of politicians there weren't enough supplies for them all.'

Williams nodded. The story was so familiar. 'Yet clearly he has taken the field, and to great effect.'

'Yes, in spite of those self-serving fools. Our first battalion is complete and has been active since the autumn. Between that ruddy bishop and a German blackguard, only God knows what has happened to the second battalion.

'Damned shame. If we had all the men we should the chief wouldn't half be playing merry hell with the French. He still is, truth be told, but we could do so much more.' The captain's almost cherubic face seethed with frustration at such folly. He expanded on the theme at considerable length, and Williams could not help being relieved when Wilson returned and sent Charles and Corporal Evans off to patrol ahead of them.

'No sign of the French,' said Sir Robert. 'I suspect that we have given them the slip for the moment. Or more likely they have learned caution and we must take advantage of the fact. If we can keep to this pace then I believe we shall reach your comrades not long after nightfall.'

'That is good news, sir,' said Williams, and meant it, although his heart sank at the thought of having to tell Pringle that their friend was either dead or a prisoner of the French.

'The good captain told me that you ran into a storm after sailing from Corunna?'

Williams nodded. 'I confess that I am not the best of sailors, and the ferocity of the weather and the waves overwhelmed me.'

'Yes, I know. For reasons best known to himself old Father Neptune has conceived a great dislike for poor Sir R W. As soon as he glimpses me on a boat he unleashes his savage gales and flings me about every which way. Given sailors and their superstitions, it's a wonder I haven't been tipped overboard on some of the rougher nights!'

He changed the subject abruptly. 'So you charged at Sahagun, Mr Williams?'

'My horse did rather run away with me that morning.' At the moment he was struggling to control the carriage horse, unused as it was to a saddle. The animal was continually shifting under him, tossing its head and threatening to surge away at a gallop. Williams clung on to the reins to keep a nominal control.

'You are too modest, I am sure. It was a gallant action and I am proud of my old corps.'

'You served in the Fifteenth, sir?'

'Aye, till I transferred to the Twentieth. In my day we made almost as gallant a charge at Villers-en-Cauchies back in '94. Did the French cavalry meet you at the halt? By the way, if I were you I would lengthen the reins and use less force. At the moment he's fighting you every inch.'

Williams followed the advice, and the horse lurched into an awkward trot. He pulled back hard. For a moment the animal threw up its head and he had no control, but then it sullenly slowed back to a walk. Wilson suspected that the rider's nervousness was communicating itself to the mount and making him skittish. Yet for all his evident inexperience as a horseman, Sir Robert liked the young ensign, with his open face and remarkable bashfulness, but most of all for his impression of confidence and ability as a soldier.

'Yes, the French waited and fired volleys as we approached. I could not understand why. Surely impetus is the great strength of the cavalryman.' Wilson liked the ensign's lack of bluster.

'It is indeed, as long as order is retained. Once the enemy break then a regiment will split up in the chase. We went eight miles or more in Flanders. My horse and most of the others were lathered in sweat. I have rarely felt so elated and weary at the same instant. One of our farriers killed twenty-two Frenchmen by himself.'

Williams had an image of an axe dripping blood, then realised that was absurd for the man must surely have used his sabre.

'You never saw such slaughter,' continued Sir Robert. 'Well, of course you probably have, for your corps was in the thick of things in Portugal, was it not?'

'I was commissioned there,' said Williams, for there was something about the colonel's enthusiasm which made him ready to speak. 'I was also at Medellín, and saw the French slaughter the Spanish.'

Sir Robert looked grim for a moment, and then smiled. 'A dreadful day, but I have no doubt Don Gregorio will dust himself down and rise again. He's a tough old bird. Your commission is the first step of many, I am sure. Villers-en-Cauchies got me my knighthood, or did you think me some scion of ancient lineage?' He laughed out loud, and continued before an answer could be given. 'There is something pure and very right in a title won by battle. We were under Austrian command that day, so, believe it or not, you are looking at a Knight of the Order of Maria Theresa and Baron of the Holy Roman Emperor. There is something fine in being a modern crusader. Although I dare say Boney would claim the title has lapsed now that he has dissolved the Holy Roman Empire. Damned cheek.'

'The truest form of nobility is surely the reward for courage,' said the ensign with obvious sincerity.

'I am proud of the honour, but doubt that our own country will copy such an example. Just imagine if the Lords was filled only by the heroes of our nation.' Wilson shook his head. 'Instead I fear we blame our heroes. It is truly shameful how ministers now condemn Sir John Moore for their own failure to support him.'

'He was a great man,' said Williams with a note almost of awe in his voice.

'Your regiment served in his last campaign.' Sir Robert caught something in the voice, and was curious. 'Did you meet him?'

'Yes, I was beside him when he received his mortal wound, and waited and watched with the others during his final hours.' Reluctantly, and with considerable encouragement and cajoling from the colonel, Williams told the story. It seemed more like an age than little more than three months ago.

'A great man, and a great loss. His was a clear mind, who knew that this war could only be won in Spain. Portugal cannot be defended. Its border is too long, its fortresses too few and easy to pass. It is in Spain that we must beat the French, and we must beat them by attacking, always attacking.

'My Legion is merely the start. With more men and more regiments we could hound the French from dawn till dusk!' Williams was reminded of Charles's recent passion.

'Can a light corps achieve so much, sir?' Williams asked with genuine interest.

'Even on its own it can achieve a great deal. Is that not the lesson from America, where the Yankees showed us how it was done? We could win battles and yet lost the war. They controlled the country. Our outposts, our foragers and our sympathisers were always at risk of attack. The only way to challenge such partisans was with fast-moving and well-led bodies of horse and light foot. Numbers mattered less than speed.

'I have ridden with the Turks and the Cossacks. It is an ancient way of fighting, and we can learn much from them. Boldness is what matters, as I believe I said to you some hours ago.' Sir Robert chuckled. 'I fear I have been up on my hobby horse once again. You have shown commendable patience in listening with such courtesy.'

'You are too kind in your judgement, for I have listened in fascination. Indeed, I believe the speed of your campaign has readily overcome any chance of my disagreeing.'

Sir Robert laughed.

'May I ask where the main body of the Legion is at the moment?' asked Williams.

'Moving fast, I trust, and waiting for the right moment to harry Lapisse. We have been occupying his corps and now they have grown tired of our hospitality. Do you know we captured nearly a thousand of them last week? The prisoners should be on their way to Ciudad Rodrigo by now.

'Once I have seen La Doña Margarita safely to her escort I shall ride to join them. I am only out so far to spy out the land. Knowledge, Mr Williams, knowledge. That is what a commander most needs, and often the best way is to see with his own eyes.'

'Are we to escort the lady farther, sir? There remains the question of our own orders.'

'Your famous shells? All gone, I am happy to say. They were taken to Ciudad Rodrigo and my own Colonel Mayne dealt with them. They were the wrong calibre for the Spanish guns, so he blew the lot up. So now that you are unoccupied you can perform a task for me, and for our allies.'

'An honour, sir,' said Williams, for there was no real choice.

The last hour passed with little talk, but without any alarm. The land seemed empty. Houses had their shutters tightly closed and it was not until they reached the bottom of the valley and looked up to see the village that they spotted silhouettes in the fading light. There were soldiers forming a piquet beside the road. Captain Charles rode forward to hail them.

As they passed up the track Williams felt at home to see the familiar uniforms of his regiment, and faces he knew. They went between the first houses of the village itself, and Williams saw

Pringle – plump, reassuring Pringle with his round glasses and ready smile. He saluted and exchanged courtesies with Sir Robert and Captain Charles, before grinning at Williams.

'So you have been off wandering again, my friend. And leading poor Hanley astray. Where is he, by the way?'

CHAPTER 9

Hanley's forehead throbbed. His eyes did not want to open and when they did it was hard to focus. The light was white and piercingly bright. His tongue felt rough and so swollen that it pressed against the inside of his mouth, rubbing over teeth which felt as if they were clogged with great lumps of food.

With his right hand he managed to push aside the sheet covering his face and saw the open window and the dark timbers of the roof of the room. He blinked in the bright sunlight. His hand ran across his face and chin and felt the wiry stubble of two days or more.

Hanley was not a heavy drinker. Billy Pringle and most of his fellow officers soaked the stuff up like sponges, but Hanley was content to soften the hard edges of the world rather than wash them away altogether.

He could not remember where he was. He was hungry and oh so very thirsty.

'I need a drink,' he said as the door opened.

'Señor?' It was a woman's voice.

His thoughts trudged wearily up a long slope

until he found the Spanish words. 'I need a drink.'

There were footsteps and the door closed. Hanley felt that he had done enough work for the moment and lay there. A year may have passed before the door opened again.

'Well, I see you have returned to us after all,' drawled Espinosa. A maid came over to the bed and offered him a cup of water. Hanley drank with difficulty, dribbling down his chin.

'Behold the highest form of creation,' muttered Espinosa.

Hanley took the maid's wrist, making her gasp. He stared at her for a moment. She was scarcely more than a child, her brown eyes nervous. 'I do not remember you,' he said. Then he smiled. 'But thank you for your kindness.' He let her go. The girl gave a faint smile in return, but was obviously still frightened of the strange foreigner. She left the room, leaving behind a tray with a bowl of soup.

'Have something to eat and then get dressed,' said Espinosa. 'You have lain in sloth for too long. The barber is on his way. When he has finished I shall come back and then we can talk.'

Hanley forced himself to sit up, and swung his legs down from the bed. He looked around the room. Dim memories were coming back of Lasalle and his officers, and of the blonde.

'I cannot see my uniform,' he said, noticing only a brown suit draped over the back of a chair.

'Burned,' said Espinosa. 'You were very ill indeed and your jacket and breeches were sorely stained when you spewed up the contents of your stomach. It was simply not worth trying to save those rags.'

'I do not remember.'

'On balance, I imagine that is just as well.'

'How long have I been asleep?' Hanley asked.

'Two days, so you should feel well rested. Now eat. We shall talk when I return.'

By the early afternoon they were on the road. Espinosa returned as promised, but although they spoke for half an hour Hanley had learned very little. He had fallen ill two nights ago. First he had sunk into the deepest of sleeps, and a little later woken and purged himself for the first of several times. Lasalle and the column could not wait for one sick prisoner and pressed on.

Hanley still had his own well-worn and comfortable boots, but was now clad in a black shirt, brown jacket and breeches after the Castilian style, and a tall round hat, with a wider brim than the top hats beginning to be worn by the beaus in England. At his waist was a long scarlet sash. His sword belt ran over the sash, for there was nothing out of place in a Spanish gentleman carrying a blade. Espinosa similarly kept his sword and had a pistol in his belt, although he had changed his uniform for a black civilian suit.

'There is no need to attract unnecessary attention,' he said, although since they were accompanied by two hussars in the brown and sky blue of the

Chamborant, that hope seemed futile. Both men rode horses suspected of lameness, and so had stayed at the inn in the hope that rest would permit a recovery. They were wary of pushing the animals too far, and Espinosa clearly found this frustrating.

'There is no need for you to stay with us, Guindet,' he said to the older of the two hussars.

'Orders, sir,' came the reply. Hanley began to wonder who was being guarded. He could sense that neither Guindet nor the youngster with him relished the idea of being out on their own.

Espinosa said little as they rode. They saw no other French soldiers and scarcely any civilians. By nightfall they reached a farm overlooking the road, and with Espinosa's authority demanded rooms. The farmer had grey hair and skin the texture of leather. He did not seem especially impressed by the name of the King, but the two soldiers were enough to convince him to comply. He was relieved that they wanted so little, as since the start of the year passing soldiers had slaughtered and eaten a quarter of his pigs.

'Worse than that,' he told Hanley later in the night after they had shared the family's stew. 'One lot burned the shafts of my spades and hoes for firewood. Can you dream of such folly? Where is a man supposed to buy new tools in these times?'

They rode on the next morning, and after an hour passed a march company of convalescents going the other way as they returned to their regiments with Marshal Victor's main body at Merida. The lieutenant in charge said that they had had trouble with peasants firing at them as they passed.

'We caught one, but the rest of the scoundrels fled,' he said with contempt. 'Be careful when you pass that way.'

At noon they saw a corpse hanging from the branch of an old dead tree.

'The one the lieutenant caught,' said Espinosa without any particular emotion.

A few hours later they dismounted and let the horses drink from a pond. On either side of the road were walled vineyards. There were a few farms, a small chapel on a hillside, but most of the people evidently lived in the village they could see about two miles away.

Espinosa seemed on edge, and started up when Hanley accidentally brushed against his sleeve.

'I am sorry,' said the Englishman, more than a little surprised at the reaction.

The Spaniard said nothing, and then there was a shot and a ball flew over their heads. Hanley spun around and saw a puff of smoke from the corner of one of the vineyards, and glimpsed movement behind it. Another deep-throated boom and a musket ball flicked up a plume of dust in the dirt beside them.

The hussars quickly sprang back into the saddle.

'Catch them!' yelled Espinosa. Guindet gave him a glance, but then the two men were off, pounding along the path to the open archway of the walled yard. Sabres drawn, the hussars sped through the entrance, and they heard cries from beyond.

Espinosa grasped Hanley by the shoulders.

'There is not much time. Inside the lining of your sash you will find an envelope sewn into the material. It bears a list of all the regiments in Marshal Victor's army, and their strengths, as well as the numbers and station of the regiments under King Joseph's direct command. The numbers for the other corps are much older, and their positions have no doubt changed considerably. One thing I do know is that Marshal Soult has already attacked Portugal from the north. He will have Oporto by now, and perhaps be farther south.

'There, you have just heard something King Joseph himself will not learn for another day or two. This is all I have had time to prepare. Better information will come at greater expense.

'Take it to your own superiors. Either to Lisbon if you go due west or if you go more to the north then to your Colonel Wilson, who patrols the border. There will be more. If someone comes to you and speaks a certain word, then you will know that they speak for me and can reach me.'

There was a shot from behind the high wall, and then a scream.

'Why?' asked Hanley.

'Does it matter? There is food for four or five days in the saddlebags and a map.'

'Then what is the word your men will say?'

Espinosa smiled. 'Mapi.'

That was like the man to choose something personal, intimate and, in the circumstances, somewhat cruel.

'Now, hit me and go.'

Hanley looked blank.

'It must look as if you took me unawares and escaped. So you must . . .'

Hanley put all his weight behind the blow, slamming his right fist under Espinosa's chin, so that the man's head snapped back. Hanley was not a violent man. Even as a soldier he had rarely raised his hand against the enemy. Yet he was big, and had been confused and angered enough in the last week or more to relish the opportunity of venting some of his rage.

Before Espinosa fell, Hanley hit him again on the side of the face, and then kicked him for good measure as he lay on the ground. Reaching down, he grabbed the pistol from the Spaniard's belt and tucked it into his own. He put a foot in the stirrup and swung himself up on to the horse. Glancing back, he saw the two hussars returning, a captive walking between their horses.

Hanley kicked his heels and set the horse running up the slope to the left of the road. The animal was strong and fresh and surged up the hillside. He did not look back until he was a good half-mile away and saw that the hussars had already given up the pursuit. Even so, the Englishman kept the horse cantering for another ten minutes, before he slowed to a trot. The awkwardness of that bouncing motion helped to make him focus on the present and the realisation sank in that he was now no longer a prisoner.

His right hand ached badly and he began to wonder whether he had broken a bone. That night he slept in a copse near a stream. He did not dare light a fire, and for all his efficiency Espinosa had not thought to roll a blanket on the back of the saddle. He was cold and got little sleep, but neither saw nor heard any sign of other human beings. Before he tried to rest he tended to the horse, and then ripped open the sash where he thought he could feel a lump. The papers were there, just as Espinosa had said.

It was hard to know what to make of the Spaniard. Hanley was wary of trusting the man, but could see no immediate advantage for Espinosa to have set him free only to have him hunted down. There seemed no reason for the man to want his death, and surely that could have been easily arranged in the long hours of his unconsciousness at the inn. That was presumably deliberate drugging, and he thought back to the blonde girl taking him off to her room. Everything suggested a careful plan to employ him as courier for this information. Was Velarde part of it all? Espinosa had not seemed surprised when the man was mentioned. Yet the whole thing appeared unnecessarily elaborate.

He scanned the papers in the last rays of sunlight.

Some of what he read fitted with his own memories of the French battalions marching across the bridge at Merida. If he was a judge – and he was still willing to concede his ignorance of many aspects of martial science – then the lists looked both genuine and useful.

He had no means of sewing the envelope back into his sash. Part of him also felt that there was little point. If Espinosa was playing a game and would betray him, then it might be better not to keep the evidence where it was supposed to be. Hanley reached into the inside breast pocket of his coat and was surprised to find a piece of well-folded paper already there.

Opening it, he saw a sketch of a girl, sitting on a stool. It was one of his own works, and immediately his mind went back to the camp in Dorset and Jenny Dobson sitting for a portrait in the new dress she had got for her wedding. She had been widowed in the winter's campaign, and had then struck off on her own. For a moment he was baffled.

Suddenly Hanley snapped his fingers and immediately felt searing pain. 'Bugger,' he hissed. He no longer thought that he had broken a bone when he punched Espinosa, but his hand was bruised and sore whenever he flexed it.

'It was Jenny.' He laughed as the pain died down. 'Little Jenny Dobson.' He shook his head. She was the blonde whore. Appeared from nowhere and then vanished to goodness knows where just as soon.

Did Espinosa know? Perhaps he realised that the girl was English and that was why he had bribed or persuaded her to help him.

It seemed the girl wanted him to know her, but there was no other message. Still, as far as he knew, Jenny could neither read nor write, but then perhaps he was simply assuming such ignorance. Williams would probably know.

Hanley could do no more for the moment. He slipped the envelope into the saddlebag he used as a pillow, and tried to rest.

The next day Hanley rode on through a country occupied by an invader and ravaged by marching armies. He saw no trace of the war anywhere, and there was an unreality to everything as he passed through the sparsely populated land. That evening he stopped in a small town preparing for market the next day. Espinosa had left a purse of money in the saddlebags, and he was able to procure the share of a room with a lawyer's clerk from Talavera travelling north to visit his family in their pueblo.

He rode hard the following day. This time there were signs of war, and he passed dozens of boys trudging along the road in answer to the junta's proclamation of conscription. Having seen the corpses strewn on the plain of Medellín he found it hard to look in the faces of these children.

Hanley rode on. A thick cloud of dust hovered over the country to the west and he began to see patrols of French cavalry. Most could be avoided, although it meant looping around in a wide arc to the north.

Then he came around a bend in the road between two orchards and saw a dozen French dragoons leading their horses. They were well over a hundred yards away and perhaps he could have outrun them. Instead he urged his horse into a trot and waved in enthusiastic greeting as he went to meet them.

A corporal led the patrol. He wore a round forage cap instead of his heavy helmet and his long-nosed, thin face was full of suspicion.

'I am Major Velarde of King Joseph's staff,' said Hanley. His French was impeccable, and his steady voice belied the pounding of his heart. The name was the first which sprang to mind, and nearly made him grin with sheer mischief.

The corporal waved his hand in the most casual of salutes. 'Sir,' he said.

'Stand to attention when you speak to me!' bellowed Hanley in his best impression of a proper officer.

The tone prompted the habit of obedience. The corporal slammed the heels of his high boots together.

'Sir!' This time it was a shout of fervent obedience. The other dragoons all snapped to attention, although one of the fathest away glanced at his neighbour and rolled his eyes.

'That's better,' said Hanley, and wondered whether his hand was shaking as much as he feared. 'Now take me to your officer,' he commanded.

'Sir.' The corporal turned to his men. 'Larpent, Schwartz. Escort the gentleman to the lieutenant.'

They both rode to his left, and Hanley felt that more suspicious men would have kept him between them. He tried to appear utterly confident and careless, and decided that a proud Spanish officer would not deign to chat to common soldiers. In a few minutes they found a larger party of forty men led by a young officer.

'Good day to you, Lieutenant . . .?' Hanley gave a gentle smile.

'Hollandais.' The officer's uniform was neat and seemed less spotted with dust than those of his men. He had dark freckles all over his tanned face and eyes which gave no hint of significant intelligence. Hanley guessed that he was a fairly new arrival, so would probably be either officious or gullible.

'I am Major Velarde of King Joseph's staff, lately come from Marshal Victor's headquarters with a message for the senior magistrate in Leon.' The lies came readily, and Hanley deliberately restrained the urge to appear over-friendly. Part of his mind screamed out that he was a British officer wearing civilian clothes and carrying secret information back to his own army. His heart had calmed down, as had his hand, but now a muscle in his thigh started to twitch and he longed to rub it. It was as well that he was mounted as he was sure that his leg would otherwise have been shaking.

'I see, sir,' said the French officer, his well-polished

brass helmet gleaming in the sunlight. He turned to one of the escorting cavalryman. 'Report, Dragoon.'

'This peasant came riding up to us and claims to be a major,' said the man without any emotion or sign of interest.

The officer looked at Hanley again. 'Forgive him. Any civilian is a peasant to a French soldier. However, you must excuse me, sir,' he said, 'if I ask whether you have proof of your identity?'

'That would be a most foolish thing to carry with me, would it not?' Hanley tried to sound patient. His life was hanging by a precarious thread. What surprised him was that he found this exhilarating. The dangers of battle had never struck him in this way. 'I have my dispatches concealed about my person. I could perhaps show them to your general, but I fear I would be failing in my duty to reveal their contents to anyone less senior.'

There, the gamble was made. *Iacta alea est* indeed, and the quote would no doubt have delighted Williams. If a French general appeared at that moment, or was close by, then it was likely that Hanley would hang or be placed in front of a firing squad. If he was fortunate they would not interrogate him too brutally beforehand. Hanley now felt that his heart was not beating at all.

'I see.' The officer's face showed little emotion and indeed little interest. 'Do you wish for an escort?'

144

'That is kind, but it is better that I ride alone,' said Hanley. 'I am a Spaniard, unlikely to attract attention.' Hanley was a big man, but so were some Spaniards. His clothes were local, his hair was black and since his years in Madrid his already dark complexion had permanently tanned.

'Of course.' The dragoon officer seemed truly relieved, and Hanley realised that his greatest fear had been facing a demand to provide some of his men to accompany the Spanish officer. 'Then how may I be of assistance?'

'I simply wished to ask whether you know of bandits on the road to Leon. I do not wish to court more danger than is essential.'

'We have brushed most aside.' The lieutenant's assurance confirmed that he had not been long in Spain. 'General Lapisse is advancing to bring the corps into closer support of Marshal Victor.' Hanley knew that meant the French were also retreating from the Portuguese border, but the young lieutenant seemed wholly sincere in his optimism and utterly uninterested in the fate of a lone courier sent by his emperor's brother. A sergeant who knew better was equally lacking in concern and was not moved to contradict his officer.

'Good,' said Hanley. 'That is good to know. I shall ride by the main roads without fear.'

He rode away. There were no shouts, no pursuing horsemen. Nor had there been searching questions, and still less a search of his bags, disclosing the documents he carried. It was so very easy. Confidence was the key. Pringle always said that a plausible rogue had the world at his feet.

Hanley waited until he had ridden for more than a mile and was sure no one was following him. Then he laughed out loud, startling his horse, which flicked her head up and twitched her ears in surprise.

He managed to avoid other patrols, and a group of men in drab civilian clothes who rode mules and had muskets slung over their backs. They were probably guerrillas and patriots, but he suspected that it might well be harder to convince them that he was genuinely an ally.

As the sun was setting two horsemen appeared on the road ahead of him. He glanced behind, and saw two more gently walking their horses on either side of the track behind. The men were in dark jackets, but he did not think he had ever seen the uniform before. One wore a helmet like the British dragoons, and when they came close Hanley could see that his uniform was ornate and was a dark blue rather than the green of the others.

'Well, what have we here?' the man said in Spanish that was good and yet still betrayed the intonation of an Englishman. The soldier beside him challenged Hanley in Portuguese.

Hanley took another gamble, remembering the name Espinosa had mentioned.

'I am looking for Colonel Wilson,' he said in Spanish.

'I am Wilson,' replied the man in the blue cavalry uniform. There was no hint of surprise in his voice. 'And who may you be, señor?'

'Hanley, lieutenant of the 106th, and most pleased to see you, sir.' It was almost strange to speak English again after so many days. 'I carry information about the enemy which I believe will be most useful.'

'Do you indeed! Well, my dear fellow, then I am all the more happy to meet you!'

CHAPTER 10

'It must be a truly remarkable place,' said Pringle with genuine enthusiasm. He paused to take a sip of port. 'A land of harsh beauty, strange creatures, and wonderful and yet savage peoples.'

'Indeed,' replied the Doña Margarita, toying with the food on her plate without actually eating very much at all. 'It is harsh enough. There are hundreds – perhaps thousands – of leagues with nothing but bare rock and sand. Then there are mountains higher than anything I had seen before, and rivers wider. Grandeur perhaps is there. I am not sure that I would speak of beauty.'

'And yet one so fair must naturally be the finest judge of beauty – if only when peering into a looking glass.' Major Wickham paid the compliment smoothly.

They had marched a good twenty-five miles escorting the carriage, before stopping for the night in another village. Colonel Wilson had given Pringle clear orders on the route to be taken by the two companies of the 106th, listing the distances of each stage. One of his men had ridden on to arrange for their billets.

'Don't want you running foul of Lapisse's men,' Sir Robert had said with a grin. 'Not that I am sure you fellows could not each handle a dozen Frenchmen, but simply because I do not wish the lady to run any further risks.'

The villagers were prepared for their arrival, as the colonel had promised. There seemed little enthusiasm for the shabbily uniformed redcoats – even Pringle had to admit that his own men were scarcely the most prepossessing sight at present. The fine carriage and even finer name of the daughter-in-law of the Conde de Madrigal de las Altas Torres produced both deference and a good deal of excitement. The prior of the monastery on the edge of the village greeted them in person, and insisted on providing a sumptuous meal for the lady and the officers of her escort. It was laid out in the main room of the house kept for visiting fathers of the church. Evidently, thought Pringle, such men did themselves proud, for the room was well furnished, the food rich and the wine flowed generously.

'If you will forgive me, my lady.' That was Lieutenant Hopwood, the acting commander of Number Three Company since Captain Mosley had not yet recovered from the wound he suffered last August. Pringle suspected that only the copious stream of wine and now port had given the snub-nosed and freckle-faced subaltern the boldness to address the lady at all. 'But have you seen the natives of the land? Is it true they ride like centaurs?

And that they wear skins and feathers – and indeed precious little else!'

Pringle noticed Williams frown in disapproval at such indelicacy in the company of a lady. Yes, Hopwood was very red in the face, flushed with courage and dulled in his wits.

'I doubt that a lady has occasion to spend much time in the company of savages,' said Wickham quickly. 'Although perhaps that is no longer true, now that she is the guest of our humble mess.'

The laughter was loud – indeed very loud, thought Pringle, detecting another sign that his fellow officers were taking full advantage of the prior's hospitality.

'I have already endured one savage wilderness, Major Wickham.' The lady spoke as soon as there was a break in the guffawing. 'No doubt I shall survive another – and one that I must say is a good deal more convivial.' Her teeth where very bright as she opened her red lips into the warmest of smiles.

La Dona Margarita had them all under her sway. Pringle watched his comrades – suave Wickham, the reserved but readily enthusiastic Williams, shy Hopwood, and the frequently snide and rarely fully sober Hatch. Each was entranced by the Spanish lady and her dark good looks. In truth the presence of any woman, let alone an elegant and mysterious lady, invariably stimulated a group of young officers like the sparks and vigour of one of those electric shows performed on the London stage.

Pringle readily confessed that he was equally fascinated. On his first clear sight of the lady he had revelled in her beauty. Imagination quickly rolled time back a few months to before her pregnancy, and as promptly stripped and bedded her. It was an intensely pleasing thought. Not long afterwards his daydreams had as happily conjured a similar encounter with the maid, and even the cook, whose long hair was more grey than black, but who remained plump and cheerful in a rustic way.

Billy Pringle liked women, and felt no guilt in the knowledge of this simple truth. Opportunity to go beyond vivid imaginings seemed unlikely in the days to come. Command brought responsibility, and the need to set an example. It would not feel right to pursue his own pleasures when his fellow officers would not have similar opportunities. It was a pity, though, he thought, as La Doña Margarita turned to answer another enquiry about the Red Man from the persistent Hopwood. The line of the lady's neck had a natural grace, her skin looked soft and smooth, and beneath swelled the lines of an ample . . .

Pringle took another long drink of port.

'You must speak to my driver,' said the Spanish lady with commendable patience. 'Ramón served under my late husband in campaigns against the Comanches. They are a most warlike people.'

'May we once again join together in extending our fullest commiserations at your dreadful loss.'

151

Wickham appeared full of sympathy and concern. Hopwood looked down, aware that he had clumsily provoked an unpleasant memory, but he and the other officers all echoed a chorus of 'hear, hear'.

'It is simply war,' replied the Doña Margarita. Her eyes glistened with moisture, but her gaze was resolute. 'My husband was a soldier. It was his duty to return and fight for his country. I am sure I do not have to tell soldiers of the risks inherent in their calling.'

'I am sure he was a most gallant gentleman, whose fall was not in vain,' said Williams. That was typical of his friend, thought Pringle, naturally both kind and expecting to see nobility wherever he looked.

'My husband was taken by yellow fever on the voyage back from Mexico.' The lady's voice betrayed no obvious emotion. Pringle was sure he saw Hatch smirk at Williams' immediate embarrassed confusion. 'Most of our servants died as well, including a maid who had been with me since she was little more than a girl.'

'A foe as terrible as any Frenchman,' declared Wickham, 'and one against which even the highest valour cannot always prevail. Fate has not been kind, but that must not diminish the high reputation of a great hero, nor indeed the respect we pay to a living heroine. Gentlemen, I give you a toast, La Condesa de Madrigal.'

'La Condesa de Madrigal!' they chorused, hearty

enthusiasm struggling with the respect considered appropriate for a brave lady and a widow.

'Both of my husband's older brothers were killed.'

Pringle barely restrained a laugh. There was the faintest hint in the lady's tone that almost made him believe she jestingly offered this as an achievement to balance her husband's modest fate.

'Tragic,' he said, as solemnly as he could.

'So many sons of Spain have fallen at the hands of the French,' added Williams, thinking again of the collapse of the army at Medellín.

'The second brother, Fernando, was killed by the English.' Pringle was sure there was a brightness in her eyes that hinted at mischief far more than bitterness. Hatch's pleasure at Williams' discomfiture was also more obvious, although he doubted that his friend noticed. Pringle himself was uncertain of the root of so deep a loathing.

'A man's duty is to his country,' said Williams, with surprising determination in the circumstances. 'Even enemies can be respected for their gallantry and honourable conduct.'

The lady smiled. 'A sentiment my husband shared and often expressed. He respected brave enemies, whether French or English – or indeed Comanche.'

'I would guess there is rough-hewn virtue among the savages,' said Hopwood, who had read some wildly romantic stories of the tribes of America.

'Not sure I'd want to meet one of the fellahs,

though!' snorted Hatch, breaking his long silence. 'Or a damned Frenchman for that matter!'

Williams, who was sitting beside the other ensign, kicked him under the table for cursing in the presence of a lady. Hatch looked at him in outrage, and then his face wrinkled.

'Perhaps they smell better than some civilised men.' At the end of the day's march Williams and Dobson had hung their clothes over a wood fire to smoke out the lice. The method was effective, but did mean that the ensign now walked surrounded by a pungent odour of charcoal. The others had courteously pretended not to notice.

'Civilised Frenchmen have behaved with all the cruelty of savages,' said the Doña Margarita in a clear voice, which immediately drew all the attention back to her. Pringle felt she wanted to help Williams, perhaps through an instinctive dislike of the other ensign. 'In spite of this I have met with courtesy from them on many occasions, in Toledo and Madrid, and during my travels. Even the worst of enemies can show kindness.'

'Yet it is better still to meet as allies and friends,' said Wickham. 'Gentlemen, I give you another toast. To allies and to Spain!' He inclined his head and glass to salute the Doña Margarita. 'And most of all to its fairest flower!'

'Thank you, Major Wickham. And thank you to you all. Now the hour is late and I am weary from another long day in the carriage. I shall bid you all good night.'

As the lady rose, the officers all sprang to their feet, prompting a stifled hiss from Williams, who had banged his knee on the table as he did so.

'I do hope you are not injured, Mr Williams,' she said fondly. Pringle began to wonder whether there was more to her attitude than simple dislike of the drunken Hatch. La Doña Margarita allowed Wickham to take her arm and escort her to the foot of the stairs. Before she ascended she thanked him and then once again smiled at the whole company. 'Good night, gentlemen,' she said, and was gone.

Pringle realised he was whistling silently through his teeth. If Hanley were there, Billy might have said something. Williams was too prim for such conversation, and the others not sufficiently close friends. Pringle missed Hanley and hoped desperately that he was at least alive. Even if he was, it seemed unlikely that they would see him again for a long while.

Billy knew that Williams missed their friend just as much, but they had not discussed the matter. The ensign told him what had happened and then listened with a wooden expression to Wickham's account of the chaos when the Spanish army had collapsed and Hanley had fallen from his horse. Pringle was not sure whether the major had done all that he could to bring away their friend.

There was nothing they could do to change things, and it was the soldier's lot to lose comrades. Last August Lieutenant Truscott had fallen in the last moments of the fighting at Vimeiro. He was an old and good friend, and lost his arm to the surgeon's knife. They had to march on. Then in the winter Williams himself had been left behind when the army retreated. He and Hanley looked for him each time they stopped, hoping that he would catch up, and both had feared for him, until he did finally reappear, with Miss MacAndrews and Jenny Dobson's abandoned baby in tow. He had to hope that Hanley would still surprise them all. Wallowing in their sorrow would not help that to happen.

'I must go and relieve Mr Clarke in charge of the piquets,' said Williams, reaching for his straw hat, which was the only headgear left to him. An officer should not go about his duties bare headed, even at night.

'Thank you,' said Pringle as the ensign departed. 'Tell Clarke there is food waiting for him before he turns in.' Hopwood and Hatch were already walking somewhat unsteadily towards the room they shared. Wickham looked fresh. He was also the senior officer and thus in charge of the detachment. Wickham's commission as captain in the 106th dated to several months before Pringle's own promotion. Thus he was undoubtedly in command, even if his brevet majority was army rank, held only while on duties away from his own regiment. Pringle was not sure whether the two companies of the 106th counted as the battalion. Such a concern was academic in the extreme.

It would no doubt have intrigued the fastidious and precise Truscott, now recovered from his wound and back on duty with a detachment of the regiment in Lisbon.

Whether captain or major in this situation, Wickham had shown no inclination to take charge. Pringle regulated the column on the march, settled the men into their billets, and set sentries and a piquet on the roads leading into the village.

'I don't want to get in your way,' said Wickham with earnest goodwill, 'and have every confidence in your diligence.'

Pringle did not mind. His subalterns were capable men – even Hatch and young Clarke if no great initiative or industry was required. The men had been hardened by two campaigns and were no longer the fresh-faced recruits who had drilled in the green lanes of Dorset the previous spring.

Escorting such a fine lady was a pleasant enough duty, although he wondered whether two companies were necessary for such a task. Colonel Wilson had appeared from nowhere, and his infectious enthusiasm made his orders easy to obey. The whole business still struck Pringle as a little odd, and that unease increased when Williams had whispered to him of Dobson's suspicions. Something did not make sense, but then their original orders to find and destroy a store of shrapnel shells had never struck him as other than a wild goose chase, dreamt up by a nervous quartermaster.

'Have you read any of Sir Robert's books?' asked Wickham suddenly. The two senior officers were enjoying a peaceful smoke before they too retired.

'Only the pamphlet about Bonaparte's mistreatment of the Turks.' Pringle chuckled. 'My mother sent it to me. Said I ought to know what sort of monsters I would be fighting and act accordingly. She's a cheerful old soul. Not sure whether she meant me to fall on my sword rather than face capture.'

'Good to inspire the masses, no doubt.'

'No doubt.' Pringle drew deeply on his cigar, relishing the taste of the good tobacco – another gift from their host. He wondered how to broach the subject, and in the end could think of no more subtle method. 'Does our current task in service of Sir Robert seem entirely justified?'

Wickham looked surprised. 'It is unorthodox, but I believe it to be worthwhile. Colonel D'Urban spoke of the great importance of the reports and letters being carried. I have no doubt we are falling in with his desires.

'Besides,' he smiled, 'there is a great opportunity here. We are of service to a member of one of the greatest families in all of Spain. That in itself is good. Even better we are performing a duty that will be greatly appreciated by our own government. It is a chance to win the gratitude of important men.'

'I see.' Pringle felt there was little purpose to be served in pursuing the matter farther. 'Well, I believe I shall get an hour's sleep before doing my rounds.'

There was no offer to share the burden, only best wishes for the night.

Pringle was asleep almost as soon as he lay down. He did not know what woke him, but guessed that he had been asleep for no more than half an hour. It was moments before he heard a door creak softly open and then footsteps crossing the hall outside. His room lay next to Wickham's, with the larger main guest chamber occupied by La Doña Margarita opposite.

There was silence, and then again the sound of a door opening, and closing a moment later. Pringle sat up, and carefully got out of bed. In spite of his size and girth, he was light on his feet and moved silently across the floor, scooping up his boots as he passed. It was a luxury he would never have granted himself during the winter's retreat to sleep in only his stockings.

As slowly and gently as he could, Billy Pringle opened the door of his own room. Then he froze and listened. There was a man's voice, muffled so that he could not catch the words. A woman's voice was a little louder, but still beyond comprehension.

Pringle listened for a while. Then he eased open the door to Wickham's room. The bed was empty.

There seemed no cause for alarm – a little jealousy perhaps, but not alarm. The lady had not cried out. Pringle waited for some minutes in case that changed. The voices had stopped and he could hear nothing distinct.

Finally, he walked as softly as he could along the hall and down the stairs. At the table where they had eaten he donned his boots, straightened his uniform and put on his cocked hat. Then he went to inspect the piquets.

At the east side of the village Williams was waiting, with Sergeant Probert and a file of grenadiers.

'Ah, I was just about to send for you, sir,' said the ensign in greeting. Beyond him, in the far distance, the underside of the clouds glowed red from many fires.

'How far do you reckon. Bills?' asked Pringle, as much to have his own judgement confirmed as anything else.

'Hard to say. Twenty miles? Perhaps a little more or a little less?'

Pringle nodded. 'Make sure everyone stays on their toes and keeps their eyes open, but no need to stand to arms.'

'Sir.'

'I rather think the war is coming to us,' Pringle said.

CHAPTER 11

They marched two hours before dawn because Pringle wanted to cover a good few miles while it was still cool. In fact it proved to be a dull day, with grey cloud blocking out all save occasional glimpses of sunshine. Yet as the morning drew on the air became humid and heavy, and the redcoats of the 106th sweated in their woollen coats and felt the straps of their packs grasping tightly at their chests.

'It must be a large village. Perhaps even a town?' he said.

'Sir?' Ensign Hatch's eyes were bloodshot, and Pringle wondered whether the man had continued to drink on his own for a long time after the previous night's dinner.

They could see dark smoke from the direction where they had seen the glow reflected off the clouds the night before. There was simply too much of it to have been the reflections of campfires.

Billy Pringle pointed towards the black plumes of smoke. 'Perhaps even Alcantara?' It was the only place marked on his map in roughly the right direction.

'The work of the French?' Hatch asked, frowning as he concentrated. Pringle was very familiar with the throbbing discomforts of the morning after a festive evening and so guessed what the man was going through. It did not incline him towards sympathy.

'Them or fat old Father Lopez smoking in bed,' he snapped. 'Of course it's the damned French!'

Pringle had decided to alternate the companies in the order of march, and so today the grenadiers were behind the carriage. Williams kept a file of men two hundred yards to the rear – and even farther when there was a better position from which to observe the land behind and to the flanks. Lieutenant Hopwood was in charge of the advance party. Wickham rode with La Doña Margarita in the carriage and they saw little of him after he had clambered in when they left the village. Pringle gave the orders, decided when they needed to halt for rests, and worried about how they could protect the carriage, let alone themselves, should they encounter any sizeable body of French.

'Send out flankers from each company,' Pringle ordered. 'Four men to each flank. Tell them to keep us in sight at all times, but maintain a good watch.'

Billy Pringle was nervous. He also wondered at the apparent intimacy between his superior officer and the Spanish lady. Wickham was a rake, and were it not for the lady's condition, Pringle would simply have assumed that the pair were lovers. If so, then Billy Pringle was neither inclined nor

162

dishonest enough to feel himself entitled to judge them. Yet the lady was heavily with child and while such things were possible, it did not strike him as in keeping with Wickham's sense of style.

Something – perhaps many things – were being kept from him, and he did not care for it. Pringle was a soldier and used to obeying orders. There was much that a battalion commander did not choose to share with his officers. Generals such as Sir Arthur Wellesley last August or Sir John Moore in the winter were even more reticent.

Yet that did not matter. The army and the regiment surrounded him, and he was content to wait and see what happened, tolerably confident that those in authority would do their best not to throw him too deeply into the soup.

This time he was in charge. His two companies were deep in Spain, a very long way from the modest British army left in Portugal. There was unlikely to be any significant Spanish force within hundreds of miles. The enigmatic Wilson and his 'Legion' were somewhere out there to the north. Any aid from them was uncertain at the very least, and yet Pringle knew that not too far away there were French regiments in numbers strong enough to put a large settlement to the torch.

There was no particular reason why the French should stumble upon his little column. There was also no particular reason why they should not.

Billy Pringle worried as he marched along at the head of the Grenadier Company. The lives of over one hundred men depended on the decisions he made. He resented anything he did not know which might help him decide well.

It was almost a relief when the shot came, sudden and loud above the tramp of marching feet and the rattle of the carriage.

Williams and his rearguard were on the crest behind the little column. One man had fired into the air to attract attention and now Williams himself was signalling. Pringle shaded his eyes to see better, but they were close enough for him not to need his telescope. Arm raised with thumb pointing down was the signal for enemy. The next gesture meant cavalry, and then Williams pointed in the direction beyond the ridge behind them.

Pringle signalled back, calling them down to join the main body. Williams sent his men jogging down the slope, but waited before following them. They did not run, and that was a good sign because it meant the French could not be too close.

'Sergeant Probert, recall the flankers,' said Pringle. 'Mr Hatch, we shall form rally square three ranks deep around the coach. Three Company will compose the front and left face of the formation. The grenadiers will form the rear and right side.' Scattered men on foot were at the mercy of cavalry. Pringle needed to make a rough square so that all sides were protected against the fast-moving horsemen.

Hatch nodded. The man looked pale, but that was more than likely the mark of his hangover rather than any undue nervousness.

'Corporal Dobson.'

'Sir!'

'Take three men and help the driver unhitch the horses.' With barely one hundred and twenty men, Pringle could not hope to form a square around the carriage and its team. With the horses standing beside the coach they might be just able to protect them. It would mean keeping the animals calm and so a man to hold each one. Panicking horses might well push aside the redcoats and open up one side of the square. Once the French were close then it would take no more than a brief instant of confusion to let them in and turn a fight into a massacre.

Pringle, soft hearted by nature and fond of animals in general and horses in particular, resolved to shoot the team at the first sign of trouble.

'French lights, your honour,' said Lance Corporal Murphy, stamping to attention next to Pringle. 'A mile away, but coming straight down the road. Two squadrons.' The tall, lanky Irishman looked almost pleasantly surprised to encounter the enemy. His infant son had died during the retreat to Corunna, and Pringle wondered whether this gave the man a new eagerness to knock over a few more Frenchmen. Mrs Murphy had taken the loss hard, and Pringle was suddenly glad that the companies' wives had been left with the rest of the detachment back in Lisbon. He had seen enough dead women and infants during the retreat not to relish the prospect of any more.

'Thank you, Murphy, join the company,' said

Pringle. He turned to see Lieutenant Hopwood and the advance guard. The officer raised his arms with the palms down flat to show that he could see nothing. Pringle called them back to the main body. It was good that there were no Frenchmen coming from that direction, but there was no prospect of outrunning cavalry on the road and he could not cut across the fields and risk the coach bogging down.

Williams loped up, one hand pressed to his straw hat to stop it blowing off.

'Chasseurs,' he said, confirming Murphy's report. 'Two squadrons. Perhaps two hundred or a little less.'

'Anything else?' Pringle meant whether there was any sign of guns or infantry.

'Just the chasseurs.'

That at least was something. They might be able to hold off cavalry if the square remained firm. They would also be a dense target and the arrival of even a single cannon or a company of infantry would slaughter them where they stood.

'What is happening, Billy?'

Pringle had forgotten about Wickham. The man was now leaning out of the carriage window, with that familiar half-smile and careful poise. He had obviously heard the shot and the commotion around him and yet it had taken minutes for him to roll up the blind and investigate.

'French cavalry, sir. Two squadrons coming up behind so I am forming square to hold them off.'

'Good God,' said Wickham. 'I'll . . . I shall be out in a moment.'

Putting his breeches back on no doubt, thought Pringle sourly.

The square was formed, with each side composed of three ranks of ten, the front rank kneeling with the butts of their muskets on the ground. The second and third ranks stood. All of the men had already loaded.

'Fix bayonets,' Pringle ordered. There was something reassuringly determined and a little savage about the metallic clicks as the sockets were fastened on to the muzzles of the firelocks.

There was barely enough room inside the square for the coach and horses. Wickham stepped down from the coach, and then paused to straighten his sash and adjust his sword belt. His right boot stood squarely in a pile of fresh dung from one of the horses and he looked down in distaste. The animal was barely a foot away from him and he had to look over its back to see Pringle.

'Everything in hand, I see.' The major sounded almost uninterested. 'I should not think they will attack.'

La Doña Margarita appeared in the carriage door behind him.

'Best if you stay hidden, ma'am,' said Wickham. Pringle was surprised by the hatred in the lady's expression as she obeyed.

A horseman appeared on the crest where Williams and his men had been. In silhouette they could not see the deep green of his jacket and overalls, but the wide top of his shako marked him out as a Frenchman. They did not have long.

One of the carriage horses reared up, and had Ramón not had a firm grip on its reins it would have got free. Men looked behind nervously.

'Dobson, kill the horses,' said Pringle, amazed that he could speak so steadily.

Wickham looked shocked. 'Don't be absurd, man, that team is worth a thousand dollars if it is a penny.'

Dobson was already leading one of the horses out the front of the square and did not pause. Nor did Ramón. The redcoats parted to let them through. Two privates, both of them countrymen well used to animals, led the rest of the team.

'We can't protect them, sir, and cannot risk them bolting and breaking the square.' Pringle kept his voice level and entirely reasonable, but then raised it so that it carried to all the men. 'As long as the square remains steady the French cannot harm us.' The redcoats did not need the explanation, but a statement of confidence never did any harm.

Seven or eight yards ahead of the front rank, Ramón calmed the horse he was leading, talking softly to it. Then he sliced very precisely through the blood vessels in its neck. Hot blood jetted out in a red stream and the animal's eyes rolled as it shuddered and began to sink down. The driver still talked softly to the dying beast, guiding it to the ground.

Up on the ridge, the chasseur circled his horse. Pringle guessed it was a signal, but did not know how the French system worked. Give me a few minutes, he prayed. If the French charged now, then they might catch them before the rear face of the square was reformed. Ramón had moved on to the second horse and killed it with the same gentle efficiency. Pringle guessed some of the men were unnerved by the sight.

'There they are!' Wickham's shout was a little high pitched.

A line of French horsemen now crowned the ridge, looking down at them. They were stationary and Pringle was relieved to see that they were not yet coming on.

'Fifty in the front rank,' commented Williams in a matter-of-fact way, before Pringle had finished adding in his head. 'The trick is to count the horses' legs and divide by four.' Pringle chuckled at the ensign's peculiar sense of humour.

'Or you could count their heads and divide by one,' suggested Murphy, and the laughter rippled along the ranks of grenadiers.

'I bow to superior Irish wisdom, Corporal.'

The third horse was down, but Pringle did not want to leave the men out any longer.

'Let it go!' he called. Ramón slapped the remaining horse on the rump and it jerked into a trot, heading off to the right. The three dead animals formed an awkward barrier a short distance in front of the square's rear face.

As the redcoats and the Spaniard scampered back into the formation, Pringle felt happier. If only these chasseurs faced them then they ought to be safe barring dreadful ill-luck. They should be safe, but they could not move. It was possible to march in square – or at least a column ready to turn into a square at a moment's notice. The drill in the 106th was of a decently high standard and he was confident the men could do it, but it would mean abandoning the coach and its suspiciously heavy concealed load. There was also bound to be disorder if they retreated from around the carriage.

'Worth a volley from the rear ranks?' Wickham scarcely sounded as if he was in command, and yet did not seem concerned about this. It was almost as if he did not feel personally involved in proceedings. 'Show them that we are not to be intimidated?'

'Better not to waste it, sir,' said Pringle levelly. The leading French squadron walked down the slope before stopping. They were now some two hundred yards away, and the supporting squadron was just visible on the crest itself. At this range they would be lucky to bring down one or two chasseurs. The rest could cover the ground to them quicker than the redcoats could reload, which meant it was a question of which side flinched. Pringle trusted his men, but saw no sense in taking unnecessary risks. A rally square lacked the assurance and strength of a more formal formation.

'As you wish,' said Major Wickham, as if such decisions were of minor importance. 'We all know

that cavalry cannot break properly formed infantry.'
Pringle was not sure whether the major was trying
to reassure the soldiers or himself.

'Well I'm damned.'

It was so rare for Williams to swear that Pringle
spun around to stare at his friend. The ensign had
his long glass to his eye. He also had an immense
smile across his face.

'It's Hanley. As I live and breathe it is William
James Hanley, Esquire, hale and hearty and dressed
like a don!'

Pringle scanned the slope and saw a handful of
horsemen in a cluster to the left flank of the rear
squadron. Even with the naked eye he could clearly
see the epaulettes and lace of senior officers. One
was in light blue, there was a trumpeter in pink,
a dragoon officer in a brass helmet and three chasseurs in green. There was also a figure in drab
civilian clothes. There was something familiar
about the ungainly posture and slightly slumped
shoulders of the man in the saddle. It was undoubtedly their lost friend. How or why he had come
here Pringle could not even guess.

'Perhaps the French made him a better offer
than King George!' he said.

Williams roared with laughter, relief washing
over him with the knowledge that their friend was
not dead.

Then a trumpet sounded and the chasseurs
began to advance.

CHAPTER 12

The leading squadron walked for a few yards then speeded into a trot when the trumpet sounded again.

'Steady, boys,' said Williams to the grenadiers in the rear face of the square just before Pringle could say the very same thing. The captain smiled, and glanced around at the two companies. Hopwood was behind the rear face and Hatch just where he should be on the left. Wickham stood with one hand on the hilt of his sword and the other bent at the elbow, fist pressed against his hip as if posing for a portrait in the heroic style.

'We must show the men we are unafraid,' he whispered, noticing Pringle's gaze.

'Well, hurrah and three times three,' muttered Pringle beneath his breath at such an obvious statement, and then turned all his attention to the French.

'Hold your fire, lads,' he called.

The chasseurs were close, barely eighty yards away and surely soon to surge forward into a canter and then a gallop to sweep over the little square.

He did not hear the order or trumpet call, but suddenly the line split in the centre and those on the left wheeled away in that direction, while those on the right went to the right.

'Hold your fire.'

The men on the ends of the two wheeling lines came as close as forty yards to the square, offering an enticing target.

'Hold your fire, boys,' said Williams over the thunder of hoofs and clinking of harness. It would take only one man to pull the trigger and the shot would surely prompt everyone else to do the same.

Pringle dragged his attention away from the wheeling chasseurs and saw that the supporting squadron had come up behind and was heading straight at them. This time he heard the trumpet and saw as the horses began to run, and then men stood in the stirrups, holding their curved sabres so that the tips thrust forward.

'Steady, lads, wait for the order.' Pringle's throat was dry and he would have given anything for a drink.

The chasseurs were close. He could see each man's face, mouths open under their drooping moustaches. The horses looked wild eyed, their teeth bared as they pounded through the long grass.

'Fire!' yelled Pringle, and all four sides of the square exploded in a cloud of dirty powder smoke, blotting the enemy from sight. He had not meant for everyone to fire, but in the excitement had forgotten to give a more precise order.

Through the thinning smoke Pringle saw two more dead horses piled against the corpses of the coach team. A green-coated chasseur lay beside them and another man staggered away. The French stopped, horses refusing to press on, no matter how much the riders urged.

'Third rank reload!' called Pringle. It was better for the second rank to be ready to support the first with their bayonets than to be fumbling with cartridges and ramrods. If the French came on then it was just possible they could overwhelm the little line. All it might take would be one man flinching, or still worse a wild or dying horse pressing on and crushing the ranks to tear them open.

'*Vive l'Empereur!*' A chasseur officer managed to jump his horse over the barrier of the dead animals and came forward, knowing that the fight was balanced on a knife edge. No one followed him, but it was as if British and French alike were holding their breath. The only sound was the footfalls of his horse as the man came right up to the front rank and then raked back his spurs to make the animal rear up, hoofs thrashing in the air. The tips of the bayonets kept the horse back too far to reach the men holding them, but even so the two closest grenadiers ducked instinctively.

Pringle remembered that he had a pistol and reached to pull it from his sash. Williams had already unslung the musket he carried and brought it up to his shoulder. The French officer was edging his mount a little closer into the gap where the two grenadiers' bayonet points had dipped. One lost his shako as a hoof passed perilously close to his head. Still the other chasseurs hung back and Pringle could not understand why because they were so close to winning. Men in the second rank jabbed at the horse with their bayonets, but could not drive the big bay or its rider back.

Williams fired over the heads of the men in front and the ball struck the French officer on his chin-strap, driving up through his mouth and into his brain. He died instantly, his body slumping limply, sabre falling from nerveless hand to hang on its wrist strap. The corpse dropped to the left, and perhaps this turned the horse away from the staggering line of British soldiers. The other way and it would surely have barged through even if it died in the act.

The line had held and Pringle finally felt he could breathe.

'Well done, Bills,' he said, and then louder, 'Well done, lads.'

'*Vive l'Empereur!*' The shout was loud and from behind him, and this time it was taken up by dozens of chasseurs as another officer led them against the right rear corner of the square. Corners were weak spots because it was hard for men to aim their muskets to the right and so few could bear. Pringle ran the few paces to the spot, but Sergeant Probert already had things in hand.

'Present!' he called, and the men in the third rank levelled their firelocks, pointing the muzzles through the narrow gaps between the men ahead of them. Pringle was amazed that they had loaded so quickly.

The French officer saw the movement and swerved, leading his men away.

'Hold your fire! Hold your fire!' called Probert, who had spotted ten more chasseurs coming in from another angle towards the same point. 'Wait for the order.' Once again the French did not press home against loaded muskets.

There was a lull for a good ten minutes as the French reorganised. The men of the 106th were all able to reload and dress the ranks. Pringle paced around behind the lines, complimenting his officers and NCOs and encouraging the men. As he passed the carriage he noticed La Doña Margarita standing in the opened door. The lady had a small pistol heavily decorated with silverwork.

'Hope we won't need that, ma'am,' said Pringle, raising his hat to her. 'Although I am most glad to know that we have you in reserve, should the need arrive.'

She smiled and he could not help thinking how uncommonly handsome she looked today.

'It will not, my lady,' added Wickham, who never wandered more than a pace or so from the coach. 'I am sure Captain Pringle will agree that we have seen the French off and should have no more trouble with them.'

'I believe they will attack again soon,' said Pringle, feeling no need to hide the truth from either a heroine of Saragossa or a British major.

'Then never fear, we shall drive them off as smartly next time.' Pringle was not sure, but felt that Wickham's expression was a little strained. He walked on to check the rest of the square.

Williams looked cheerful. Having seen to his men he was now finishing off loading his own musket. He spat the ball down the barrel and then grinned at Pringle as he drove it down with his ramrod. 'Good to see that Hanley is unscathed.'

'Yes.'

'Cannot help wondering what he is doing here, though?'

'Indeed.'

'I wish we could . . .' Williams left the thought unfinished.

'I know you do, but we cannot think of going out to get him.'

They were interrupted by a new trumpet call. Parties of fifteen or so chasseurs walked their horses into positions facing each of the corners of the square and no more than a long musket shot away. Two larger bodies of some fifty men apiece were back about two hundred and fifty yards facing the right and left sides of the little formation. Individual skirmishers came forward with carbines ready between the formed groups.

'It is always somewhat disillusioning to meet a clever cavalryman,' said Pringle.

The first of the skirmishers fired, the ball going high over their heads.

'If he was genuinely clever he would dismount some of them,' said Williams.

'Always hard to separate a cavalryman from his horse.' Pringle spoke more in hope than expectation. 'Ah well, work to do. Select one man from the second rank to return fire, Mr Williams. No one else is to fire unless they make a charge and then only under orders.'

'Sir.'

Pringle went around the other sides of the square giving the same instructions. A man from Three Company was down, with a carbine ball buried in his left shoulder close to the joint. He hissed in pain as he was pulled inside the square, and yet rallied when he saw Pringle.

'I'll be all right, sir, don't you worry,' he said. The man's face was pale and his eyes glazing.

The chasseur skirmishers continued to squib away. The nominated redcoats periodically fired in reply without hitting anyone. The French fared little better, but in spite of several near-misses there were no more casualties for five minutes. Shots struck the carriage repeatedly. La Dona Margarita no longer stood in the doorway, but when Pringle continued his walk around the square he was surprised to see the lady bending over the wounded man to give him a drink. Her servant tied off the bandage, working with practised skill.

Over time, the chasseurs risked coming closer. They were joined by a dozen troopers on foot, running awkwardly because of the long belts on their sabres, but able to fire their stubby carbines with more accuracy, kneeling or lying on the ground to make themselves poorer targets.

A grenadier in the front rank was hit on the kneecap and screamed until Murphy yelled a reproof. Almost immediately the man next to the lance corporal had his shako knocked off by another ball. The grenadiers laughed, and then they cheered because the man told off to fire pitched a chasseur off his horse.

'Good shot, Hope,' said Williams.

One of the mounted groups made to charge at the left front corner of the square, but shied away before they came too close. The first redcoat died, hit squarely in the chest as he cheered their retreat. Another man from Number Three Company lost his left index finger as it clasped his musket.

'Flag of truce!' Williams called to attract Pringle's attention. The French had ceased fire, their mounted skirmishers pulling back a little and the men on foot lying down so that they were hard to see in the long grass.

'No closer, messieurs,' called Pringle when the French were ten yards away. The dragoon officer and one of the chasseurs formed the party, followed by a trumpeter in a pink jacket with an almost white handkerchief tied to his sabre. It surprised him that the French had taken so long before demanding a surrender. The directness of their attack reminded him of Williams' account of the attack on the coach.

'Good day, gentlemen.' The dragoon spoke slow, heavily accented English. 'Your position is hopeless. If you stay here you will die one by one. I call on you to surrender.'

'We could cut our way out,' said Pringle in purely conventional defiance.

'You would die on our sabres. But we both know you will not leave that.' The French officer pointed at the carriage.

'Would I not?'

There was no answer.

'What are your terms?' Pringle had not noticed Wickham come up beside him.

'Honourable surrender. That and nothing more. You are scarcely in a position to bargain.'

'We could give you the coach,' said Pringle. Wickham started, obviously surprised by such an offer.

'We will take that now or later,' said the dragoon. 'It is simply a matter of whether you wish to be prisoners or die.'

'We will take plenty of your men with us.'

The Frenchman shrugged as if that was a small matter. 'You will still die.' He turned his horse away. 'Ten minutes, gentlemen, until we open fire once again.'

'Cocky rascal, don't you think,' said Pringle softly to Wickham.

'I fear we must consider his offer.' Wickham spoke as quietly. 'We have done all that honour demands. No one would blame us . . .'

'I would,' said Pringle. 'We are not beaten yet. If we can last until nightfall then we may break out.'

'It would mean leaving the coach, and how would La Doña Margarita keep up?'

'We should carry her if necessary. Her coach would no doubt be a loss, but surely not too terrible for so great a family. Or she could remain and rely on French protection.'

'The coach is important.' Wickham dropped his voice to be only just audible. 'A considerable sum of gold is carried in a hidden compartment, intended for the use of Sir Robert Wilson.'

Pringle had guessed as much, as had Williams and no doubt Dobson. It was almost a disappointment to have the mystery finally revealed. 'Then let us trust he is deeply concerned about its safety.'

Billy Pringle was sure they were being used as the bait in a trap, which meant that they were probably not supposed to be left to die and lose the gold. Hanley was there with the French, and in some way he could not fathom he was equally convinced his friend was part of the wider deceit.

'If we hold long enough, then help will come.'

'I am senior here,' said Wickham, almost as if the idea were a new one.

'You are, and you are a gallant officer with a fine reputation,' lied Pringle. 'There is a good chance that today you will add to it.' The fellow would, too, the captain thought, for he had powerful friends and the knack of presenting his own actions in the most favourable of lights.

Pringle retained the feeling that Wickham somehow felt uninvolved with the rest of them.

'We'll show these French rogues!' the major called out to the men. A handful gave a limp cheer.

On time the French skirmishers resumed shooting at the little square. Over half of them fired at once and it seemed a miracle that no one was hit in the dense mass of men. The slower, steady shots, where more care was taken over aim, proved deadly. A grenadier was struck in the cheek by a ball which smashed two of his teeth. He screamed horribly until dragged back from the line. The arrival of the lady made him stop, as if he did not want to seem weak in front of her. Ramón cleaned and bound the wound.

A few minutes later another man standing in almost the same spot was hit in the throat. As he was pulled back behind the line, Williams forced his way to stand in the gap.

'Do you see him?' he asked.

'Next to that hat.' Dobson nodded at a chasseur's shako just visible in the long grass some fifty yards away. 'Reckon he's to the right, down in a dip. Do you mark him, Hope?'

'The two of you and Rafferty fire at the mark as soon as he pops up for his next shot,' said Williams.

Pringle kept glancing back, hoping that he would not see his friend pitched back on the ground.

'I can see him moving,' said Dobson quietly. Williams saw a slight twitching in the grass that could as easily have been the wind.

Then he saw a man's head and there was a flame and then an eruption of smoke from the spot before he could call out, but he ducked his head. A ball plucked the air inches above him.

Three muskets fired almost together and flicked the long grass around the thinning puff of smoke. There was no cry, no sign of any success, but Williams waited a good ten minutes that seemed like an hour and no shot came from the same spot.

'Good shooting, lads,' he said, and felt able to return to his station at the rear of the company.

'That's a clever trick, Bills,' said Pringle. 'I am sure it must work at least one time out of ten.'

'As often as that! Cannot say I enjoyed it.'

The coach was scarred again and again.

'Remember MacAndrews telling us about how people fire high,' said Williams. Pringle was pleased to see that mention of the major's name did not prompt melancholy thoughts of his daughter.

'Wish the old fellow was with us now – ideally with the rest of the battalion!'

'Amen to that.'

An hour dragged on for an age, so that Billy Pringle began to wonder whether his watch had stopped. Two more men were wounded, one so badly that it was likely he would last no more than a few hours.

The French made several rushes, and once instead of a feint the chasseurs clapped their spurs against their horses' sides and flew at the corner held by Three Company. Lieutenant Hopwood timed the volley well, tumbling a man from the saddle and knocking down a horse. The French came on, but the square was solid and the horses baulked at the row of bayonets held steadily by the front rank. They stopped and no amount of urging could get them to move on. By the time the redcoats had almost reloaded the chasseurs had peeled away. The skirmishers resumed fire immediately.

Wickham stood beside the carriage most of the time. The vehicle seemed to draw the shots, but none came near him, and Pringle wondered whether the man felt he was sheltered from at least one side.

Sunset was well over two hours away. Pringle was not sure they could last, but there was nothing he could do and it was simply a case of standing and suffering. If French reserves arrived then that would be it. He wondered whether there was any basis for his hope that Wilson might arrive to save them. Hanley was still there up on the hill with the senior officers and it was so odd to think of his friend watching them die.

Pringle wondered about breaking open the hidden chest and putting as many of the coins into each man's pack as they could readily carry. It would not do. They would be hard enough put to it to break out even if unencumbered. All they could do was wait – or surrender? The men's spirit was good, still amazingly so, but he wondered how many more would drop before darkness fell.

More shots, and a grenadier was grazed across the forehead. He winced in pain, but there was no real harm done and he was soon back in the line, his head bandaged. Ramón seemed to have no shortage of bandages.

A ball glanced against the metal rail on the back of the carriage and deflected down, thudding into the belly of La Doña Margarita. Pringle happened to be looking at the lady and saw it in one horrible moment, watched as there was a puff of white from the material of her dress almost in the centre of her stomach. She clamped a hand to the spot, fear in her eyes, feeling for the wound, but made no sound. Ramón rushed to her side, dropping the wine bottle he had raised to the lips of a wounded man. Wickham was looking the other way and did not notice.

The lady held up her hand to stop the servant from assisting her. There was no blood on fingers or palm. She stood up straight, brushed some white fluff off her dress, and continued as if nothing had happened.

La Doña Margarita was evidently not with child after all. That explained Wickham's conduct if not the need for such subterfuge.

Another great cheer from the French and they came on against all four corners of the square simultaneously. Pringle was needed, and dismissed the deception for the moment.

'Wait for the order,' he called. 'Second and third ranks, present!'

The chasseurs pressed on, going straight from a walk into a canter, the men rising in the stirrups, arm up and wrist turned so that their sabre points thrust forward.

This was no feint, and the mere threat of presented muskets was not enough to halt them. A trumpet called and behind them the main reserves began to walk forward.

Pringle tried to judge the distance.

'Wait for the order!' They were fifty yards away, then forty and now thirty.

Pringle made himself hold his breath for two heartbeats.

'Fire!'

It was the largest volley they had fired since the first, as over seventy muskets flamed almost as one.

'Steady, lads!' he said in the stunned silence that followed. Men and horses were down. One chasseur was flung from his dying horse and landed just a few paces from the front rank. A horse rode across the rear face of the square, its side a sheet of blood and a lumpen bag of forage bouncing from the back of the saddle.

The reserves pressed on.

'Steady, lads!' That was Hopwood's voice.

'We're holding them, boys!' That was Williams.

A few of the skirmishers still dared to fire past their own comrades milling around the square and a carbine ball smacked into the forehead of a redcoat, who slumped down with a sigh just beside Pringle.

'*Vive l'Empereur!*' The French raised their familiar chant and the trumpet sounded the charge.

'Hold 'em!' shouted Pringle. 'Keep your bayonets ready for when they lift their skirts.'

Men grinned. This time there was no volley, and it was just a question of looking so solid that the horses would not plunge to destruction on the steel-tipped line.

The French came on, coming from the left and right, each formation two ranks of twenty-five men. The dragoon officer led one, and Pringle wished someone was loaded so that at least they could shoot that arrogant swine.

'Steady, lads,' he said. 'Steady.'

'Should we not fire?' whispered Wickham anxiously, and Pringle wondered at the man's ignorance, and then had a wild idea.

'Third rank, present!'

A few men hesitated before bringing empty firelocks up to their shoulders.

Perhaps the threat helped. The chasseurs reached the debris of the first wave and horses slowed as they tried to avoid wounded and dead riders and mounts scattered on the ground. The volley had brought down almost a dozen of each.

The lines were ragged now, and made worse by survivors of the first attack standing their horses and staring dumbly or screaming abuse at the square. Horses saw a wall of red edged by gleaming rows of sharp spikes and those that could veered to left or right to go around. Others stopped.

There were horsemen all around the square. They were so close that Pringle could see every detail of their uniforms and faces. One chasseur was surprisingly plump and red faced as he cursed the redcoats. The man's sabre hung from his wrist strap and he levelled a pistol. The muzzle seemed big and Pringle was sure it was pointing directly at him. He saw the hammer slam down and spark, but nothing happened.

Pringle let his breath out.

'Hold 'em, lads,' he said. 'They can't harm us.'

A loud explosion came from behind, and Pringle glanced back over his shoulder to see Ramón on the roof of the carriage, the blunderbuss in his hand.

The dragoon officer went past the side of the square, flailing with his long sword, but unable to reach the redcoats.

'Good job there are no lancers,' said Pringle to the major, who was standing beside them, his face heavily flushed and his knuckle white as he gripped the hilt of his sword. Men armed with lances had a longer reach than muskets and bayonets.

Wickham looked uncomprehendingly at him, and Pringle did not bother to explain.

A French trumpeter was sounding the same notes over and over again and Pringle guessed it must be the recall. Some of the chasseurs went reluctantly. A few fired pistols. More hurled abuse, and the fat trooper flung his pistol.

'Bastard!' yelled a grenadier who was hit on the shoulder by the awkwardly tumbling missile.

Men laughed.

'Third rank reload!' Williams gave the order and Hopwood, Hatch and Sergeant Probert repeated it to the other faces of the square.

'Well done, boys.' Pringle's throat was parched and his voice cracked as he called to the men. 'They shall not break us. They are only Frenchies after all!'

'Nearly as bad as Welshmen,' came an Irish voice from the ranks of the grenadiers, and Williams laughed with the rest.

'Steady, lads!' added Wickham, and Pringle thought that the major had never made any effort to understand the men.

Pringle felt a gentle touch on his arm, and there was the Spanish lady offering him a bottle of wine.

'Thank you,' he said with a broad smile, 'but it is better kept for the wounded.' He noticed Wickham dabbing a handkerchief against his lips. Pringle had lost the energy to think much about the major's conduct, and for the moment did not care to ponder about the lady, and whether her nobility was as much a fraud as her pregnancy.

The French were reforming as two squadrons

back at the top of the crest. Pringle wondered what they would try next. It seemed unlikely that they would give up. He tried to think of what he would do in their place. Perhaps dismount half – or even more – and bring the square under a heavier fire until it could be ridden down by the rest. How many cartridges did French horsemen carry for that matter?

'Mr Pringle, sir!' The call came from Hopwood. He noticed that the man called him rather than Wickham. It was odd how easily men ignored a superior who was so supine. If Wickham noticed he did not seem to care.

Pringle walked to join the lieutenant.

'More of them,' said Hopwood, his voice steady, but little hope in his eyes. Down in the valley a column of horsemen was trotting along the road. There was a troop in the lead in dark uniforms, but at this distance it was impossible to tell their colour or nationality. Behind was another, larger squadron, so lost in dust that it was hard to say anything at all about them.

'Mr Williams, may I have loan of your glass?' Pringle scrambled up on to the top of the carriage and hoped the French skirmishers would hold off for a while. He took off his hat, lifted his glasses up on to his forehead and then tried to hold the heavy telescope steady as he adjusted the lens.

The leading men were in blue or green so dark that it looked almost black. There were fifty or sixty of them. He raised the glass and caught a glimpse of something red before the dust cloud again enveloped the squadron behind. Pringle had never heard of French or Spanish cavalry in red, but there were so many gaudily dressed regiments in the world that this probably meant little.

Pringle tried to run the glass across the column, but inevitably moved too jerkily and lost it. He found the front of the lead squadron again, and then caught movement to the side and was surprised to see a pair of hounds bounding through the grass. He followed them and then twisted the lens to sharpen the image of a lone horsemen they followed.

Billy Pringle smiled as the relief flooded over him. He watched for a moment to be sure, and then stood up, pushing his spectacles back down on to his nose.

'They're friends, my lucky lads!' All of the officers and many of the men turned their heads to look at him. 'It is Colonel Wilson.'

A carbine ball ripped a splinter from the roof next to his right boot.

'Damned cheek!' said Pringle, and the redcoats cheered happily as he jumped down.

CHAPTER 13

'It seemed a worthwhile risk,' said Hanley, and then winced as Dobson pulled the bandage tight around his forehead.

'Keep still, sir.'

Pringle and Williams scarcely brimmed over with sympathy as the three of them sat around a little fire. It was dark and the cold was getting worse so that it became difficult to remember the feel of the day's heat.

'You nearly got yourself killed,' said Williams. That was true. Hanley had spurred away from the French when the squadron of Spanish cavalry attacked them from the rear in support of Wilson's men. A chasseur officer had given chase, slashing and missing as he passed. The man had turned his horse on a farthing. Hanley could not make his mount swerve far enough, and so flung himself to the side, losing balance and his stirrups as he fell to the ground. The tip of the Frenchman's sabre grazed his head. If the Spanish had not come up so quickly then he would surely have been killed.

'Oh, this is just a scratch, I assure . . . Oh God

damn it all to bloody hell!' Hanley spat the words as Dobson turned the bandage slightly, pulling at the clotted blood on the long scar.

'Cursing will not help, sir,' said the corporal softly. 'Just you keep still.' Williams marvelled at the transformation in the veteran since the arrival of the new Mrs Dobson and her firm ideas of respectable behaviour.

'I am sorry, Corporal,' said the officer meekly.

'Nearly done, sir.'

'I am more concerned about the danger to the detachment,' said Pringle, no longer light-hearted old Billy, but the officer commanding a detachment of his regiment who had just watched two of his men buried, and suspected that a third would join them soon. 'It was close.' The captain thought for a moment. 'Damned close,' he added.

Williams noticed that Dobson made no protest this time, and suspected that the corporal's sentiments echoed those of his captain – and indeed of Williams himself. They had lost men, and if the relief had not arrived then they would have lost more and perhaps all gone to the grave or French captivity.

'Colonel Wilson was delayed by bad luck,' offered Hanley in weak defence.

'Misfortune is in the nature of war,' said Williams, who was fond of such pronouncements and trying to be fair.

'Indeed it is.' Pringle was less sympathetic. 'And it was surely possible that farther obstacles might well have postponed his appearance until it was too late.'

'It seemed . . .' Hanley struggled for an answer.

'A worthwhile risk?' Pringle's voice was bitter, his gaze harder than Williams had ever seen in the past.

Hanley met it. 'So it seemed. And so it still seems.'

Dobson coughed. 'It's done, sir.' Williams was not sure whether he meant that the bandage was in place or something else. 'If you will excuse me.' He did not salute, as none of the officers wore their hats. Instead the corporal stiffened to attention, about-faced, and walked rather than marched away.

'You are probably right,' said Billy Pringle, and broke into his familiar smile. Williams let his breath out, and had not realised that he had been holding it.

Sir Robert Wilson had no doubts about their success.

'Caught 'em on the hop!' he called out delightedly as he returned from leading the pursuit. The gentlest of motions brought his horse to an abrupt stop, and a moment later he sprang lightly down. 'Capital sport.'

His two dogs scampered after him as he strolled over to join them.

'Any chance of tea?' he said, and waved them down as they moved to stand.

Jenkins, Pringle's soldier servant, appeared

miraculously with a steaming mug in hand. A devotee of the merits of the brown leaf, he struggled manfully with the misfortune of caring for an officer who could not stand tea in any form. This never prevented him from brewing the liquid at every opportunity and urging the captain to reconsider.

'Thank you,' said Sir Robert, and sipped from the mug with such evident pleasure that delight was brought into Private Jenkins' heart.

The colonel nuzzled the heads of the hounds with his free hand.

'Good fellows, both of them,' he said as the dogs licked his fingers. 'Plenty of heart. Remind me of a couple of pugs I have at home. So ugly they're beautiful.'

Sir Robert took another long sip and then passed the mug to Pringle. The captain noticed Jenkins watching with expectation. Knowing that he would regret such weakness, he nevertheless felt obliged to drink a little before passing it on to Hanley.

'Thank you, Jenkins,' he said, dismissing the quietly ecstatic private.

One of the dogs wandered over to sniff at Williams. He would have thought the smell of charcoal was so strong that there was no need for such close inspection, but the animal seemed fascinated.

'How many poor fellows have you lost?' Sir Robert asked, noticing the wounded men lying around another fire.

'Two dead, half a dozen wounded, one of them most likely mortally.' The colonel's sympathy sounded genuine, but Pringle did not soften the news because of this. 'Oh, and a few scratches here and there.'

'A great shame. However, I have no doubt that if you and Major Wickham had not commanded with such resolution then the cost would have been far higher.' Williams noticed that Wickham was already receiving credit for their stand. 'Where is the major, by the way?'

'Deeply asleep,' said Pringle. Williams suspected that Wickham would have been assiduously dancing attention had he known of Sir Robert's return. 'Shall I send to wake him?'

'No, no. Let the good fellow rest. I count myself a good judge of men, and have no doubt that I am already sharing tea with the true heroes of the day.'

Williams was pleased to hear this. It was Pringle who had kept them going and Sir Robert who had saved them. It was also Sir Robert who had put them in such a fix in the first place.

'Is La Doña Margarita well?'

'Resting as best she may in her carriage. As well as can be expected given her condition.' Williams noticed the emphasis in Pringle's words. The captain had revealed to him that the lady was not with child. Sir Robert betrayed no sign of recognition in his face, but perhaps the flickering red light concealed his thoughts.

'She is a fine lady and a dedicated patriot,' said the colonel. 'And has played her part well, as have you all. No doubt Hanley has explained our little ruse?' That seemed too mild a term for using them all as bait to draw the French down on them and give time for Sir Robert to gather his horsemen.

'Yes, sir,' Hanley confirmed.

'You must accept my apologies, Mr Pringle, for not taking you into my confidence. When we met and I arranged for you to escort the carriage I was not sure that there would be any need. I had knowledge that the lady was on her way.' No doubt from Mr Baynes, thought Williams, and carried by Velarde. 'It was a happy chance to discover your two companies so near. The Legion and our Spanish allies are spread so very thinly and there was no one available.

'And I hope you will understand that it is prudent to be secretive when such a sum of money is involved.'

'Then we are carrying gold?' asked Pringle.

This time Williams saw a flicker of amusement from the colonel. 'Yes, indeed yes. Although I did wonder whether to send the coin by mule more secretly, and perhaps fill the chest with lead bars.'

'Is that a mark of confidence?' said Williams boldly. The dog was slobbering over his trousers.

'I could not find sufficient good mules in so short a time,' said Sir Robert with disarming honesty. 'But in truth my faith in your corps is complete in every regard. So it was prudence, and not the slightest doubt, that led to my concealment of the whole truth, and for that I once again crave your forgiveness.'

'Of course, sir,' said Pringle after only the slightest hesitation. Williams echoed his approval. The dog suddenly sprang to press its front paws against him. The scent of meat with just a hint of mud and dung wafted over him.

'Push him down if he is bothering you,' said the colonel with the cheerful unconcern of the true dog lover. Williams had a general benevolence towards animals, without particular regard for all things canine.

'You may well have slipped past the French without any trouble. General Lapisse is retreating with his tail between his legs. I cannot stop him, and all I can do is harry their flight, snapping at small detachments. The Legion has cost him a lot of men, a lot of time, and shown the Spanish hereabouts that the French can be beaten.

'The French knew about the lady and the gold. I don't know how they found out. Perhaps a traitor or a mere mercenary with Cuesta or any one of a dozen garrison commanders or leaders on the juntas.' It seemed to Williams that the colonel scarcely lamented the escape of this secret, and he could not help wondering whether his ignorance was feigned.

'Hence the attack on the carriage, which we helped Mr Williams here to thwart.'

Williams smiled at the compliment. 'We were lost

if you had not arrived. Such good fortune was hard to accept as coincidence.'

'You have shrewd judgement,' continued Sir Robert. 'One of my patrols noticed their dragoons fanning out in small groups to sweep along the roads, so we split up and tried to find you first. It was a close thing.

'After that failure the French seemed to lose interest. Lapisse was not hanging around, and we were making life difficult for his outposts, but skipping back out of the way as soon as they gathered any sizeable force.

'Then your Mr Hanley turned up after his remarkable escape from captivity and . . .!'

Williams' startled yelp interrupted the explanation. The dog had nipped him as puppies will, not hard enough to break the skin, but with sufficient force to make their presence known. He stood up, half crouched, with both hands clasped protectively over his crotch.

Hanley looked almost as shocked by the suddenness of the exclamation. Pringle was struggling to restrain his mirth.

'As I say, just push him aside if he is a nuisance,' said Sir Robert calmly. He snapped his fingers and the dog slunk back to join its companion sprawled at their master's feet. 'Now where was I? Oh yes, the return of the prodigal son. So in comes this saucy fellow with his story of how he had brazened his way through the French lines. It seemed a shame not to take advantage of the opportunity.

'Off he goes again, telling the French he is Sancho Panza or some such and a loyal servant of King Joseph – God rot his benighted soul – and has news of the treasure they had so narrowly missed. There ain't a French general in the world who can resist loot. Call them princes or counts for five minutes and it doesn't turn 'em from the bandits they are. The rascals have been filling their pockets with anything they could find since they got here.

'Here was certain knowledge and an agent to show them the way. Didn't take 'em long, did it, Hanley?'

'No, sir. Thought that I would have to go to Lapisse himself, but the head of the cavalry brigade snapped at the bait at once and sent these squadrons under the same officer who had led the first attempt.'

'The dragoon,' said Williams, who as part of the bait found himself less than enthused by the story.

'That's the lad,' confirmed Sir Robert. '*Chef d'esquadron* Dupont and no doubt *Duque de nom de chien* now that Boney is doling out titles with the rations. They peel away from the main column and sneak through our outposts. Well, that doesn't take much since we have so few men, but we'll let the rogues have that deed to boast.

'You pretty much know the rest. Hanley and these French scoundrels come dashing down here after you. My lads – including Lieutenant Dawney and his mule-borne knights – are off thundering

200

to the rescue.' Sir Robert had led the cavalry of his own Legion. Behind came a company he had raised from stragglers cut off from Sir John Moore's army. Altogether he had rounded up nearly one hundred redcoats, with facings of every colour known to the British Army, and put them on donkeys, mules or nags to turn them into mounted infantry.

'My legionaries are all prime young soldiers,' continued Sir Robert, 'but it is good to have some solid British regulars for the toughest jobs.'

Williams began to worry that Wilson would do his best to keep the 106th to bolster his private army.

'So we come from the east, while Colonel D'Espagne leads his Spanish dragoons around from the west to cut them off. He is a Frenchman, although you would never think it. Left when the Revolution came, and has been fighting them ever since. We would all have been here sooner if the bridge hadn't been down and forced us to ride a couple of leagues farther to the next ford. Still, no great harm done.' Sir Robert conveniently forgot the wounded and the two graves. 'All worth it in the end.

'Just think, a whole regiment of French cavalry broken and badly mauled!' Sir Robert's voice rose in his passion and his dogs looked up, surprised by the noise. He leaned down to pat their heads. 'With the fellows you toppled and the dozen we caught in the chase that's nearly forty men knocked down. A splendid day's work!'

Williams felt the arithmetic was optimistic, while two squadrons were scarcely a regiment. The French butcher's bill was certainly higher than their own, but the affair could so easily have left all of the 106th dead or captive. As calculated risks went, this one seemed out of proportion to the stakes on the table. What was that old saying – breaking windows with guineas!

'That's the way we must fight until those damned fools in London have the sense to send the army back to Spain. Beresford is a solid fellow, and will do wonders now that the Portuguese have made him marshal of their army, but the war can only be won here. That's what I'll tell him when we meet in a few days. Won't do any harm to slip into the conversation that I have just ridden down some chasseurs and cut nearly fifty of them out of the saddles!'

None of them bothered to mention the steady climb of the total.

'Are you to go to Portugal, Sir Robert?' asked Pringle.

'Indeed. I have been summoned, no less.'

'Then shall you require us to accompany the lady on the rest of her journey?'

'No need, although of course most grateful for the kind offer. D'Espagne's men will take her all the way to Ciudad Rodrigo.'

'Then,' said Pringle, 'have I your permission to march before dawn on my way back to Lisbon?'

Sir Robert smiled. One of his dogs stretched and

he rubbed his hand along its back. The animal yawned massively. 'The day after you may go. Tomorrow I need you. Or rather I need these,' he said, and pointed an elegantly gloved finger at Pringle's red coat.

They marched at three in the morning. Some of Wilson's men and the Spanish remained behind and they left the wounded with them to collect on their return. The one redcoat hit in the chest still lingered, but there were bubbles of blood when he breathed and it seemed doubtful that he would meet them on their return.

Pringle set a rapid pace and the two companies of the 106th grumbled as they trudged along the ten miles they needed to cover before the sun came up. They saw little of Wilson, who had ridden ahead. Wickham went with him, but Hanley marched with the grenadiers. He was still in his civilian clothes, but was pleased to be back with his friends and also felt that sharing the toil of a march might complete his redemption in their eyes.

'I can see a couple of sentries,' said Williams, studying the convent through his glass. General Lapisse had left a company of infantry as garrison to this little outpost. The walls were strong, and there was no doubt a good supply of food and water inside the compound, so that the commander ought to be able to hold out against any likely attack from partisans or light troops.

'It will not be easy if the bluff does not work,' said Pringle softly. Only Hanley, Hopwood and Williams had come forward to the crest of the hill to look down at the village and the convent on the high ground outside it. 'Well, we had better get on with it. You go first, Mr Hopwood.'

Five minutes later Three Company marched along the very top of the ridge, easily visible to the French post. They followed the crest, until they reached a walled orchard which covered them from the enemy's view. A sunken lane led down from there into the main road leading into the valley. Some of the Legion cavalry were waiting and trotted down to send up a cloud of dust and make it look as if the company of redcoats was heading along to the road. Hopwood took his men back along the reverse slope of the ridge until he formed up behind the grenadiers. Then Pringle led both companies back along the ridge. More horsemen were waiting to create the necessary dust.

A little later each company marched across individually before they again went as a group. This time Wickham and Sir Robert joined them and rode conspicuously at their head. Two grinning grenadiers carried long poles with blankets fixed to hang from them in the hope that the French would see the Colours of a full battalion.

This time they followed the road and were joined by Lieutenant Dawney's scratch company.

The French saw several hundred infantry appear

outside the village and halt before the whole 'battalion' was in the open. Wilson and several of his staff rode forward under a flag of truce to call upon the garrison to surrender, announcing that he had a British regiment and Portuguese auxiliaries and would storm the place in an hour if they did not agree.

'Do you think they will believe him?' asked Hanley, somewhat disappointed to be left behind.

'Perhaps,' said Pringle. 'Depends how suspicious they are. Or how stupid.'

'Or brave,' added Williams.

'Aye, that too.'

'I cannot see any timber good enough for making ladders,' said Williams after a moment.

'Pray it does not come to that,' replied Pringle.

'It will work,' said Hanley, with greater confidence than he felt.

The wish proved true, and forty minutes later some ninety French infantrymen processed out of the convent gate and laid down their muskets.

'That is a true success,' conceded Pringle.

Sir Robert was his usual jovial self. 'Smoked 'em again,' he said delightedly. 'This is how to fight the war. Let those fools replace me now!'

Dawney's men took charge of the prisoners. The two companies of the 106th were given bread and wine by the villagers and the chance to eat and rest for the afternoon. They marched back to retrieve their wounded that same night, in time to bury the man with the chest wound.

The next morning Pringle set off early. The men were tired, but shared their officer's desire to leave such chaotic warfare behind them. They marched heartily, and kept a quick pace for several days.

'Be good to see Lisbon again,' said Pringle.

CHAPTER 14

The mouth of the River Tagus was bright blue and sparkled in the sunlight as Hanley and Williams walked down from the remains of the Roman theatre. They had visited the site before in the previous autumn, and even now Williams struggled to make sense of it. In the last century an earthquake had split the ruins into slices which lay on different parts of the slope rather than joined together.

It was the second week in May and they had returned five days ago to find far fewer British soldiers in Lisbon than when they had left. That meant the remaining officers were finding plenty of tasks for the men of the 106th – both the company that had stayed in Lisbon and the other formed of convalescents and stragglers left behind the previous year.

'I think it is good that Sir Arthur Wellesley is back,' said Williams, breaking their companionable silence. 'He knows how to win.' Wellesley had beaten the French at Vimeiro, but then been immediately superseded by a cautious superior who had squandered the victory.

207

One general seemed much like another to Hanley. 'He certainly has not chosen to tarry overmuch.'

Wellesley had arrived while they were with Wilson. By the time Pringle had marched the detachment back to Lisbon, the newly arrived general had gathered all available regiments and led them north against Marshal Soult at Oporto. Hence the enthusiasm with which commissaries, quartermasters and sundry other officers had pounced on his detachment as a source of sentries and escorts. This was the first free morning the Grenadier Company had enjoyed since their return.

'I hope the lists I brought from Espinosa prove both accurate and useful,' said Hanley.

Williams could tell that his friend was not boasting of the exploit, but was genuinely concerned. 'By the sound of things they were. And he did tell you the French were in Oporto before anyone knew of it.'

'Yes, although no doubt the news would have reached us in time. It has always struck me that the finest way to convince someone of a lie is to wrap it in truth.'

'Is that the voice of experience?' asked Williams mischievously.

'Certainly not.' Hanley paused for a moment. 'Well, assuming that I am telling the truth now.'

They strolled along the hill, the road wide and well paved. Everything had been rebuilt after the earthquake and this part of the city was grand and carefully planned. The cathedral with its big arched doorway, high roof and two low towers stood just where the road ran down the slope towards the sea and the pavements outside were crowded with people leaving after morning mass. It was not the wealthiest area of the city, but men and women alike were dressed in whatever respectable finery they possessed. The women – and there were far more women in the crowds than men – walked proudly and gracefully, their dresses shorter than was the English fashion so that slippered feet were clearly visible.

Pringle's voice hallooed them from amid the throng. It took them a while to make their way through to the far side of the street, stopping time and again to raise their hats and let ladies pass. Male companions greeted them with smiles, the women with chaste nods, for the British were once again very popular in the city since Wellesley had returned and acted so smartly.

When they came closer they realised that their friend was not alone. Pringle stood arm in arm with a lady dressed in a pale pink dress that would not have been out of place in a market town in Oxfordshire. It had puff sleeves, the high waist of current fashion, and a neck decorated in lace. Her gloves were white, as was the lace mantilla which now rested back on her shoulders. A pink parasol gave shade to the dark skin of her slim face with its full lips and grey eyes so pale as to seem almost without colour. Her free hand held her skirt off the ground, which even in this main street was liberally smeared in dirt and other filth.

'Maria and I have just come from the cathedral,' announced Pringle happily.

'It is good to see you again, Mr Hanley, and Mr Williams,' said the girl in English that was clear, and just tinted with enough of an accent to appear exotic. Maria was a courtesan. Not a common whore – Williams was surprised that the expression came to his mind since he would never have voiced it. Indeed, an uncommon one of great panache, whose clients were the wealthy and powerful. The previous August she had appeared in the guise of a nun and lured them into helping her retrieve a rich treasure left by a lover who had fled abroad. They had killed for her, and nearly died themselves.

Maria was very persuasive. It was not simply her remarkable good looks, for every movement carried an entrancing grace. That it was a studied performance made it no less powerful. She shifted slightly, turning to stare up into Pringle's face, and somehow the new posture set off the curves of her figure more clearly.

'Mr Williams.' Maria's voice broke in on his thoughts. 'I am still greatly in your debt and must find a way to make recompense.'

'An honour to be of service.' That was not quite true, for they had been duped into helping, and then the affair became a challenge none of them could ignore. Since then, it was obvious that Billy

Pringle – and he suspected Hanley – had enjoyed Maria's gratitude in the most obvious way.

'Surely there is something. Perhaps advice on clothes.'

Williams laughed. He still wore his threadbare jacket and trousers for he could not afford anything else. An ensign's pay was modest, and as with all the rest of the 106th stranded in Portugal, his was months in arrears.

'There is perhaps one way you might help me,' he ventured. His friends exchanged incredulous glances. Neither would blame him, nor feel jealous, since no one could own Maria. It was simply a surprise that their pious friend with his devoted adoration of Miss MacAndrews had even noticed the existence of another woman. 'It is just that . . . perhaps, if you did not mind to assist . . .' Williams struggled to find the right words and knew that he was blushing. 'I would seek tuition in the Portuguese tongue.'

Pringle bit his lower lip to stop himself laughing. Is that what you call it? he thought.

'Then call on me at three tomorrow afternoon,' said Maria, showing mild pleasure at his acceptance and no trace of amusement.

Williams looked at Pringle, who just managed to control himself.

'I am sure we can spare you,' he said, 'although it may mean taking charge of the overnight guard at the warehouses.' That's assuming you have the energy to stay awake, he added to himself.

'Then that is settled,' said the girl. 'Now, I must leave you.'

Pringle bowed to kiss her hand, and the others followed suit. Maria nodded to them, and ignored the disdainful glances of passers-by.

The three officers strolled off down a winding side street which led to their billet nearer the harbour. Tall houses towered on either side of the path, and although they could see the blue skies above them they walked shaded from the powerful sun.

'A surprisingly popish excursion for you,' said Hanley. Billy Pringle's family had once intended him to become a vicar until his clear unsuitability was finally admitted on all sides. He nevertheless retained a distinct loyalty and fondness for Anglican ritual. Hanley had no religion, but the years in Madrid gave him some pleasure in the splendid theatre of Spanish Catholicism.

'Maria was keen, and it was pleasant enough. It continues to surprise me how much chatter there is among the congregation during the quieter parts of the service.'

'You did not attend confession?'

'My dear boy, what on earth could an innocent lad like myself have to tell?'

'Of course.' Hanley saw no need to mention that Pringle had left to see Maria the previous night.

'They would not let a heretic take part,' said Williams a little solemnly. He appeared to think for a moment. 'Well, in your own case, one cannot entirely blame them.'

'Thank you kindly,' replied Pringle, joining in the merriment. 'Maria went.'

They thought about this in silence for some time.

'Bet if you published that in London it would make you a fortune,' said Hanley eventually. Then he caught movement above them. 'Look out!' he yelled, wrenching Williams back by the shoulders.

A woman was leaning out from a high window, a pail in her hand. They just managed to spring back before she poured out the contents and a rank-smelling stream of yellow-brown night soil splashed on the cobblestones where they had been standing.

'I cannot help wondering whether that actually might make your coat just a little cleaner,' said Hanley, his nose wrinkled at the stench which for the moment overcame the wider odours of the city. There was a dead dog on the far side of the alley, its stomach swollen to bursting point, and it brought back grim memories of a field of corpses. 'Let us press on quickly.'

'Oh yes, I do not know how I can have forgotten, but there is additional cause for haste,' said Pringle. 'Truscott sent word to say that he is bringing post for us. A navy sloop arrived this morning with official dispatches and a good deal of private correspondence.'

Williams set off at something more akin to a jog than a walk.

★   ★   ★

Truscott was waiting in the room they used as a temporary mess. The left sleeve of his shirt, like that of his jacket, was sewn against the chest following the amputation of his arm after Vimeiro. A slow recovery meant that he missed the winter's campaign, but had not prevented his promotion to captain and assumption of command over the hundred and twenty or so convalescents and others left behind by the regiment. With the three companies blown back to Portugal on the *Corbridge* he had become the officer commanding a substantial detachment of some three hundred men. That was assuming that Wickham did not return, since he was senior.

Williams almost flung the door open.

'Ah, Billy told you about the letters, I presume,' said Truscott with a quizzical look. Williams felt that his face, always thin, had become haggard since his wound. Several neatly written pages were spread out and weighted down on the table in front of the captain. A clean page was similarly held down with quill and inkpot waiting for him to compose a reply.

'He did mention it,' replied Williams somewhat abashed. Pringle and Hanley finally caught up with him and came into the mess.

'Anything to drink?' asked Pringle. 'I'm parched beyond belief.'

Truscott pointed the quill at an open wine bottle and some glasses on the side table.

Pringle grinned happily.

'Before I pass over the letters, we ought to deal with official business,' said Truscott solemnly. 'It may vex your soul at the ever-changing world once again turned upside down, Mr Williams, but you ought to see this.' He handed over a copy of the London *Gazette*.

Williams saw that it dated to the beginning of April. He had never seen the *Gazette* which listed his commissioning as an ensign, but the date quickly dissuaded him from the hope that he would now see those glorious words in print.

'Am I searching for something in particular?' he asked.

Truscott looked at Pringle and shook his head. 'One truly deplores the impatience of young subalterns in these modern times. They scarcely understand the burdens placed on their seniors!'

'"Uneasy lies the head that wears the crown,"' said Hanley.

'You poor martyred captain,' added Pringle.

Williams scanned the pages listing every promotion in the army. He spotted Wickham's brevet and frowned. Surely that was not what Truscott wanted him to see. The latter watched him closely and finally saw the first shock, the long uncertainty and then the birth of excitement.

'May I be the first to offer my congratulations.'

Williams wordlessly handed the paper to Hanley, who stood beside him.

'Well I'm damned.' Hanley passed it on to Pringle, pointing at the notable paragraph.

Ensign H. Williams of the One Hundred and Sixth Regiment of Foot promoted Lieutenant in the Second West Indies Regiment without purchase.

'The army's going to the dogs,' said Billy Pringle with a broad grin, and then began pumping Williams' hand with the greatest enthusiasm. 'Well done, old boy, well done indeed.' Hanley followed suit.

'Bills, you old rogue, in six months' time you will no doubt be ordering us all around.'

'I fear you gentlemen may be in for a disappointment.' Truscott raised his voice to cut across their celebration. 'For our friend is not bound for the islands of palm trees and dusky maidens.'

'And fevers,' said Pringle. The prospect of so unhealthy a posting suddenly chilled Williams to the bone. So did the thought of leaving his friends – and even more being taken yet farther afield from the girl who formed the centre of his world.

'Major MacAndrews writes to say that an exchange has been arranged with Mr Deacon, who is going on half-pay due to declining health. It will not matter to him in which corps he does not serve. So the 106th has not yet seen the back of our Bills! I trust you enjoyed your brief moment of exoticism?'

Williams felt a huge relief and then the joy of the step in rank. 'But why?' he asked, the doubt rising in case it was all some misunderstanding. 'Others are senior.' Two new ensigns had appeared on the regiment's books since Williams was commissioned after Vimeiro, but every other subaltern was senior to him and ought to have received promotion before him.

'The major does explain. Apparently it is on the recommendation of Sir John Moore no less, in recognition of your actions in January.' Williams had rallied a group of stragglers from the main army and on his own initiative defended a bridge which protected the flank of the entire army. The general, and several of his staff, had complimented him afterwards, but he had not expected any formal reward. A lot of men had died at the bridge and he could not help wondering whether their families received anything.

'Others deserve promotion more,' he said.

'Yes, I do,' chipped in Pringle cheerfully. 'But this is the army, Lieutenant Williams, and you must do as you are told!'

It was the first time anyone had used the title and Williams could not help grinning.

'However, now that we have dealt with this trifle, let us hear the more important news of the regiment,' said Pringle. 'Has Toye sold out?' Lieutenant Colonel Toye succeeded to command of the 106th after their previous colonel was killed at Roliça. Toye was wounded and captured in the same action. He returned to them just a few weeks later when the Convention of Cintra suspended hostilities, only to succumb to fever. Toye was unable to lead the battalion in the winter's campaign. Now, his health irreparably shattered, he was selling his commission to help support his retirement.

'Yes, the matter has been arranged. The regiment is now in the charge of Colonel FitzWilliam, late of the Guards, and younger son of a lord.'

Pringle whistled softly through his teeth. 'God bless all here,' he said.

'Amen to that,' said Truscott.

'So MacAndrews is just a major again.' The elderly Scotsman had led the battalion with great success at Vimeiro and during the winter. Formerly in charge of the Grenadier Company, he had taught Williams, Pringle and Hanley a good deal about soldiering.

Truscott shrugged. 'He may get his chance one day.' Vacancies caused by battle went to the next most senior officer and avoided the need for the substantial sums required to purchase rank. 'They want us back with the battalion.'

'Good to be popular,' said Pringle. 'Any idea when we might sail?'

'No. What the new colonel wants and what actually happens in the immediate future may not coincide.' Truscott had always had a precise, if somewhat opaque manner of speaking. 'I suspect we may not get away for some months.'

'Be a shame to sit here guarding stores while the rest of the army is in the field,' said Williams.

'Ambition rearing its ugly head once again, eh!' Pringle laughed.

'We may not sit things out,' said Truscott, always happy to reveal greater knowledge than his fellows. 'They have already formed two battalions of detachments and both are in the field with Wellesley. We only escaped because your two companies were gallivanting off escorting mysterious ladies. Now that you are here, I would not be surprised if there was talk of a third battalion.'

'Any news of our pay?' asked Hanley.

'Mercenary dog,' said Pringle.

'The matter is being given attention.'

'As bad as that,' said Hanley. They were issued with rations, but none of the 106th received any pay. Borrowing money was possible, but expensive, and so their mess here was a modest affair and there was little or no money for pleasant extras.

'At least they did not say "close attention",' said Pringle. 'That way we would never see it.'

'Probably true,' said Truscott gloomily. 'However, on a brighter note there are letters for both you and Williams. Nothing for you, I am afraid, my dear Hanley.'

'I do not really have any family. The closest are you fellows.'

'He's looking for sympathy again,' said Pringle with a thin smile, taking the half-dozen letters for him. There were two for Williams, both in the cautious, circular script of Anne, the eldest of his sisters. There was nothing from Miss MacAndrews and he tried to convince himself that he had never hoped for such a message.

'If you will forgive me,' he said to the others, and retired to a chair. In her methodical way, Anne had numbered the envelopes. He opened the one marked *11* first, leaving *12* to follow so that he would get the news in order.

Dearest brother
It was with such joy and relief that we received your letter telling us that you were safe and sound. I cannot describe my relief to know you were well and to see your words and stop worrying. Oh joy you are well and soon we will see you again. Mr Hopkins [an elderly master's mate who was a regular boarder at Mrs Williams' house when not at sea] *was at Portsmouth when the ships came back from Spain and said that he had never seen anything like it on land or sea when so many men like scarecrows came off the ships with officers no better than the men and all with beards and holes in their breeches.*

He suspected his modest sister had blushed to write the last word.

He says it is terrible and so we were worried and then we were more frightened when you sent no word and your regiment told us that you were not with them and your ship was missing so that no one knew whether or not you were safe and sound. Mama had a very kind letter from Major MacAndrews saying that we should not be concerned and that he would write as soon as news arrived and also to say that you were so very gallant during the war and won praises from the general before that poor man fell like a hero in defence of our country. We were all so very proud of you and I wished all the more to see you and kiss my fine brother. And so we worried and fretted. Mama worried most of all . . .

Williams wondered a little about that.

. . . although she put the bravest of faces on it and no one who did not know her well would have realised.

That he could certainly believe, for Mrs Williams, widowed at a young age and left to raise her children as best she could, was most skilful at masking whatever emotions she felt.

And then came that glorious day when your letter arrived and on the very same day one from Major MacAndrews' wife saying that her husband was busy about his duties, but that she wishes us to hear the good news without delay so took the liberty of writing to us herself.

Esther MacAndrews was a formidable lady and he could well believe her impatience, but he was extremely grateful for her kindness. His heart hoped that this reflected a favourable disposition towards him on the part of Jane MacAndrews' parents.

The rest was small news, recounted in Anne's breathless and enthusiastic style, and once again he lamented his inability to convince her of the merit of writing in paragraphs. He laid it down, knowing that he would read it again and again as news from home was such a rare and precious thing, and for a while even the minor details of his family's life in Bristol would fascinate as glimpses of a world left behind.

Williams opened the second letter, which continued for over a page in the same vein. Kitty and Charlotte, the middle and youngest sisters, each had new bonnets and Mama had managed to find enough money for all three girls to have dancing lessons.

> . . . *It is with great anticipation and excitement that we look forward to the chance to attend balls in the summer months.*

There was considerably more on this, with details and even a rough diagram of what they had learned. He skimmed through quickly, although on later readings he would make the most even of such a topic.

*. . . And then we returned home one day from
our classes to find Mama receiving visitors in
the parlour with her finest china and can you
guess who were the two fine ladies who sat with
Mama and took tea and some pieces of cake?
I am sure you cannot guess, and can you
imagine our excitement when Mama presented
us to Mrs and Miss MacAndrews and they
spoke so very kindly to each of us. I have never
seen such elegant and fine and beautiful and
well dressed ladies in my whole life. Mrs
MacAndrews is taller even than Mama – well
you must know this, but imagine my surprise
and yet she is like Mama in her poise and
bearing so that they almost seemed sisters
and so very friendly that I do not think I have
heard Mama laugh so much for a long time.*

That was hard to imagine, although Williams
conceded that his mother laughed so seldom that
perhaps it did not take much to impress his sister.
His mind thrilled at the evident goodwill shown
by the visit. He dared to hope and his eyes ran
along the lines.

*Mrs and Miss MacAndrews were on their way
to Bath for the season, where they will be joined
by Major MacAndrews when his duty permits.*

Or when he can no longer think of excuses good
enough to satisfy his wife, thought Williams.

It was so wonderful an afternoon and they spoke a little of the war in Spain and the high esteem in which you are held by the regiment. Miss MacAndrews is the most beautiful young lady I have ever seen.

Williams agreed with that verdict, but was also aware that many things were for the moment 'the most beautiful' things Anne had ever seen.

. . . And she spoke for a very long time to me and to Kitty and Charlotte and praised the bonnets we were wearing which are the ones we made last spring with the ribbons we bought from the market and said how much they became us and how she wished she had fair hair like mine and I said that her own hair was so lovely and surely far finer with its curls and colour. They stayed with us for almost an hour and then said that if we were to come to Bath we should call on them and accompany them to some of the functions and we all thanked them so very much for their kindness and said how very wonderful that would be . . .

The letter ended with a series of plans for somehow taking advantage of this offer by accompanying neighbours such as the Baxters or old Mrs Waters, who would surely benefit from 'taking the waters' (the joke was underlined three times to make the point) and who ought not to go without a companion or companions.

Williams finished the letter and tried to get his breath back. It had become such a wonderful day that he ceased to be embarrassed as other officers came in and gave him their congratulations. With the general shortage of funds no great celebration was possible, but they toasted his health and in a moment of weakness he took a glass of port himself and drank it quickly. Euphoria did not prevent his throat from burning and his stomach rebelling at the infusion of alcohol. With the heat of the crowded room he felt nauseous and pushed his way to the door. Outside, in the almost fresh air of the street, he took deep breaths, leaning against the wall.

Ensign Hatch watched him, a look of pure hatred on his face, which vanished as Williams looked up.

'Congratulations, Lieutenant, sir,' he said.

CHAPTER 15

'There, at least now I shall not be ashamed.' Maria walked around behind him, inspecting the new uniform. Williams was not sure whether he ought to feel shame for escorting a known lady of the town to the theatre, but knew that he did not. Judge not, lest ye be judged, he thought to himself.

'Stop grinning like a fool!' Maria ordered sharply. 'You are supposed to look like a hero. Now sit down.'

Williams obeyed.

'Yes, that is good work.' She ran a finger along the top of his collar, ruffling his fair hair, and the simple gesture instantly put him on edge. Everything about Maria was sensual, and although in the last week their friendship had never extended to greater intimacy, Williams was kept constantly aware that she was a woman. Miss MacAndrews had the same effect on him – perhaps an even more overwhelming one – but he was in love with her and that seemed right. He liked Maria and she was true to her word in instructing him in Portuguese. There was no more than that.

Now it was her turn to ask for another favour,

and as part of this she had insisted on purchasing for him a new uniform. 'I could not possibly be seen with you as you are,' she said, and sent him to one of the many Lisbon tailors who now catered for the requirements of British officers. Two days later, the new uniform was waiting for him, and it seemed that it had passed inspection.

'That will do. It is a pity that the cuffs are red and not bright yellow like some others I have seen.'

'It is the colour of my regiment,' said Williams. The 106th had red facings, so that cuffs and collar matched the rest of the jacket. In keeping with his status as an officer, Williams' new jacket was made in brighter scarlet than the coats of the ordinary soldiers.

'They should have asked a woman to devise it. Well, too late for that now.' She walked beside him. 'These are good.' For the first time in his life Williams was the owner of the tight-fitting white breeches worn in full dress uniform and a pair of new and highly polished black hessian boots, complete with tassels at the top. The leather was stiff, and it would be a while before they softened enough to be comfortable, but there was something very pleasant about being dressed like the most fashionable of officers.

'Yes, I think this will do. You look almost dashing. It will please his vanity to take me from you.' Maria planned to capture the affections of a certain Mr Howarth, who was in Lisbon as part of the British legation and also had an interest in several of the companies under contract to supply the army. Howarth was small, pale and short sighted, but considered himself something of a buck. Maria was sure the man resented the presence of so many handsome men whose uniforms outshone his own civilian finery. 'Now, you must look as if you desire me above all things.'

She walked in front of him, the long windows opening on to the balcony behind her. Bright afternoon sunlight streamed into the room. Her white cotton dress was modest, with a high neckline and very little decoration. In the bright sunlight it was also almost transparent. Williams' eyes widened. He glanced down for an instant, but only for an instant. The curves of her legs and body were all in dark silhouette, stark, clear and very lovely. An image flashed into his mind of Jane MacAndrews, naked after her drenching in the icy river as he tried to stop her from dying of cold, and other images of his ardent dreams. They could not quite blot out the immediacy of the woman in front of him. His nobler affections had little say in the matter.

'Yes, that is a little better,' said Maria. 'You may stand up again.'

Williams did not move. Maria smiled with satisfaction.

Three hours later, Williams walked Maria into the theatre. Her dress was a brilliant white, with its top for the moment covered in a tight crimson jacket. Her thick black hair was piled high and topped with a black ostrich feather. 'Your Scottish

228

soldiers sell the ones from their hats to buy wine,' she explained.

They had a small box to themselves. He helped her to her seat, dancing attendance upon her with only a little of his accustomed clumsiness. Somehow he did not feel nervous around her, perhaps because this was all an act. He helped her to remove the jacket, revealing a plunging neckline displaying a good deal of her out-thrust bosom. Williams' throat felt dry.

'At least you will be able to practise your Portuguese,' she said. 'Ah, there he is as usual. In the largest box on the far side.' Williams was surprised to see a younger man than he expected. He was dressed in a light blue jacket and immense kerchief. Howarth was an ill-favoured fellow with an expression ever shifting from disdain to petulance and back again.

'Are you sure you want to bother?' he asked.

'He is rich,' she said. 'And will do for a few weeks.'

Williams struggled to follow the play. It was clearly a comedy, and he recognised the stern guardian, the dull tutor and the handsome nobleman disguised as a simple student to woo the beautiful maiden. There was also a villainous rival, who wore a hat with a French cockade and a false nose adorned with a wart. The actor was hissed on each appearance.

Maria was not inclined to explain. 'Whisper in my ear,' she commanded. When he did so, she gave a little laugh and fluttered her fan.

A few minutes later she repeated the instruction. This time her response was to flush. Williams noticed Howarth looking in their direction. He was not the only one, and many of the men kept glancing at his companion.

'Kiss me!' she ordered.

'I beg your pardon,' was all he could manage.

'On the cheek, kiss me!'

'I . . .'

'Get on with it, while we have his attention.'

Williams leaned over and pecked her lightly on the cheek. Maria recoiled, looking surprised and shocked.

Lieutenant Williams panicked, sure he had misunderstood. 'I am so sorry, but I thought . . .'

'Again. On the lips this time,' she whispered. 'I will struggle, but force me until I say.'

'If you are sure . . .'

'Do it.'

He slid his arms around her and tilted his head as he pressed his mouth firmly against hers. Maria's perfume was intoxicating, her lips smooth and soft. She squirmed, her left hand with the fan smacking his head in apparent protest, while her unseen right grasped his shoulder firmly and pulled him ever tighter towards her. They struggled, Williams unsure quite what he was supposed to do and very conscious of the beautiful young woman held in his arms. Maria twisted her mouth away from his, and so he kissed her neck instead.

'Enough,' she whispered in his ear. 'I said

enough,' she repeated as he continued to press his lips against her skin.

She was breathing hard, a fact all the more evident because somehow his right hand now cupped her left breast through the thin silk of her dress. Williams looked down and stared as if somehow this would help him to understand. Maria also looked down, then her face filled with anger. Williams at last withdrew, and the girl slapped him hard on the cheek.

'I am sorry . . . I do not know . . .' he stammered.

''You are doing well,' she hissed. 'Wait a little and we will try again.'

There was a burst of unnaturally loud laughter from the stalls beneath them. It did not seem to be provoked by anything the rest of the audience found amusing.

'Why did you not ask Pringle or Hanley to help you with this?' asked Williams in an effort to recover his balance.

'Pringle has glasses and you have blond hair. You also look like a bold man,' she said bluntly.

'So does Hanley.'

'But I could not be sure of stopping either of them! You are safer.'

Williams was not sure whether he was being complimented or insulted.

Maria saw his confusion. 'I trust you because you are in love,' she said quietly.

'Did one of the others tell you?'

'Yes, but I did not need to hear that. It is so easy to see.'

He was pleased at that, even if part of him knew that she was very good at pleasing men and doubted her sincerity.

'You're looking in the wrong place, old cock!' The shout was loud and came from beneath them. On stage the guardian was patrolling with his faithful retainer and looking for the lover, who was now disguised as the tutor.

Maria turned to Williams. 'Some of your countrymen. Is such boorishness accepted in England?'

Williams had rarely had the funds or inclination to attend the theatres. 'Perhaps in the lower halls, but no, I do not believe so.'

'Look under the stairs!' came another helpful comment in English. The cast tried to ignore the heckling, raising their voices in an effort to be heard.

'Silly old sod, he's not listening.'

'Let's help the poor old dog out!'

There was commotion beneath them, with chairs falling and voices raised in protest. Williams leaned forward to see and was dismayed when two British officers scrambled up on to the stage. There was relief when he spotted that one was in the blue facings of a royal regiment and the other in white, and then they turned to help a third redcoat up and his heart sank as he saw the coat of the 106th. It was Hatch. Williams put his hand over his eyes.

'It would be,' he muttered.

Hatch was bare headed, his long brown hair not

yet trimmed back after the month or more spent on the march to Spain and back. He was swaying visibly, as were his associates. The man in white facings dropped something which rolled noisily across the stage. He crouched down on all fours searching for it. The man from the royal regiment took a swig from a brandy bottle, and then generously offered it to the actor playing the servant.

'Please yourself,' he said when the man declined. 'I was only being civil.'

Ensign Hatch appeared to notice the audience properly for the first time. He smiled broadly and took a bow, but the motion brought a wave of nausea and for one horrible moment Williams thought the man was going to vomit. He staggered back a few steps before recovering and bumped into the guardian. Hatch appeared offended.

'Look where you are going,' he said. 'No way to treat a guest.'

Someone was obviously calling and gesturing to the officers from the wings. The officer in blue facings noticed and turned to the servant. 'I think they want you,' he said helpfully.

With a fortitude that Williams could not but admire, the cast did their best to continue, pretending the drunken Englishmen were not there. Two maids appeared, one very plump and white haired and obviously played by a man.

'My darling,' said Hatch, spreading his arms in greeting, and lurched towards them. The actress dodged him, but the man was not so fortunate and was taken in an embrace. 'Together again at last,' said the ensign.

Meanwhile the officer from the royal regiment had finally realised that the people in the wings were calling to him and he wandered offstage to see what was so damned urgent. The man from the regiment with white facings continued to crawl around the stage, almost tripping the guardian and the disguised suitor.

'It's all a fraud,' yelled Hatch, as the actor managed to free himself, but lost his mobcap and wig in the process. With surprising speed the officer lunged forward and jabbed at the maid's bosom. 'Look, a fraud,' he said, as if making a great discovery.

Maria seemed more amused than angry. 'They are not very good actors at the best of times,' she explained. 'Still, ought you not to do something to restrain your comrades?'

'Get off the stage, you fellows!' he called as loudly as he could.

Hatch nudged the actor playing the maid. 'They don't seem to like you.'

There was shouting from the wings. 'Don't think they like you either,' added the ensign. He jabbed his index finger against the man's bosom again. 'A fraud, you see, it's simply no good.' Then he edged towards the actress playing the pretty maid, who squealed at the sight of his outstretched finger and retreated behind the guardian, who was promptly prodded in the ribs.

'Get off!' shouted another English voice from beneath them.

'Leave 'em, this is better than the damned play!' chipped in another.

'You must make them,' said Maria.

'Must I?'

'Yes, it is time for you to leave my side and give him his chance. Earn your new rank,' she added after a moment. 'After all, you are the hero.'

'So you keep saying.' Williams rose reluctantly. Reasoning with drunks was rarely profitable, and he could not help thinking that a situation like this could all too readily end in scandal. What if one of the drunks called him out? He knew Hatch disliked him intensely, although was never sure why. 'I'll go, then.'

'Do.'

Williams walked slowly, hoping that the matter would resolve itself. He studied the walls of the corridor as if they were works of art, taking his time.

As he came out at the back of the stalls a woman's scream cut through the commotion. Hatch raised his hand high. 'The call of honour,' he shouted before tripping over the crawling officer and falling offstage.

Suddenly the actress playing the daughter ran out on to the stage, wearing only her stays, petticoats and the old-fashioned hoop which would support her skirts when she was wearing them. She was closely pursued by the ensign from the royal regiment, who in turn was followed by several angry men.

'View halloo!' The man dodged the guardian, knocked the servant down and took the opportunity to kiss the pretty maid as the daughter tried to hide behind the others.

Most of the audience were yelling protests, apart from a few English voices, and then a red-faced major barged through the doors and led a file of redcoats with muskets past Williams. The curtain fell and ended the first half.

'You, sir!' The major pointed at Williams. 'This one is one of yours, isn't he?' A soldier was lifting Hatch to his feet. 'Take him away and see that he does not get into any more scrapes.'

'Sir,' said Williams without any enthusiasm, but he dutifully supported the ensign.

'Who are you?' said Hatch, his eyes clearly unable to focus.

'A sad man,' replied Williams, thinking that he had arrived with a beautiful woman on his arm and was leaving with a drunken lout. He hoped the man would not throw up over his new uniform.

There was a press of people outside the theatre, where men were selling wine, pastries and cool lemon juice sweetened with sugar. The buzz of conversation ceased for a moment when the two officers appeared, before redoubling in volume.

'Wasn't much of a play,' muttered Hatch.

Williams saw that Maria was there, with the diminutive Howarth attending her. He marvelled that she had worked her magic so quickly. The girl feigned alarm at the sight of him, and the small civilian moved protectively in front of her. Well, the fellow had pluck at least, and good luck to them both. Yet there was something wounding about being seen to lose to such a man – or indeed to lose at all, even if Maria meant nothing to him.

'Look at those tits,' said Hatch with slow reverence, his eyes evidently responding better.

Howarth glared at them with a mixture of distaste and triumph and took Maria's arm to lead her away.

The next night, Williams found himself in charge of the guard placed on the rear doors of the theatre. Sir Arthur Wellesley himself had given the order for this after similar displays to that of the previous night, but the practice had lapsed when he set off on campaign and soldiers were in short supply. It was also hoped that there were too few British officers left in Lisbon with the energy to cause such mischief.

Lance Corporal Murphy himself stood outside the dressing room used by the actresses.

'You may have to assure my Mary that I behaved like a gentleman, your honour,' he said when Williams did his rounds.

'Of course.' They both tried to ignore the girl wearing only a loose robe who walked out of one of the rooms, looked them up and down and then returned through the door. 'I trust Mrs Murphy is well.'

'Thank you, sir, that she is.' Having lost an infant to the winter's cold, Mary Murphy was now once again expecting. 'She's sad as well, but happy, if you know what I mean.'

No rowdy officers appeared and Williams was glad for he had no particular desire for confrontation. Howarth brought Maria to the performance and he was surprised that he found it disturbing to see them together. When the man was not looking, Maria blew him a kiss. Williams smiled, shaking his head, and returned to his duties.

'Be good to be back in the field again,' he remarked to Murphy at the end of the night. The same girl appeared again, this time clad in only a flimsy shift.

'Aye,' said the corporal. 'In a way.'

Ensign Hatch stayed in his room that night. In part this was because he had neither duties nor funds with which to enjoy himself. He also had something important to do.

He hated Williams, and the man's elevation to lieutenant was especially wounding. Hatch was sure that the man had murdered his closest friend in the chaos of Roliça. That was not true, for Dobson had done the killing in revenge for Ensign Redman's seduction of his daughter, but Hatch did not know this.

Hatch dared not call Williams out. Duelling

was against the Army Act. Sympathetic fellow officers who felt the quarrel was justified might forget what they had seen and so a court martial would collapse. Hatch doubted his comrades would protect him in this way, especially since he had no evidence to offer them. More importantly, Williams was a killer, and he suspected that his prowess as a duellist would be as formidable as his ferocity in battle.

Ensign Hatch had no wish to die. He must wound his enemy in secrecy and so for months he took every opportunity to make jokes at Williams' expense, in the hope that his respect in the world of the regiment would crumble. Success was so far modest, but now he realised that there was a better way.

This time he would write a letter. It was addressed to Captain and Mrs Davenport. Mrs Davenport was an intimate of Mrs Wickham, sure to pass on any gossip about mutual acquaintances to her friend. Telling such stories to Lydia Wickham was much the same as shouting them from the top of a church tower.

Hatch began slowly, telling of their recent march into Spain. His account suggested a cheerful picnic rather than a grim skirmish.

Our Mr Williams was much taken by the Spanish lady. She was a handsome lady, no doubt, although her grace diminished by the advanced state of a certain condition. Sadly for our Sir Galahad, she was immune to his rustic charms, which also seemed poor in the company of other, more gallant officers.

On our return to Lisbon, Mr W set his cap at more attainable goals, and began to be seen in company with a woman – I cannot say lady – famed throughout the city for the mercantile nature of her charms – although I would not mention the title for such a one in a letter or polite society. It appears he had some success, so much so that she paid to dress him in a new uniform of finest materials and he became quite the buck. However, once again fate was not on the side of our brave macaroni, for the female as promptly threw him over for a civilian no less, and a tiny, ugly little brute to be sure. All our Mr W could do was gnash his teeth.

He was soon consoled for his loss! For now he stands special guard over the actresses in the theatre to protect these damsels from who knows what peril.

There, that should do it. In time the stories would circulate. There would be laughter, and when the tales reached Miss MacAndrews no doubt there would be anger.

Hatch laid down his pen with considerable satisfaction.

CHAPTER 16

News came from the north and it was good.
'Soult's beaten,' announced Truscott to
the assembled officers of the 106th.
'General Wellesley slipped across the River Douro
under his very nose and hounded him out of
Oporto and back through the mountains. He has
lost a few thousand men and all his guns.'

That was indeed good news and particularly
satisfying since it was Marshal Soult who had
pursued Sir John Moore's army all the way to
Corunna.

'That begins to even the score,' said Pringle.

'We may have a chance to do more soon,'
continued Truscott. 'The formation of the Third
Battalion of Detachments is confirmed and we are
to be part of it – indeed, the largest single contingent of the battalion. We are to march to Abrantes
at the end of the week.

'As you may gather, this means that there will
be a good deal to achieve in a very short time. We
are relieved of some of our duties, which will be
taken on by the advance party of a new battalion
just landed. I fear, Mr Williams, that this means

your participation in the theatrical arts is terminated.'

They laughed, and then Hopwood raised the question on almost every mind.

'Who will command, sir?'

'I understand that an officer is to be appointed. Until he arrives our senior captain will oversee the formation of the battalion.'

'Many congratulations,' said Pringle heartily.

'Misplaced actually. Major Wickham has returned from attachment to the staff and of course naturally takes over.'

Pringle said nothing, but felt his heart sink and exchanged meaningful glances with Williams and Hopwood. Wickham was usually affable – untrustworthy with money or women, but pleasant enough as company. Yet his lack of interest during the fight with the French chasseurs was worrying. Pringle did not seriously doubt Wickham's courage, although he knew Williams had stronger feelings on the matter. He was unsure about the major's ability and judgement and that was not encouraging. Yet Wickham's apparent unwillingness to exert himself unless in the presence of persons of influence was profoundly worrying. A battalion drawn together from the flotsam and jetsam left behind by other corps needed strong leadership, which in the beginning it did not get.

'I trust you, old boy,' Wickham told Truscott. 'And I had better keep my ears open at headquarters to find out what they want us to do.'

They saw little of the major. Truscott did most of the work, assisted by Pringle and several of the others. Some of the officers drawn from other corps were just as eager and capable. Others struck Pringle as the kind of men their regiments had probably been happy to leave behind. A few were willing, but barely fit enough for their duties.

The same was true of the men. The hospitals were combed for men well enough for active duty and this yielded a harvest of the genuinely recovered, the unmasked malingerers and good, keen soldiers trying desperately to hide their physical weakness. Others came from the parties posted to the stores and other services, where duties were often light and the prospects of profit frequent. One sergeant proved so obese that he was unable to fasten the buttons of his jacket around his stomach.

Pringle burst out laughing when the man was dismissed and stamped out of the room in a passable impression of discipline. 'Clearly the fruits of a righteous life,' he said to Williams. 'God help us if he breaks down on the march and we have to carry him.'

On the second day they received the most welcome addition of Mr Dawney's improvised company of mounted men, finally released by Sir Robert Wilson after a series of increasingly strident orders to this effect. Wilson kept the mules and horses for his own purposes, so the redcoats were infantry once again by the time they reached

Lisbon. They were good men, if inclined to independence, and the months of skirmishing along the border had forged them into a good unit.

There were seventy men from the 4th Battalion of the 60th Regiment who had somehow found their way to Portugal instead of joining their fellows as garrison of Corunna at the end of the previous year. Officially the Royal Americans, almost all were Germans or Swiss.

'Will they be able to understand us?' wondered Truscott.

'The lieutenant speaks pretty good English, and the ensign is an Irishman,' said Pringle. 'The sergeants ought to be able to comprehend orders at least. Although I cannot help wondering why their Fifth Battalion hasn't taken them – or the German Legion?'

'The Fifth Battalion are riflemen, trained and equipped as such, so I doubt they would welcome men from a marching regiment.'

'Perhaps that explains it,' conceded Pringle. 'However, I wonder whether they have asserted their independence too zealously.'

'Good. We need men with pride. Shall we add them to our strength, sir?' Truscott took advantage of a rare appearance by Wickham to seek his opinion.

'By all means take them. Now I fear I must leave you.'

Pringle presumed such active involvement had left the major fatigued. Truscott was not inclined to sympathy.

'There is the question of the new muskets, sir.'
'Muskets?'

'For the convalescents, sir. The stores assure me that these men should have kept the firelocks issued by their own corps, but very few have them. They will not issue new ones without the signature of the officer commanding this battalion.' Truscott beckoned to a clerk and the corporal dutifully held up a piece of paper.

'Very well.' Wickham signed and was off before greater burdens could be placed upon him.

'Thank you, sir,' called Truscott after the retreating figure. He turned to the corporal. 'Take it to Browne and have him copy it on to the other requisitions. Oh, and tell him if Major Wickham's signature appears anywhere else I'll have the hide off his back.' The captain noticed Pringle's curious expression and explained. 'Private Browne came to us courtesy of the provosts and has considerable dexterity with pen and ink. That should allow us to prise everything else we need from the most reluctant of quartermasters.'

Pringle smiled at his friend. 'It is a good job you are mostly honest.'

Altogether they had enough men from the 106th to form four decently strong companies. With Dawney's men and Lieutenant Shroeder's Germans that made six. The convalescents made up a seventh and a party of twenty-five light infantrymen from the 43rd and thirty men from the Royal Highlanders formed the nucleus of an eighth. Truscott preferred to keep the companies relatively strong and of similar size and so threaded additional men into them rather than attempting to form the full ten companies of a proper battalion.

In just a few days the 3rd Battalion of Detachments had a ration strength of 748 sergeants, corporals, drummers and privates. The men of the 106th were in their ragged uniforms, and some of the other men no better, and somewhere in the ranks was to be found virtually every facing colour known to the army. Some men had no shakos and wore forage caps instead. Their trousers were of brown, black, grey and blue as often as the regulation white, and most were heavily patched. A few of the Highlanders had their kilts, but most had replaced the thick wool garments with cooler cotton trousers.

'You're a magician,' said Pringle to Truscott when the whole battalion paraded for inspection for the first time.

'Pity there are no Colours,' Truscott said wistfully. 'Well, cannot be helped. Take post, Mr Pringle.'

'Sir.' Billy Pringle saluted and marched smartly back to the right flank of his Grenadier Company, which formed the right of the whole line. Hanley stood behind the company with the sergeants. Williams was at the far end of the battalion, attached now to their 'Light Company', consisting mainly of the men from the 42nd and 43rd. They were short of officers and could not afford the luxury of two lieutenants as well as a captain with the grenadiers.

'Present arms!' The voice echoed across the parade ground from the acting sergeant major, a neat and capable Yorkshireman from the 9th Foot. Sergeant Major Fisher was already making his presence felt. Pringle believed him to be a godsend and Truscott was of much the same opinion.

The movements were scarcely immaculate. There had been little time to drill as companies and none as a battalion, but the men were all experienced enough and if there was some variation in the timing it was certainly not disgraceful.

Wickham rode past beside the newly arrived officer commanding, a brevet lieutenant colonel with the deep green facings of the 24th. He was a small, stocky man, with thick and very black eyebrows spreading over the wide forehead of his large face. Together the colonel and the major took the salute, walking their horses along the line before wheeling back to face the centre.

'Men of the Third Battalion,' said the colonel. 'My name is Pritchard Jones and I have the honour to command you.' His voice was deep, with a musical tone and the soft accent of North Wales. 'You come from many corps, all with fine reputations. Do honour to your regiments by your conduct here and return to them with pride when the campaign is done and the French driven from the field!

'Dismiss the men, Sergeant Major.'

Pringle felt himself warming to the colonel when the officers were gathered an hour later. There was a confidence and bustle about the man without his seeming overbearing. He was full of praise for the work of Wickham, which was a little disappointing if unsurprising, and also of Truscott and the others, which was deeply satisfying.

'We march tomorrow, gentlemen,' he announced, 'so I will not detain you long as I know you have much to prepare. I simply want to meet you all and for you to meet me. We are strangers, sadly, and must somehow manage to create in weeks the trust in each other which in a regular corps is the product of many years.

'I mean to drill as we march. One hour of drill, every day, after camp has been pitched. Longer, if ever we get to rest.'

Pringle noticed that Pritchard Jones was watching their faces to judge their reaction, already gauging the mettle of his subordinates.

'Any idea where we are going, sir?' asked Captain Grant of the 42nd, who commanded the Light Company. He was a tall man, almost as big as Williams, but his frame was sadly shrunken and his skin left with a yellowish tinge by the fever which had kept him in Lisbon the previous autumn.

'The border first. The orders are for the army to concentrate at Abrantes on the River Tagus. After that everything adds up to Spain,' answered Pritchard Jones, and then he grinned. 'Although

I fear the general has yet to tell a mere brevet colonel of his plans in any detail!'

He had something to say to each of the officers, including the subalterns, praising their regiments or asking after acquaintances within them. It struck Pringle again how small the army was. He took its tribalism for granted.

When greeting Williams and hearing he was from Cardiff he launched into a language no one understood.

'I fear I do not speak Welsh, sir,' apologised Williams.

The colonel added another comment in the same language and then reverted to English. 'That is a shame, but no fault of your own. In any event they do not speak well in Glamorganshire and have the most heathen accent from living so close to English Monmouthshire.

'I am glad to have a fellow countryman with us – and also one promoted for gallantry, if I am not mistaken. And smartly uniformed too. Do you sing?'

'At every opportunity,' said Hanley cheerfully before Williams could reply.

'Excellent, truly excellent, for no Welshman should lack music in his soul.'

Pritchard Jones was true to his word. They marched long before dawn the next morning, and covered a good fifteen miles before laying out a camp. Only the colonel and a few of the officers had tents, but since the nights were now warmer it was comfortable enough to be wrapped in a blanket and lie under the stars. Before they could rest, the drums beat to muster and they drilled. For three evenings they practised as companies before training as a battalion on the fourth. By the end of the week they had improved a little, which was just as well as they were now close to Abrantes.

'Any of the wives of your company good with needle and thread?' the colonel had asked Pringle after the first day's parade was dismissed.

'A few of them,' he replied, more than a little puzzled. The colonel's uniform was well tailored and did not appear in need of repair. Standing next to Pritchard Jones, Pringle was struck by how very short he was. He could not have been more than five foot one or two, and yet had a huge head and very broad shoulders which spoke of great physical strength.

'Send two of them to my tent in half an hour.'

'Yes, sir.' That was a little unusual, and made him think how little they knew about their new commander. Regiments were families, and like families often did their best to conceal from outsiders the eccentricities and weaknesses of their members.

'Tell them to bring their husbands,' Pritchard Jones added, and his thick eyebrows seemed to leap up his forehead as he chuckled to himself. 'Just in case anyone has a squalid imagination.'

They kept up a good pace each day, continued

to train after they camped, and every night Mrs Murphy and Mrs Dobson with their husbands were summoned to the colonel's tent. Pritchard Jones would then take one of his horses out for a lively hack. The women disappeared inside and Dobson and Murphy smoked and told yarns outside. When Pringle tried to find out what was going on the answer was always the same.

'Regretfully unable to answer, sir. Colonel's orders, sir. No disrespect meant, sir.'

'Carry on,' was the best Billy Pringle could come up with in response.

The sun seemed to grow hotter each day. Many of the men were already burned to that dark brick-red shade which only the British seemed to develop. They marched covered in a thin shroud of pale dust, lips as dry as sandpaper and parched tongues filling their mouths. The sensible ones tried to make their canteens last as long as possible, and some of the veterans put a stone in their mouth to suck on and keep the thirst at bay.

The battalion lost twenty men on the march and that was fewer than Pringle had feared. The weary were lifted on to pack mules to ride when they could not keep up, but the health of some of the convalescents broke down in spite of this care and the men had to be left behind. A pair of healthy men tried to fall out until the sergeant major found them and expressed his opinion forcibly.

On 12th June they saw Abrantes ahead of them. Before they marched the last two miles into camp,

Pritchard Jones halted them and formed them into a hollow square.

'Well done, my brave boys, well done indeed. We will soon be joining Sir Arthur Wellesley's army. Those of you who were there will remember how he hammered the French last year. We will make sure that he does it again this summer.

'We don't have Colours in a provisional regiment, but I thought there ought to be something to show the Frogs who we are.

'Here is our flag!'

Dobson and Murphy, along with two of the Germans from the 60th, marched in through the open corner of the square, their faded and patched coats brushed and their belts bright white with pipe clay. They escorted fifteen-year-old Ensign Castle, a lad of truly startling ugliness and boundless ignorance who had proved himself unsuited to any of the duties so far assigned to him. Truscott was doing his best to tutor the boy in the barest rudiments of drill and was finding the task frustratingly slow. 'I do believe he even forgets his own name,' he had told Pringle wearily. 'Yet he is willing enough, and eager to please.'

Now the young officer looked as proud as a king as he failed to keep step between the escorting corporals and held aloft the new banner. It was smaller than the standards properly carried, both for lack of material and Pritchard Jones' desire not to do anything so presumptuous as make proper Colours. Three foot high and three and a half foot long, it was fixed to a plain staff without spearhead or tassels.

Pringle suspected that Williams would be delighted, for the flag was of a red dragon on a green field. Actually, Pringle thought it looked more like a dog, but even if it did, it was a noble, fierce-looking beast and he liked it.

'Three cheers for the colonel!' The voice was the sergeant major's and the response was genuinely enthusiastic.

Behind their new flag, the 3rd Battalion of Detachments marched in to join Sir Arthur Wellesley's army, which was mustering again after the defeat of Soult. For many regiments that had meant long marches over bad roads and through mountains. They had the confidence of fresh victory, and the lean faces of weeks on poor rations. Pringle knew most of his men envied them, even if many were barefoot or had toes sticking out and soles flapping from worn-out boots. One of Private Browne's convincing forgeries had given every man in the Provisional Battalion two new pairs of boots.

'Make sure no one sells their spare pair,' ordered the colonel. The men of the 3rd were mainly away from their regiments and officers and NCOs who knew them well. Some may well have worked for such an inconspicuous position, but even the good men were apt to have less respect and fear for authorities who were strangers. There had been some looting, and a nasty incident where a private had threatened a Portuguese peasant because the man would not hand over his mule to carry a footsore comrade.

'By the sound of it things have been worse in the corps marching down from Oporto,' Pritchard Jones told his officers. 'Especially some of the regiments full of Irish militiamen. Fortunately they fight as well as they rob otherwise they would be sent home.'

They continued to drill. Sir Arthur Wellesley had decided to group his brigades into divisions and the 3rd Battalion of Detachments found themselves assigned to the Third Division under Major General MacKenzie. Soon there was brigade and divisional training as well as battalion drills.

'I think I have marched farther than we did on the road to get here,' said Hanley to Pringle after an especially long day under a sweltering sun.

'Well, you know the army – keep on moving even if you aren't going anywhere.'

'Major MacAndrews would be proud,' said Williams cheerfully. He longed for another letter from home in the hope that his sister would write of more contact with the major's family.

'Yes, I rather think he and Colonel Jones are two of a kind,' said Hanley.

Pringle nodded thoughtfully. 'I surely hope so.'

CHAPTER 17

anley waited in the hall of the house occupied by the general's headquarters. It was cool, and that was something, for the heat of the day was oppressive and Pritchard Jones had kept the battalion at drill throughout the long morning.

'The general bids you attend upon him,' the colonel had said to him afterwards, his big mouth and wide face once again split into an impish grin. 'Whatever he asks, refuse at all costs. Spit in his eye if necessary. I have already lost too many officers to spare another to the whim of our commander-in-chief.'

An ensign and a lieutenant had collapsed on the march and had to be left behind. Captain Grant had made it to Abrantes by sheer willpower alone, for the man looked more and more like a moving skeleton and could not keep his food down. He was now in the hospital. Wickham, presuming on distant acquaintance, had secured himself a place as an additional ADC to General Hill of the Second Division.

Hanley waited, sitting on a chair with its back

against the wall. A tall clock noisily ticked the seconds away as nothing happened. The noise from the street was more muted, with muffled voices, and then for a good ten minutes the maniacal screams of the ungreased axles of local ox carts.

A servant in civilian clothes came past and offered him a glass of water, waited for him to drain it, and then carried the empty vessel away. This excitement did not last long, but it was reassuring that at least someone had noticed his presence.

The clock ticked on and Hanley waited. He presumed his summons had something to do with the business of Espinosa, although perhaps there was simply a need for someone able to speak Spanish. The pride so many of his fellows took in being unable to understand any language other than their own continued to baffle him.

He wondered about learning Welsh, and that kept him occupied for a good five minutes before he decided that the opportunity to practise it would be too rare for true accomplishment.

The clock ticked on and so he had to accept the fact that time was passing. There was no other evidence of this. Hanley was tired, and had the chair not been so uncomfortable he suspected that he would have fallen asleep.

A cavalry officer appeared from one of the rooms along the corridor, nodded affably to him and then went on his way.

The clock informed him that another ten minutes passed before a captain in the jacket of the Foot Guards came from the same room.

'Lieutenant Hanley?'

Hanley stood up.

'Please follow me. I must apologise for the wait. We are all rather on the hop today.' He led Hanley up the stairs and along another corridor. Rather ominously there were three chairs in a row outside the grand double doors to what was presumably one of the main rooms of the house.

'If you would like to sit, they will call for you in a few minutes.' The captain vanished and Hanley sat and waited. He was beginning to feel that he was very good at it. This chair had arms and a padded seat. He was sure that he could doze here if he could just get comfortable.

'Hanley, dear boy, it is grand to see you again.' Baynes' cheerful red face had appeared around the now opened door. 'Come in, dear boy, come in, we need your advice.

'May I present Colonel Murray.'

'We are old acquaintances,' said the colonel with a warm smile. 'Welcome.' Murray had a thin face with high cheekbones and dark expressive eyes. His brown hair was neatly combed apart from one unruly patch above his forehead. Hanley had met him the previous autumn, but was surprised to be remembered with such warmth. It reminded him of Velarde's and Espinosa's equally surprising enthusiasm, and made him wonder whether this man had any greater sincerity.

'Thank you, sir.' There was silence as they looked at him. He noticed a map spread out on the table. A door to a side room was ajar and he could faintly hear a sharp authoritative voice dictating a letter. The colonel and the merchant paid it no attention and simply watched Hanley for a while.

'Talkative, ain't he?' said Murray to Baynes.

'Isn't that an advantage? Perhaps it is better if you explain the situation.'

'Just so. Well, come over here, Mr Hanley, and I will show you our problem.' Murray stood on the far side of the table, and pointed the worn stub of a pencil at the map. 'We are here.'

'Abrantes,' said Baynes helpfully. 'That's in Portugal.'

'That is useful to know.' Hanley grinned.

Murray smiled briefly. 'Well, it might soon be in France if we make a mess of this, so pay attention.

'We will have twenty thousand men when all the brigades have arrived. Thanks in part to the papers you brought us from this Espinosa, we have some idea of the enemy's dispositions. Soult should not trouble us for a month or more until he has licked his army back into shape and found himself some guns. Ney and Mortier are too far to the north to be an immediate threat. We need to keep an eye on them, in case they do move, but there has been no sign of it yet.

'Marshal Victor is still mainly concentrated

258

around Merida and General Lapisse has retired to join him. Well, you saw something of that. A few weeks ago Victor sent a strong force north to drive back some of Wilson's men who had seized the bridge at Alcantara.' Hanley followed the line of the River Tagus eastwards into Spain. Alcantara was not far from the border. 'His fellows put up a good struggle, but took a real pounding and in the end retreated. Wilson was not with them, and Sir Arthur has just decided to reinforce him with a fresh Portuguese battalion so that he will have a full brigade for the coming campaign.

'Any questions before I continue?'

Hanley shook his head. It was a lot to take in and he wanted to concentrate.

'Good. Now that Lapisse is back Marshal Victor has his full corps of three divisions. We hear he has supply problems – and no doubt Bonaparte is barking orders at him from all the way away there in Austria and wanting him to attack. He will probably move soon, but we do not know which way he will go. There is another corps under General Sebastiani – he is a mere general and not a marshal or a prince so I don't know how the poor fellow upset Boney not to get his promotion and a few new baubles. Probably told him the truth or some other damned fool thing like that. Well, whatever his fault may be, *General* Sebastiani is farther east, around Toledo.

'King Joseph has a smaller force of one division or so stationed near Madrid itself. All told, we judge them to have some forty thousand men in the valley of the Tagus. We cannot deal with such numbers unless we co-ordinate our action with the Spanish. General Cuesta's army watches Victor from a safe distance. A smaller army under General Venegas is to the south-east, somewhere well down here.' Murray circled the pencil well to the south of Toledo.

'We need the Spanish and they want to attack. Well, so do we, but after what happened to Moore we want to make sure we know what is happening before we charge deep into Spain.'

'That is where you can assist us,' said Baynes. 'How do you know Espinosa?'

Hanley told them of his years spent in Madrid, a little embarrassed these days to speak of his artistic ambitions, but conscious that only the truth would serve.

Baynes and Murray exchanged glances, and the latter gave the gentlest of nods, before the merchant continued. 'How well did you know him? Velarde tells me you were all friends.'

'We knew each other, and knew many of the same people. I would not have said we were especially close.' He could not help wondering what Velarde had said.

'Acquaintances rather than friends.'

Hanley nodded.

'Do you trust him?' asked Baynes.

'No.'

'Do you mean Espinosa or Velarde?' asked Murray, who had obviously been listening intently.

Hanley smiled. 'I meant Espinosa, but the answer applies with equal vigour to both of them.' He thought for a moment. 'I strongly suspect that Velarde knocked me from my horse and so caused my capture by the French.'

'Imaginative fellow,' said Baynes without great surprise. 'Do you believe he and Espinosa are in league?'

Hanley had wondered about this more than once. 'Perhaps,' he said. 'Although I doubt very closely.'

'Why?' Murray was watching him intently.

'They both know the other is quite clever and neither has a trusting nature.'

Baynes snorted with laughter at this judgement. 'I told you Hanley has the right sort of mind for our business,' he said. 'So do you believe they trust you?'

'They have no reason to do so.'

Murray's gaze never left Hanley. 'So tell us, are they patriots or *afrancesados* – those who welcome the French? Which side are they really on?'

'I believe both will endeavour to be on the winning side. Whatever it takes.'

'Good, then I suppose our concern is to ensure that we are victorious.' Murray rubbed his chin thoughtfully. 'Well, Major Velarde is officially on our side. Espinosa is not, and we should take advantage of his willingness to deal with us, even if we don't actually trust the little rogue farther than we can kick him.'

'He did ask for payment,' Hanley reminded them.

'Him and every other rascal in these wretched countries,' said Murray with a flash of anger.

'Sir Arthur is desperately short of funds,' explained Baynes. 'Bankers drafts are of little use, and the army needs Portuguese coins to pay the merchants here and Spanish dollars once we cross the border.'

'Well, we won't be doing that until we have paid our debts here and somehow hired enough muleteers, carters and animals to lug our supplies with us. That is of course assuming we can buy enough grain, meat and fodder in the first place.' Murray's tone expressed a deep weariness. 'Still, that, God help me, is my difficulty. Yours is to reach Espinosa or his agent and find out what he has to tell us.'

'Word is already on its way to him along with a small sum of money. I managed to keep back a few hundred dollars before we exchanged them for escudos,' said Baynes, taking over the explanation.

'La Doña Margarita is our agent again. Her family has houses in Talavera and Toledo as well as Madrid itself. The message will reach him soon if it has not already done so.

'It will also inform him that you will be riding along the north road and will be near Coria for a week from tomorrow. We will give you an escort and a guide. There is a band of irregulars led by a Captain Rodriguez who will also help.'

'Will that be enough for his man to find me?'

'Yes, if Espinosa is any good,' said Baynes, 'and

if he is not then we may all be wasting our time. If he just has letters then there are other ways he could reach us. Yet nothing has come from him since the papers you brought. So for whatever reason he appears to want to work solely through you. You might want to think about why, but for the moment we must accept it and find out whether he can be of further use.'

They were interrupted when the side door opened fully and a slim man in a plain blue frock coat, buff breeches and well-polished riding boots strode into the room.

'Well, Murray, that is one more letter trying to make the captain general see reason. Have you finished arranging matters?'

'Almost, Sir Arthur. May I present Lieutenant Hanley.'

Hanley had seen Sir Arthur Wellesley once or twice before, but never been so close. The general was of little more than average height, but seemed bigger. His grey-blue eyes spoke of restless energy and little warmth.

'May I wish you good fortune,' said the general formally. 'Get as much from this fellow as you can. I will not fight this war blindly and so must see what the French are up to on their side of the hill.' Hanley started when without warning the general bayed with laughter. 'Hard enough trying to work out what our allies are doing without the French being difficult! Baynes, I need your assistance in composing a letter to the junta. Perhaps they can find us a less obstinate general. Murray, I shall need you in half an hour. We must find more carts from somewhere. Good day to you, Mr Hanley.'

Wellesley was gone and the room now seemed empty.

'Can you deal with the rest?' Baynes asked Colonel Murray.

'Yes.'

'Well, Hanley, I look forward to what you can bring us. Please try not to get killed in the process.'

'If you do, send the information back to us first,' added Murray cheerfully as the merchant knocked on the door to Sir Arthur's office and then went in.

'I have other work for you so that you can earn your pay properly,' continued the colonel. 'It is less dramatic, but in time will be almost as useful. You can draw, can you not?'

'Yes, sir.'

Then at the end of each day you travel I want a map. I want to know the route of the road and how good it is, the ground to either side, the places of note, the bridges, fords and passes. Whenever there is time I want sketches of the topography. In short I need all the facts that our useless maps fail to tell us. This is how I want it all done.' He produced a bundle of papers and went through each in detail. Then he went through it all again. Hanley felt like a schoolboy.

*   *   *

Two hours later he left Abrantes with a corporal's guard of light dragoons as escort and still felt like a child, albeit one pretending to be a soldier as part of some over-imaginative game.

'Nice to be out in the country,' said the corporal when they had gone three miles.

Hanley grunted assent, and they rode on in silence.

CHAPTER 18

'**P**ermission to speak, sir?'
The two sergeants stood rigidly to attention. The older man, his black hair flecked
with grey, was Sergeant McNaught of the 42nd,
and it was he who had spoken. Sergeant Rudden
of the 43rd was probably no more than twenty-five
and his fair hair made him appear younger.
Williams had heard the men calling him 'the kid'
and could understand why, although Rudden
evidently deserved his rank and was a capable
NCO. He and McNaught were also clearly unhappy
and it had shown in the lethargic way the Light
Company had practised skirmishing.

'Yes, Sergeant McNaught, please say what is
on your mind.' Williams already guessed what
they wanted and knew he could not give it to
them.

'Thank you, sir. We mean no disrespect, but there
are contingents from both of our corps with the
First Battalion of Detachments.'

'Indeed.'

McNaught hesitated and the light infantry
sergeant took over. 'We would like to be transferred

to join them, sir. Fight alongside our own.' Rudden looked nervous but determined.

'I see.'

'Meaning no offence to yourself, sir,'

'None at all, sir,' added McNaught.

'But now we are with the army instead of on our own.' Rudden was staring just to the left of Williams' head, avoiding looking him in the eyes and any punishable challenge or insubordination.

'And with Mr Grant in the hospital, sir,' said the Highlander. He left unspoken the obvious implication that the men felt happier with their 'own' officer. Williams knew that he remained a stranger.

'The colonel says no, and the general wants to keep the battalions as they are. It is too late to change. If your corps were here in full strength then it would be a different matter.'

Actually Pritchard Jones had suggested that the score of Royal Highlanders with the First Battalion of Detachments ought to be transferred to his own command, but had failed to get approval for this.

'The First Forty-Third are on their way, sir,' said Rudden determinedly.

Williams was amazed at how quickly the word had spread. After what he had said he could scarcely change tack. 'When they arrive I promise to speak to the colonel about having you transferred to them.'

'Thank you, sir.' Rudden looked marginally less aggrieved. 'Any word on our pay, sir?'

'I am afraid not. The pay of the entire army is in arrears.' They must have known that, and also known that there was nothing he could do about it. For a brief moment he regretted his new uniform, the colour of the jacket still bright, its buttons all in place and gleaming. Perhaps they believed he was wealthy and beyond such concerns. Then Williams began to resent being blamed for problems beyond his control.

He knew that he could not say that. Rudden's protest seemed to be over, but McNaught was clearly not satisfied. 'None of my men are from the Light Company, sir,' he said, raising yet another grievance.

'I realise that, Sergeant, and understand that the training is new to you. Yet most of your lads are good soldiers and have natural aptitude. Did not the Ninety-fifth draw heavily on the Highland regiments when they were formed?' So Pritchard Jones had assured him when explaining why he wanted Williams' company to act as skirmishers for the battalion.

'Maybe, sir.' McNaught, like a lot of pipe smokers, had one of his stained lower teeth missing and Williams found himself obsessively staring at the gap. He also fought with a powerful desire to make these men like him. Both appeared to be good soldiers, and in their place he would no doubt have also preferred to be back with the 106th rather than serving in a mixed unit. Soldiers relied on their comrades, and trusted their officers and

NCOs. None of them was given any choice about joining this battalion and there were simply too many strangers – some of them even foreign to make the discomfort worse.

It was a little surprising to see the two NCOs approaching him together and only a shared dissatisfaction made it possible. Williams had noticed that the two contingents were keen to do everything their own way. At every opportunity the redcoats from the 43rd marched at the quicker light infantry pace, their muskets held at trail rather than on the shoulder. The Black Watch responded by speaking Gaelic among themselves – even though there were a handful of Irish and English soldiers in their ranks. The number wearing kilts had increased to almost half, and Williams was baffled as to where they had found the tartan. Then he happened to notice that some of the men's wives, who had formerly worn regimental skirts, were now wearing local brown cloth instead and the mystery was solved.

Williams also had two dozen men and a corporal drawn from convalescents released by the hospitals. The rivalry of the 42nd and 43rd and their deep suspicion of all outsiders had bonded these men into another distinct faction. As the only officer left to the company, he had to rely on his NCOs, especially when they deployed as skirmishers, for he could not be everywhere. At the moment he did not lead a company, but three hostile tribes.

'You could split them up,' suggested Pringle, when Williams asked his advice later that evening. 'Mix 'em all together and so they cannot simply stay with their own.'

'No. I thought of that, but cannot help thinking that the bond of the regiment is the strongest we have. They will fight better beside their comrades.'

'Do you want me to send you Dobson? I have raised him to lance sergeant.'

'Is he happy about doing a sergeant's job for a corporal's pay?' asked Williams with a smile.

'He did mention it. Then he said since no one was getting paid he supposed he would just have to get on with it. I suspect he was pleased – if only because the new Mrs Dobson is delighted.'

'Again, thank you, but no. I suspect it would be a mistake to bring in anyone else from outside the company. Apart from which both of my sergeants would be senior.'

'I am not sure mere seniority would prevent old Dob from making an impression on those around him,' said Pringle wryly.

'Probably,' and for a moment Williams was tempted to accept the offer. 'No, it must be resolved within the company.'

'Well, at least take some of Dobson's advice. He has told this to me and I dare say to you as well, but there is no harm in saying it again. If you don't know what you are doing then act as if you do. Play the part, and never for a moment even hint that you could imagine anyone not following you and jumping to every order.

'Keep them busy, too.'

'Oh, I shall most surely do that. There will be extra drill for the Light Company until we make a better show of forming, advancing and withdrawing to command. If they are discontented now, then wait until I have really worked them. After all, they do not need to like me.'

'Spoken like a true tyrant,' Pringle laughed.

When they trained he tried not to yell too much. Taking over from the sergeants and doing their job for them would not help. There was a slow improvement, and when Williams got permission from the colonel to expend cartridges in some live firing there was even a little excitement. He had them firing at paper targets at one hundred paces and let them shoot in competition as three groups. The Highlanders loaded more quickly, and to everyone's surprise the convalescents scored the most bulls in the first round. They took a break to replace the targets and it was clear that Rudden had harangued his men for they took the second session far more seriously. So did the other two groups, and the light infantrymen from the 43rd only narrowly scraped a victory in marksmanship.

Pritchard Jones was inspired to order a battalion sports day as a break from the normal routine. It added to the rivalries among the different contingents and introduced a new level of company competitiveness. Williams was pleased that his light bobs won more than their fair share of events. The culmination was a tug of war. They won the first two contests easily, and as a novelty it was decided that officers would take part in this, adding another stake to the rivalry. The struggle with the Grenadier Company was long and arduous, but ended when Pringle slipped and brought down Murphy, Dobson and several of the other key men. In the final, Williams' men were soundly trounced by the disciplined skill of the Germans from the 60th.

The colonel bought barrels of wine at his own expense and the weary men ended the day in a cheerful mood. The men of the Light Company even took their drink off to sit together. The three groups remained distinct and did not mix to any extent, but at least there was a desire to set themselves aside from the rest of the battalion.

Williams kept driving them in the days that followed. There was more progress, but now he wished that the army would move. The prospect of action ought to give the men a stronger sense of the purpose of it all.

Hanley trotted past the Light Company as it trained, and saw Williams blowing a whistle so that half of the company jogged forward in pairs. MacAndrews had put them through the same drills in England almost a year ago. The realisation that he had been a soldier for a year surprised

Hanley. It was getting harder and harder to imagine himself part of the world outside.

Williams spotted him and nodded, but then quickly returned to the practice. Hanley could not tarry to watch and nudged the horse with his heels to keep the tired animal in trot. Behind him the corporal and his escort kept pace, knowing that they would soon be dismissed and back in the comforting world of the squadron.

Colonel Murray was waiting for him at headquarters.

'Victor is retreating,' said Hanley after he had drained two glasses of iced water. A servant brought him a brandy and he was sufficiently restored after the long ride to take pleasure in sipping it slowly. 'He was desperately short of supplies and has petitioned King Joseph for weeks for permission to leave Merida.' He handed Murray a copy of a letter from the marshal.

The colonel scanned the pages, and smiled as he read aloud. '"The troops are on half rations of bread. They can get little meat – often none at all. The results of starvation are making themselves felt in the most deplorable way. The men are going into hospital at the rate of several hundred a day." Yes, well, we have some idea of what that is like. "The whole population of this region has retired within Cuesta's lines, after destroying the ovens and mills, and removing every scrap of food. It seems the enemy is resolved to starve us out, and to leave a desert in front of us if we advance."

Laying it on a bit thickly, isn't he? I doubt the land is as empty as he claims.'

'There were certainly plenty of folk left in the city and some of the villages when I was there,' said Hanley.

'Well, many cannot risk leaving all that they have. Oh, this bit is good. "Carefully estimating all my stores I find that I have barely enough to last for five days in hand. We are menaced with absolute famine, which we can only avoid by moving off, and there is no suitable cantonment to be found in the whole space between the Tagus and Guadiana: the entire country is ruined." Hmm, well, perhaps they should not have robbed the country blind in the first place.

'That confirms what Baynes tells me. He has returned to Cuesta's army for the moment. Does your fellow Espinosa have any word on where Victor is going?'

'Back north of the Tagus. The corps is to concentrate and hold the bridges from Almaraz to Talavera de la Reina. They are probably there by now. The bridge at Alcantara is destroyed.'

'Yes, Wilson's fellows blew it up.'

'Well, Victor says that without it he cannot advance against Portugal. They wanted him to help Soult, and have only lately learned of his defeat. So he has put the river between himself and Cuesta. They do not seem to know about Sir Arthur's army and believe that only a small Portuguese force is here at Abrantes.'

'Good to know they are even more blind than we are.' Murray beamed happily. 'Well done, Hanley, this is splendid stuff. It fits with everything we know and fills in quite a few gaps. Yes, Mr Espinosa is earning his pay – at least at the moment. Did the fellow turn up in person?'

'He sent a servant. The man seemed to know the country. The guerrillas tell me he used to be a smuggler.'

'How appropriate.'

'Espinosa writes to say that he will send a new message on the ides of each month and use Caesar's cipher.'

'Gone all classical on us, has he?'

'Probably for my benefit,' said Hanley.

'Is he being clever or witty, do you think?'

'He probably feels both.'

Murray nodded. 'Good, let him keep thinking that way.' He looked Hanley up and down. There was dust on his boots and clothes, and smudges from where he had wiped the dirt from his face with a wet towel. 'You must be greatly fatigued. Let me have your observations on the roads and then go and take some rest. But well done, man, well done indeed.'

The training for the day over and his duties complete until he did his evening rounds of the men's billets, Williams sat in the shade of an orchard wall and read the letter again. It was hard now to share his sister's excitement in the early pages.

275

Oh joy, dearest brother, our heart's desire has come true! Mrs Waters did decide to take the <u>waters</u>!!! and asked us to accompany her. Mama would not let Charlotte go this year, saying that she was still too young and needed about the house, but said that Kitty and I should go and that it would be good for us. So we waved our poor sister goodbye and she wished us joy . . .

Williams suspected this was through gritted teeth.

. . . and have been in rooms in Bath for ten days now. Kitty was all for calling on Mrs MacAndrews at once, but I felt it incumbent on us to spend our first days attending on Mrs Waters since only her generous invitation had allowed us to come at all. Bath is a far more handsome town than Bristol, although most hilly and Mrs Waters soon became tired on each of our walks and would stop and sit for a long while . . .

Williams skimmed through the lines.

. . . On the fourth day we went to the Assembly rooms, but I cannot speak with warmth of the lack of kindness we encountered there for no one came to speak to us. Mrs Waters lacks acquaintances. But then Miss MacAndrews

appeared from nowhere – a picture of beauty, elegance and friendship. She expressed her great delight in our coming to Bath and chided us sweetly for not yet calling upon herself and her mother.

The sinister hint came late.

. . . Also in Bath was a party including Colonel Fitz William and so through Mrs MacAndrews two of your little sisters have now been presented to the head of your regiment! Oh think of that!! He is not as tall as you, dearest brother, and though I speak as a sister I would not say so handsomely furnished by nature. Yet he is the most gentlemanly person I have ever met, not at all afflicted with pride or disdain and open in his friendship without ever demeaning his position in life.

And he danced with us!! On the next evening he came and asked both Kitty and I for the 'honour' – not once, but twice!! He is a most accomplished dancer and attentive as a partner, with an elegant poise and leg. He danced with Miss MacAndrews more often – and they stood out in every set as by far the most elegant of couples. She was in a deep blue gown . . .

Much as he was fond of picturing Jane MacAndrews, Williams skipped the extensive description of her costume, followed by comparisons with those of his sisters and apparently each one of the other one hundred and fifty or so ladies present.

> *Kitty is sure that they are in love and that they make the most perfect pair that anyone could imagine, but Kitty is young* [a full fifteen months separated the sisters] *and inclined to fancy. Yet I believe she is correct to see a considerable partiality on the part of the colonel beyond simple good manners. Who could not fall in love with so fine a lady as your major's daughter . . .*

Who indeed, thought Williams bitterly, and how could he compete with a colonel, an aristocrat and a man by all accounts generally held in high esteem. His elevation to lieutenant seemed hollow and perhaps his failure to inspire the company was deserved. Miss MacAndrews was beautiful, kind and courageous – he had seen her fortitude and inventiveness in the winter's retreat. She was admirable in every way. If he were honest then she surely deserved better than he was able to offer.

He wished some word would come from her. They had no promise, and the girl admitted nothing beyond friendship. He just wished she would write to him, even as a friend. For the hundredth time he wondered about sending a letter to her. Over and over again he had composed it in his mind, trying the phrases, testing them and refining each word in desperate quest for perfection.

He could not. He had proposed and she had turned him down. The warmth with which she waved to him from the passing ship still thrilled him with the hope of a change of heart, but perhaps that was merely a presumptuous dream. The letter remained unwritten.

Williams shook the thoughts away. It was time to visit the company, to see their rigid faces. He still did not know these men, however much he tried. In the winter he had led a band of stragglers, but then there had been no time to learn even the names of some, and yet they had responded to fight like tigers.

The men of the Light Company – the Highlanders, the 43rd and the mixture of men from the hospitals all alike – struck him as good soldiers. It could be a most excellent command. Williams wondered gloomily whether he was good enough to lead them.

He passed a cheerful Pringle, out visiting the billets of his grenadiers.

'Rumour has it we will soon be off,' said Billy. 'Take a stab at Marshal Victor.'

'Good,' said Williams, and glumly wondered whether a battle might solve all his worries.

Hatch paused and absent-mindedly licked the tip of his pencil. The lead tasted sour, making him grimace, and he reached for the wine and took a sip straight out of the bottle. His funds were low, and when faced with the choice of buying ink or wine the decision had been easy. A moth flirted with the candle flame, casting weird flickering shadows against the canvas of his borrowed tent, but the ensign ignored it and stared fixedly at the paper before him. He skimmed over the first few pages of pleasantries and small news and decided that they were engaging enough, imagining Mrs Davenport's demure chuckles and Lydia Wickham's brazen giggles.

The last page was the one that mattered and he studied it closely. The tone must be light, that of a well-meaning friend, amused and generously tolerant of the failings of others.

Our Mr W continues to provide amusement throughout the battalion and army for his misadventures. Elevated in rank, and now in responsibility since the illness of an experienced officer leaves him at the head of a company – the Light Company, no less! As you know, our 'light bobs' as we call them are chosen from slight, agile men with quick wits. Poor W is a slow giant among them, puffing as he runs to keep up, bellowing out orders five minutes after the men have obeyed them. 'They must learn,' says he, by which we all know that he must discover for himself what his men already know, and so the weary fellows of the Light Company must run about in the evening sun or under the light of the moon, training an officer who most earnestly believes he is training them! They indulge him generously, for they know the lieutenant means well and is doing his poor best.

'A company must be ordered,' W declares, his brow furrowed in the sober cares of high command, for even Sir Arthur appears less sensible of his heavy responsibility. The Light Company are regulated in every aspect, and even the soldiers' wives ordered to starch their petticoats just so, and lay their infants down to rest at seven o'clock precisely. W is always inspecting the company lines and passing the time of day talking to their women. No doubt he is pleased to find them fascinated by his conversation – especially following his previous disappointments with the fair ones (although this term scarcely extends to the followers!). He is quite the success, and these sweet damsels smoke their pipes and listen to his stories of his bravery. If this continues I dare say some husbands will be jealous of their new rival!

Hatch was tempted to add more, and kept his pencil poised over the page for a while before laying it down. The moth, its wings irreparably burned, tumbled on the table beside him.

No, that was enough. He would wait and write more strongly in the next letter – for he was determined that there would be more letters. Let

Williams be a poltroon for the moment, paving the way to blackguarding him thoroughly in the future. Mockery would readily turn to disdain and contempt. Hatch feared to fight the man, but he would kill his character and reputation stone dead.

Flicking the dying insect aside, Ensign Hatch folded the pages and slipped them into an envelope. He used the candle's heat to melt his stick of wax and sealed the letter. Pritchard Jones had arranged for all officers' correspondence to be carried in a single packet that would leave the next morning.

Satisfied with a task well begun, Hatch smiled to himself and reached again for the bottle.

CHAPTER 19

The salvo rolled along the line as Spanish gunners touched the burning match of the linstock to the tube of powder thrust into the touch hole of each dark bronze cannon. It flared and an instant later the main charge boomed out and the cannon jumped back a good two feet. The charge was small, for there was no ball or shell loaded in the barrel, and so there was not the dreadful violence of artillery firing in battle. The booms were flatter, the plumes of smoke smaller and the recoil gentler, but still this was a powerful battery and the flames were vivid against the darkness of night.

Hanley's horse flicked its ears back at the noise and stirred underneath him. He patted its neck to calm it and pressed slightly with his heels to stay at a steady pace, trailing at the rear of Sir Arthur Wellesley's party.

'We've woken someone up,' muttered Sir Charles Stewart, an immaculately dressed cavalryman riding beside the general.

Torches flamed into light and bonfires were

ignited across the rolling plain. They began to walk their horses along the front of the parade.

Hanley smiled. The sight was dramatic – well worth a picture if he could impress the scene on his memory. It reminded him of the stories of Austerlitz, where Napoleon's veterans were supposed to have lit torches to cheer their Emperor the night before the battle. Before he had seen the French massacre a crowd in Madrid, Hanley had possessed a great enthusiasm for Bonaparte, and followed his legend with eagerness.

'Must have taken a quick bit of organising to be ready to do this in the dark,' he said.

'Pity they did not simply give the dragoons a map!' replied Colonel Murray mischievously. Sir Arthur had been invited to review Cuesta's army, and a squadron of Spanish cavalry sent to escort the British officers fittingly. Unfortunately, the dragoon officer lost his way on the return trip to his own army. They rode for miles and arrived over four hours late, by which time the sun had set.

The cavalry were first. Each squadron was in two ranks, officers to front and rear, dark standards hanging limply from their shafts, and drawn sabres flickering redly in the firelight. On and on the line stretched, squadron next to squadron, some six thousand men with a frontage almost two miles long.

'Assuming they did not plan it this way from the start,' mused Hanley. 'Darkness hides many sins.'

Murray grinned at such cynicism. 'Not

completely.' Plenty of the troopers were having to fight their mounts to keep them in position. The shadows only hinted at ragged uniforms and missing equipment, but Hanley saw bare feet in stirrups, horses of all shapes and sizes mingled together, and he could not help thinking back to the almost instant collapse of many of these squadrons at Medellín barely three months ago. Baynes rode beside them and he wondered whether the merchant was also thinking back to that day.

High mounds of fresh excrement lay in long lines beneath the horses and the smell was penetrating.

'Botched the feeding,' said Sir Charles Stewart loudly. Hanley suspected he suffered from the familiar British conceit that no foreigner would understand criticism voiced in English. Sir Charles was supposed to oversee the gathering of intelligence for General Wellesley. From the little Hanley had seen of him it was hard to imagine anyone less suited to the task, and he was glad that his own dealings were with Murray. 'Need to give the brutes four hours or more to digest their grain before bringing them on parade,' continued Sir Charles. 'That's how the Life Guards stop St James's getting covered in dung.'

'Perhaps not a planned deception, then,' said Hanley.

'Human frailties explain a good deal more of this world than human ingenuity,' conceded Murray.

Hanley lowered his voice. 'May I ask, sir, your opinion of General Stewart?'

Baynes snorted with laughter, but let Murray reply. 'I trust you are not asking me to comment on a superior.'

'I see.' Hanley's teeth caught the light as he smiled.

'The general is a gallant officer.'

'Indeed, most gallant, and does not know the meaning of fear,' added Baynes, unable to resist.

'Which has unfortunately led him to injudicious and costly affairs at the head of our own cavalry,' conceded Murray.

'He is also the brother of Lord Castlereagh. Who is by all accounts a man of considerable intellect,' said Baynes, his voice heavy with implication, 'and a most efficient Secretary of State.'

'We have not troubled Sir Charles overmuch with the detail of your activities,' said Murray, his voice just audible over the creak of leather and jingle of harness as the Spanish and British senior officers at last reached the end of the cavalry squadrons and turned to the right to process along the front of the infantry battalions.

'Tall fellows.' Sir Charles appeared to have been struck by a sudden diplomatic urge, and raised his voice until he was almost shouting. 'As fine material as ever I saw.' The compliment did not carry great conviction. Even Hanley could see the rawness of the foot soldiers. Their faces were so desperately young, what uniforms they had were ill fitting and evidently uncomfortable. Muskets were held awkwardly by boys more used to pitchfork and scythe.

'Poor devils,' said Hanley before he could stop himself. Noticing Murray's glance, he felt obliged to explain. 'They look so much younger than the cavalry.'

'They do. Inevitable, I suppose.'

Hanley did not understand.

'Much easier to get away when you're mounted,' explained Baynes.

'Of course.' Hanley was surprised that he had not recognised that grim and obvious truth. 'At least they all look willing.'

'They do,' said Murray. 'So does the old boy up front.' He nodded in the direction of the Spanish commander. Captain General Don Gregorio de la Cuesta looked a pale shadow of the bullishly confident man Hanley had seen in March. He looked thin and ancient, and moved only with difficulty and in obvious pain. Two servants walked on either side of his horse to support him in the saddle. They kept a slow pace, and therefore so did Sir Arthur and his staff. Hanley saw the Spanish general speak only twice and then briefly.

There were plenty of infantry. Hanley counted twenty battalions and judged that most mustered more than seven hundred bayonets. The army was as big or perhaps even bigger than the one at Medellín. It took a long time to pass them all in review and then they took up a position to witness manoeuvres preformed by parts of the army. The cavalry took more time to jostle into position and then their lines on the ride past were ragged. An infantry battalion painfully deployed from line into column and then back again, but ended with irregular gaps between the companies.

Hanley thought the Army of Estremadura looked much like its commander – defiant, but still badly hurt and only barely limping on. It was a miracle that it was in the field at all, let alone taking the offensive. Then he remembered watching another apparent miracle being cut to ribbons by the French cavalry and tried to dismiss the thought as unlucky.

It was late into the night when the generals finally began to discuss the campaign. Before they did so the Spanish divisional commanders were each presented to Sir Arthur Wellesley. In turn the senior officers approached, bowed with considerable dignity and then withdrew. They were not to be included in the council of war.

As the Duke of Alburquerque left he greeted Hanley warmly and nodded amicably to Baynes.

'I must go. Apparently our leader does not require the advice of his senior officers,' he said. Hanley found his candour even more surprising than the exclusion. The Spanish general strode off quickly to join his own staff.

'Many feel the duke ought to be in charge.' Velarde had appeared from nowhere, joining the group of British and Spanish officers waiting outside the open flaps of the tent. 'Including your own Mr Hookam Frere, I understand.'

'My dear colonel,' said Baynes, his face even redder than usual in the firelight. 'I am sure our envoy in Seville wants only to assist the junta in every way in his power.'

'I am sure.' The two men stared at each other, before Velarde smiled. 'I am glad you are safe and with us again, Guillermo.'

'Colonel?'

'Medellín brought death to many and promotion to some. I hear you have seen Espinosa?'

'He is well and loyal to King Joseph.'

'No doubt.' Velarde paused for a moment. 'I should not trust him too far if I were you.'

'That is prudent,' said Hanley. 'He is a traitor, after all. At least to somebody.'

'As you say. You may not be the only one paying him.'

'Including you?'

Velarde laughed and startled the officers near by, who glared at him. He stared back, and they spoke no more until the others lost interest and returned to their own conversations.

'They are Palafox's men,' he said with amused contempt. 'Foolish enough to believe the pamphlets and want him to guide the country.'

'Dictatorship?' said Baynes, as if he had heard the idea for the first time.

'Leadership.' Velarde shrugged. 'At least that is what they would call it. A Caesar to drive the Gauls back to their own benighted country.'

'You did not answer my question,' said Hanley.

'I believe not. However, how could a poor colonel afford the services of a man like Espinosa?'

Cuesta slammed a fist down on the table and for one brief instant stood tall before his shoulders slumped again and his whole body seemed to shrink.

'I imagine he disagrees,' said Baynes drily.

Sir Arthur and Don Gregorio had only one common language and since the Spaniard resolutely refused to speak French, his chief of staff acted as interpreter. Negotiations were slow.

'Little trust, I should guess,' observed Velarde.

'Alliance is never easy,' said Baynes in bland response. 'Yet it is in mutual interest.'

'Of our countries, yes. Of individual men, well, that is a different matter.'

There was another disagreement between the generals.

'Difficult to trust a man who has written asking for you to be replaced,' said Velarde. 'Well, I must go. Greater rank brings greater burdens. Good night to you both.'

'Is that true?' whispered Hanley after the Spaniard had departed.

There was no denial, which seemed as solid confirmation as there could be. 'Clever devil, that one,' said Baynes at last. 'Wouldn't trust him an inch, but I do rather like him.'

It was long into the next day before agreement was reached. By the time the British party returned to their own camp the sun was setting.

'We need 'em, Murray, we need 'em,' Sir Arthur told his quartermaster general on the ride back to camp. 'We have an opportunity to strike before the French concentrate their forces. It will not last, but now that London have given us permission to advance into Spain we must achieve something. Without the Spaniards we are simply too few, and we cannot wait for them to shape up.

'They probably want six months, maybe even a year, before they will be anything like a real army, but by God we need them now, although I am not sure what we will do with 'em if it comes to a fight.' He thought for a moment. 'Put them behind stone walls, and I dare say they would defend them, but to manoeuvre with such rabble under fire is impossible. I am afraid we shall find them an encumbrance rather than otherwise, but we cannot do without them. I would wish for a less obstinate fellow at their head, but nothing can be done about that quickly.

'We also rely on them for food and transport. How much has come in so far?'

'Very little,' replied Murray. 'Certainly far less than we need, let alone than we would wish. Most of the men have been issued biscuit rather than fresh bread or even grain. Meat is not yet so short, but we are consuming our own reserves quickly. Carts and mules are promised, but few have arrived. There is still no means of bringing the reserve ammunition or even the treasury forward from Abrantes.'

Hanley looked at the arid brown fields rolling away on either side. This was a poor country, even before armies began marauding through them. He could not help thinking of Marshal Victor's letters with their talk of deserts and starvation.

Sir Arthur Wellesley was not inclined to be understanding. 'We must tell Frere to press the junta to meet their promises. I shall write to Cuesta as well in the strongest terms. He is a difficult, foolish man, but must understand that I cannot advance if my men have no food. I will begin no operation till I have been supplied with the means of transport which the army requires.

'How do the men behave?'

'There have been many incidents, sir. The men are hungry and see the villagers as unwilling to help the friends risking their lives to free their country.'

'So they see this as licence to plunder.'

Murray nodded. 'All too often.'

'Infamous. This army cannot bear victory any more than Sir John Moore's army could bear defeat. The fault is all too often with the officers.'

'They are hungry too,' ventured Murray. 'There have been particular problems with the battalions of detachments. Officers and men do not know each other.'

'Well, damn them, they must learn or I shall order them to inspect their men each hour, just as I did with Donkin's brigade after those Irish rogues took to plundering. We must have discipline even if we hang dozens of the rascals. Continue as we are and soon every peasant's hand will be raised against us as it is against the French.

'Where is the fellow who is to ride to Wilson?'

Murray was used to his commander's abrupt changes of subject. 'Hanley,' he said, and gestured for him to come forward and ride beside them.

'Ah yes, I recollect. You go in the hope of receiving more information?'

Hanley nodded. 'I expect to be contacted on the fifteenth, sir.'

'Good. The more we know the better. A courier has already gone to Wilson, but you may confirm his instructions and share intelligence with him. Our army will join with the Spanish of General Cuesta at Oropesa and then advance together on Marshal Victor at Talavera. Wilson's brigade guards our northern flank. He has his Portuguese and some Spanish regiments. I wished for more, but . . .' Sir Arthur trailed off for a brief moment. 'That does not matter. We do not believe that Marshal Soult can press against us from that direction so soon. Tell Sir Robert to send word if there is the slightest hint that this is not true. Anything your man tells us in that regard is invaluable.

'A second Spanish army under General Venegas marches on Madrid from the south. Orders should reach him at the latest three days from now.' The general glanced at Murray, who nodded in confirmation. 'Very good. He is to pin the French corps of Sebastiani and King Joseph's reserves around Toledo. They must face him or Madrid will fall to him. Cuesta and I will march against Victor with more than double his men. He must fight and be beaten or retreat and let us take Madrid.'

It seemed so clear, and so very simple, and yet Hanley struggled to take it all in. In January Sir John Moore's army had escaped from Corunna on board ship. In March Cuesta was shattered at Medellín. Now, in July, there seemed every prospect that King Joseph would be chased from Madrid once again.

'Share any information you gain with Wilson. He is to use his initiative and alarm the enemy towards the rear of his right flank, but since the force of his corps is not sufficient to make a serious impression upon the enemy if he is found to be strong in that direction, Sir Robert must act according to circumstances, endeavouring to give the enemy as much jealousy in regard to his operations as possible.

'But he must also be ready always to respond to new orders – quite possibly to join the main army or cover us more closely. Tell him he must report every day so that I can be sure of his location. He must also assist in every way with regard to supplying the main army.

'You are clear?' Hanley nodded. 'Good. You will ride as soon as you have a fresh horse. Murray will detail an escort from the Fourteenth Light Dragoons.'

Before he left, Murray had another word with him. 'The general has good reason to insist on Brigadier Wilson reporting to us each day. Sir

Robert is . . .' the colonel struggled to find the right words, 'particularly inclined to independence. For months he has told the authorities in Lisbon that his Legion is part of the British Army and so not subject to their orders, although he earnestly wishes to co-operate with them. He then tried to convince Sir Arthur that the Legion were Portuguese troops and so not under the control of the British.

'We really do need him to cover our flank and guard against any surprise from the north.'

'Will he not do that?'

'He should,' said Murray. 'Indeed he should, and probably will. Yet he is by nature a gambler and may not tell us if he scents the prospect of some dramatic stroke.' Murray smiled ruefully. 'You were not to know, Hanley, but in many ways it is to be regretted that Wilson received the chest of gold smuggled to him by the lady.'

'I understood the money went to the Spanish at Ciudad Rodrigo.'

'Well, some of it probably did. Some went to pay Sir Robert's soldiers and secure supplies and new clothing for them. It means we have one less means of exerting control over him.'

'Where did the money come from?' asked Hanley, who had simply assumed it was sent by the Spanish high command to their garrison.

'The junta in Seville.' Murray spread his hands. 'Or at least someone or some group in the junta. I fear we began this war with the grave misapprehension that there actually was a single government or leadership guiding the Spanish cause. Perhaps they are now reaching the same conviction in regard to us.'

'I am not sure I follow,' said Hanley.

'Sir Robert Wilson and his little band may be readier to join in certain schemes than a British lieutenant general with heavier responsibilities and far greater prudence. Brigadier Wilson has prodigious talent and great dash, but I do not believe he can be accused of prudence.'

A day of hard riding took Hanley to Wilson's column, where he found Sir Robert enthusiastic and impatient. 'The Spanish were late and as slow as snails in arriving, while my own fellows spent almost a week repairing worn uniforms, but I am now ready to advance. Praise God, but this is the opportunity of a lifetime. At last we fight this war as we should.'

The messenger from Espinosa was already waiting, held in custody after announcing himself a friend at the outposts.

'Soult is given command of Ney and Mortier as well as his own corps and is to prepare for a fresh occupation of northern Portugal. He is tasked with capturing Braganza,' said Hanley as he summarised the letters.

'Good. That will keep Soult far away and unable to intervene.' The news did not appear to come as a surprise, and Hanley had the sense that Sir Robert was feigning interest. 'The man brought duplicates directly to me,' he explained. 'I suspect that rogue Espinosa is receiving double pay for the same documents. It does not do any harm to review what he says just to ensure that he tells us both the same, but I am already planning accordingly.

'Who knows,' he added, and his eyes sparkled with excitement. 'We may beat everyone else into Madrid.'

Hanley decided to keep one secret, for he guessed that a ciphered note included in the packet of letters gave two addresses where Espinosa might leave a new message before the next monthly delivery. If Sir Robert already knew then no harm was done. If not, then perhaps it would be better to carry the information to Wellesley and Murray first and then pass on anything important to Wilson.

'General Wellesley did ask me to remind you to stay close to the army.'

'Oh my dear fellow, of course, of course. But when each of us is close to the city, then I think you will have to race hard to snatch the lead from my little column. I'll make the French believe there is a third big army coming against them and they will not know which way to face.' He laughed for sheer joy. 'We'll smoke 'em out again, just like last time!'

CHAPTER 20

'It is a pity we do not have a band,' said Pritchard Jones as the 3rd Battalion of Detachments paraded ready to march out from Plasencia with the rest of the Third Division. The other two battalions in their brigade each had their musicians who would march at their head playing a spirited tune. 'Pity we do not have some decent bread as well,' he added to his assembled company commanders. 'Sadly we do not, and from today the ration is to be halved. You had better warn the men before it is issued to them.'

Williams did not relish the task, suspecting that many of the men in the Light Company would see him as personally to blame. He knew that he had not won their affection, and yet the weeks at Abrantes and the shorter rest at Plasencia had done much to improve the men's close and open-order drill. They resented being driven so hard, but dislike or hatred of a lieutenant who made them train when others were resting had become a bond between the three groups. Williams took them on runs and long marches, carrying pack and musket as they did, and the men took fierce delight in competing with the officer. They were turning into a good company, but he was sure they did not thank him for it. It was becoming more and more of an effort not to respond to their hatred in acts of petty vindictiveness.

The army marched early in the morning of 18th July, following the road as it swung gradually back south towards the Tagus. The sun's heat was savage, beating down like a hammer on the anvil of the hard-baked soil. Mostly the infantry marched in the fields either side of the road, leaving it to the army's thirty guns, their caissons and wagons and what little transport had been gathered.

A thick cloud of dust hung in the still air. Williams' new jacket looked a pale sandy colour rather than its bright scarlet. He had folded his new breeches and carried them in his pack along with a pair of soldier's boots, a spare shirt, drawers, cleaning tools and other necessaries, his Bible, a translation of *The Gallic Commentaries* and a copy of *Tom Jones*, which he jealously guarded from Hanley's predatory glances because it was a book for which Jane MacAndrews had expressed fondness.

Williams stopped to watch the company march past. One of the kilted Highlanders was flagging, his face ruddy and its covering of dust washed by little rivulets of sweat. He looked close to collapse, chest pressed hard by the tight belts of the army's awkward and uncomfortable pack.

'Not far now, Patterson,' he said encouragingly,

'we will be getting a rest soon. Here, let me carry your musket for a while.'

The soldier looked at him, his face blank, but his eyes suddenly hard. 'No thank you, sir. I'll manage, sir.' The man beside him glanced at his comrade and then at Williams.

'He'll be fine, sir, he'll be fine. No need to trouble yourself, sir.'

There was no point in making an issue of it. 'Good man. Keep an eye on him, Skerret.'

Patterson staggered on. It was good that they were so determined, and not a man had fallen behind from the company since they crossed into Spain. Yet Williams still found the resentment troubling. He was sure that even the men from other corps had more readily accepted Captain Grant. Would they fight for him?

The colonel stopped his horse alongside.

'Not as green as Wales,' he said, as if noticing the brown fields for the first time. 'I'll wager you never thought that you would miss the rain, eh?'

'Or the sea,' said Williams wistfully. 'I have never liked being on the water, but to walk beside it gives such peace, even on the rough days.'

'Well, I imagine it will be hotter work for all of us soon. Do you realise Madrid is little more than seventy miles away? I do not believe they will let us march there unmolested. Still, that is for the days to come. The Light Company has shaped up well.'

'Thank you, sir. They are good men, even if all

would be happier with their own regiments.' Williams wondered about mentioning his fears.

'That is true of the whole battalion. You have done well, Mr Williams, so keep on earning such accolades.' Pritchard Jones leaned down more from the saddle and lowered his voice. 'It is never easy to lead a company, and harder still when the arrangement is temporary and you are the only officer present. Best not to expect too much after so short a time.'

Williams wondered how much the colonel knew and how he knew it. Was his own worry – or the men's hostility – so very obvious? If he was visibly lacking in confidence then perhaps that was feeding the poor spirit.

Pritchard Jones straightened up again. 'We are about to rest for ten minutes around that hamlet. Keep a close eye on the men. The First and Second Battalions have bad reputations for plundering. I do not want us to match them. Good day to you, Mr Williams.'

As far as Williams could see no one had the energy to wander. He suspected the main risk would be when they camped for the day and the men rested and had more opportunity to slip away unseen.

When the march resumed he noticed that Skerret was soon carrying Patterson's firelock as well as his own, and that Sergeant Rudden of the 43rd had the man's pack. There was some encouragement in the willingness to help a soldier who was not from his own group.

The second and third days were as blazingly hot as the first. The landscape rolled along with little change and it became hard to judge distance in any way apart from blistered feet and sore muscles. The 3rd Battalion lost a few stragglers, but fewer than some regiments, and this made Pritchard Jones happy. 'I suspect we have already lost our weakest men.'

Throughout the day another thick dust cloud rose to the south, and by the evening British and Spanish armies were both camped outside Oropesa. There were over fifty thousand men in the combined armies when the advance resumed the next morning. Williams had never seen so large a force. The British followed a northern, lesser road, which wandered across the line of little hills and meant that at times he could look down and see the Spanish columns stretched out on either side of the main road. Once or twice the sun caught the sluggish waters of the Tagus itself.

Talavera was nineteen miles away and the French were still there.

'Think Marshal Victor has had a bit of a shock, seeing the Dons marching against him so boldly,' Wickham explained as he stopped to pass the time with the 106th's officers during one of the hourly halts. 'We are letting the Spanish take the lead and push in his outposts so that he won't yet know that we are with them. There is a good chance he will stay to fight.'

'Well, it will make a change from walking,' said

Billy Pringle, using his sash to rub the grime off his spectacles. He lifted them up and peered at the lenses. 'Hmm, think I may have made them worse.' A very faint rumble of cannon fire drifted towards them. 'Apparently you are right.'

'There is no need to sound surprised as you say that.' Wickham laughed, and merriment clearly made him think of something else. He laughed even more. 'Have any of you fellows received letters from home in the last days?'

'No, nothing for us,' said Truscott, flapping his good arm in a vain attempt to brush away the flies buzzing around his face. The tiny insects seemed to multiply with every minute of the day.

Williams simply shook his head, but listened intently.

'Oh well, perhaps they will come soon,' said Wickham.

'If all carriers are not devoted solely to the comfort of the staff, that is,' quipped Pringle. 'We mere mortals of the marching regiments live a more frugal life in every way.'

Wickham smiled with the others. 'Well, if we spend any time in Talavera I believe there is somewhere where I may treat you fellows to a good dinner at least.

'However, my wife has written and tells me that everything is well with the regiment back in England. There is general satisfaction with the arrival of Colonel FitzWilliam.'

'You have a connection, I recollect,' said Truscott.

'Yes, although less close than perhaps it ought to be. I doubt that decided his choice on purchasing command!'

'Any other news?' asked Hopwood.

'There is general amusement at the tales of Mr Williams here and his romantic exploits – nights at the theatre in the company of such a "distinguished" lady companion. I believe you are now seen as quite the roistering young blade.' Wickham clearly thought it hilarious and almost all the other officers were equally beside themselves with laughter. Pringle was amused because it was so ridiculous. Truscott merely smiled faintly, for he both knew Maria and the truth of the matter and also disapproved of open vulgarity. Hatch mingled triumph with almost hysterical laughter. His letter had worked and he knew now that this was a way to hurt his enemy. He would write again soon, and damn the truth if he could not dream up better stories to tell.

Williams said nothing, but could no longer bear to stay with them. He turned and walked back towards his company.

'Off for another conquest, no doubt.' Hopwood laughed without any malice.

Williams struggled to hold down his surging temper. Worries of Miss MacAndrews being swept away by the dashing and wealthy new colonel were now overwhelmed by the horror that she would hear these stories and think him faithless. He wanted to believe that she was wiser than that and knew him better than to believe him a rake. Yet for all her intelligence and wit, Jane MacAndrews was both young and of high spirits. Williams still winced at the memory of her rage when he had proposed marriage in Corunna.

The drums began to beat.

'On your feet!' bellowed Williams at the Light Company. 'Up, you idle rabble, up!' The men responded to the bark of command even though they were surprised and baffled by the ferocity of his onslaught. His two sergeants happened to be next to each other and exchanged glances, but knew enough to join in.

'Fall in!' shouted Rudden.

'Get moving!' called McNaught in his hoarse voice.

A few moments later the Highlander sergeant stamped to attention in front of Williams and yelled his report. 'Company fallen in and ready to move, sir!'

Williams returned the salute absent-mindedly, but merely grunted in acknowledgement. They were at the rear of the battalion's column and it was taking longer for the other companies to prepare. He took the briefest of pleasures in that.

'Carry on, Sergeant. We shall be moving in a moment.'

As they marched the wind picked up a little. It brought no relief from the heat, and instead the hot air swirled the dust around and blew it into faces and eyes. At times it carried the distant popping of musketry as the Spanish vanguard skirmished with the French. Then a brigade of light dragoons passed them at the trot and flung up even more muck and dust into the breeze.

'Damned donkey-wallopers,' muttered one of the men from the 43rd.

'Silence in the ranks!' snapped Williams for no other reason than that he felt like shouting.

They marched on, and he brooded and once again wondered whether he had lost the only woman he had ever loved. Another letter from his sister might tell him more of Miss MacAndrews' mood, and then he worried that the news would be bad.

He noticed that one of the convalescents had stepped out of the ranks and was leaning on his musket, panting for breath. For a moment Williams wanted to savage the man for his weakness or ignore him rather than risk another snub. He took a deep breath.

'Come on, Hawkins, let me help you. Give me your musket.' The redcoat handed over the firelock with some reluctance, but looked so ready to drop that it was a relief to pass it across. Williams slung the musket over his own. 'Now, lean on me.' They followed the company. Hawkins was a small man, so that it was a little awkward to reach up and put his arm round Williams' shoulder.

'Thank you, sir,' he said.

McNaught dropped back from his station behind the rear rank. 'I'll take his other side, sir. Hughes!'

He called to another of the recovered convalescents. 'Get his pack off. Carry it for ten minutes then pass it on to someone else.'

'Well done, Sergeant.'

'It's my job, sir,' came the blunt reply.

They marched past the town with its medieval walls, but did not go closer than threading their way through some lanes running between walled gardens. Following the light dragoons, the Third Division marched across a wide rolling plain of parched yellow grass. There were a few Spanish outposts ahead of them, but most of Cuesta's army was farther south.

For a while the Third Division halted, and the men were given permission to sit on their packs and rest. Few had water left in their canteens and a stream running across their path proved to have dried up apart from a few foul-looking pools infested with insects. Snakes slithered in the grass along its banks, and one the 43rd gave a yell when he tipped a big stone and uncovered a couple of scorpions.

The redcoats were more careful after that. Some started looking for the poisonous creatures and fashioned little nooses out of thread. Then, when one man tipped over a stone, another looped the noose around the creature's tail. A quick prod with a stick and the scorpion arched its tail over its head ready to sting. The noose was pulled tight and the beast was caught. In half an hour, several dozen were hung up and left dangling from branches on trees.

'Serve the little sods right,' said a redcoat with the yellow facings and back badge on his shako of the 28th Foot.

Gallopers rode up to the divisional commander, Major General MacKenzie, who then summoned the commander of his second brigade. Fifteen minutes later the men were marching forward again, most stepping gingerly in the grass now that the word of snakes had spread.

They advanced for a mile and found themselves among rows of vines and clusters of cork trees. There was the sound of artillery firing. Williams counted five, perhaps six, guns, which suggested a battery, and from the direction they were probably Spanish. He could see nothing of the fighting, but more guns responded.

'Sounds as if the French are not going back too quickly,' he said to McNaught.

The sergeant seemed to think about it, and Williams was not sure whether he was going to reply at all.

'Aye,' said the Highlander, as if at the end of long consideration. 'They took some shifting in Egypt. We did it, though.'

'That you did.'

'Aye.' No more seemed to be forthcoming.

The battalion halted, as did the only other visible battalion from the brigade. Williams could see the Grenadier Company of the 1/45th Foot over to their left. The regiment had green facings and a high reputation for discipline. He could barely see the end of the Battalion of Detachments' own line in the other direction, and nothing of the 2/31st beyond them to the right.

As the sun dropped down over the horizon the trees cast long shadows and soon it was too dark to see much at all. Piquets went forward from each battalion, but after half an hour orders were passed for the remainder to stand down.

'No fires,' said Pritchard Jones.

'Good,' muttered Pringle to Williams, 'at least that will stop Jenkins from concocting his foul brew.'

There was also no food, apart from whatever was left in the men's packs, and there was little enough of that. A few still had remnants of hard tack. There was water from the River Albreche, some way to the front, but strict orders were given for only small parties of men to take bundles of canteens forward and fill them.

The night turned cold. Until the moon rose there was only a pale starlight. Men did their best to check their muskets and flints and look to their equipment. Williams could hear rhythmic scraping from all around him as men worked obsessively on their bayonets, honing the points. The sound was reassuring and reminded him of other nights before an action. Men worked in quiet determination as if the better the point the better they would fight, and in desperation, as if a sharp bayonet would keep them alive.

A strangely high-pitched gurgle squeezed on to the night air.

'Skerret, you pig,' said someone.

'I'm hungry,' said a plaintive voice in justification.

More squeaks and gurgles followed and then a sudden explosive breaking of wind.

'That's told them Frenchies we're here!'

They were woken at three in the morning – at least those who had managed to get any sleep. Bugles and drums were forbidden and sergeants went around shaking each man by the shoulder. All around were the distinctly masculine noises of waking, as redcoats yawned and groaned, stretched and scratched, and finally stamped or rubbed life into their limbs. The Third Division's women had been ordered to stay with the baggage train outside the town itself.

'The French are on the high ground east of the river,' explained Pritchard Jones to his officers. 'We march south and join the First Division to attack across the fords. The Spanish will be to the south again, on our right. Together we outnumber Victor's men more than two to one. Even if they realise we are coming they will not be able to stop a determined assault.

'Back to your companies. The Thirty-first will lead off in column and we will follow.'

It was still too early for much talk in the ranks. The men marched in silence, but Williams could feel their tense excitement because it mirrored his own feelings. Fear remained a vague, lurking presence on the edge of his mind, and he imagined French volleys or blasts of canister from their guns scything through the battalion as they splashed through the river.

The route was not simple, winding between vineyards, copses and scrub. Several times they halted and waited, not knowing why they were delayed. The sky grew lighter. It was an hour before they were in position, ready to advance through a line of cork trees beyond which was the river. The sun rose red and brooding behind the black pillars of smoke from the French campfires.

The 3rd Battalion waited, formed in ranks, but with the men standing at ease. Nothing happened. They heard a French sentry giving a distant challenge of 'qui vive!', but then it was silent again. As the sun climbed higher the heat grew. Williams could feel sweat all down his spine. He never sweated on his face, but any warmth soon made his back wet with perspiration.

Bugles sounded and drums beat in the French camp without any particular urgency. Pritchard Jones and the other battalion commanders were summoned by General MacKenzie.

Williams and the rest of the battalion waited. They were all hungry, having gone more than a day without hot food and very little that was cold.

Pritchard Jones rode back and reached the Light Company on the left of his battalion first. 'It's called off,' he said to Williams as he passed. 'It seems the Spanish are not coming.' He spoke calmly, as if this

311

were a minor change to social plans between a few intimate friends. 'Our brigade is to stay here for the moment and remain stood to.'

Williams felt flat and very tired.

'Any chance of some hot food, sir?' asked Sergeant Rudden.

'Not yet,' he replied. 'Not until we are relieved.'

'Sir.'

Williams felt the brief relenting of the men's hostility was fading as quickly as the prospect of an engagement. Well, damn them, he thought, and damn the Spanish, and damn whoever was gossiping about him back in England. Damn Jane MacAndrews too, if she believed such lies about him. His rebellious anger lasted all of five minutes.

CHAPTER 21

Talavera was bustling that evening, Spanish soldiers in white, brown, blue, green and yellow uniforms mingling with the redcoats. Then there were the followers of both armies, women and children of all shapes and sizes looking for food or anything useful or unguarded. Many of the townsfolk who had fled the French occupation had returned. They and the ones who had lived through the days when Marshal Victor's regiments marched through the streets now looked with almost equal suspicion at the throngs of newcomers. There were soldiers and their women from distant kingdoms of Spain, with strange accents and odd manners.

Then there were the English, and they were heretics and came from a distant island of rain and cold, and what man could understand their speech or their heathen ways. Many looked like thieves, and the stallkeepers in the market kept a close watch on their wares whenever the odd men in their patched red jackets or their grubby women sidled up.

Hanley was dressed in the dark suit of civilian

clothes provided by Espinosa. He turned the corner into an alley and then stopped because a Highlander and his family were coming the other way. The man was tall and lanky, his knees bronzed and bony beneath his dark kilt. His jacket had green facings and was faded to look more purple than red, and patched with brown cloth on the sleeves. He had long since lost or sold the feathers from his bonnet and now wore it as a plain blue cap. His wife had a hard face, lined with care, worry and days and nights spent out in all weather. Her drab brown skirt was tattered and stained, her hair greying and dirty where it peeked out from underneath her frayed straw hat. Husband and wife alike showed teeth stained brown as their lips parted in what was perhaps intended to be a polite smile, but came across as a grimace. A small boy scampered beside his mother, and his single tooth was at least a wholesome colour as he stared open mouthed at all around him. A girl a few years older walked with the pride of a queen beside them and a third child was strapped to the mother's back.

'Mary, mother of God,' whispered a well-dressed man beside him. When the Scots had passed he turned to Hanley and crossed himself. 'They say these men are forced to wear such clothes because they are criminals. Pray God they leave soon, with all the other intruders.' Hanley was not sure whether the man meant the French or Spain's own soldiers. He had heard the story about Highland dress before. Billy Pringle reckoned that it was first spread by one of the Scottish regiments who did not wear kilts.

Hanley pushed on. There were fewer people in the alley, but it was still busy. He was reassured that the man had taken him for a Spaniard, and then he saw a group of British officers coming towards him and worried that they might be men he knew and greet him openly.

It was a relief to see that they were strangers, and one of them – a man who was elderly for an ensign and had a sour expression – glared at him in the disdainful way that showed the man saw him as a foreigner, a civilian and no doubt a fool.

'The buggers wouldn't fight on a Sunday,' said one of his companions, a lieutenant with a pronounced stoop and arms which swung in an ungainly way as he walked.

'Cowardly devils!' said the ensign. 'Want others to die to save their precious country.' He almost spat the words in Hanley's direction.

Plenty of rumours were spreading throughout the army since the cancellation of the morning's attack. Hanley had already heard the one about Cuesta refusing to fight on the Sabbath. Baynes had told him it was false. 'He gave plenty of excuses, but that was not one of them.'

The Spanish general would not attack. Every request, every reminder of their agreement by Sir Arthur, every plea, met the same stubborn response. The Army of Estremadura would not attack today and probably not tomorrow either.

'He's a damned old fool,' Murray said angrily. 'A craven relic of a man not fit to command a corporal's guard.'

'The Spanish say that the enemy position is formidable,' Baynes responded, without any conviction.

'Was it any stronger yesterday when he agreed to the plan?'

'Then perhaps he knows something – or believes he knows something we do not.' The merchant had then looked at Hanley. 'See what your man has to say.'

'If the messenger turns up.' Espinosa's note had said that he would try to reach him with more intelligence at the same time in the yard of an old tannery on one of three nights. No one had appeared on the first two although Hanley had waited for more than two hours after the set time.

'Well, we can but try.' Murray smiled. 'Or rather you can but try. Different factions are busy accusing each other of treachery. We need to know as much as we can learn.'

It was dark by the time Hanley walked through the gateway into the courtyard. It had been years since the tannery had last been in proper use and only the faintest of odours lingered. It was a quiet part of the town, the alleys less busy, and the only houses near by were small and occupied by those who could not find or afford better. Most seemed to be empty and there was no light from any window.

The smell of horses, leather and dung was fresher inside the courtyard. Just a few days before it had served as billets to a French battery and all its horses and mules. They had chopped up the few remaining doors and shutters to burn.

'Mapi,' hissed a voice from the shadows.

Hanley started in surprise. He was early, and after two days with no sign of a messenger he really had not expected anyone to appear.

'Follow me.' The voice was familiar, and so was something about the way the dark shape moved towards the door of the main building.

Hanley was nervous and did not really know why. He followed the man into the hall and off to a small side room which reeked of rotting meat. His boots crunched softly on something. The man lit a lamp on the table and as the light flared hordes of beetles and other vermin scuttled across the floor. There were bones in the corners of the room, and a dish with water.

'I suspect the officers kept dogs.' It was Espinosa himself, dressed all in black and with a hooded cloak which gave him a theatrical air. 'How are you?'

'Impressed by your luxurious residence.'

'You cannot be paying me enough.' Espinosa's smile was faint and nervous.

'You have papers?'

'Nothing written. That is why I came myself. Victor knows you are here and that he is outnumbered. He began to withdraw several hours ago.'

'He would be a fool not to, and blind if he had not realised that British as well as Spanish faced him.'

'That is true, but he was also told early this morning. A dawn attack would still have caught him, even though surprise had gone, but as the hours passed he had his chance and so slipped away.'

'Who told him?' asked Hanley.

'I do not know.'

Hanley grunted.

'You are surely capable of working out that it would not have been in my interest to do so.'

Hanley let that pass. 'So what else do you have to tell me? We could have guessed all of this.'

'You have the money?'

'What else do you have for me?' said the Englishman, ignoring the question.

'Plenty.'

'I have the money,' said Hanley.

'Good. Commerce is so much better than mere trust. Venegas has moved.'

'As he was supposed to.'

'Perhaps, but I doubt he was supposed to stop. He is a long way away and no threat to Joseph or his capital. They know you are here and Victor is moving back towards them. The French may soon be able to match your numbers.'

That was bad news. The plan rested on keeping the French armies apart and beating them separately. Espinosa waited for some reaction. 'You know, you have become more English, my friend.

'Venegas may be about to move again,' he said after a long pause.

'How do you know?' asked Hanley. It seemed that the Spaniard was aware of far more than the plans of King Joseph and the French commanders.

'I listen, and people bring me or sell me things, so that I know the Junta in Seville has promised Venegas supreme command if he is the first one to reach Madrid. Cuesta will learn of this by tomorrow if he does not already know. You cannot expect him to care very much for the idea. So no doubt there will soon be two Spanish generals changing from lambs into lions.'

'What of the French?'

'Ah yes, it is so easy to forget them with so many different sides in this war. Joseph cannot flee Madrid for a second time, and so when he hears from Marshal Victor he will want to fight, but he must not lose. So he will want all the force he can find. I made one mistake in my earlier reports.'

Hanley smiled. 'An error? You do surprise me.'

'*Errare est humanum* after all, even for me. Sebastiani's corps is twice as big as I thought.' He started patting his pockets. 'No, cannot find it. I did have a list. Perhaps twenty thousand men is a better estimate.'

That was important, and shifted the balance between the armies in favour of the French. 'Then perhaps General Venegas was wise not to press him too hard,' said Hanley.

'Well, he is a hero of the war so he must also be wise, I am sure. A true hero with a pure heart and a wooden head.

'There is more news. Soult is in charge of all the armies in the north.'

'You have told us that already.'

'Yes, I have, but then he was ordered to attack Portugal once more. That has changed. When he is ready he is to drive south. Napoleon writes from all the way there in Austria to tell his generals that the most important thing is to destroy the British Army.'

'Then when will he be ready?'

'That I do not know.' Espinosa shrugged when he saw the Englishman's expression. 'Yes, I confess there are many things I do not know. He writes to Joseph asking for artillery and the horses to pull the guns. Silly fellow. Perhaps the King should write back and say that he ought to have looked after his own better in the first place.'

That suggested it would not be soon. Perhaps they had weeks before the odds would begin to shift more heavily against them.

'I think you have time,' said Espinosa, apparently reading Hanley's thoughts. 'Some time anyway. All of Spain is there to be won – or lost.'

'And you?'

'I do my small part.'

'That you do,' said Hanley thoughtfully. He reached into an inside pocket and pulled out a purse. 'Thank you. This is well worth your price.'

'My dear Hanley, it is worth ten times that much.' Espinosa smiled, spreading his hands wide, before taking the money. 'But I am not a greedy man and I love my country.'

'It is as we agreed.'

'Oh, I trust the English,' said Espinosa, slipping the bag into his own pocket without looking inside. 'However, in a spirit of trust I must now ask you to wait for ten minutes before you leave.'

'Afraid I'll see what you're up to?'

'Let us just say that I prefer to keep my dealings private. Now, I will take your hand, and bid you good night. We shall not use this place again, nor can I say whether I will come in person. In three nights go to the Church of the Holy Trinity and tell the priest that you want to light a candle and pray to St Mary of the Pillar. He will pass more information or tell you how it will come.'

'Are you going to see Wilson?' said Hanley abruptly as the other man was in the doorway.

'The good Sir Robert? Why not, he is on your side.' Espinosa pulled the hood back over his head. 'Ten minutes, Guillermo, before you leave.'

Hanley took out his fob watch and tried to remember the game where he had won it from a captain in the light dragoons. There was no particular reason not to wait. Espinosa was no doubt dealing with others, and surely Spaniards as well as the British. None of that made his information of less value. It was barely nine, so he would not have to feel guilty about waking Colonel Murray as the man was bound to be still hard at work.

When the time passed he blew out the lamp and left, glad to leave behind the stench and the crawling things. There was a torch burning in a wall bracket out in the courtyard and that surprised him because it had not been there before. Hanley could still see the faint yellow glow of the snuffed-out lamp as he came through the black darkness of the hallway and now the torch seemed almost painfully bright.

Something was wrong. A shape moved under the arch of the gateway and he flung himself to the side as a flint sparked, powder flared and then the main charge of the musket split the night apart. Something seared his right side and Hanley fell with a grunt of pain, banging his elbow hard against the flagstones. He lay still.

The man approached cautiously, stopping after each step. He slung his musket and drew a long, slim-bladed knife. Through half-closed eyes Hanley could see that he was dark haired and had a moustache and was probably Spanish.

Hanley watched, still stunned and hurting and not knowing what to do. He had a pistol in his belt, but if he moved the assassin would surely be on him in a moment.

Boots pounded down the alley outside and there were shouts – thankfully English shouts.

'Down here, sir, down here!'

The man ran past Hanley and into the building as a corporal and two men in greatcoats appeared under the arch.

There were explanations and delay before Hanley convinced the ensign and his patrol to look for the assassin.

'We're out to try to stop any theft by our fellows,' explained the young officer. His men found nothing in the house and Hanley was not surprised. He refused their offer to take him to the surgeon.

'It's nothing,' he said, 'just a graze.' He hoped he was right. His side throbbed and he should probably get it bound up, but he wanted to explore behind the tannery just in case there was any indication of where the man had gone.

'Thank you again,' Hanley said as he waved goodbye and then tried to find his way through the alleyways until he was in the right spot. He did not want to go through the house just in case the would-be assassin was watching and waiting for him. Hanley found the back door as he expected – or at least a doorway since the door itself had probably been another victim of French cooking fires.

There were no footprints or obvious trail and he was not really sure what he sought. Most of the lanes were empty, the shadows very dark, and Hanley began to wonder whether he was being wise. He followed a lane which seemed to be heading towards the more prosperous parts of town and came to the high wall of a garden. It was obviously big and belonged to a grand house and when he came to the main road, which was well lit, he could see a grand entrance with a crest carved into the stone archway.

Hanley smiled to himself and walked past before doubling back to crouch in a lane opening opposite the main entrance. This must be the house of the Conde de Madrigal de las Altas Torres. He wondered whether La Doña Margarita was in residence, and his suspicions were confirmed when five minutes later he saw Major George Wickham swagger out into the road. Pringle and Williams had told him of the lady's deception and the officer's association with her.

Others passed along the street, but for a long time no one else went in or out of the house. Hanley felt a stab of pain from his side every time he shifted slightly. His elbow was sore from where it had hit the ground and he knew that he ought to take his information to Murray and Baynes. Still he waited. Then Velarde walked down the road and into the house, nodding amicably to a doorman who presumably sat unseen behind the gateway.

It was becoming so much easier for Ensign Hatch and all that Wickham had said delighted his heart. These days Hatch found himself often thinking of things to write in his next letter, playing with phrases and ideas as he went about his duties. Tonight he was in Talavera in charge of a party sent to guard the artillery park, but his sergeant had proved more than capable of regulating the sentries, and Hatch had just heard a story so wonderful that he felt the words instantly forming in his mind. An old acquaintance from the wagon train was generously obliging, giving him pen, ink and paper, and the peace of the room in use by day as their office to write in. Best of all was the rich port his host provided, for good liquor certainly aided composition. No wonder so many poets were sots!

Hatch laughed out loud at the thought, but then forced himself to concentrate now that he had reached the heart of the letter.

> *At Talavera we found that the famous Spanish lady of our acquaintance is in residence. Mr W grew instantly excited, forgetting his amours of the past months, and once again began his ardent pursuit of the dark eyed – and wealthy! – Dulcinea. Soon he was seen, haunting the street outside her grand house, mixing with the pedlars and wastrels of the town, in the hope of a glimpse of the lady or better yet some words with her. He waited outside, because he was not permitted within – the servants forbidding him whenever he requested an audience and the lady ignoring his pleas when she drove past in her coach. Poor simple fellow, W is unable to understand just how unwelcome his attentions are, and is convinced that the servants, and not the mistress, are to blame! He cannot see that so fine a lady – and she a widow and soon to be a mother – would at no time even glance in the direction of so uncouth a suitor, or indeed any foreign officer save of the most exalted rank.*

Actually, Hatch had happened to pass the house and seen Major Wickham being ushered in by the doorman, but there was no reason to concern his readers with such details. Nor need the knowledge that Williams had been nowhere near the place even for a moment spoil a good story.

No doubt due to his frustrated passion, Mr W's manner has grown rougher and it is the unfortunate soldiers of the Light Company who suffer as a result. He bawls and shouts at them in a savage manner and still they train for hours on end as the poor fellow struggles to understand his duties and vents his spleen.

He has also become more distant in his relations [that was a good and suggestive word] *with the soldiers' wives and no longer spends as much time regaling them with tales of his exploits. Opinion is uncertain as to whether he now spurns such companions in the hope of better, or if those stalwart souls grew weary of his boasting. Whatever the cause, his anger now extends to these women as much as their husbands. Marauding is a serious problem in the army, and often the female followers are the worst culprits. Each day new orders come for ceaseless vigilance to prevent them riding on their donkeys ahead of the column and buying or stealing provisions intended for the commissaries, or simply abusing the inhabitants. In another division of the army, some wives were arrested and trussed up to the halberds in the public square to be flogged on their lower back. W is much taken by the story, and openly dares the wives of the Light Company to misbehave in like manner, boasting that he will 'take his cane and himself give them six and thirty strokes on the bare — if they be caught in the act'.*

Hatch wondered whether the unwritten, but suggested, word was too much. Mrs Davenport would blush, he had no doubt, but he judged that she would read on none the less. Mrs Wickham would pretend to be as shocked and all the while laugh uncontrollably. In fact, Hatch had heard the dour Caledonian sergeant in the Light Company give this stern warning to the followers, and the man – he neither knew nor cared to know the fellow's name – had said 'bare doup', which presumably was some Scotch vulgarism. A dash was better, allowing the reader to be as chaste or coarse as their imagination permitted.

W is a simple fellow, and perhaps little is to be expected from one of his background, but there was a gleam in his eye when he spoke which hinted at dark instincts, mingling rage with disappointed passion. An unkind observer might wonder if he longed for the chance to commit such brutality, and whether or not he had his eye on one or two comely victims, but I think that this is mere gossip.

And so to less amusing themes. May I pass on the best wishes of . . .

He closed with a few lines of pleasantries, and then leaned back in his chair well satisfied. The words had simply flowed, and he had finished this longer letter far more quickly than its predecessors. Hatch drank happily and wondered whether his fiction of an ardent, brutish Williams would actually excite passion in the bosom of Lydia Wickham. The girl was an outrageous flirt, and he suspected would prove willing for more in the right circumstances. A comical image of her pursuing the confused Williams took shape and delighted him, one scene following another. Wickham calling the lieutenant out – perhaps drilling him through the heart with a ball, for the major was reputed to be a fine shot – and even if he survived ruining his career.

His friend reappeared, a fresh bottle in each hand.

'Have you finished?' he asked.

'Yes.' Hatch sealed the letter. 'Although I am pondering whether I have it in me to write a romance,' he said more than half seriously.

The officer grinned, revealing small and misshapen teeth. 'An admirable ambition, I am sure, and there was I planning to idle my time away in drinking.'

'An even better enterprise, and you inspire me to join you!'

His wound cleaned and bandaged, Hanley went through his story once again.

'Espinosa?' asked Murray.

'It seems unlikely and I cannot see what he would gain from killing me.'

'If he meant to do so,' said Baynes.

Hanley touched his side ruefully. 'The man appeared to be serious.'

'Yes, but not competent. If the man was any good you would not be here now. You admit that you were surprised?' There was little trace of the jovial merchant as Baynes spoke with cold reason.

'Yes, I suspected nothing until I came out into the courtyard.'

'Then either he was no good or he was not really trying. It would make us more inclined to believe his story.'

'Perhaps,' said Hanley, 'but is the story not plausible enough?'

'Oh, aye, it all adds up,' conceded Murray, 'although God alone knows how he found out about it. Spying on Joseph's court is one thing. Knowing what the Junta or Venegas are up to is another. Makes you wonder how much he knows about us – and who he's telling. For the laddie spoke no less than the truth when he said this is all worth more than we are paying.'

'He also spoke of a traitor in the Spanish camp warning the French of our attack,' said Hanley.

Baynes rubbed his chin thoughtfully. 'He did, and there may be one, or indeed several.'

'Cuesta may just be an old fool and no general,' said Murray.

'And he fears rivals – Alburquerque, Venegas and

half a dozen others generals, let alone our own Sir Arthur. Any one of them could take his command and he is convinced that he is the only man able to save Spain.' Baynes shrugged. 'It could be jealousy, or simple malice.'

'Or it could be his bad instincts as a general. There need be no great mystery in any of it,' said Murray pragmatically, 'least of all in Victor realising he is facing long odds. He's a sly old fox.' It was now clear that the French corps had retreated.

'Do you trust Velarde, or La Doña Margarita?' asked Hanley.

'Trust is a very grand word,' said Baynes with a smile.

'She has lied about her condition. Presumably without the prospect of an heir her importance to the old count is greatly diminished.'

Baynes nodded his head. 'Yes, although I am told the old man was fond of her as a child. She and her husband were distant cousins. It may simply be that she wishes to keep his favour, although surely such a deception would be unmasked in due course, unless . . .'

Hanley thought of Wickham. 'Would the late appearance of a child not cause comment?'

'No doubt, no doubt.' Murray tried to bring them back to the matter in hand. 'She has been a useful courier, let us leave it at that since we know no more at present. Velarde is considered loyal by at least some senior Spanish officers. They may be in league, they may be lovers, or they may be loyal patriots working to free their country.'

'They may indeed be all of those things and more,' added Baynes.

Murray frowned. 'The news of Soult is worrying, since it may in time pose a grave danger. Time is the key. From what I saw of the state of his army during the retreat from Oporto I cannot credit him ready to take the field for another fortnight at the very earliest. Now I cannot but regret the obstinacy of General Cuesta in not placing stronger garrisons to hold the passes.' If Soult were to move against them rather than attacking Portugal, then the most direct route ran through the passes in the mountains to the north.

'We can do no more now,' said Murray decisively. 'Temper trust with secret suspicion. There is a big lie somewhere, I am sure of it, a great deception. Pray God we do not discover it when it is too late.'

'Amen to that,' said Baynes, and then laughed when Hanley crossed himself. 'You are getting used to playing the Spaniard!'

CHAPTER 22

Black smoke blew dirty embers into Williams' eyes and made him blink.

'On reflection, it may have been unwise,' he said to a captain from the 5/60th foot, whose green-jacketed riflemen extended the piquet line on the flank of the Light Company.

'Too much of a temptation,' said the captain. It was four days after the aborted attack and Williams and the 3rd Battalion of Detachments were once again on the west bank of the Alberche. 'The lads would not like to think of the Frenchies sleeping snugly in their old camp.'

Marshal Victor's men had made themselves very comfortable during their stay, running up row on row of little thatched huts. The British had now burned them because the French were coming back. Williams had also felt that the redcoats – and many officers – had enjoyed the simple boyish destructiveness of setting torches to the roofs. Then the wind picked up and blew strongly from the east, sweeping the clouds of thick smoke across the river. As outposts of the division, the Light Company could see very little.

The Spanish were behind them once again, having passed through them earlier in the day. On 24th July General Cuesta had led his army in pursuit of the French. The British stayed at Talavera. Sir Arthur would not advance until the promised supplies and transport were delivered and none had appeared. Daily rations were reduced once again. In three days the Spanish were back, chased by a heavily reinforced Marshal Victor, and the Third Division was part of a British covering force sent out to protect them as they retreated. The redcoats burned the old French huts because they were there, and because it would have seemed a shame to let them stand.

'If you will excuse me, I had better check on my left flank,' said Williams.

'Well, good day to you. Do not forget that we'll be going back any minute now so make sure the order is passed along.'

Williams passed Rudden. 'Anything to report, Sergeant?'

'No, sir. Can't see a lot, though.' There was the faintest hint of disapproval in his voice, as if Williams were personally responsible for the smoke.

'I know. Be ready to pull back to the brigade.'
'Sir.'

The brigade major appeared, riding carefully between the stunted trees and scrub. With him was Hanley, who hailed his friend and dismounted to walk with him as the piquet line pulled back.

'What news?' asked Williams as soon as the Light Company was formed up and moving. He let McNaught lead them, and walked at the rear.

'The French are coming. Forty-five, maybe fifty thousand of them with King Joseph and Sebastiani's corps as well as our old friend Marshal Victor.'

Williams whistled softly. The numbers were daunting, far bigger than anything he had ever seen. With the Spanish and British there might soon be almost one hundred thousand men meeting to shoot and stab each other. 'Will the Spanish fight?' he asked.

'Cuesta was all for making a stand on the other bank of the river.'

Williams shook his head at such folly.

'It took hours for Wellesley to persuade him to cross to this side,' continued Hanley. 'The old man is boasting that he made Sir Arthur go down on his knees and beg.'

'Why?' Williams was genuinely baffled.

'Well, he has so few victories to his name.'

'Maybe Dobson and I should not have rescued the old fool.'

Hanley laughed. There was a simplicity about his friend which was so very refreshing after the last few days. 'He is grateful. Indeed, there is a gift waiting for you – at least if any of his staff remember about it. It is a fine Andalusian mare.'

'Side of beef might be more welcome.' Williams and the others had watched the Spanish drovers and servants driving large flocks of sheep and herds of pigs and cattle ahead of their army. Their allies appeared to be enjoying everything they failed to provide for the redcoats.

The Light Company marched for a mile, following the main track through the trees until they reached a patch of more open ground filled with parties of redcoats. Several battalions were there, their arms piled into neat pyramids, their packs off and laid out in rows for each company. Some groups had already lit fires and were starting to cook, although no doubt the stews they were making were short on everything apart from water and wistful hope.

'Looks like we are settling in for a while,' said Williams. It was barely one o'clock and seemed too early to halt for the night, but perhaps they would rest for a few hours. 'Will you stay and see Billy?'

'Afraid not, so give him my best.' Hanley had spotted the general and his staff riding up to a walled farmhouse with a pair of high towers. No doubt Sir Arthur wanted to look out from the position and see whether there were signs of the enemy. 'I had better report to Colonel Murray.'

Williams watched his friend ride away and then glanced back the way they had come. There were small groups of soldiers stood to arms as an outpost line to protect the camp. The men were not far away, on the edge of the clearing where the groves of low trees again started to become thick.

'Sergeant Rudden, Sergeant McNaught!' he called. 'Would you join me for a moment.'

The two sergeants looked startled to be summoned. Williams suspected they were wondering what new folly their officer had dreamed up to keep them and the men from rest. Nevertheless, discipline took over, and the two NCOs marched over to join him. 'Corporal, lead the men in, we shall catch you up shortly.'

Williams pointed along the line of outposts. 'What do you think of our piquets?' he asked. 'Would the Forty-third have them posted there?' He wanted Rudden's advice for his regiment had been trained as light troops by Sir John Moore himself. McNaught was experienced, but was a battalion company man. Even so he saw the same thing that Williams had spotted.

'They cannot see anything,' he said with his usual air of long deliberation.

'Yes, it would not have done at Shorncliffe,' added Rudden. 'The line should be farther out or the bivouac set up farther back. And that is fine for the support line, but I did not see sentries set in advance. There should be an outpost line. One man can see as well as ten so individuals should be farther out to give early warning. I doubt that any of our sentries can see the river and the fords. Not with the smoke, any road.' He thought for a moment, judging whether or not to ask a question, but the officer seemed to want his opinion. 'Do we expect the French, sir?'

'They are close, that we do know. I confess I do not know how close. There may be no immediate danger, but . . .' Williams made up his mind. 'When we reach the battalion let the men stand at ease, but keep them together, keep their packs on and muskets with them.'

'The laddies will not thank us, sir,' said McNaught. 'It's been a long day.'

Williams grinned at him. 'Then blame the officer – and pray I am wrong. Join the company. I shall find the colonel and see if something can be done.'

Hanley ran up the spiral staircase to the tower. He had just glimpsed Velarde tying up his horse in the yard and ducked into the doorway of the tower before he was spotted. There were no other Spanish officers around and he wondered what the man was doing here. Hanley himself was waiting for a message. The priest had told him to go to the Casa de Salinas three miles east of the town and wait for a messenger from two o'clock.

The steps wound around in a tight circle and seemed to go on and on. His thighs ached and he was breathing hard, so that it was a great relief to see the bright light of day and come out on to the top of the tower. Sir Arthur was looking with his glass towards the east and with him were Stewart, General MacKenzie and a staff officer he did not recognise.

'Oh, hello, Hanley,' said Stewart affably. 'Anything to report?'

'No, sir, I was looking for Colonel Murray.'

'In the other tower. Too much of a squeeze to fit us all in here. Still, now that you have joined us take a squint through your glass and tell us if you can see anything, because I am damned if I can.'

Hanley did as he was told, looking out of the opening facing northwards, since the other three men filled the one looking east towards the French.

'Have we seen anything apart from cavalry, MacKenzie?' barked Wellesley in sudden question.

'Only cavalry patrols so far, Sir Arthur,' came the reply.

Hanley waved to Murray in the tower at the far corner of the courtyard, but could not attract his attention. He glanced down, but could not spot Velarde anywhere below, and so obeyed his instructions and panned the telescope over the redcoats milling in the camp. It was always strange to see men shouting, laughing and singing and yet be too far away to hear the noise. A file of Germans in their green coats faced with red, and grey trousers, jogged through the tent lines, their short rifles held at the trail. Another group – redcoats with yellow facings this time – walked along carrying pails of water. Farther ahead he saw the line of outposts. Thin smoke drifted between the trees beyond them and he spotted some soldiers in blue with tall green and yellow plumes walking casually back towards the camp.

Another quick look down into the courtyard and

there was still no sign of the Spanish officer, but Hanley did see a civilian in a dark green jacket and russet headscarf strolling confidently through the open gate. The man was one of Espinosa's couriers. He could not see Velarde, and then a chill thought struck him.

Hanley lifted his telescope again and looked where he had seen the men in blue. There was no sign of them, for the smoke was blowing thickly again. Then something wavered on the edge of vision and he shifted his gaze, focused and saw them clearly – wide-topped shakos with high, nodding plumes, green epaulettes, white belts and blue tunic and trousers. There could be no doubt.

'French voltigeurs, sir!' Hanley had not meant to shout, but needed to draw the generals' attention and his voice ended up louder than he had meant.

'Don't be a damned fool,' said Stewart.

'Where?' cut in Sir Arthur.

'There, sir!' Hanley pointed. 'Just beyond our piquet line.'

'By God, you are right,' said Sir Arthur and the first volley rippled along the edge of the scrub.

Redcoats dropped. Hanley was looking straight at a man wearing his white shirt and carrying his jacket over his shoulder and suddenly there was a wide red stain spreading across his back and his arms went high and wide, head back, as the man toppled forward.

Another volley of some thirty or so muskets and

then isolated, aimed shots from skirmishers. More men fell. Others stood staring dumbly at the enemy, who had come from nowhere.

'By God, they are French,' said Stewart in a strained voice.

A ragged line of French light infantrymen advanced through the scrub and into the clearing. They halted and a sergeant dressed the three-deep line as an officer swished his sabre impatiently on the flank of his company. More shots came from skirmishers, and another formed company pushed its way through a grove of cork trees. The French light infantry reached back to draw their bayonets and screw them to the muzzles of their muskets. Light glinted off the points. The officer raised his sword and the line came forward.

The British were not ready. The piquets were weak and several had already been overrun. A few men died when they tried to fight, but they were still sluggish with surprise, and slowed the enemy not at all. Most gave in and were pushed to the rear under the guard of a few French sentries.

The men in the camp had no weapons. Some fell beneath the bayonets of the advancing French or held up their hands and were taken prisoner if the first Frenchman to reach them was calm and under orders, or were stabbed when the enemy were not and the passion of the attack was too great.

Most ran. They could not fight and several quickly saw no reason to die or be taken without purpose. Redcoats fled, stamping through or jumping over campfires and barging anyone out of their way. They ignored the shouts of officers and sergeants or even their friends and they ran. More and more joined them. Hundreds were fleeing.

The French pushed onwards, killing anyone who tried to stop them. Skirmishers still fired and men died as they ran. Hanley saw one pitched into a cooking fire and even from this distance could hear his screams as his clothes caught fire and he tried to roll and douse the flames. No one helped him. A whole brigade had gone from an ordered camp to a fleeing mob in a matter of moments.

'Time to go, gentlemen,' said Sir Arthur, and bounded towards the doorway. Stewart and MacKenzie followed him. Hanley waited, knowing the stairs were narrow and transfixed by the scene. There was something unreal about watching from this high tower, like a spectator in the Roman arena. Thank God the French could not get cavalry through the thickets for the British were helpless. Hanley turned to go, and saw more French coming round from the other side, and fear gripped him for he might have left it too late and had no wish to be a prisoner again.

He bounded down the stairs, slipped, banged hard against a wall, but kept going down and somehow recovered his balance so that he pelted out through the door and into the courtyard. A body lay beside the wall, and he saw that it was Espinosa's messenger, and it seemed an age ago that he had spotted the man. His pockets were turned out and there was a ghastly wound to his neck which left a pool of blood around him.

A musket banged from close by and plaster was flicked from the farm wall beside him as a ball dug into it. Hanley knew the dead man had had his throat cut by a blade and not a shot, but he could not wait longer and ran for his horse, glancing behind him to see a single French light infantryman kneeling in the gateway to the east. Then with a shout half a dozen more Frenchmen appeared and began to level their muskets.

Hanley ran for his horse. Sir Arthur and the other senior officers were already mounted. He saw Murray among them, and then Hanley unhitched his own mount, struggling to hold it as shots flew past so close that he could feel them snapping through the air. The general and his staff set off at a canter through the far gateway. Hanley had a foot in the stirrup, and hauled himself up as his mount started to trot after them. He lost his balance, his right foot slammed down on to the ground again, but he managed to turn this into a bounce and swung himself up. There were shouts from the French, running footsteps, and then Hanley was in the saddle, his right foot over the horse but swinging free, and there was no time to look for the stirrup and he kicked his horse hard, so that it ran on, and he grabbed its mane with one hand to keep himself on as the animal jerkily pounded through the gateway after the senior officers.

★　　★　　★

Williams met the brigade major before he found Pritchard Jones.

'Oh, I shouldn't worry yourself about that,' came the reply when he explained his concern. 'We shall not be here all that long. Just an hour or two until the Spanish are out of our way.' Then he noticed a captain of the 31st walking past and immediately gave him a warm greeting. 'Oh, hello, Ned, good to see you.'

The captain's head was jerked back as a neat hole was punched in his forehead. The ball continued and ripped a great chunk out of the rear of his skull, spraying blood and brains like a burst wineskin. Williams heard the bang of the shot almost immediately and that meant it was close.

He ran back towards his company, pulling his musket from his shoulder as he did so. He saw Frenchmen off to his left, but ignored them, and there were plenty of others to keep them busy. The camp stirred like a disturbed anthill and there was a strange buzzing noise as men asked what was going on or shouted to each other. Then they started to run. Williams heard French cheers and shouted orders, and the sound of rustling as redcoats fled through the long grass and scrub.

Some redcoats were formed two deep, the front rank kneeling, and as Williams sprinted towards them he saw the white facings, and then spotted Rudden. The line fired a disciplined volley, blanketing their front in white smoke. There were more redcoats to their right in another group, and then beyond them McNaught and his Highlanders.

'Well done!' Williams called to Rudden as he reached the line. The men were loading, ramrods scraping in barrels as they thrust down. 'Keep at it.'

There was no one to their left. Williams glanced in the other direction and saw green-jacketed riflemen. He was about to order Rudden's men to wheel back and face at more of an angle to cover the open flank until he saw another company of the green-jacketed Germans running up to extend the line. Their captain smiled as he passed. 'Uninvited guests, *ja!*'

The 3rd Battalion of Detachments ran, just like all the other battalions save one. The Light Company fought alongside the Germans of the 5/60th for a good ten minutes. They gave a little ground, but not much, and Williams lost only one man wounded in the leg. He wondered why the French did not push harder, but so far he had seen only men in the blue of the light infantry so perhaps there was only one regiment close enough to attack. If so then it had done enough damage. Over to the left Williams could see dozens of bundles of red rags dotted in the grass throughout the camp. More had been taken.

The Germans began to cheer and Williams turned back to see an intact battalion advancing steadily to support them. Beside the big union flag or King's Colour was a Regimental Colour with a deep green field matching the shade of the men's facings. That meant the 1/45th, who had a reputation as a disciplined and steady corps.

Williams blew his whistle. 'Send out skirmishers!' he ordered, and half of the Light Company ran forward of the line, spreading themselves into a chain. The men moved as pairs, just as they had practised, and when one man fired his companion waited for him to reload before discharging his own weapon.

'Forward!' The rest of the company formed the supports to protect against a determined enemy attack and to feed men forward into the firing line if there were casualties. Three groups of a dozen men, each formed two deep, marched through the grass.

Williams did not go far. The French gave ground a little. Skirmishers fired on both sides and bullets thumped into the many vines and cork trees, which gave both sides good cover. Few men fell on either side. Patterson of the Highlanders had the tip of his nose torn off by a ball just as he turned to talk to his rear rank man. He screamed a stream of Gaelic oaths at the French, and at his comrades, many of whom could not resist laughing.

'Always sticking your nose in the wrong place, Pat!' called one.

The enemy were far from beaten and kept up a steady fire, but had not been reinforced. The British were able to recover the packs and muskets abandoned in the camp and pick up most of their wounded. Then they began to withdraw.

A somewhat chagrined brigade major ordered Williams back to his battalion. 'Leave the riflemen to cover with the Forty-fifth as supports,' he said. 'And well done, old boy. Pity I didn't see what you saw.'

The Light Company marched back and found Pritchard Jones forming the other companies in column at half-distance. Williams brought his men into their correct position at the rear. They swaggered into the formation, conscious that they were the only ones to stand their ground and hold the enemy back.

Sergeant Major Fisher stamped to attention and reported to the colonel that five men from a water-carrying party were missing, presumed taken, one dead and seven wounded. A dozen casualties was much less than in the three corps that had taken the brunt of the attack. Few French had come near the 3rd Battalion of Detachments, but the officers and men had fallen into confusion anyway and fled with the rest.

'Bloody shambles,' said Pringle in the brief moment he and Williams had to talk. 'Never seen anything like it.' All of the grenadiers had kept their muskets, even during the flight, but the battalion had gone back four or five hundred yards before anyone could get them to stop. 'Wellesley himself galloped up to rally us. We were all trying to show we didn't need his help and had it all in hand. Hanley was with him, so at least he managed not to get captured this time!'

Sergeant Major Fisher raised his voice. ''Talion, 'shun!'

Williams and Pringle dashed back to their companies, the grenadiers at the front and the lights at the rear of the column.

'Forward march!'

The 3rd Battalion of Detachments and the rest of the Third Division marched back towards the town in sullen silence, ashamed of the suddenness with which they had collapsed.

One of the Highlanders started to whistle a Scottish air. It was a familiar tune, and soon all the Light Company joined in, even Private Patterson, with a bandage tied around his face and over his nose. The other companies strode on silently through the dry grass and scrub.

CHAPTER 23

This time it was the Spanish who ran. A whole brigade of some two thousand men lined an earthwork built to extend the stone-walled gardens outside Talavera. Then they saw some French cavalrymen more than half a mile away. There were little puffs of white smoke as the dragoons popped away with their pistols.

'Firing at the snakes?' wondered Hanley aloud.

'Or testing the Dons' discipline?' suggested Murray.

It was an absurd, impossible range for a musket, and yet one Spanish infantryman raised his firelock to his shoulders, took no sort of aim and fired. The dull boom shattered the evening's peace and then another man fired and another. Two thousand men pulled their triggers in a drumming thunder of noise, flames and smoke. Half the men had been with the army for only a few short weeks. None had ever heard so loud and so terrible a noise. More regiments farther down the line poured a volley at the horizon as the firing rolled along over the mile or so held by Cuesta's army.

'If they will fire so well tomorrow, the day is ours,' said Sir Arthur Wellesley to the Spanish general beside him. His face was amused, his beak-like nose casting a long shadow across his face in the light of the early evening sun. 'But as there is nobody to fire at just now, I wish you would stop it.'

'Well, that has revealed the position,' said Murray drily.

'Treason!' shouted a voice. Hanley could not see who called out. Just like the contagious first shot, others swiftly joined in until it became a great chant. 'Treason!', 'Treason!'

Two thousand men dropped their muskets and fled from the noise of their own shooting and from an enemy too far away even to know what was happening. They pushed at each other to force their way through the press, tearing off their packs and throwing down anything that would slow them. Their faces looked blank and unnaturally pale, eyes staring at nothing, and arms pumping as they ran.

Sir Arthur shook his head slightly, as if disappointed at the behaviour of a hound. 'Only look at the ugly hole those fellows have left.' He smiled at the Spanish general and spoke as if asking for the most minor of favours. 'I wish you would go to the second line and try to fill it up.'

Orders were shouted, and staff officers set off at speed to see them carried out.

'It took a lot of work to make Cuesta stay and fight,' said Baynes quietly to Hanley. 'We had thought them safe behind walls and earth banks.'

The Spanish Army was bigger than the British, but Sir Arthur had arranged with his ally for them to hold little more than a mile of frontage. 'At least that will permit them to have one or even two lines of reserves. Your Mr Williams should approve!' Hanley looked baffled. 'My apologies, I recall a conversation with your friend a long time ago and on a different field.'

'Then let us hope things go better this time.'

'Well, they could not go much worse. I just saw the fellow, by the way.' Hanley looked puzzled. 'Your earnest Mr Williams,' explained Baynes. 'He is helping to build a redoubt, or whatever you military gentlemen call it, near the end of Wellesley's line.' The British would hold the rest of the frontage, more than twice as long and with few natural advantages, and that would be the place the French would attack if they had any sense. Even the rawest of Cuesta's regiments could prove formidable behind walls. The British would mainly fight in the open.

'We do not need to bother Colonel Murray, I think. He will have plenty to do helping Sir Arthur to organise his army. In fact I rather suspect Sir Arthur will end up organising Cuesta's army as well. Can't blame him after this farce.'

Hanley had told Baynes and Murray of the dead messenger, the lost message, and seeing Velarde.

'He may be a traitor, but can you be sure it was not the French who killed the courier? Their soldiers were swarming all over that place.'

'I mean to go to the church,' said Hanley. 'The

priest may be able to tell me how to reach Espinosa or when the next messenger will come.'

'Assuming Espinosa knows what has happened so soon.'

'He seems to know a lot,' said Hanley, 'and know it quickly.'

Baynes said nothing for a moment. 'Yes, so be it. It is not wise to go alone. Talavera will be a shambles with all these stragglers. It will no doubt get even worse when darkness falls. Even if there are no other perils it is better not to be alone.' The merchant looked suddenly old and very weary, almost sinking down in his saddle.

'Find out what is happening, William.' It was the first time he had used Hanley's Christian name. 'We must survive and win this next day, and then we must survive the weeks to come. Everything is coming to a head. I sense it somehow.' He smiled. 'Forgive an old man his fancies, but we may lose the game in the hours to come – or win it, or perhaps just stay for the next trick.'

'Where shall I find you?'

'With Wellesley, and I suspect that for the next hours that will mean with the Spanish Army. I may be of some small use to him.' Baynes looked the lieutenant in the eyes. 'Good luck, Hanley. Good luck to all of us.'

Hanley rode to the redoubt and was disappointed by its diminutive size. The land rose so slightly that even with the piled earth its walls were barely at waist height.

'Where is Billy?' he asked Williams, after they had expressed mutual pleasure that the other was unscathed.

'Back with the battalion. There are only two companies of us helping with the work here. They are behind the Guards Brigade, and were in the second line of our own brigade. Expect he is loafing somewhere while others toil!

'Yes, typical lazy grenadiers!'

Hanley pressed on, and found Pringle with a fatigue party from the Grenadier Company gathering firewood. 'Goodness knows what we are going to cook, but I suppose at least we won't freeze.'

'May I borrow Dobson?' said Hanley.

Pringle frowned, pulled off his glasses and wiped them on his sash before putting them back on and replying. 'Trouble?'

'There may be.'

'Is it official?'

'Almost.'

'Then I cannot order him, but suspect he will come along. Try not to get him killed. Mrs Dobson would never let me hear the end of it! Do you want anyone else?'

Hanley shook his head.

'Well, bring him back before it is too late. He has a wife and the girl.' Dobson's younger daughter Sal was with the couple. His son was a drummer and with the rest of the 106th back in England, and who knew where Jenny Dobson was now. Hanley wondered for a moment whether she might be just a few miles away, waiting to service French officers in a tent or the bedroom of an inn. He could not help wishing he was one of them.

'Give them a few hours together, just in case.' Pringle's tone was grim.

It was hard for Hanley to imagine anything ever touching the old veteran. Then he remembered how the man had drunkenly wept after his previous wife was killed in the retreat. Reason told him that no one was safe, even if his heart did not want to believe it. Williams has it easy, he thought, with his simple faith in God. Must be nice to be so confident.

'They say we have two full French army corps up against us,' said Pringle, interrupting his thoughts.

'Yes, and some of Joseph's own regiments.'

'Then there are at least two of them to every one of us – probably more.'

'Only if we do not take the Spanish into account. Sir Arthur believes they will fight from behind their defences.'

'So why should the French attack them?' Pringle took off his glasses to give them another polish. 'Oh, I am sure the day will go well. Just wish there was more in my belly! I'll send for Dobson.'

The lance sergeant arrived and readily agreed.

'I'll look after Mr Hanley, don't you worry, sir,' he told Pringle.

'Thank you, Dobson.' The Grenadier Captain

smiled. 'He may not look much, but I have grown fond of him.'

They walked into town. Hanley had no horse to offer Dobson and so he left his with Pringle. The baggage of the British Army showed all the signs of an orgy of looting. Packs lay with their contents strewn across the ground around them, and officers' valises had their locks broken and contents stolen or tossed aside. Parties of redcoats and women went about trying to tidy up and find things precious to them. They passed a group of soldiers' wives doing their best to comfort a sobbing, fair-haired girl whose dress was torn to rags and whose face was bruised.

Truscott nodded to Hanley as he passed. He and a half-company of the 106th were guarding one of the medieval gateways into the town. 'Sorry to say some of our fellows joined in. Not the battalion, but men from other corps. Watch yourselves,' he said when Hanley explained that they had business in the town.

Hanley took them through the side streets. Some were untouched. Others showed broken windows and signs of marauders, but they saw no riotous soldiers in any uniform. Then they turned on to one of the main roads for a short distance and saw a well-dressed British officer strolling away from them. It was Wickham. Hanley did not need to see his face to recognise the straight back, right hand pressed just so against his waist, while the left held the hilt of his sword to stop it trailing, and the languid stride which appeared careless, but was surely conscious. Wickham had style, there was no doubt about that, whatever his personal character.

William Hanley was a gambler by nature. He liked cards, and played well enough to win more hands than he lost, but the thought that he could lose made it all worthwhile. Now he changed his plan and took a chance.

'Major Wickham!' he called. The other man turned, and nodded in recognition. 'May I have a word?' Hanley was walking quickly to catch up.

'Certainly, old boy, certainly, although make it quick as I am due to dine with the general. We are all to be fed before we go and join the division up on the big hill.'

'This should not take long, and I believe it will be in your own interest.' Hanley's voice had a hard edge.

Wickham laughed. 'You sound very solemn, my dear boy, very solemn indeed.'

'It is a serious matter, I am afraid.'

Wickham's eyes darted. He saw Dobson behind Hanley, but paid no attention to a common soldier, and instead wondered whether there was anyone who knew him near by. A few civilians walked briskly along, heads down and not wanting to look any soldier in the eye. 'If it is about the fifty guineas,' he said, recovering himself and once again with an easy smile, 'you know that I am good for it. You will have the money as soon as our arrears in pay turn up.'

Hanley doubted that promise, and had almost forgotten the loan made more than a year ago. 'That is not my concern. I wish to speak to you about a lady.'

'Of course, yes,' said Wickham lasciviously. 'I believe there is a good house just off the main square.'

'I mean La Doña Margarita.' Hanley was trying to make his questions blunt, almost brutal, but doubted he was being convincing. He needed to frighten Wickham because the major could tell him something that might just help.

'Bit late for you there, old boy, given her state.'

'She is not with child, and she is your mistress.'

Wickham looked shocked for a moment, but only for a brief instant. 'You should not listen to gossip, old boy.'

'You are lovers. Shall I write to your wife and tell her?'

'Scarcely the act of a gentleman, my dear fellow.' Wickham looked him up and down. 'Yes, we are intimate. What business is that of you or anyone else? I know you and your friends keep that flash whore in Lisbon. Why should you care?'

Hanley stared at him, but Wickham stared back. The man was probably no stranger to confrontations like this. 'Because of who she is.'

'Bit late to worry about her honour, old boy. That ship sank without trace long ago.'

'I am concerned about your honour.'

'You have spent too long with that old Methodist Williams. Who will care?'

'They may care enough to end your career. They may care enough to put you on trial.'

'You're raving, old man.'

'She is a spy for the enemy.' Hanley did not know that, but finally Wickham looked surprised and worried. 'What have you told her?'

'Oh my God.' Wickham spoke quickly, nervously. 'That bitch, that trollop . . . Oh no, damn it, man, you cannot mean that my loyalty is suspected. Oh God, you can't think that.' He rallied a little. 'I am an English gentleman.'

Hanley thought he heard Dobson mutter, 'Well, that's all right, then.'

'Does she ask you about the army?'

'We don't talk a lot. Look, the whore lured me on, but I have taken pleasure with her and no more.'

'Tell me about her body.' Hanley snapped the words like a command.

'What?' Wickham was baffled. 'What the hell do you want to know that for? She is a woman, for God's sake, a damned woman with all the usual meat on offer.'

'Her arms?' Hanley thought of the story of the burning hospital and the heroine of Saragossa.

'What about her damned arms? She has two of them just like any other dollymop. They're smooth and they reach from her shoulders to her hands.'

'Not scarred?'

357

Wickham looked baffled. Presumably he had not heard the story or simply did not care.

'Of course they are not damned well scarred, although they will be if I get my hands on the trollop. I'll flog the bitch until she is raw.'

'You will not.' Hanley could not help noticing that Wickham had not questioned being interrogated by a mere lieutenant. The sign of a guilty conscience, no doubt. 'Major Wickham, you shall not see the lady again. Stay away from her and do not communicate with her in any way. Your reputation, and indeed your career, depends on this. So may the success of the army.' Hanley felt he might as well lay it on thickly.

'Of course, of course, you have my word on that. And I swear I told her nothing, nothing at all.'

Hanley let himself smile. 'I am sure of it. None of this need go any farther. Enjoy your dinner.'

Wickham was white faced as he walked away and Hanley thought he was even shaking slightly. 'I must be better at this than I thought,' he said softly to himself.

He would see the lady later. For the moment, Hanley needed to find the priest at Holy Trinity and see if the man could tell him anything.

They were near the church before Dobson broke the silence.

'Is the lady a French spy, sir?' he asked, his voice matter-of-fact.

'I do not honestly know,' said Hanley. Dobson had good instincts and broad experience. 'You know that she is a spy of sorts, carrying messages and money. Whether she is really on our side or works for the enemy is hard to say.' He gave Dobson a quick summary of his suspicions.

'I'll not hurt a lass, sir. Not for you, not for anybody.'

'It should not come to that.'

'Just so you know, sir.' The veteran thought for a moment. 'That driver of hers, Ramón, is a good lad. Knows how to handle himself. May not be able to put him down unless it is permanent.'

'Hopefully she is innocent and there will be no need to try to deal with him.'

The priest did have a message, and Hanley marvelled that Espinosa had reached him so quickly. Another courier was coming. At sunset he was to be waiting at a cattle pen just to the south of the highest crest of the big ridge, the Cerro de Medellín. The name sounded like a bad omen.

'There is a carving in the wall of Saint John the Baptist. It is very old, my son,' explained the father, who himself must have been seventy or more.

'What time is sunset, Dob?'

'About an hour, give or take,' said the veteran, mildly surprised that the officer did not know this.

There was time. 'We've got some walking to do.'

They went quickly, for Hanley saw that the sun was indeed low in the sky. For a while the two men followed the road, but soon this veered to their right towards the stream cutting across the plain, and so they went straight on, heading for the hill. By the time they were beginning to climb they saw a column of weary redcoats ahead of them. The men had blue facings and were covered in dust.

'KGL,' said Dobson.

There were two brigades of King's German Legion infantry in Wellesley's army. The officers and many of the men were King George's Hanoverian subjects, who had chosen not to accept Bonaparte's occupation of their country.

A staff officer rode back along the column and noticed Hanley. It was one of Colonel Murray's men, and he waved and stopped for a moment. 'Some damned fool sent them to the wrong place. The poor devils marched extra miles, began to set up camp, and then had to pack up and march again.'

'Goddamned staff!' said Hanley cheerfully.

'Wastrels and tomfools the lot of them,' said the officer, and set his horse off down the slope. 'Best to you, Hanley!'

They kept on up the slopes. The Germans marched down into a dip and vanished for a while, but when Hanley and Dobson were higher they looked and could see the leading battalion halted, ready to be dismissed to their much-anticipated rest. There were troops moving elsewhere on the rolling hill, and others settling down or settled for the night. They passed through the camp of an Irish regiment, the men chattering to each other happily. Hanley avoided looking any of them in the eye, as he did not want to force them to notice an officer and so have to react and show him proper respect. The redcoats were equally keen not to have to stand to attention and salute and so interrupt their rest, and thus by mutual consent the lieutenant and the lance sergeant walked through the camp without disturbing anyone. Hanley was puzzled by the packs of a group still formed up and marching to mount guard.

'Kerry Militia?' he read from the badge painted on the pack. 'What the blazes are the militia doing here?' Britain's second army of the militia regiments served full time with the colours, but were not required to serve overseas.

'Volunteers,' said Dobson. 'There's lots of them transferred into the real army. Good boys, most of them, once they toughen up. A lot haven't been in long enough to be issued with packs by their new regiments. You see plenty of them wearing their old jackets as well.'

Hanley thought for a while and then stopped when they were through the camp and no one was near. He shaded his eyes for a moment and looked across beyond the valley and the stream where another, lower hill stood. Troops moved there as well, but these were French, and he saw them as dark masses or shadows in the grass. A few wisps of smoke and some much thicker clouds drifted in the light air from where the enemy guns had fired for a while at the British as they took up position. Beyond the smoke he saw a group of riders racing towards the top of the hill. No doubt they were enemy officers, perhaps even King Joseph himself.

'Are we ready for the French, Dob?'

Hanley saw Dobson frown in the red light of the setting sun. They could still see it, but lower down the slope the sun must have gone and the shadows were thickening.

'They're good lads, sir. A lot of second battalions, so plenty of them are young and this will be their first fight. Not too many of us who have seen how it's done.'

'Can we beat the French? There are a lot of them.'

'Well, they'll know they've been in a scrap.'

Hanley said no more and they began walking once again. The round peak of the Medellín Hill was a good landmark, and they pushed on towards it as straight as they could for a good five minutes.

'I reckon that is it,' said Hanley, pointing up the slope towards a low stone enclosure. He followed the wall, and found the carved stone with the figure of a bearded man. It was badly worn, and in the fading light he would have to take the priest's word for it that it was supposed to be John the Baptist.

Dobson stiffened. He had been carrying his musket down low. Now he raised it slowly and eased back the hammer to cock it with a firm click. He nodded at two vine trees at the far corner of the pen.

'I could shoot you down where you stand,' said a voice. 'Perhaps both of you. I have two pistols.'

Dobson said nothing, but kept raising his musket. With a sudden rush the butt was couched against his shoulder, the muzzle aimed squarely at the trees.

'You could try,' said Hanley, with a confidence he did not feel. He imagined a pistol or musket aimed at his chest. Would he see the spark of the flint, the flare of the powder and then the explosion as a ball hurtled towards him to sink deep into his flesh?

He gulped, hoped no one heard him and then gambled again. 'Or you could come out and talk, Luiz.'

There was a pause, then a laugh, and the barely audible sound of a hammer being gently lowered back into place.

'Of course,' said Velarde, as he stepped from the cover of the trees. 'We are on the same side, after all. Well, more or less.' The sun began to sink below the hills to the west.

Dobson made no move, not understanding the Spanish words. His firelock followed the Spanish colonel, his finger still poised on the trigger.

'It's all right, Dob,' said Hanley. The veteran lowered his musket, but kept it cocked and ready.

'I presume we are waiting for the same thing,' said Velarde. 'You really do impress me, Guillermo, with your talent for finding things out.'

'We may not be waiting for the same reason.'

363

'Really.'

Some distance away a musket fired, the sound soft. It was followed by several more.

'The piquets showing their hate,' pronounced Velarde.

Dobson's eyes flicked down the slope towards the French, but only for a moment.

'And what about you, Luiz? Why did you kill the messenger this morning?'

'Why blame me, and not the French?'

Hanley said nothing. There was another shot from down the slope of the hill and then silence once again.

'He recognised me,' said Velarde with the slightest of shrugs. 'It was unfortunate, but could not be helped. He was not a bright man and would have told everyone that I was a French spy. Someone would probably have been stupid enough to kill me if the word spread.

'You do not seem surprised. Well done indeed, Guillermo.'

'So now I know, why should I not kill you?'

'Because you are smart.' Velarde shrugged. 'I tell things to the French. Or rather I tell them to Espinosa and he tells the French. We tell them some nonsense, but more truth even if it is some-times too late to be of much value. That way we both are trusted and so they give us their own secrets. That way we can fight them.'

'Who is we?'

'I want a new Spain. One country, not divided

364

into the old kingdoms. I want it enlightened and liberal, where men of worth choose their leaders and the king rules by consent. You must remember our talks.'

'I believe King Joseph wants the same thing,' said Hanley.

'Yes, or so he says, but this new country cannot be made by outsiders. Do you think Bonaparte truly gives anything and does not come simply to take?'

'Which leader promises what you want? Or do you wish to lead this new Spain yourself?'

'They could do worse.' Velarde chuckled. 'They could do a lot worse. But no, I do not belong to any faction. Nor does Espinosa. Nor do we agree on the new Spain, but we do agree that it must be made by Spaniards – not Castilians or Andalusians or anyone else, but by Spaniards. So we must beat the French first, and so we help anyone who fights them strongly. Too many of our people are more concerned to outwit their rivals than the real enemy. I will not get caught up in that. I will certainly not die for that. If I must die for my country then so be it, but not for Cuesta, or Palafox or the Junta or anyone else.'

'A good speech,' said Hanley. 'How much is true? You never struck me as the stuff martyrs are made from.'

'Still the same.' Velarde laughed again. 'I believe what I have said. I believe other things too. I fully plan to survive this war, and it would be nice to be wealthy. Is that what you want to hear, Guillermo? It is just as true.'

'So what do you plan to tell the French tonight?'

'That the Spanish position is impregnable from the front, but that the British Army is stretched thin and vulnerable. Is that not what your General Wellesley wants them to know? Cuesta's men may panic again. If the battle is to be won then the British must do most of the fighting. None of that is a secret, or at least more than they could work out from their patrols. Yet it is enough to convince them of my usefulness. You may see the note, if you like. It is in cipher, but that should not slow a man like you. Or I could just tell you the key if you do not relish the challenge!'

'Sir!' Dobson had noticed the darker shape of a figure stumbling down towards them from the crest. The man was running, making the long grass swish about his legs. 'Up there, sir!' Dobson was looking higher now. Silhouetted on the highest point of the hill were more figures – a lot more figures. There was a dense crowd of men where there had been none before and where it seemed none were supposed to be.

Dobson's musket snapped up to cover the man, leading a little to allow for his movement. He was close now, and they could just make out the shape of a wide-brimmed hat.

'Wait!' hissed Hanley.

The running man stumbled, recovered and ran straight into Hanley, who grabbed him to hold him upright. He could see the whites of his eyes as the man looked up in terror. His head flicked from side to side, surprised to see three men where he had expected one.

'Mapi,' said Hanley. One of his hands was soaking wet and sticky as it touched the man's side. The messenger was breathing only with difficulty and not because he was tired.

'The French,' he said, and then his whole body went slack.

A moment later dozens of muskets shattered the night with flame and noise.

CHAPTER 24

'That will be the old Buffs making a blunder as usual,' said General Rowland Hill wearily. Wickham looked up towards the crest and saw the flashes, so very bright in the dim light. He and the general's staff had ridden after their early dinner to find that the Second Division was in the wrong place, and were doing their best to sort out the mess. Now it looked as if chaos was turning into farce.

'Well, Donellan, I'd be obliged if you put the Forty-eighth into line ready to occupy the hill.' The order sounded like a polite request to a neighbour in the general's beloved Shropshire.

'Come on, we had better calm them down.' The general clapped his spurs into his horse and set off like the bold hunter he was. General Hill – known as Daddy to not just his division, but half the army – looked like an affable country squire. Wickham had begun to realise that his kind nature hid an active and fearless commander. Reluctantly he followed the half-dozen horsemen as their mounts eagerly ran up the slope.

A battalion in open column of companies was beside them, the lines of men dark shadows. Beyond them another was deploying into line, while the third battalion from the brigade pressed up towards the crest, breaking up into clumps of men as it hurried.

'Be careful. No sense being shot by our own fellows!' called the general as he and his staff made their way through the dark and straggling line.

Wickham's horse could never resist a race. He tried to hold the mare back, but it surged up until it was level with the general and his brigade major. There were men scattered in front of the mass at the top of the rise.

'Cease fire, my good fellows! Cease fire!' called General Hill. 'You are firing on our own side!'

Men milled around them. They had wider tops to their shakos than usual. One grabbed hold of the general's bridle.

'My God, they're French!' yelled the brigade major.

The gout of flame from the musket seared across Wickham's vision, so that for a moment all he could see was the glow against pitch black. There was a soft thump and a gasp and the brigade major was flung from his saddle. General Hill yanked hard on his reins and his horse reared, knocking the French infantryman down and making him let go.

Another shot and a bullet smacked into the horse's chest, so that the general felt it shudder beneath him. He rammed his heels against its flanks and pulled it round, and the animal leapt away from the cluster of French skirmishers. More shots and one of his staff cried out, but did not fall. Wickham rode with them, but his mare never liked going downhill and would not go faster than a slow and bumpy canter.

The general and his staff vanished into the darkness ahead of him.

More flame and a deeper-throated boom than that of a normal musket and something hit him hard on his right arm and shoulder, flinging him sideways. His mare lost her footing at the same moment, stumbling forward, and Wickham was falling, spinning as he dropped to land flat on his back in the grass. His arm hurt savagely and there was blood on his cheek. The frightened mare ran on.

Wickham looked up at the starry sky, for the moment stunned and so dimly aware of what was happening that he felt no fear, only pain. A figure loomed above him, dark against the sky, and it raised in its hand an axe which glinted faintly and looked small, but very heavy.

'Bastard,' hissed a voice in strongly accented English.

Wickham had just the strength to plead. 'No, please, no.'

A shot struck the ground just beside him.

'Prisonnier! En avant, mes braves!' came a voice from farther away, and there was the sound of men trampling the grass as they ran.

The man standing over him vanished, fleeing into the night.

'*Eh coquin, un officier!*' said one of the French infantrymen. Wickham hissed in pain as another began to run his hands through his pockets.

'I'll wait for you here,' said Velarde.

'We ought to help, sir.' Lance Sergeant's Dobson's tone stopped just short of being a command.

Hanley and Dobson ran along the slope. Volleys slashed the darkness on each side. There were screams and shouted orders. Darker shapes came up the slope and then seemed to stop. Men fired, but the heavier volleys came from higher up.

'What the hell is going on?' shouted a voice ahead of them.

'Who is in charge?' This time it was another voice – a distinctly Scottish voice.

They got closer. Men fired again, and for an instant Hanley saw the silhouettes of two ranks of men clearly as they shot up the slope at the French.

'Don't fire!' came a voice. 'We are Germans!'

'Bugger! Damn it all! Sergeant Hawkins, cease firing, they're ours. Where the hell are you, Hawkins?'

'We're Germans!' came the cry again.

There was a break in the firing. Hanley and Dobson heard the rattle of ramrods in the barrels of muskets.

'Who the hell is in charge?' It was the Scotsman again. 'Give us orders.'

Dobson held out an arm to stop Hanley. 'Down, sir,' he hissed. They were almost behind the end of what seemed to be the British line, but now that the shooting had stopped the veteran had spotted movement coming up at an angle behind them. There was a dark mass, the head of a column and smaller shapes flitting ahead of it.

'Look out, French to the rear,' yelled Dobson.

'Who the devil are you?'

'*Españoles! Españoles!*' shouted a higher shadow – an officer riding at the head of the column. Hanley thought the accent distinctly French.

'Lying sods,' whispered Dobson. He eased his bayonet out of its scabbard and fixed it to the muzzle of the musket lying beside him.

The column pushed up the slope and the skirmishers were flowing around the back of the British line.

'Surrender, you are our prisoners,' called a voice used to command.

'They're bloody French!'

'Drop your muskets! You are prisoners.'

'I'm bloody not!' There was the sound of fighting and blows with the butts of muskets. The British formation broke up. Shots flamed in the night as some fled. Others were being hustled to the rear as prisoners. Some still struggled as Frenchmen grabbed their collars and dragged them down.

Farther along the slope, another row of flames stabbed up the hill. Closest to them the line had gone, but elsewhere parts of the battalion still fought.

'Give us an order and we will dare anything. For God's sake give us an order!' The shouting was more distant now.

Men ran past them.

Dobson sprang up. 'Stop, you buggers!' he commanded in a voice unmistakably British.

'Who the hell are you?' asked a voice, but already a dozen men had stopped.

'Who is loaded?' asked Dobson, ignoring the questions. No one answered. 'Then fix your spikes, lads.'

Hanley stood and drew his sword. He did not feel he could do anything better than the lance sergeant, but wanted to show willing. There were more shapes coming towards them, but it was harder for the French to see down the slope than it was for them to pick out the shapes above them.

'*Merde! Les anglais!*'

Dobson fired. 'Charge!' he screamed, and rushed on through the smoke of his own shot. 'Come on, lads!'

Hanley went with them. There was a hiss of pain as Dobson ran a French infantryman through the stomach, and then twisted the blade free as he kicked the man over. All around him men stabbed, hacked and struck at each other with bayonet and musket butt. One redcoat without a weapon pushed a Frenchman's musket aside with his right hand and then punched the man with all his weight behind his left fist. Another British soldier died as an enemy thrust the muzzle of his musket against his face and then pulled the trigger. Hanley cut at a man with his sword. The blow was clumsy, for he had never really practised with the blade and all of his movements seemed so very slow. His opponent ducked beneath the slash, and then jabbed forward with the butt of his musket. Hanley gasped and struggled to breathe as he folded double. He collapsed kneeling on to the grass.

The French infantryman hit him again on the head, knocking him face down on the grass so that he did not see and only felt someone come and place his feet either side of him. With a clang the man parried the French light infantryman's bayoneted musket as he thrust down to finish off the officer. Then something wet and hot flowed on to Hanley's head, stirring him to consciousness as the Frenchman screamed in intense agony.

The French withdrew, leaving three of their number stretched in the grass.

'Stay here, lads. Don't follow!' Dobson was still giving the orders, which meant that he was unscathed. 'We can't beat the lot of them on our own, but we can give time for our boys to come up and see 'em off properly. Now, kneel down and get them muskets loaded.' Hanley felt a hand on his shoulder. 'You all right, Mr Hanley?'

He pushed himself up. 'I believe so.' He saw a face that looked familiar kneeling beside Dobson and grinning at him.

'It's Ramón, sir. The Spanish lady's coachman. Told you he's a handy lad. That Frenchie would have done for you if he hadn't turned up.'

'*Gracias*,' said Hanley hoarsely. His throat seemed so very dry and there was a faint taste of vomit.

'I hate the goddamned French!' said Ramón, not bothering to use his own language.

Shots came from the darkness ahead of them. The volleys were aimed elsewhere, but there was clearly a line of skirmishers facing them. A redcoat was hit on the kneecap and cried out in pain.

'Bastards. They hit me!' He sounded surprised and angry more than anything else.

'Lie down, lads, once you're loaded. Only fire when you can see a mark clearly.' Dobson patted a man on the shoulder. 'You. Drag him back five paces and then come back here. We'll look after you when it's over, son,' he said to the wounded man.

Hanley rubbed his throbbing head as Dobson gave the orders. The officer did not understand this, or see how men like Dobson – or Williams or Pringle for that matter – saw a shape to it all and a form which they could control. He was more comfortable with the cleverness and deceit of men like Baynes and Espinosa.

The firing grew heavier around the peak above them.

'Who are you, lads?' asked Dobson.

'Second Battalion of Detachments.' That explained much of the chaos. It was always confusing to fight at night, but all the harder with unfamiliar officers and sergeants in charge.

A heavy company volley lashed at the French

column nearest to them. Then there was a distinctly British cheer and a line of men, clear and stark shapes in the growing starlight, ran straight at the enemy, bayonets reaching out and glinting dully. The French mass quivered and then broke up as men fled. Another cheer came from the far side of the crest and then the higher French column collapsed into rout.

'Up, lads,' said Dobson. 'With your permission, Mr Hanley, I think we should go forward. Steady, boys. Don't want to rush and have some damn fool take us for Frogs. We'll just clear up any of these light bobs who hang around.'

The French had gone, save for the dead and wounded. There were plenty of these, both British and French, dotted all over the slopes of the hill. Some moaned, or sobbed, or cried out for their mothers. The less badly hurt yelled for help or for their friends to come and fetch them.

More redcoats joined them, and Hanley set them to work collecting the wounded.

'Where shall we take them, sir?'

An officer was always expected to know, but Hanley had no idea. Thankfully a corporal from one of the light infantry regiments had the answer.

'A hospital has been set up in a farm on the back of the hill,' he said.

'Good, take them there.'

A surly officer from the 95th passed them, smelling of fresh blood.

'Hard fight,' said Hanley.

The only response was a grunt.

'Hanley,' a voice called. 'Help me, Hanley. Oh God, please help me!'

It was Wickham, his jacket and boots stolen along with his purse, and the right sleeve of his shirt dark with blood.

'Carry the major to the surgeons.'

'Thank you, Hanley, thank you. You are a true friend. They robbed me, Hanley. The rogues robbed me.' The voice faded as four men carried Wickham away in a blanket taken from the top of an abandoned French pack.

'You stay with us, Ramón,' said Hanley without looking at the Spaniard.

There was a cry of pain. 'Oh my God, keep steady, you damned rascals, or I'll have you all flogged!' Wickham's shout carried back to them. Hanley thought he saw Ramón grin wickedly.

General Hill passed, mounted on a new horse, and doing his best to bring order. The French had gone, and the high ground was now heavily occupied by the British, but that did not mean the enemy would not try again. Their surprise attack had so very nearly worked.

Officers appeared from the 2nd Battalion of Detachments and began to rally their men.

Hanley and Dobson with Ramón by their side walked back to the sheep pen where they had left Velarde and the wounded messenger.

'He is dead,' said the Spanish colonel. 'I bound

him up as best I could, but he had bled so much. It is a pity.'

'A pity?'

'Yes, does that surprise you? Why would I want the man dead? But it does mean I have no means of sending a message to Espinosa. Here is the packet. I have left the seal on it in case you still do not trust me.'

Hanley slipped the packet into his pocket. 'We cannot read it up here.'

They followed the parties of men carrying wounded down to the farm on the western slopes of the hill. There was light there, but Hanley wished somewhere else was nearer.

'Keep an eye on Ramón,' he said quietly to Dobson as they arrived. 'Make sure he goes nowhere near Major Wickham.'

'Aye, sir.'

The two officers found a spot under a lantern and tried their best to ignore the smell of blood, the soft noises of the hurt men and the buzzing of flies.

Hanley broke the seal and read, passing each page to Velarde when he had finished.

'This changes everything,' he said softly at the end.

Velarde simply nodded, and finished going through the last page. 'We must tell General Wellesley.'

'Yes. He will probably be on the hill somewhere trying to sort things out. You go and find him or

Colonel Murray. I shall go back to the town and find Baynes.'

The Spanish officer looked at him. 'Is this a test?'

'Should it be?'

Velarde spread his hands. 'As you wish. I'd be glad of your sergeant as escort. The sentries may be jumpy at the moment and better not to sound too foreign.'

'Certainly.' They walked over to Dobson and the Spanish coachman. The veteran was feeling the heft of a short axe.

'Nasty brute, sir. Ramón tells me the savages use them in America.'

'The Comanches,' confirmed the coachman, who had once been an hussar, taking back his tomahawk.

'Sergeant Dobson.' Hanley did not bother to use the full rank.

'Sir!' Dobson stiffened to attention, sensing that the officer wanted to be formal.

'I need you to take Colonel Velarde to find General Wellesley. He carries important dispatches. My guess is that the general will be somewhere on this hill, making sure that everything is in order. Once you have taken him to the general and his staff you may return to the battalion.'

'Sir?'

'I need to go back to the town and Ramón will be able to guide me there. I assure you that I shall be fine on my own.'

'Yes, sir.' Hanley wondered how two words still

managed to convey the lance sergeant's opinion that while the lieutenant was no doubt a splendid fellow, he was incapable of putting his own breeches on without assistance. 'Are you sure, sir?'

'I am, Lance Sergeant Dobson. I think at last I am.'

Hanley and Ramón went down the slope and then followed one of the main roads into town.

'I need to speak with your mistress,' he told the coachman. After that they exchanged no more words.

It was eleven o'clock by the time they reached the house. The doorman let them in without question. The housekeeper was a good deal less helpful. 'The lady has retired and is asleep.' She repeated the phrase over and over again. Hanley doubted it was true. The town was still noisy and full of stragglers; many of whom were now drunk.

Ramón supported him, and finally the old woman gave in.

La Doña Margarita appeared, in one of her fine widow's dresses. She appeared so rapidly that it was clear she had not yet gone to bed.

'Lieutenant Hanley, to what do I owe this unexpected visit?' Her voice was calm. Her face seemed a little drawn as if from fatigue. She sat in one smooth motion, hands adjusting her skirts to the shape of the carved wooden chair with its high arms. 'Please sit.'

'I regret disturbing you at this hour, and indeed calling unannounced and uninvited.'

'And yet you do so. Perhaps that rather weakens any apology.' She smiled and turned to her coachman. 'You may leave us.'

Ramón looked uncertain. 'I am not accustomed to repeating instructions,' said the lady. The coachman glanced at Hanley, then back at his mistress. La Doña Margarita inclined her head slightly, and Ramón left.

'He is a good man,' said Hanley, narrowly avoiding calling him a lad.

'That is true, but paying that compliment appears inadequate cause for disturbing me at such an hour.'

Hanley looked at the lady. Her olive skin seemed darker in the lamplight, her curves fuller and her lips even more inviting.

She raised an eyebrow.

'Forgive me.' Hanley was sure he knew the answers, but needed to ask the questions. 'I spoke to Major Wickham earlier this evening.'

The poise cracked for a moment and there was a flash of anger. 'If he thinks he can simply send his friends to seek my company!' Then the dignified façade reasserted itself. 'It is late, and I do not believe I can offer what you want.' She rose.

'Sit, madam!' Hanley had not meant to shout. He saw a flicker of fear in her eyes, but she stopped. Hanley had not moved from his seat. 'You misunderstand. I do assure you that I am no great friend to Major Wickham. Please, please sit down.' She did so reluctantly, and her glance remained filled with anger.

'I know you are not with child. I know that you are not scarred from the flames after your heroism at Saragossa.' Hanley spoke evenly. He was sure of all of this, and only the last piece of the puzzle would be a guess. 'I also know that you are not the lady you claim to be, although I believe you were once her maid.'

He let the words hang in the air.

She was breathing deeply, her chest surging and falling. The silence was heavy, and in the far distance Hanley could hear a voice singing drunkenly.

'Wickham did not tell you all that,' she said at last.

'No.'

'He realised I was not having a baby when the carriage fell into the ditch all those months ago. His arm pushed aside the padding I wear.' She gently slapped her enlarged belly.

'Captain Pringle saw you shot in the same place.'

'And he said nothing? A different man to your major.'

'Yes.'

'Wickham knew that a baby was important and could be the heir to a title and great fortune. My own place in society depends on the child. He threatened to reveal my secret and unmask the deception unless I let him take his pleasure with me. He wanted money as well, and then joked that he might solve my problem for me and give me a baby.' Her voice was bitter. 'What was I to do?'

'I believe Ramón tried to kill him this evening.'

La Doña Margarita smiled thinly. 'Only tried?' She stared at the Englishman and read no threat there. 'That was a great risk,' she said.

'I doubt even Wickham suspects anyone apart from the French.'

'He is my father.' Hanley's face must have betrayed his surprise. 'There, for the first time I reveal something you did not know. My mother died of fever in Mexico. When I was old enough the captain took me on and trained me to be his wife's maid. Will you betray him?'

'No. I cannot let him complete the task, but I do not feel Wickham or anyone else needs to know. The major will not bother you again.'

'Your doing? Then I thank you on both counts.

'The real widow died of fever just like her husband. Neither survived to reach the shores of Spain. I was at Saragossa, and this,' she pointed at the wreath on her sleeve, 'is mine by right. The story of the burns helps to keep men at a distance, even those not deterred by the baby.'

'Why the deception?'

'I have lived most of my life in the New World, and yet my heart is Castilian.' Her voice was strong and proud. 'As a maid without an employer what could I do? She hated the French, and she would approve. As a noblewoman I can be useful.'

Hanley stared at her for a long time. Neither said anything.

'Yes,' he said at last. 'Indeed you can. I shall tell no one what I know.'

'And the price?'

He thought for a moment of Wickham's bargain. The temptation was strong.

'Punish the French,' he said. 'In your own way keep hurting them.'

La Doña Margarita watched him as he stood, bowed politely and walked to the door.

'I like you, Mr Hanley,' she said softly as he left the room. Hanley caught the words and could not help smiling.

It was cold when he stood out in the street. The moon was rising and the night was bright. Hanley shivered and wished he had his cloak. Part of him felt noble, and that was a novel sense for him to have. More importantly he was pleased with his cleverness and revelling in the joy of gambles that paid off. It was a feeling he had always enjoyed.

'Good evening, William.' Baynes sat on horseback beside him, leading a saddled mule. It did not surprise him. 'Best I could do, I am afraid. We should be able to find your horse when we reach the general's staff.'

Hanley hauled himself up on to the mule. 'Where is he?'

'Up on the Medellín hill, sorting things out. One of the German brigades broke. They thought that they were in the second line so had not set pickets. I strongly suspect that Sir Arthur will spend the night there. Therefore so must we.'

'Has the general received the dispatches?'

'He has, and as you may guess has plenty to

think about. Soult is closer than we think – at most a week away. It is worrying that he was expected to be behind us at Plasencia even earlier and that we knew nothing about it. At least the report that Venegas is finally threatening Madrid is something.'

'What will happen?'

'My dear Hanley, you are the military man, so you tell me.'

They rode through the streets in silence after that, until they left through one of the gateways and began to climb the hill.

Finally Hanley asked, 'You knew who she was, didn't you?'

'I did.'

'Then why did you say nothing?'

'Secrets are better kept than broadcast. Would it have changed anything if you had known? Besides, it never does any harm to see how hard it is for anyone else to find something out.' Baynes' voice sounded full of contentment. 'I am fully reassured.'

'I might have made a mistake, have revealed her as a fraud or proclaimed her a spy.'

'But you did not. You really should have more faith in yourself, my dear boy, more faith.'

Hanley could not think of anything more to say.

CHAPTER 25

The French tried again in daylight. The same division launched its three regiments up the slopes of the Medellín. There was an early morning mist down in the valley. On the lower hill held by the enemy there were also French guns, some sixty of them placed in a long line each one ten yards apart so that the battery stretched all along the top of the hill and down on to the plain. Their smoke fed the mist and made one great drifting cloud, so for a long time Hanley could not see the columns advancing.

Roundshot scarred the earth, flinging up dirt and stones and sometimes bloody fragments of the men caught in their path. Shells exploded in a circle of jagged metal shards. The British infantry were ordered to lie down, and this and the slope itself made them difficult targets for the French gunners. Yet France's emperor was himself a gunner, and so was Marshal Victor, and the French artillery boasted that they were the finest in the world. Difficult did not mean impossible. Battery commanders ordered the crews to reduce the powder in each charge and so the balls no longer sank deep into the soil or bounced high overhead, but skidded lightly up the slope, grazing past it. The redcoats died or were maimed by ones and twos and many shots were fired before one struck home, but the enemy kept firing and none of the men on the hill had ever seen or heard so many French guns pounding away. This was the Emperor's way of war, deluging one stretch of the enemy line with fire, pulverising it so that the stunned survivors cracked when his infantry struck like a hammer at the weakened spot.

Every now and again there was a slight pause in the appalling crashing and destruction of the guns, and it seemed so unreal that Hanley wondered whether his ears were too beaten to hear anything until he caught the faint sound of drums and cheering. He knew the sound of French infantry advancing from Vimeiro and he had seen them beaten there, but then there had not been so many guns. The barrage resumed and the redcoats on the hill suffered.

The sixty guns pounded the Medellín. Hanley saw a shell explode squarely on a line of prone figures. The man in the front rank had the back of his skull sheared off by a whirling fragment of the casing. To the right another man's back was ripped open, while on the left a redcoat screamed because one leg had gone beneath the knee and the other was a mangled mess of broken bone and flesh. The sergeant in his place behind the double rank lay dead without a mark on him. In the middle of it all a soldier sat up, and could not believe that he was unharmed. The man shook as they dragged the dead and wounded back and closed up the formation, but took his place lying down again in line.

The guns ceased fire as they were blocked by their own infantry pushing up the slope. Skirmishers from each side fought their own private battle amid the mist and smoke. The British held back the French voltigeurs, but had to give way as the main columns came close. Bugles called, whistles blew, and officers and sergeants shouted for the light bobs to fall back on to the main line. They went reluctantly, stopping to fire down the slope. Men dropped in the front ranks of the columns, but they were far too few to hold them up.

'Damn their filing, let them come in anyhow,' shouted General Hill, impatient because the light companies were retreating so slowly that they were in the way of his main line.

Colonel Murray laughed out loud. Hanley did not understand.

'That's the first time I have ever heard Daddy Hill swear,' Murray explained. 'Damned good work by the way, getting those dispatches.' It was not the first time the colonel had congratulated him on getting the package from Espinosa. 'Puts us in a tight spot, but at least we know what is happening and can try to figure a way out. First thing is to beat Victor, of course!'

Orders were shouted and the battalions stood

up, dressed ranks and prepared to meet the enemy. Hanley saw more than one soldier cross himself. Others knocked the embers out of pipes they had somehow managed to smoke as they lay under the pounding of the guns.

The French drums were clear now that the noise had slackened, every pause in the rhythm filled by chanting. Men from the light companies and German riflemen from the 60th jogged back through the gaps between the battalions to reform.

'*Vive l'Empereur! Vive l'Empereur!*' shouted the French infantrymen, faces red and hearts pounding as they slogged up the slope towards the waiting enemy.

'Come on, we have work to do,' said Murray to Hanley and the other officers with him. 'Can't just stay here and watch the fun.' He led them away behind the line to a point where they could see the valley to the north of the Medellín. There was high ground covered in scrub on the far side, but the valley itself was fairly open and could offer the French a way around the Allied position.

The French drums and chanting rose to a crescendo behind them. The enemy was close.

'Good, it's clear,' said Murray. There was no sign of any French troops in the valley.

Hanley flinched as a sound like thick cloth being ripped violently in two erupted from behind them. He had heard volleys before, had stood in the ranks of the 106th as the noise battered at his senses, but even so it took him by surprise.

'Our fellows,' said Murray, as if commenting on a cricket match.

A few shots replied, then a smaller, ragged volley.

'The French.'

A cheer came faintly on the air, and Hanley thought how odd it was that you could tell it was British even without catching any words. Each nation seemed to shout in its own distinctive way. There were more heavy battalion volleys, and the steady drum roll of platoon volleys as individual companies fired by alternate sections, so that fire flickered up and down the whole line.

'Someone's showing off,' muttered Murray.

There were more British cheers, much nearer this time, and the closest turned into a long scream of rage. Hanley imagined the men surging forward, rushing at the enemy.

'That should do it,' said the colonel. 'Thompson, you stay and keep an eye on things here. Sir Arthur is to be informed instantly if any French formations approach the valley.' The staff officer nodded. 'We shall go and look at the other side.' Murray set off towards the crest. At the highest point Hanley glanced down and could see redcoats streaming down the slope, Frenchmen in blue running ahead of them. The attack was clearly shattered and once the French were far enough downhill the guns resumed.

'Warming up,' said Murray with a mischievous grin. He reined in where they could look to the south. This time the land was not empty. They could see all of Wellesley's army stretched across the plain, with the infantry in two lines, the second line much smaller than the first, and the cavalry brigades behind them. Hanley tried to make out the 3rd Battalion of Detachments, but knew that he was only guessing. Beyond them were the Spanish, barely visible among the groves and enclosures on the edge of Talavera itself.

The line of the Portina stream was hard to follow. Hanley could see a few glimmers off the little pools left in some stretches, but otherwise guessed where the brook ran from the denser growth of bushes around it. For most of its line it was ahead of the British position, before it curved down towards Talavera itself.

It was easy to see the French. The whole wide plain to the east was covered in battalion after battalion. Hanley counted at least thirty and more were arriving. Dust clouds showed the approach of new units still marching to join the army. There were cavalry too, probing to the south in front of the Spanish position or waiting in reserve. The ground was not open, and sometimes the French columns disappeared among the groves and orchards, betrayed only by the glint of sunlight on musket barrels and bayonets.

Hanley had never seen so many soldiers and so many guns. He knew the numbers, and had known for days that there would be as many French as there were British and Spanish soldiers combined, and yet somehow nothing had prepared him for actually seeing the great host waiting.

'Veterans in the main,' said Murray, beside him. 'Or what is left of the veterans each time Napoleon wins a victory and pays a bloody price for it. Well, at least they'll be confident, and more likely to make a mistake.'

Hanley found it hard to be encouraged. There were so many of the enemy and they seemed to know what they were doing. Everyone told him that they would not attack Cuesta's army and that his raw soldiers were not capable of advancing to threaten the French. So the whole weight of this massive army would hit the British sooner or later.

'Five divisions,' said Murray, lowering his glass after a long look at the French positions. 'Oh, and the one that has already attacked twice. We've given them a mauling, but should not count them out. And plenty of cavalry if they do break through. Not a bad little army,' he said with cheerful admiration.

'Well, we had better report to the general and find out what he needs doing.'

They went back up to the summit for Murray had spotted the general and his staff sitting their horses up there. The French gunners had ceased fire and the silence seemed unnaturally still, almost as overwhelming as the noise of the fighting.

Hanley's horse stepped carefully. There were bodies everywhere. Some had not been gathered from the night's fighting, but many were fresh.

Higher up the hill they were mainly in red, until red and blue mingled at a gruesome high-water mark of the French assault, and lowest of all the corpses were all in blue.

Murray went to tell the general what he had seen and the others waited a few paces to the rear. Baynes nodded cheerfully to Hanley. Velarde was with him, stubble thick on his chin. The sight made Hanley reach up to rub his own face and feel the bristles. There had been no time to shave. The merchant and the Spanish colonel came over to join him.

Sir Arthur Wellesley looked as neat and well groomed as ever, in spite of the fact that he had slept rolled in his cloak on the hilltop. Perhaps that was an advantage of being a general and having servants, and yet Hanley was left with the impression that it was largely a matter of willpower. Sir Arthur could not conceive of ever being less than immaculately turned out, and so it happened. Hanley hoped he could not conceive of being beaten and could somehow work the same magic.

'They must come on again,' said the general decisively. He had beckoned them closer now that Murray had completed his report. 'We need to fight them here and give them a drubbing. Time is on their side, for it seems that old fox Soult is back and will be behind us within a week. I cannot fight him and these two corps at the same time, and so I must beat them now and be free to turn against Soult. The only question is whether or not they will attack with all their force and let me thrash them.'

'King Joseph must be worried by the news that Venegas is approaching Madrid,' said Colonel Murray.

'Do we know that he has received that dispatch from his governor in Toledo?' Sir Arthur sniffed with amusement at the thought that he was reading the King's letters before the monarch himself.

'He ought to have them today if they have not already arrived,' said Murray.

'We could make sure that he does.' Baynes looked at each of them in turn.

'Without risk of discovery?' The general's question was sharp and to the point.

'With slight risk.'

'Will it make Joseph run or fight?'

'Probably he must fight.' Murray took up the argument. 'He could not leave a strong enough force to be safe against you and still have sufficient strength to beat Venegas. Soult is coming, but not quickly enough to be sure of overwhelming us by numbers alone.'

'Does he know of Wilson?' Hanley asked the question, but apart from a quick glance in his direction from Colonel Murray none of them expressed surprise at a junior officer voicing his opinion.

'Sir Robert has only a brigade,' the general mused aloud.

'Perhaps, but the French will not know that for

certain and he is close enough to Madrid to frighten the King with a new threat.' Baynes sounded genuinely delighted by this new thought.

'Not too frightened?' asked Murray.

'He still cannot afford to split his forces and cover us in sufficient strength. That is even more true if he has another threat to face. Even if he does withdraw then will that not leave Soult exposed when he does arrive?'

'It is worth the gamble,' said the general decisively. 'I leave you gentlemen to arrange the details. Now I must ride to Cuesta. The old fool wants to decimate the regiments who ran yesterday. As if shooting two hundred of his own men is not simply doing the work of the French for them!'

As Hanley, Baynes and Espinosa rode down the hill there were redcoats digging lines of graves and others forming burial parties. It was half past ten and already scorchingly hot. Hanley looked up and saw vultures circling. The faces of some of the corpses were already turning black, their bellies swelling if they had not already been ripped open by shot.

The heat oppressed him. So did the thought of what they were about to do. Hanley wondered how many of the men now digging graves would themselves be lying in similar holes by nightfall. Would he be among them? That thought troubled him less than the responsibility. They were working to make the battle happen, to stir the French into a full-scale attack five times bigger than the fighting so far. Hundreds would surely die and thousands be cut down wounded if they succeeded. They were acting for the greater cause, for the good of the army and at the command of the general. Guiltily he also knew that part of him was enjoying the cleverness of it all.

The sense that there would be no more fighting for several hours spread quickly through both armies. Parties of French soldiers came forward to retrieve their wounded. The men in red and blue mingled again, most unarmed, but all without hostile intent. French and British alike sought out the dirty pools of water in the stream bed and filled canteens and bottles or drank from the filthy liquid. Through gesture and odd phrases they spoke and laughed together.

Velarde was confused, for he saw blue and red jackets mingling peacefully around the stream and that made it hard to know just where the French lines started, but the direction was clear and he knew that he must hurry. He dug his heels into the horse's sides, his big spurs sinking into its flesh and drawing blood. The animal was tired, not in the best of health, and it stumbled as he forced it to stay at the gallop, flogging its haunches with his whip.

'Stop him, stop that man!' yelled Hanley.

Velarde pressed on.

'Out of my way!' he called at a party of redcoats, each carrying a dozen canteens back from the stream. The men looked up, unimpressed by a foreigner yelling orders. Velarde's horse slowed, and Hanley worried that the infantrymen would listen to him and seize the fleeing Spaniard, but then they jumped out of his path at the last moment.

Velarde drove his heels even harder into the flanks of his mount and it gave another burst of energy, running on down into the bed of the Portina and then scrambling up the other side.

'Watch where you're going!' yelled an ensign with green facings on his jacket.

'Bloody Dons!' commented a sergeant, the head of his halfpike thrust into the ground as he leaned over to fill his canteen.

'Stop that fellow!' called Baynes, but whether deliberately or not the merchant was some way behind. Soldiers looked up. It was hot and all suspected the battle would soon resume. No one was in a hurry to rush and obey the orders of strangers, and especially a civilian.

Hanley reined in, his horse half turning and throwing up a spray of dust as it stopped. He kicked his feet free of the stirrups and sprang down, drawing a pistol from his belt. The hammer slid back into place with a click and he folded his left arm so that he could rest the barrel to aim carefully.

The ensign saw what he was doing. 'Hey there, steady on. No need to start trouble when the Frogs are friendly.'

Baynes came up behind him.

'Be careful,' the merchant said, ignoring the snub-nosed young officer.

Hanley had never killed anyone, and rarely fired a weapon in anger. He hoped he was not about to find out what it felt like.

Velarde was forty yards away, a great distance for a pistol, even one like this whose barrel was rifled.

A French sergeant was staring at him, hands twitching as he held his musket, and it was clear the man was ready to act and tell his men to fight if the English broke the unofficial truce. The man did not care about arguments between allies.

Hanley fired, and felt the strong kick of the carefully loaded pistol.

Velarde jerked with the blow, hand going back to press against the top of his left thigh.

'That was either a very good or a very poor shot,' said Baynes. The French sergeant had his musket almost up to his shoulder, but when the English officer held up his hands he told his men to stand down.

'It was luck,' said Hanley. He put a foot in the stirrup and grabbed the top of the saddle.

'Yes, well, I believe a man could still take that either way.' Baynes tried to catch his eye and was pleased when Hanley turned and looked at him, his expression betraying no emotion. 'It should help him to convince them.'

'And if he does not?' asked Hanley.

'Well then, I should imagine a bullet in the bum will be the least of his worries, don't you?'

'The north,' said King Joseph firmly. 'Attack straight up the valley on the left of their position and then swing round to destroy the rest of their army. It is simple. If we attack the hill we give the advantage to the English. Why take more losses? If you must fight then outflank them.' The King smiled, his round face intelligent and full of concern. 'But I really do not see why we need fight at all.'

Espinosa had rarely seen the King so firm in an opinion on a military matter. His chief of staff, Marshal Jourdan, repeated the same advice.

'We do not need to fight, but surely a flanking attack is the only sensible way if we do.' General Sebastiani was just as cautious, leaving Marshal Victor heavily outnumbered. The King of Spain and the French commanders stood on the lower hill, and could clearly see the British troops on the high ground to the west and in the plain below them.

'The Emperor would want us to attack,' said Victor, playing a strong card. He had always been known for his optimism. The title Duke of Belluno, an Italian town whose name literally meant 'beautiful moon', was said to be a pun by the Emperor's sister on his old nickname of 'Sunshine'. She disapproved of the shape of Marshal Victor's legs in the court dress of breeches and silk stockings.

'My brother would want us to win,' said Joseph. In truth it was hard to know what his younger brother wanted, save that it would always be more than was humanly possible. 'If we pull back behind the River Alberche – to the very position chosen with such skill by the Duke of Belluno – we shall repulse any attack they make. It was your plan just five days ago and should be our plan now.'

Espinosa could feel the caution growing stronger, the vacillating King ready to avoid taking the risk of fighting. He wondered whether he should show them the copies of the dispatches brought back by Velarde. Surely the real ones must have arrived by now?

An ADC galloped up the hill to join them just moments later. Papers were passed to a senior staff officer, and then to Marshal Jourdan. Junior men waited uneasily, not knowing what they would be called upon to make happen as soon as a decision was reached. Jourdan handed the letters to Victor and then whispered the contents to his own master.

'Is there now any doubt as to what we must do?' asked Marshal Victor once the report had circulated. 'Soult is late, and your capital in danger, sire. We must crush the English here, this very afternoon, and drive off the Spanish so that you can return and deal with the army coming from the south. The English are the key. Your brother says that. Destroy them and your kingdom will be safe.'

Espinosa hoped he would not tip the balance

too far, but decided it was worth causing one more worry for Marshal Jourdan.

'There is another English force to the north-west of Madrid. Small, my lord, but with enough men to take the city even if they cannot hold it long.'

'You know this definitely?' asked Joseph, when told the news.

'Yes, sire. One of my men rode across from the enemy this afternoon to tell me. He risked his life and was wounded during his escape.'

'Badly?' Joseph's face radiated genuine concern. Espinosa knew him to be a sensitive, intelligent and kindly man, even if he had the morals of a Bonaparte.

'Uncomfortably, sire.'

King Joseph chuckled. 'Oh dear. Well, we must be sure to decorate him. Where is he now?'

'Having his wound dressed.'

'Good. See that he has everything he needs to make him comfortable.' A true monarch, Joseph readily dismissed the matter from his mind. 'Well, gentlemen, that leaves us no other choice. We will fight, but shall we manoeuvre around their left or attack from the front?' Espinosa noted that the certainty of earlier was gone. The decision made, the King appeared to lose interest in the detail.

'There is no time, sire. The day is already half spent. Part of my corps will advance through the valley to the north, but the main attack must come against their centre and it must be made with all our strength. Nothing must be held back. The

English are raw soldiers and badly led. We surprised them twice yesterday. Pound them with our guns for an hour and then we will march through them, shatter them and take that damned hill. If we can't do that, then we ought to give up soldiering!'

A single French gun fired from the top of the hill. The shot bounced on the slope below Sir Arthur Wellesley and his staff and then skidded just to the right, frightening some of the horses.

'Is General Anson in position?' asked Sir Arthur.

'Yes, sir,' said Murray, his glass fixed on the light dragoons moving to the far end of the valley to the north.

'And the Spanish?'

'Occupying the far side of the valley now, Sir Arthur.' The general had decided that his left looked vulnerable. He had no infantry to spare, but General Cuesta immediately responded to his request and sent Spanish battalions marching north behind their ally to reinforce the position. Cavalry regiments were following, to bolster the numbers of the British horsemen moving into the mouth of the valley. Almost as appreciated was a battery of twelve-pounder cannons, twice the weight of anything the British had with them. The oxen drawing two of these big guns were at that moment being goaded up the slope of the Medellín.

'I believe we are ready,' said Sir Arthur.

The signal gun reloaded, the sixty French guns thundered out a new salvo. Most were aimed at the men on the plain where there was no cover, but a dozen or more still pounded the Medellín itself.

'Give the order to lie down.' His brigade commanders would probably already do this on their own initiative. The order was simply to make sure that it was done and he lost no men unnecessarily. Almost no armies in the world let their men lie down to shelter from artillery fire because it smacked of cowardice and they were not sure the men would be willing to get to their feet and fight when the time came. Sir Arthur thought such ideas folly and had no doubts about the fighting spirit of his men.

The cannon thundered across the valley.

'God help us,' said a staff officer under his breath. Clouds of smoke began to drift towards the Portina stream once again.

Hanley waited for his chance to speak to Murray.

'May I return to my battalion, sir?'

'If you wish. We should not need you.'

'Feeling guilty?' asked Baynes. 'It is not a useful emotion.'

Murray glared at the merchant, who could not understand how a soldier felt.

Hanley simply shrugged, and set his horse off downhill.

CHAPTER 26

'And the soldiers likewise demanded of him saying, "And what shall we do?"' intoned Billy Pringle as they sat around the dying fire. He had a mug of tea in his hand, and knew that Private Jenkins was pretending to clean Pringle's sword while watching his officer to see that he drank.

Williams took up the quote. 'And he said unto them, "Do violence to no man, neither accuse any falsely, and be content with your wages."'

'That last would be so much easier if we were actually paid,' said Truscott.

'Yes, the doing violence to no man may also prove a little hard to achieve today,' added Pringle. He took a sip, grimaced, and passed the mug to Williams.

'Well, at least we should not have any trouble to avoid making false accusations,' said Williams, before taking a good few gulps of the tea. Out of the corner of his eye he noticed Jenkins smiling encouragingly at the setting of so good an example to his own officer.

'Oh, I don't know,' declared Truscott. 'I believe friend Pringle here is getting heavier.'

Pringle had lifted a bowl and was spooning up the contents with the greatest reluctance. They had been issued grain, but there were not enough mills and so most had boiled it like rice. It was better than no food at all, or at least that was what they had to tell themselves. The captain's distaste was obvious.

'More tea?' said Williams maliciously.

'Looks like the French are eating rather better.' Truscott set down his cup and pointed with his one arm towards the enemy lines, where smoke rose from thousands of cooking fires. 'Nice of them to stop the battle for lunch.'

Hopwood had overheard them. 'Would it not have been more fitting to speak of gentlemen in England now a-bed et cetera?'

'A-bed at two in the afternoon?' said Williams. 'The lazy dogs.'

'What I would not give for a feather bed,' said Pringle wistfully, 'and a good plum pudding.'

'And?' Truscott expected more.

'I am too tired and hungry for the and!'

The drums began to beat.

'Stand to!' bellowed Sergeant Major Fisher.

Pringle took one more tiny sip of tea to please his servant and tossed the rest into the dry grass.

The 3rd Battalion of Detachments formed line two deep at the rear of the brigade. Ahead of them were the 1/45th with their deep green regimental Colour and facings, and farther to the left the 2/31st with buff-coloured facings and a yellow flag.

The brigade – Major General MacKenzie's own, although he now also commanded the division – had crossed the Portina and then not reformed into the correct order, so that the senior corps, the 31st, was not in the place of honour on the right. The 3rd Battalion were the most junior even of the temporary regiments in the army. They would normally be in the centre of the brigade, but today the general had decided to form a second line and this had fallen to their lot. Williams remembered how on so many occasions he had tried to explain the rules of seniority to Hanley. It was doubtful his friend even now comprehended the matter, but it was really so absurdly simple. He wondered where Hanley was; it would have been good to see him. Truscott and Pringle no doubt felt the same. A man liked to have his friends near by on a day like this.

Ahead of the brigade were two battalions of His Majesty's Foot Guards and he was sure they never questioned the system, or their own place at its summit. The Guards were forming with a good deal more formality and shouting than a line battalion. They were excellent soldiers, but somehow strange and alien. Williams knew that Bonaparte recruited his own Imperial Guard from the ranks of the rest of the army. It was hard to imagine such a system working with King George's men.

The Guards were the rightmost – and so senior – part of the First Division, whose remaining three brigades took the front line up on to the slopes of the Medellín. General Hill's Second Division remained on the Medellín itself. They had repulsed the night attack and the one this morning. From the distance Williams and the others had seen little of the fighting. It was said that there were heavy losses, although those of the French were higher.

'Battalion will incline to the right by companies. Forward march!' The sergeant major's voice carried with ease and brooked no argument. Each company wheeled on its right marker, and turned to face ninety degrees so that now instead of a line they were in a column of eight small lines all facing to the right.

'Halt!' The sergeant major took a deep breath, and Williams wondered whether the spirit of the Guards' NCOs was spreading, for his next command hammered at the ears of the waiting battalion. 'Forward march!'

Pritchard Jones rode at their head and the 3rd Battalion of Detachments marched behind the rest of the brigade and then wheeled back into line. They halted to dress ranks. 'Get a move on, get a move on!' called the sergeants, copying Fisher's desire to impress any observers. Finally they marched forward one hundred paces so that they were in line and to the right of the 1/45th.

'Looks like we have become senior,' said Williams to Sergeant McNaught. The Highlander gave him a gap-toothed grin.

Pringle's Grenadier Company was at the far end

of the line, and from there he could see the Fourth Division, standing in formation among the scrub and stunted trees near to the little redoubt Williams and his men had helped to build. Spanish gunners were manhandling big cannon into the fortification to reinforce the tiny three-pounders already there.

'Look, sir,' said McNaught, and Williams turned to see a puff of smoke up on the lower ridge on the French side of the stream. A few moments later the distant bang carried to them. In less than a minute all of the French guns opened fire. Williams wished he had a watch to know what time it was. He wondered for a moment where Miss MacAndrews was and what she was doing. That concern seemed distant, but it was pleasantly if briefly distracting. A muscle in his left thigh was quivering. Williams knew it was nervousness. Waiting was almost worse than the fighting. Almost.

None of the first salvo came near them, but whether the French gunners altered their aim or new batteries joined in the bombardment, soon shot was ripping up the ground where the Guards stood ahead of them. Shells exploded and the first screams began.

A heavy twelve-pounder ball smashed two Guardsmen to bloody ruin and then skidded at waist height towards the Light Company.

'Steady, lads,' said Williams, because it was his duty, and then could not help shutting his eyes. There was a ghastly slapping sound and two of his men were sliced in two at the waist, their entrails flung out and blood spraying to soak those around them.

'Drag the bodies away,' called Sergeant Rudden from his station behind the line. 'Close up there!'

Pritchard Jones rode along the front of the battalion.

'Lie down,' he ordered. 'Lie down.' Other regiments were doing the same. Williams wondered whether the Guards had a special drill to lie down by numbers.

Officers could not lie down. Williams watched his men drop to their knees and then spread themselves flat on the ground. He knew they were grateful for it, even the ones now lying on the foul offal left by the dead men. It was his job to show no fear, and to stand or walk up and down the Light Company's line while the men took cover. They could see little through the long grass, while he was able to watch what happened, but that was not the main reason. An officer and a gentleman must show his men that there was nothing to fear and that victory was certain.

'Keep your heads down, boys,' he said. 'They cannot hit you if you stay down.' That was almost true. The French gunners were firing through an ever-growing cloud of their own smoke. With the redcoats on the ground in the long grass, and their Colours laid down beside them, there were no longer good aiming points. Cannon did not snipe at lone officers. Yet the gunners knew roughly where the British were, and they turned the screws which elevated the barrels and then lifted the trail spike to aim the whole gun at the right places. Shot and shell slammed into the fields where the redcoats hid themselves. After that, it was all a matter of chance.

A shell exploded among the company from the 4/60th and wounded two men, jagged pieces of casing slicing into their legs. Then one of the redcoats who had served with Sir Robert Wilson was struck on the hand by a bouncing shot which then skimmed over the man behind, doing no harm. The wounded man stared dumbly at an arm now ending in a wrist and just mangled fragments. His face was pale from the shock and loss of blood, but he stumbled to the rear, refusing offers of help.

'Keep your heads down.' Williams repeated the phrase. He could see that the Guards were taking worse punishment. The losses were not devastating, but the awful fury of the artillery tore men apart so that each wound or death seemed worse than two or three times as many men falling to musket shots.

The guns continued to pound. The French artillerymen had rested since the morning and they toiled with enthusiasm, reloading quickly and running the guns back into position time and time again. Many had undone or taken off their heavy blue jackets and now worked in their shirtsleeves, sweat running down their faces and backs. Williams spun around as a shell hit a caisson stationed behind the lines and the wagon exploded in a great gout of flame and black smoke, flinging debris high into the air, and with it the little figure of a man, legs and arms splayed out like a frog's and miraculously in one piece.

He lost track of time, and suddenly realised that he was singing the 'Minstrel Boy' under his breath. He wondered whether a hymn might be more appropriate, but there was something reassuringly determined about the words and the tune and he began to sing out loud.

'Quiet,' said a voice from the ranks of the Light Company. 'We can't hear the French properly!' Men laughed and Williams marvelled at how well they kept their spirits. He sang on and some of the men joined in, voices thin because they were pressed against the ground, but somehow there was a joy in the defiance.

The French guns pounded away. Williams felt the wind of shot punching the air above his head. He sang, repeating the same verse over and over again. A shell landed ten yards ahead of him, spinning crazily in the grass, its fuse throwing off sparks, and then the earth erupted as soil and red-hot fragments of iron were flung into the air. A moment later a piece that had gone high tumbled down and gently tapped the end of his boot.

More earth puffed up and this time it was a heavy shot which bounced and then skidded low straight at the Light Company. It went directly at a man leaning up on his elbow to talk to the man beside him. Williams saw the redcoat's face freeze in utter horror and then the shot struck him squarely on the neck, smashing him into pieces of flesh, bone and torn backpack, his musket broken into fragments. The man lying behind him flinched and looked upwards so that the shot shattered his skull to ruin before going higher and bouncing on behind them.

Something hit Williams hard in the chest and he fell, unable to breathe and his chest feeling as if it had been struck by a hammer. He lay on the ground staring up at the clear blue sky, unable to think or feel the seriousness of his wound.

'You're all right, sir,' said McNaught, leaning over him. 'You got hit by part of Horan's musket.'

Williams felt the lump of jagged wood and ripped barrel lying beside him. He could breathe again now, but each gulp of air was painful.

'Lie still, sir. You'll be fine in a minute.'

He struggled to say thank you, but the words were weak. McNaught gave the tiniest of nods. 'The Frogs are none too friendly today, sir.'

'No,' gasped Williams at last. McNaught helped him up. The officer's chest still throbbed and he wondered whether any ribs were broken. He swayed a little as he stood, his eyes struggling to focus. The Scottish sergeant stayed with him until he looked more steady and then went back to the rear of the company.

'Reckon the Frogs heard your singing, sir!' came a voice from the ranks.

Another shot hit the ground just ahead of the company, bounced over the lying men and smacked into the sergeant's pack as he was lowering himself into the grass. McNaught was flung into the air, flying four or five yards back and slamming into the ground, limbs spread and kilt about his waist.

Williams ran back to him, his side aching. McNaught lay still, bare buttocks much paler than his tanned face and legs.

'Sergeant, Sergeant!' Williams touched the man's shoulder. He could see no sign of blood. 'Are you hurt badly?'

'I'm fine, sir.' McNaught's voice sounded mildly puzzled. 'It just hit my pack. It's in my bloody pack.'

Williams saw that the backpack was badly torn, and rummaged among the clothes inside until his fingers sprang back from something hot. He grabbed a spare shirt and took hold of the sphere, lifting it out and rolling it in the grass beside them. He realised he was laughing nervously.

'It's a shot!' he said. 'A twelve-pounder shot!'

'Bloody Frogs!' McNaught's voice was full of wonder as he pushed himself back up. 'Those bloody French bastards shot my pack.'

'They'll stop that out your pay, McNaught,' said Rudden cheerfully.

'Show them your arse again, Sergeant,' called a voice from the ranks. 'That'll frighten 'em!'

An ADC rode up, reining in beside Williams. 'The Light Company is to advance and reinforce the skirmish line of Campbell's brigade. I will lead you.'

'Sir,' said Williams, acknowledging the order. 'Light Company on your feet.' The men moved faster than he expected, eager to do something rather than simply lie down and take punishment. The NCOs chivvied the men, but there was little need.

They jogged forward, following the staff officer as he led them to the right, into the much denser maze of vine trees and olive groves. No shot hit them as they moved and Williams guessed the French were concentrating their fire on the open ground.

A captain from the 53rd with the tall green plume of a Light Company officer in his cocked hat greeted Williams, relieved to have someone on his open flank. The ADC galloped off to carry further orders.

'We've put skirmishers fifty yards ahead,' explained the captain, 'with the support line here.' Williams just managed to glimpse some patches of red in the trees and bushes ahead of them. 'There is something of a clearing in front of the skirmishers so that should give us warning.'

Williams formed a reserve in two ranks under McNaught and took Rudden and the other half of the Light Company forward to extend the skirmish line. He did not like the ground, which reminded him too much of yesterday's surprise attack, but at least the Fourth Division men seemed to know their business.

'What do you think of the position, Sergeant?' he asked Rudden.

'It'll do, sir, it'll do.'

'Good luck. I had better return to the supports.' Williams felt guilty about that, but he was the only officer in the Light Company and he could not be everywhere. His place was with the fresh men, ready to lead them up to reinforce the skirmishers or to cover them if they retreated.

'Mr Williams, sir! Sergeant Rudden!' One of the 43rd had spotted movement ahead of them on the far edge of the clearing. Men appeared, wearing dark green-jackets and with tall green-tipped yellow plumes in their shakos. They moved stealthily, spread in pairs as skirmishers.

'*Españoles!*' shouted a voice.

'They're Spanish, sir,' said Rudden with only a slight trace of doubt. 'What the hell are they up to?' It was hard to keep much sense of direction in this dense country, but there did not seem any good reason for their allies to be coming from that side.

'Don't fire, they're Spanish!' ordered someone from the 53rd's Light Company.

The men came out of the shadows and Williams saw their buff leather crossbelts clearly and remembered the bitter fight to rescue General Cuesta.

'Make ready!' he ordered. 'They're French!'

'The lying sods!' said Rudden bitterly. 'Commence firing!'

Half of the skirmish line dropped to their knees,

some of them crouching behind the trunks of the low trees. Men pulled triggers and fired at the men in green from the Nassau Regiment in French service. Farther to his left, Williams saw men in white uniforms coming through the trees, and then they and the Germans fired a volley into the uncertain British skirmish line. A few of the 53rd dropped and the others wavered in confusion at an ally suddenly turning into an enemy.

There was weight behind the French attack. The green-jacketed men pushed on into the clearing. A couple were down, one of them screaming horribly, but pairs of skirmishers came forward. Behind them came a denser mass of men in green, but with tall red plumes and red epaulettes. Williams guessed they were grenadiers at the head of the main column – or as much of a column as it was possible to form in this broken ground.

'We'll not stop them here,' he shouted to Rudden over the noise of firing. 'Fire and retire.' The Light Company of the 53rd, less prepared for the onslaught, were already going back. 'I'll go and be ready to cover you. Give us as much time as you can.'

Rudden nodded. 'Prepare to fall back!' he shouted. 'Fire and retire!' Now each man waited for his partner to load. Then he sought a target, fired, and sprinted back ten yards before crouching to load himself. A man dropped, struck in the calf by a ball, and he cursed as his comrade dragged him back into cover.

Williams ran through the long grass. A ball smacked into the branches of a tree beside him, but he did not think anyone was aiming at him. He saw the 53rd reforming a skirmish line a little way back and that was good, but he knew that the light troops would not be able to stop this attack on their own.

McNaught was waiting with the reserve. 'The French are coming in strength.' Williams' chest still hurt and the running had only made it worse. 'Three or four battalions at least. We will try to slow them, but we don't want to get cut off and surrounded in this scrub. Take half the men back fifty yards and form to cover us. I'll wait for Rudden's men.'

'Sir.' The Highlander shouted orders.

'Right, lads, we have some rogues in green coming at us,' said Williams, standing on the right flank of the eighteen men making up his little line. 'Let our boys back through and then give the Frogs a surprise.'

They did not have to wait long. Two men appeared supporting the man hit in the leg. A moment later more redcoats followed, ran back a short way and then crouched to reload. There were shots, and the remaining men came through the trees, Rudden jogging just behind.

Williams called to him. 'Bring them back!' He could see more of the green-jacketed skirmishers pushing forward to his right as the 53rd fired and withdrew, and he did not want Rudden's men cut off. The sergeant waved his hand in acknowledgement, and shouted an order which sent all his men scurrying back past the formed line. Then he turned, took careful aim and fired his own musket back through the trees.

'Present!' Williams ordered.

The Nassau skirmishers rushed past the line of cork trees, eagerly chasing their enemy.

'Fire!' yelled Williams, and the little volley erupted in dirty smoke and the rank smell of black powder. 'Back!' he shouted. 'Back!' They ran, rushing past McNaught's group and then farther past Rudden's men. They stopped again, repeating the process. One or two men fell, but they knocked over more of the enemy even if they could not stop them.

Bugles sounded the recall. Another staff officer was bellowing at the light companies to retire on the main line and so Williams led them back into a much wider clearing. He could see the 53rd to his left, and it was good to see their red facings, just like those of his own regiment. Then another line of redcoats marched up beside them. There was a single small flag fluttering in the centre of the battalion. Williams smiled when he saw the dragon.

CHAPTER 27

Pringle grinned as Hanley ran up behind the Grenadier Company.

'Good to see you,' he said. 'Any idea what is coming our way?'

'At least three columns and a dozen guns in support. They are the Germans and Dutch of Leval's division.'

'Always nice to know who is trying to kill you!' said Pringle cheerfully. He could tell the grenadiers were glad that their lieutenant had chosen to join them. Men counted on each other at a time like this.

Billy Pringle stood to the right of his company on the very right of the battalion. The ground ahead of him led up to a low bank, and beyond that the trees were so thick that it was difficult to see anything. He heard the bugles and shouted orders and saw the red figures of the light infantry running back from the wood to reform on their battalions. Pringle spotted Williams and was glad his friend was unscathed, but the Light Company was on the far left of the battalion and there would be no chance to speak to him.

The French artillery rumbled in the distance, but the 3rd Battalion was sheltered from their fire now that it had advanced. It was a relief, and made the battlefield strangely quiet. He could hear drums beating from somewhere in the trees, coming ever closer, and there was cheering as well, but it did not sound like the usual French enthusiasm, and then he remembered that Hanley had said the enemy were from France's German allies. British, Germans and Dutch fighting each other because the French had occupied Spain after invading Portugal, he thought, and the idea seemed so absurd.

The drumming and the cheers came closer and now there was the sound of bugles blowing, different in pitch from the ones the British used.

'For what we are about to receive,' said a voice from the ranks of the company.

'Someone always has to say it,' said another.

'Silence in the ranks!' yelled Sergeant Probert with just a hint of nervousness.

Men in green appeared on the edge of the trees. Pringle could see them only from the waist up because of the bank. They hesitated for a moment, and then a great rush of men spilled over the bank and into the clearing. Ranks had broken up or bunched as the two battalions of the Nassau Regiment came through the trees, and so it was a crowd that surged into the clearing, but a determined crowd none the less. The German soldiers raised their muskets to their shoulders.

'Third Battalion, present!' called Pritchard Jones. Redcoats raised muskets to their shoulders. There was a roar of gunfire from the redoubt over to the right, the sharper cracks of the little British three-pounder cannon and then the deeper thunder of the heavy Spanish guns.

'Fire!' Smoke enveloped the front of the battalion. It took a moment before it spread to block Pringle's view and he saw the German infantry vanish behind their own cloud of powder smoke as they fired. A thump and a curse of pain and one of the grenadiers in the front rank dropped to his knees, musket falling to the ground and one hand pressed against his side, where his faded red jacket was wet.

'Bastards!' said the man. All around him the other grenadiers let the butts of their firelocks slide to the ground as they reached back to their pouches and took out a cartridge. They bit off the top, which contained the bullet, flicked the lock back to half-cock and so opened the frizzen pan of the musket, and then gently tapped the open paper tube so that a pinch of gunpowder poured in. The rest of the powder went down the barrel, the paper on top, and then they bent over and spat the ball into the muzzle. Ramrods grated as they slid from the rings holding them followed by one hard thrust down the barrel to drive ball and charge down and make sure the force of the explosion would be concentrated behind the bullet. Then the ramrod was reversed, slid back into place, and the musket came back up, the right hand bringing the flint back to full cock as the butt slid back into place at the shoulder.

'Fire!' Pritchard Jones let the sergeant major give the order this time, his voice carrying over the shots and screams. Flints sparked, powder ignited and set off the main charge so that the butt slammed back into a man's shoulder and then there was flame and more smoke to feed the cloud masking the battalion.

'Well done, boys!' shouted Pringle. 'We're hurting them!' The Germans' own volley was more ragged and did not come for a good few seconds after their own, and that was encouraging because it suggested that the 3rd Battalion was better practised.

The Grenadier Company began reloading again. The men were old hands now after almost a year of campaigning. Some of them cut corners, sticking their ramrods into the ground beside them when the soil was soft enough, or turning their pouch on its shoulder strap so that it lay in front rather than on the back of their hip.

The smoke blocked the enemy from sight, but did not hamper their bullets. One ball creased the cheek of a Grenadier, drawing blood and provoking a yelp of pain, and then the ball smashed through the teeth and lower jaw of his rear rank man. The wounded man clutched at his face, moaning horribly, but unable to scream, and spots of blood shook through the ragged hole in his cheek. Lance

Sergeant Dobson took him gently by the shoulder to pull him out of the formation and directed him back to where the surgeons waited.

Again the cannon fired from the redoubt, the tightly packed metal canisters bursting as they left the barrels to spray great arcs of musket balls and pieces of metal, shredding the ranks of the blue-coated Germans trying to push on towards the little fort.

'Fire!' The third volley was the last the 3rd Battalion fired on command. Men began to load at their own pace, raising the musket to their shoulders and firing as soon as they were ready. The noise was constant.

'Keep it up, boys!' called Pringle as encouragement.

The Nassauers managed to come forward a few yards. There was little wind, but now and again the smoke thinned and Pringle could see bodies in green dotted around the clearing, but their comrades were closer now.

'Bastards!' The first grenadier to be wounded still lay in the grass in front of the company, and he would have to stay there until the fight was over. He was in pain, but still seemed more enraged than anything else. 'Bastards!'

Pringle glanced to his right and saw that the nearest men of the 53rd had stopped firing and were fixing bayonets. Then it was as if he was kicked by a horse and he gasped as he was flung down.

Hanley was bending over him, face full of concern. Dobson stood behind.

Billy Pringle felt for the wound. It was a struggle to speak for the moment, but he managed to ask, 'Glasses?'

'Here you are.' Hanley held up the spectacles. 'You are a lucky devil, do you know that?'

'Born lucky,' said Pringle, the life returning. Hanley was holding up his sword on its belt. There was a dent and flattened metal near the top of the scabbard and beneath it the whole thing was bent out of kilter.

'Cease fire! Cease fire!' Sergeant Major Fisher's voice forced its way over the general din, and officers and NCOs took up the cry. 'Cease fire!'

'Go on,' said Pringle. 'I need a moment.'

'Grenadier Company, cease firing!' bellowed Dobson with a strength Hanley knew he could never match. A couple of men fired, but the rest responded quickly.

'Fix bayonets!' Again the order was repeated in each company. Men reached behind, slid the blades from their scabbards and turned the ring so that it locked around the muzzle. Billy Pringle stood up and rubbed his side. It was sore and no doubt bruised, but nothing seemed broken. He took hold of the hilt of his sword since an officer ought to lead a charge sword in hand. The blade would not move. Instead he pulled the pistol from the crimson sash round his waist, flicked open the pan to check that the powder was still there, and held it ready.

There was a loud British cheer from his right.

'There go the Fusiliers!' The shout carried from the ranks of the 53rd. Then that regiment had their muskets to their shoulders and fired a more ordered volley before each man yelled and went forward, bayonets extended.

'Come on, boys!' cried a voice no one recognised. One of the grenadiers in the front rank screamed and dashed forward. Another followed, then the whole company was surging ahead. Pringle, Hanley and the NCOs ran after them. The same excited urge sent the whole of the 3rd Battalion charging into the smoke before Pritchard Jones had told Sergeant Major Fisher to give the order.

'Charge!' yelled the colonel as loudly as he could, putting spurs to his horse as men ran past on either side of him, one of them the young ensign with their green flag. 'Follow me!' he added out of habit.

A grenadier stumbled, blood spreading fast just where his white crossbelts met in the centre of his jacket. Pringle felt a ball flick his sleeve as he ran, brandishing his pistol. He saw the green-jacketed enemy, but there was confusion in their ranks and more and more men turned to flee. One tripped and a redcoat drove his slim bayonet into the man's back, so that he arched his body away from the blow, screaming horribly. The grenadier could not get the blade free, and began kicking at the wounded German.

Pringle ran on, jumping over the corpse of

another Nassauer who was sprawled in that ungainly way that only those deep in sleep could ever match. The green-jacketed men were pouring back up the little bank they had come down. A few slipped or were too slow and these died as the wild-eyed grenadiers caught them. Some of the enemy had been hacking at the bank with picks and spades, trying to cut a path for the horsed gun team following the advance. Behind them was a man in a blue jacket with red tails and a strange hat cocked on the left side and flat on the right. Pringle did not recognise the uniform, but the man was clearly a driver as he had just dropped his whip and was struggling with the collar of the lead horse, desperately trying to turn the animal.

A grenadier reached him and slammed the butt of his musket against the side of the driver's head, knocking the man down so that his hat fell in the grass and was trodden on by the horse. The driver behind dropped his long whip and raised his arms in surrender. The grenadier shoved him ungently to the rear and the remaining driver followed. Other men came along with them. Pringle barged the drivers aside to get to the front, but knew that he could trust his grenadiers to deal with the prisoners.

He saw the blue-grey painted limber and field gun on the narrow track behind. A man in a shako, but with a similar blue jacket to the driver's, raised a short carbine. One of the grenadiers was flung backwards, a ball in his forehead.

The German gunner looked shocked at what he had done, and instantly dropped the carbine and raised his hands. '*Kamerad*!'

'They're giving in!' shouted Hanley, who was standing up on the bank.

Corporal Murphy pulled the trigger. He had not aimed, but the muzzle was less than a yard from the surrendering gunner and the ball drove into the man's belly and ripped a jagged hole in his back as it came out. The man screamed and then grunted as Murphy drove his bayonet deep into the wound. He twisted the blade and the gunner cried out in his agony.

'Stop, stop! They're surrendering!' shouted Hanley.

The Grenadiers flowed around the corporal and the gunners died on their bayonets. Some tried to run, but the path was narrow and the gun got in the way. Another tried to surrender, but was shot in the face, and the other three simply stared dumbly at their executioners.

Pringle uncocked his pistol, but did nothing to restrain the men because he doubted they would obey and was not sure that he should intervene.

Hanley looked appalled as he came up.

'They left it too late to change their minds,' Pringle said.

Sergeant Probert leaned his half-pike against a caisson as he opened the chest and looked at the shot. 'Wrong size for our guns,' he said.

Pringle nodded. It would have been a surprise

if the French, let alone whatever little German prince these men served, would use the same calibre guns as their own army. 'Get the horses away!' Dobson took charge and unhitched the team, before sending it and the drivers back behind the main British line. Then the grenadiers sweated as they dragged limber and gun out into the clearing. An engineer officer and a party of men were already there with hammer and nails to drive into the touch hole of this and other guns captured by the Fusiliers and the 53rd. That would render them useless for the moment. More permanent arrangements could wait until the end of the battle.

The drums began to beat. 'Form, Third Battalion, form!' Fisher's voice echoed across the clearing.

Pritchard Jones rode along in front of the reforming line. 'Well done!' he said again and again. 'Most truly well done! Sir Arthur sends to say that you are the bravest fellows in the world and that he does not have the words to express his full pleasure at our conduct. Well done, my brave lads!' The colonel was beaming.

'General Leval went in early,' said King Joseph. Espinosa thought he sounded only mildly disappointed, as if someone had used the wrong fork at a dinner in the palace.

'His orders were clear.' Marshal Jourdan sounded defensive, as if expecting to be accused of dereliction of his duties.

'Doesn't matter a damn,' insisted Victor. 'He's

tying up the enemy on that flank and that's what does matter. Hard to see much inside all those trees. Can't blame the fellow for pushing on. We won't win a battle by caution.'

Espinosa could hear the marshal's frustration and his obvious dislike of his colleagues, but also sensed his excitement. The guns thundered on in the background, but he was surprised how used he had become to their noise.

'The rosbifs on our left are busy,' continued Victor when no one said anything. 'The ones on the hill cannot move because of the threat to that flank. Now we smash the centre of this second-rate army. Don't we, General Sebastiani?'

Espinosa noted the emphasis on the word 'general'.

'As Your Grace says,' agreed the general with little enthusiasm. Yet when Espinosa looked down into the plain he felt his heart sink. He had helped to convince the French leaders to attack because the British and Spanish needed a battle. Even at the time he had realised that the French might well need one too.

Two divisions of French infantry stood side by side on the open fields beneath him. Twenty-four battalions of men who had trampled Austrians, Prussians and Russians beneath them before they came to Spain now waited to crush the British. They were in two lines, the supports several hundred yards behind the first, each battalion in its own column ready to advance. Ahead of them the gun batteries still pounded the redcoats. It was hard to believe that anything could live under such an onslaught. Harder still to think that the few stunned survivors could stand against the assault of at least double their number of French veterans. Espinosa was very afraid that he had helped to bring defeat on the cause he loved.

'Quite a sight,' said Velarde, limping up beside him. 'I think this will be a day to remember.'

Espinosa still struggled to trust the man, even though he was sure the message he had brought was genuine. This is what the English general had wanted.

Guns slammed back on their trails, jumping as they threw solid shot at the enemy lines little more than six or eight hundred yards away. They had been firing for an hour. Espinosa realised he was seeing the French Emperor's way of war. There was an appalling violence to it.

'With your permission, sire,' said Victor in a tone that made it clear the request was a formality. 'We shall order the main attack.'

'Do so,' said King Joseph, and ADCs flew off to carry the message.

The French guns thundered.

CHAPTER 28

Each company of the 3rd Battalion of Detachments wheeled to the left, changing from line back into column. General MacKenzie's ADC had come to summon them and now he led them to form up behind the Guards' brigade.

'Forward march,' called Pritchard Jones. 'At the double.'

Williams' Light Company was at the head of the column, jogging through the long grass, packs and equipment bouncing as they went. The men's faces were stained dark from the powder of their own firing. They were thirsty from the saltpetre in the gunpowder, which got into their mouths every time they bit off a cartridge, and their bodies ran with sweat from the brutal heat of the sun and the man-made warmth of musket and gun. Williams heard men panting, gulping for breath as they kept up the pace.

The French batteries could see them again when they came from behind the woodland. A bouncing shot kicked up muck from the earth just ahead of the Light Company. Another grazed the flank of the colonel's horse, somehow missing his leg, but tearing flesh from the poor beast. The horse sank down on to its haunches, its immensely long tongue hanging out of the side of its mouth and its eyes rolling.

Pritchard Jones sprang off, staggered slightly as he hit the ground, and then recovered. Williams could see the tears in his eyes as the colonel pulled a pistol from his saddle holster and aimed it at the animal's forehead. The horse stared at him, not moving, and Pritchard Jones pulled the trigger.

'Keep moving! Keep moving!' he yelled as the Light Company began to halt around the dead animal.

'Come on!' called Williams, and the men parted to flow around the corpse before reforming and jogging on. A shell exploded over to the right. Williams saw another lying in the grass unexploded and was glad it did not lie in their path because a careless kick might easily have reignited the fuse and set off the bomb.

Pritchard Jones ran at the head of his battalion, his sabre held up by his side to stop him from tripping over it.

'Come on lads!' He turned to run backwards, facing his men and encouraging them. The ADC trotted beside him and had to keep holding his horse back.

The Grenadier Company was at the rear, running past any of the men who fell. They saw the dead and wounded torn horribly by cannonballs. One man had been eviscerated when a shot hit him in the belly and his entrails, pale and already teeming with flies, were stretched across a good five or six yards. A grenadier was struggling so much to keep pace that he did not see the body and slipped on the wet meat. He staggered, staring down aghast, and then he was bending over as he vomited.

'Get back in rank!' called Dobson, who knew that it was better not to brood.

With a gentle thump a shell landed in the grass at the man's feet, spun for a moment, sparks flying from the fuse, and then erupted into flame, smoke and flying metal. The grenadier was ripped apart, limbs, flesh, blood and pieces of equipment flung amid the shards of casing.

Dobson and Hanley had their legs knocked out from under them as they were sprayed with blood and flesh. The officer could feel an appalling stabbing pain in his right thigh and he heard himself whimpering like a child. Dobson rolled over, pushing part of the dead grenadier's arm off himself, and grasped at the wounds in both of his calves. He tried to get up, but immediately the pain seared through him and his legs folded.

'Goddamn it,' he hissed.

The Grenadier Company ran on, following the battalion.

Hanley was stunned, and could not quite believe it as the redcoats kept going, without anyone even looking back. He called out, but his voice was hoarse and weak and lost in the noise of the French guns. Pushing himself up on his hands, Hanley tried to rise, but there was simply no strength in his right leg. He slumped down, sobbing, and then rolled on to his back because that eased the pain a little.

The 3rd Battalion of Detachments doubled on through the dry grass. For a moment one enemy battery was almost perfectly positioned on their flank and a single shot bounced down the rank and took the heads off half a dozen men from Truscott's company. The next man was left unmarked but stone dead and the man to his side was unconscious. Redcoats coming up behind dodged the corpses and doubled on.

'Here!' The ADC raised his arm to mark the spot.

'Sergeant Rudden, put the left marker there!' shouted Williams as the Light Company wheeled back into line. The rest of the battalion did the same. Sergeants kept the men moving and then jostled and shouted at them to redress the ranks.

'Reload!' Some of the men did not move, for their muskets were still charged, but most went automatically into the well-drilled routine, made a little more difficult because bayonets remained fixed.

The artillery fire slackened suddenly, leaving ears stunned and struggling to cope with the heaviness of silence. A few shells fell for a minute or two more, but then the battery commanders decided that even the shells fired high by the short-barrelled howitzers risked hitting the advancing French infantry, and they ordered the crews to cease fire. A twisted piece of casing from one of the last shots wounded Lieutenant Hatch in the face. Two men began helping him to the rear until a sergeant bellowed at one of them to get back into the ranks and not use this as an excuse to escape from the field.

Williams saw the Guards battalions stand up in front of him. French batteries still pounded the slopes of the Medellín Hill, but that noise was distant. Shouted orders came from behind him to the left, and he looked back to see the 45th and the 31st advancing to form line level with the 3rd Battalion of Detachments.

Then he heard the drums. 'Old trowsers! Old trowsers!' he said softly in time with the beats and drum rolls of the French *pas de charge* – the rhythm of the attack. Rudden looked at him oddly. 'Takes you back to Vimeiro,' he said, and the sergeant nodded in acknowledgement.

The drums came closer. Williams could not see the French columns beyond the Guards. Dust came up to add to the gently drifting smoke as the only trace of the enemy. The drums were louder and closer, and chanting that had only been indistinct now came as phrases.

'*Vive l'Empereur!*'

Everything was louder and stronger than in Portugal the previous summer.

'*Vive l'Empereur! Vive l'Empereur!*' More men marched and chanted in this attack than there had been in the entire French Army at Vimeiro. Far fewer redcoats waited for them.

'*En avant! Vive l'Empereur!*' The shouting was close now, and Williams saw the Guards begin to march forward to close the distance with the enemy. From farther down the line came the sound of volleys and cheering. Williams waited for the Guards to fire. They did not.

Without warning the Guards cheered and went straight into a bayonet charge.

'Typical bloody Guards,' he heard Rudden mutter. 'Have to do it their own way.'

Williams could not see it, but the French must have given way. The Guards rushed forward a couple of hundred yards, their neat lines becoming ragged as they went through the Portina stream. Only then did the battalions halt and begin firing on the enemy. He saw their front blossom into smoke. Then the Guards were going forward again.

Up on the hill with the French commanders, Espinosa had watched the French attack close with the English. There were twelve battalions in the lead, each column separated by enough distance so that they could form into line if necessary. Voltigeurs ran ahead of them and sniped at the little dots that were the English skirmishers.

The twelve battalions went forward. Soon the light troops ran back on either side and the French closed with the thin line of redcoats.

436

'My lads have broken two of their brigades already,' said Marshal Victor almost absent-mindedly.

Then things happened quickly, far faster than Espinosa expected. Some of the red lines fired at close range and then all were charging. From the distance the columns seemed to stagger, some firing back while others tried to deploy. A few men ran from the back of the formations, and then it was dozens, and in a moment entire columns turned into a loose swarm streaming to the rear.

The redcoats came after them. Espinosa saw the little flashes of colour as their flags streamed behind them.

'Damn,' said Marshal Victor.

British battalions became crowds of men almost as confused as their fleeing enemies. They came on, across the stream and on to the plain beyond. Below them, in front of the great battery, some redcoats were even running up the slopes of the big hill.

'Ruddy fools think they have won,' said Marshal Victor, his assurance returning.

The fleeing French infantry came through their own gun line. Crews had already loaded with canister, and were waiting for this moment. Officers shouted orders, but the targets were getting so close that they were scarcely needed.

'Fire!' yelled battery commanders. Guns slammed back and sprayed the lethal swarm of musket-sized balls at the enemy. Redcoats fell as men were snatched back by the blasts of canister. The battalions stopped in their tracks. Men started to load and fire back. Then the guns fired again and more men dropped into the dry grass.

Drums beat the *pas de charge* and the second line – another twelve battalions of fresh and first-rate infantry – moved forward. Voltigeurs ran out ahead of them, the tall yellow and green plumes on their shakos bobbing with the motion. As they got closer the light infantrymen would halt, sometimes kneel to steady their aim, and the muskets would fire and bullets pluck men down.

'It looks like our friends are winning,' said Velarde tonelessly.

'Oh my dear God.' Colonel Murray grimaced as he sat on his horse with the general's staff on the highest point of the Medellín Hill. They could see almost the entire battlefield from this position and now they could see a disaster.

The King's German Legion battalions broke first. They had chased the French across the valley and up the other side until they were only a few hundred yards from the enemy's artillery line, and now those guns cut great swathes through the disordered Germans. A new line of infantry columns came through the smoke and the Germans at last ran back.

Within minutes most of the First Division, four battalions of the Legion and two of British line were streaming back across the stream as fast as they had chased the French. The Guards were more stubborn. In rough groups they clustered together and fired at the enemy.

It did not slow the French advance for very long. Tall Guardsmen dropped as they were shot by the voltigeurs, who were in open order and used cover well and so made themselves elusive targets. The columns of the second line came on steadily as many from the broken leading battalions stopped running and began to rally. Dragoons in dark green coats and with brass helmets manoeuvred to hunt down the little groups of Guardsmen. One of the columns fired a volley.

The Guards came back, all order gone, and although some still turned and fired at the enemy, they kept going back and the French came after them.

Sir Arthur Wellesley looked out and saw that the centre of his army was gone. On the far right was MacKenzie's brigade. He glanced in the other direction, and saw the French beginning a cautious advance into the valley north of the Medellín. It was too dangerous to take many troops from the hill in case the attack developed.

'Tell Donellan to double his battalion down on to the plain and form behind the Germans. Tell him to let them through and then stop the French.' It was a simple order. General MacKenzie seemed to know what he was doing without needing to be told. That would make four British battalions to halt twelve French. He must hope that they could do this long enough for the First Division to rally and re-enter the fight. Another ADC went to bring a cavalry brigade forward to plug some of the gap, but cavalry could not drive back good infantry on their own. At best it would slow the French.

'We did want this battle, did we not?' whispered Baynes in Murray's ear.

The Guards came back, running to either side of the 3rd Battalion of Detachments.

'We'll be back to help you soon, sir,' said a sergeant as he passed Williams. Roundshot flicked one huge Guardsman aside like a rag doll and then skidded low to take the legs off two men standing beside Ensign Castle carrying the flag.

'Close up to the front!' ordered Pritchard Jones.

Sergeants repeated the instruction all along the line. 'Close up to the front!' When men fell the normal practice was to pull the wounded or dead behind the line and then edge towards the centre to fill the gap. If losses were heavy, this would keep the line two deep but make the frontage ever narrower. Pritchard Jones wanted his battalion to hold the same width of ground no matter how many men he lost, and so if the front rank man fell, the man behind was to step into his place.

'*Vive l'Empereur! Vive l'Empereur!*' Williams could see the French columns. Their voltigeurs had run back to join their regiments, for the French commanders wanted to press their advantage and smash these last formed English battalions.

The drums beat and they were louder now

because once again the guns had friendly troops in front of them and stopped firing.

'*Vive l'Empereur! En avant, mes enfants!*' Officers flourished their swords as they went ahead of the front rank, trying to inspire their men to win glory. The senior men were in their heavy blue jackets, but the soldiers of the closest battalion had wrapped these and folded them into their packs. Instead they wore their belts and equipment over the white-sleeved waistcoats that went under the jackets in normal times. Even so they sweated in the searing heat of the sun.

'*Vive l'Empereur!*' Mouths opened wide as the men chanted. The French marched with their muskets resting on their shoulders, as if they did not even need to fight to brush any enemy aside.

There was shouting and cannon fire from over on the far right, and Williams guessed that the Germans and Dutch were attacking again, but that was not his fight. Two columns were coming at the 3rd Battalion, their heads facing either end of the line, so that one was almost directly in front of him. The other must have faced Pringle and the grenadiers, and Williams made himself say a silent prayer for them.

'*Vive l'Empereur!*' The French were close now. At the head of the column rode an officer with an ornate shako topped by a tall white and red plume. He had an immense moustache, and an even bigger belly.

'*En avant, mes amis!*' His mouth opened to show

badly stained teeth as he urged his men on. '*Ne tirez pas!*' Men who fired tended to stop to reload rather than pressing the attack, and the fat *chef de battalion* was determined his men would not make that mistake.

'Make ready!' There was a rattle as muskets were brought up to shoulders and levelled at the oncoming column. The French saw the British line ripple, almost as if the men were turning to the right.

'*Ils se rendent!*' called the officer optimistically and spurred his horse forward. '*Ne tirez pas!*'

'Fire!' shouted Pritchard Jones.

Hanley groaned. Neither he nor Dobson could walk. They were more than four hundred yards from the battalion and Hanley had to push himself up on his arm to be able to see them through the long grass. It was uncomfortable, and most of the time he simply lay on his back and stared up at the sky. He could hear the flies buzzing even over the noise of battle as they covered the mangled remains of the two soldiers.

Dobson sat up just next to the officer, propping himself up on his pack.

'Looks like the lads are giving them hell, sir,' he said. With some difficulty he went through the motions of loading his musket.

'What are you doing?' asked the officer.

'Best to be careful, sir.'

CHAPTER 29

The front of the column was a shambles. Men lay in the grass, blood dark red on their white waistcoats. The plump *chef de battalion* had been plucked from his saddle and his frightened horse dragged him along until his foot came free and the body dropped to the ground, the right boot still dangling in the stirrup as the animal sped away.

'Reload!' The men of the Light Company were already reaching back for new cartridges.

'*Ne tirez pas!*' Williams distinctly heard the shout and yet the two companies at the head of the French column fired anyway. It was less of a volley than a few shots turning into a cascade.

One of the 43rd was hit in the throat, the ball punching through the leather stock he wore according to regulation. The man clutched at the wound, but the blood was pumping out like a fountain and his face was already pale.

'Close up!' shouted Sergeant Rudden, tapping the rear rank man on the shoulder to indicate he should step into his comrade's place.

Another man, this time one of the Highlanders,

was shot through the bowels and was dragged back behind the line before the space was filled.

'Steady, lads,' called Williams. He had his own musket in his hands and pulled back the hammer ready to fire. Seeing the men were ready, he gave the order. 'Present!' His own firelock nestled against his shoulder. Williams gave the men a moment. 'Aim low, boys! Aim low!'

'Fire!' Sergeant Major Fisher gave the order and the whole of the battalion loosed its volley.

Williams felt the musket slam back on to his shoulder, and then slipped easily into the old routine of loading. He fired once more, like everyone else simply levelling and firing as soon as he was ready. They could not aim. The smoke was so thick that no one could see the enemy, and it was simply a question of pointing the muzzle in roughly the right direction and pulling the trigger.

'Aim low!' called the officers over and over again because instinct made men fire too high and it was so very easy to miss even the densest of columns.

Men fell. Williams saw some of the men in his company as they were hit. A man with yellow facings on his jacket had the fingers smashed on his left hand as he held his musket. Patterson, his nose still bandaged from yesterday's skirmish, was shot through both thighs as he stood with his side towards the enemy. He was dragged back, crying out even though he tried to bite down on his lip to stop himself. Skerret stepped forward into his place and within minutes a ball took him in the right eye and drove deep into his brain. Sergeant McNaught pushed another Highlander forward into the front rank.

The French drums had stopped and there was no more chanting. Bullets continued to snap through the smoke. One struck the firelock of a man from the 43rd, smashing the wood so that the butt hung down limply. Williams gave the man his own musket.

'Keep firing, boys! Aim low!'

A figure came through the smoke, eyes wild and teeth bared. '*En avant, mes enfants,*' shouted the officer, trying to drag his men forward. Williams reached for his sword.

'Look out, sir!' yelled Rudden, and then half a dozen muskets banged and the white front of the Frenchman's jacket bloomed scarlet as he was pitched back. Two more shapes loomed out of the smoke; one was a sergeant.

Williams' sword slid readily from his scabbard and he turned the motion into a parry that knocked aside the sergeant's bayonet. The other Frenchman raised his musket to his shoulder and pulled the trigger, the ball taking the man using Williams' musket in the chest so that he sank down with a sigh.

The sergeant moved to lunge again, but he slipped on the pool of blood gushing from the dying officer and Williams dodged the blade. His sword flicked up to bite into the man's neck and he raked the wickedly sharp point to slice through the man's throat and come free. He revelled in the balance of the Russian sword as he spun back to block a tentative jab from the other Frenchman. Rudden was coming up beside him, as was another man, but Williams yelled in anger as he beat the man's musket aside and drove his sword into the Frenchman's belly. The man grabbed at the metal, cutting his fingers on its well-honed edge, and the officer kicked him over as he pulled the blade free.

'Keep firing!' shouted Williams. It had all taken so very little time and already the fight seemed almost unreal. His sword was dripping with blood and the French infantryman sobbed as he lay in the grass until a bullet from one of his own comrades smacked into the back of his head. No more Frenchmen seemed to have followed through the smoke and it was hard to know whether they could have held them if they had.

'Well done, sir,' said Rudden, and was then knocked down as a ball thudded into his right arm. He dropped his musket. 'I'm hit,' he said, as Williams had heard so many others utter the same phrase. The sergeant's arm hung uselessly.

'Go to the rear, Sergeant Rudden,' said Williams, and tried to smile. 'I'll look after your fellows.'

Men were falling all along the line. Some were able to walk back to the surgeons, and others were simply pulled back behind the line to wait as best they could. Some would never move again. In the rare moments when no one fired, the air was filled with moaning and cries of pain.

The lieutenant in charge of the Germans of the 4/60th was hit in the leg, and hobbled to the rear with his arm around the shoulders of one of his men, who had a ball in the side. His ensign, a popular, eager youth who had just celebrated his nineteenth birthday a week ago, was hit badly, ribs broken and a wound to the chest which bubbled with foam. Four of the Germans carried him away in a blanket, moving as gently as they could.

Sergeant Major Fisher took a ball through the neck, which somehow managed not to cut any of the vital blood vessels, and when he was bandaged, he walked stiffly and unaided back to the surgeons.

Still the men loaded and fired. Their shoulders were bruised from the kick of their muskets. McNaught caught one of his men tipping some of the cartridge on to the ground to reduce the recoil and screamed at the man, telling him that he was on a charge and a disgrace to his regiment. Men skinned their knuckles as they rammed down and caught their hands against their fixed bayonets.

Williams had lost all sense of time. He did not know how long they had fought or how many times the men fired. His corporal was dead, and that left McNaught as the only NCO, and so he made one of the 43rd an acting sergeant, but then that man was hit in the foot and used his musket as a crutch to go back to the rear.

'Keep firing, boys, keep firing!' Williams' voice was hoarse from shouting, his mouth dry, even though he had fired only a few rounds.

News came that the colonel was down. Truscott walked along behind the Light Company.

'Well done, lads, well done, we're hurting them. Take more than Frogs to beat us!' he shouted encouragingly. 'Aim low!'

'Pritchard Jones took one through the lungs,' he said to Williams. He spoke more softly, but still loud enough to be heard over the din. 'So I'm in charge.'

'Congratulations,' said Williams, and meant it, even though it seemed a little foolish under the circumstances.

'Well, the way things are going you might be in charge soon enough! An officer from the Guards has come and says they will be back in line soon, but General MacKenzie is dead so I am not sure who has the brigade.'

'Good. Is Billy unscathed?'

'Was the last time I saw him.' Truscott looked solemn. 'I'm afraid Hanley was hit and left behind when we moved up. Sergeant Dobson too.'

'Badly?'

'No idea.' He patted Williams on the shoulder with his one hand. 'Keep up the good work, Bills.' Truscott glanced along the rear of the Light Company. There were barely a dozen men left in the second rank. 'Like that everywhere,' he said. 'Well, good luck to you.'

'Keep firing, lads, keep firing,' Captain Truscott called as he walked back to the centre of the line.

The men loaded and fired. Throats were parched, limbs weary and faces black with powder smoke, and still they found the strength to load and bring their muskets back up to their shoulders.

'Steady, boys, pour it into them!' croaked Williams as loudly as he could.

He heard the slapping sound as a ball struck a redcoat and flung him backwards. There was no man left in the rear rank at that spot, and it took McNaught a moment to yell at someone else to step into the gap.

A corporal ran up. 'Mr Williams, sir?' The man was from the 106th, but although he recognised the face Williams could not think of his name.

'Yes, what is it?'

'Mr Truscott's compliments, sir, and you are to prepare to charge. The men are to take off their packs first.'

'Fine.' Williams turned and strolled out to the flank of the company. There had been a wide gap between his men and the grenadiers on the right of the 45th. Now there were several hundred Guardsmen formed in two ranks filling the space.

'Well, hallelujah,' said Williams to himself. He tried to shout and then coughed to clear his throat. 'Cease fire! Cease fire!' All along the line the order was being repeated. One of his men fell screaming as a ball broke his femur.

'Take off your packs!'

The men looked puzzled and reluctant. Everything they possessed was in their packs and no man wanted his lost or stolen. Then they began to push the straps back and let the heavy burdens sink to the ground.

'Fox!' shouted McNaught at the wounded man. 'Stop that caterwauling and stay here to watch the Light Company's packs. Lose anything and I'll have the hide off your back.'

'Yes, Sergeant,' came the response, as habit took over.

'Get ready, boys,' called Williams. 'Let's chase these French rascals off our land!'

A bullet whipped through the air beside him.

'The Third Battalion will advance. Forward march!' Truscott's voice carried along the line and Williams thought that he had never heard his friend shout so loud.

The line was ragged. Some of the men had slight wounds, bound up with stained cloth from whatever they could find. They were in almost a single rank, with just a few men here and there walking behind.

Williams could see nothing because the smoke cloud was so thick. He held his sword out and had to think before he could remember why there was dried blood on the blade. Another man cried out as he was struck, but the rest pressed on and the dirty white smoke began to thin. The men felt far lighter and strangely refreshed without their heavy packs.

He came through the bank of smoke and there were the enemy, no longer in ordered columns, but clustered, the braver souls near the front, the rest flinching away from the appalling fire. Many lay on the ground, dozens, probably hundreds of them, more it seemed than the redcoats had lost.

'Charge!' shouted Truscott, and officers took up the cry.

'Charge!' yelled Williams, and he ran forward, sword thrusting towards the masses of men in white. Muskets fired. One ball plucked at the long tails of his coat as it streamed behind him. A man from the 43rd doubled up as he was hit in the groin, but his sharp cries were lost as the battalion cheered.

The French seemed to quiver and they were close when the remnants of the columns dissolved into rout. Not all of them fled. Two men in front of Williams were loading and one brought his musket up and pulled the trigger before he was ready so that his ramrod cartwheeled past the officer's head with a weird thrumming sound. Then the man dropped his firelock and fled.

Williams yelled as he hacked across the face of the other man, sending him reeling back. Around him the men of the Light Company stabbed or clubbed down any of the French infantry who stayed to fight or failed to run quickly enough. The spirit seemed to have gone from even those who did not retreat, and Williams knew that it had been a very close thing and that he and the other redcoats might well have been in the same position if the French had managed to charge.

Fear and exhaustion fed the British anger, and the men killed hungrily, as if in payment for the pain they had suffered. One quiet soldier from among the convalescents stabbed three French fusiliers until his bayonet was bent back on itself from striking too hard against bone.

The French broke. All of the second line and the rallied men from the first fled as the British battalions came forward at them. They ran to the rear, dropping muskets and flinging down their packs to go faster.

'Grab the packs, boys!' shouted McNaught practically. 'They've got food!'

They reached the stream, running past the dead and wounded of the earlier fighting.

'Halt!' Truscott was shouting. 'Don't cross the stream!'

'Stop, lads!' shouted Williams. They did not want to sweep on too far like the First Division in case more French waited for them. Yet in truth the men were so weary that it was easy to halt them.

The French guns began to fire. Batteries had targets again and the gunners took advantage for they did not know that the British were too weak to keep advancing.

Ensign Castle's head was shattered by a twelve-pounder shot. His torso stood for a moment, blood fountaining up on to the little flag he had carried so proudly. Private Hope from the Grenadier

452

Company lost both his legs below the knee to another ball which skimmed low through the grass.

'Lie down!' ordered Truscott. 'Take cover in the stream bed!' Williams and McNaught got the Light Company moving, but the men were reacting sluggishly, the brief surge of passion from the charge now spent and only exhaustion left.

Billy Pringle was giving the same order when a bullet fired at absurdly long range by a sullen voltigeur smacked into his stomach. The force was mostly spent, but even so it slashed a long groove through jacket and flesh. Pringle sobbed in pain as he slumped down.

CHAPTER 30

The ground was parched, the grass and bushes dry as tinder after months of baking sunshine. Every time a musket was fired, pieces of burning paper from the cartridge dropped on to the fields. The big guns threw their smouldering wadding even farther. No one knew where the first grass fire broke out or whose embers started it, but as the fighting slackened on both sides of the river thick clouds of dark smoke rose up in several places. The wind, which had scarcely blown during the day, now began to gust, sweeping the flames quickly as the fires spread.

'Can you crawl, sir?' asked Dobson urgently.

'Should we not wait to be found?' Hanley replied.

'Not unless you want to roast, sir. Come on. That way.' Dobson pointed in the direction the battalion had gone. 'And pray someone comes looking for us.'

Guns still fired. They could not see the Germans and Dutch repulsed for a second time, but did hear the trumpets as some Spanish cavalry charged and cut down the fleeing enemy. Farther away in the north valley more guns fired and more cavalry – British this time – charged so recklessly that they seemed to stun the French, so that the enemy attack stalled and came to nothing.

Dobson and Hanley were more concerned with the closer noises. The grass fire roared as it came on quickly, and then there were the dreadful screams as wounded men were caught and burned alive. There seemed to be corpses everywhere. Hanley dragged himself past one stripped almost naked by looters, and he was sure he knew the boy's face. Then suddenly he realised it was Lebeque, the cheerful conscript who had guarded him on the bridge at Merida.

'Poor devil,' he said aloud, and then dragged himself on through the grass.

'There you are, I have found you, Mr Dobson.' It was a woman's voice, and Hanley was surprised to see the very proper Mrs Dobson. She was dressed in a plain but neat brown dress and was fanning her face with her straw hat. A pin had shaken loose from her long hair, which hung down to her shoulder on one side.

'Annie, get away, girl, you should not be here,' said her husband, his pride mingling with fear, for it was getting hot now as the flames came closer.

'Don't you tell me what to do, Mr Dobson,' came the stern reply, and Hanley could not help laughing out loud.

'Help Mr Hanley, lass!'

'He is managing. It's you, you old fool, who needs help!' Mrs Dobson was small, her husband tall and heavy. Somehow she lifted his shoulder and dragged him foot by foot.

They struggled on, and soon Hanley felt as if he were standing next to a furnace for the heat was so great. More men screamed as they died in the flames.

'Praise the Lord,' said Mrs Dobson as redcoats came towards them. 'It's our Mr Williams.'

'Take your pouches off, you daft sods!' yelled Dobson.

'Mr Dobson, there is no call for such language,' snapped his wife automatically.

Williams understood. 'Pouches off, boys. Throw them that way, away from the fire.' The heat was so great that it could easily have set off a man's cartridges, blowing up his pouch and wounding or even killing him.

'Lift 'em up!' he shouted, and he and a Highlander took Hanley while two men from the 43rd lifted Dobson. 'Quick as you can!'

They fled from the fire, Mrs Dobson scooping up her husband's pack and carrying it with them even though she did not have the strength to put it properly on her back. Williams wished they could run fast enough to free their nostrils from the smell of roasting flesh.

There were wounded everywhere, far more than any of them had ever seen. Thousands lay across the plain and there were not enough fit men left to gather them up quickly. The lucky ones were carried along the tracks leading to the hospitals set up in the convent and some of the other big buildings. Others hobbled or crawled, dragging wounds through the dust and grime.

The convent was worse. Rows and rows of wounded soldiers waited for the surgeon, filling the courtyard and the road outside. A steady stream of orderlies came from the buildings with amputated legs and arms wrapped in ever filthier covers and tipped the limbs on to a steadily growing pile. Dogs howled at the smell and had to be kept at bay by the bayonets of the sentries. A few men screamed. Most sighed softly or moaned, and some lay still, and unless they had a friend near them their wounds became covered with flies.

Hanley remembered little. They laid him down on his front in a pile of straw. He always slept that way, and with the weariness and the heat he quickly lost consciousness. They woke him up when a surgeon came and probed for the fragments of the shell. The pain was worse than anything he had ever known, even when his arm had been smashed at Roliça, and he could remember yelling and cursing at the doctor as his thigh and all of his leg were stabbed repeatedly by a white hot poker. Then he fainted and there was nothing for hours or days or years. Once or twice he came half awake and there were the sounds of gentle movement around him. The room he was in seemed large, but there was only a single candle flickering far away. He saw Billy Pringle beside him, his face looking white and his breathing so soft that Hanley had to stare for a long time before he was convinced his friend still lived.

'Oh dear!' Again and again he heard voices sighing the same words. 'Oh dear.' Sometimes they called for their mothers, and on the first night a man screamed again and again for Emma, calling for forgiveness and one last kiss. Then the voice went silent.

'Oh dear, oh dear!' The smell assaulted his nostrils. There was the stink of excrement and blood, and a growing odour of decay that made him gag if ever he took a strong gulp of air.

Hanley drifted in and out of consciousness. He heard Billy talking to him at one point, but he could not understand the words or remember how to reply. His wound did not hurt as long as he remained still. Whenever he moved the pain savaged him and he knew that sometimes he wept.

Williams and the rest of the 3rd Battalion spent days dealing with the debris of battle. They dug graves and dragged the already decaying corpses into them. Sometimes the bodies came apart when men tried to lift them by the arms.

There were too many, and so the order came to burn the remaining corpses. They built pyres with any wood they could find, but the orders were not to touch the vine trees, and apart from that there were not enough axes so some of the fires were too small. Many bodies were left as shrunken dolls half the size of a man, and these had to be buried by the weary survivors.

Truscott gave Williams the task of putting together the casualty list for the battalion.

'One officer and forty-four men killed,' he read. 'The officer being poor Mr Castle. Then eight officers wounded, six of them severely.' Williams struggled to take the numbers in even as he went through the list. 'Two hundred and sixty-eight other ranks wounded, and twenty-one missing.'

'Any idea where?' asked Truscott, trying to be practical rather than face the full scale of the appalling losses.

'I fear that some are among the dead, but were unrecognisable. Let us hope they were killed outright before the grass fires reached them.'

'Amen to that.'

'I do not know of any taken prisoner. Some may have run.' Williams shrugged. No one wanted to admit such a thing, but all knew that a few men snapped under the strain of battle and would find some way of escaping to the rear in all the confusion. They might return in time. 'Grand total,' he continued, 'nine officers and three hundred and thirty-three other ranks.'

'Dear God alive,' said Truscott softly, and it was rare for him to swear. 'From what I hear the loss for the army amounts to well over five thousand.' That was around a quarter of the total, but all save one brigade of the cavalry had taken little part in the fighting and the bulk of the fallen were from the infantry battalions.

'The French have lost more,' said Williams.

'They had more to start off with.'

'True. Oh yes, we have also lost the twelve remaining men from the forty-third who have returned to their regiment.'

The day after the battle a fresh brigade of three first-rate light infantry battalions joined the army. Williams hoped that Sergeant Rudden would recover quickly and be able to return to his precious regiment. He felt guilty now for doubting the men of his company. None could have fought better, and it did not really matter whether they did it for him or in spite of him, for their regiments, their own pride or sheer damned stubbornness.

'We beat them,' said Williams firmly.

'Yes, we did.' The French Army had withdrawn, but the Allies were in no state to follow them. 'Sadly I fear this achievement will be the last for our battalion. The men from other corps are to be sent to the First and Second Battalions of Detachments, pending either their return to their own regiments when these arrive in Portugal or a return to England.'

'And us?'

'In due course the officers and men of the One Hundred and Sixth are to return to England, although I dare say they will keep us busy in the meantime. That should give time for some of the wounded to recovery sufficiently for the voyage.'

'Any word?' Williams had been to the hospital once during a brief break from duty, but with so few officers left and so much to do he had had no more time.

'Only indirectly. I think Pringle and Hanley have a good chance. The colonel is grievously wounded.' Truscott's tone conveyed his lack of hope. 'Still, he is a tough one.'

'He is Welsh,' said Williams, but his confidence was thin.

Hanley was sitting up and able to eat and keep it down by the time Baynes came to see him.

'I am glad to find you on the path to recovery,' said the merchant, who thought the lieutenant still looked pale and weak.

'Still hurts,' came the reply.

'Well, you should be pleased to know that our deception worked. King Joseph is off chasing Venegas, while Victor is looking for the "great army" led by Sir Robert Wilson.'

'Was not the original plan to keep the French armies apart and fight them individually?'

Baynes smiled at the evident bitterness in Hanley's voice.

'Indeed it was. Then that did not work and we needed a battle, even though it meant fighting them all in one place. Sir Arthur and you fellows won the battle and so we are still in the game.'

'Madrid?' Hanley looked excited, life coming back to his face.

461

'Not yet, but perhaps in a few weeks. First we must deal with Marshal Soult, who has forced his way through the mountains and is behind us. He may have a few of Ney's men with him. Sir Arthur estimates their force as no bigger than his remaining men. So tomorrow the British Army marches back east towards Plasencia to beat Soult. Cuesta and the Spanish will stay here. They can guard the hospitals and block any move from Victor or the others.'

Hanley waited for a moment. 'There must be more.'

'There is.' Baynes brought up a handkerchief to cover his mouth. The air stank and was no doubt poisonous. Then he realised how this must look and took the handkerchief away. 'Do you have any way of reaching Espinosa that you have not told me?'

'You have tried the priest?'

'His body was found last night. The throat had been cut.'

'Poor devil.' Hanley had liked the old man. 'La Doña Margarita?'

'Her driver killed an assassin who had broken into the house last night,' said Baynes.

Hanley thought of Dobson's verdict on Ramón and nodded. 'Is she hurt?'

'A little shaken, but unscathed.'

'There may be a way. That is assuming Espinosa himself is still alive?'

'I am making that assumption, but you may be right. Perhaps the French have discovered him. At the moment we cannot know.'

'Velarde?'

Baynes looked him in the eyes. 'Who knows?'

Hanley was silent for a moment, trying to decide whether the merchant was really so unsure. No doubt the man was still holding back, out of habit certainly, but after the last weeks Hanley found it hard to trust anyone wholly.

'Well,' he said in the end, 'perhaps that does not matter for the moment. Tell me, is it day or night? I am inclined to lose track and there is no window in this room.'

'It is just after nine in the morning,' answered Baynes slowly.

'Good, then we have time to make plenty of ground today. You must fetch me a horse and a small escort of reliable men.'

'Must I?' The merchant smiled. 'For what purpose?'

'I shall ride to Captain Rodriguez and his guerrillas. They will not be far away and it should not be too difficult to find them. With his aid, I believe that I can reach Espinosa.'

Now it was Baynes' turn to lapse into silence and watch the other for several minutes. Hanley waited, for he was finding so serious a conversation fatiguing and he knew that he would soon need all his strength for one last effort.

'Can you ride, William? Indeed, my friend, can you even stand?'

'It seems that I must,' said Hanley. He pushed himself up with his arms, keeping all the weight on his good leg, and with effort was able to stand up. 'There. Good as new.' He was struggling to breathe.

'Most impressive.' Baynes remained seated, watching him closely. Pringle snored loudly where he lay on a mattress of straw beside the wall.

Hanley smiled and let himself balance more naturally before he took his first step. Sudden agony engulfed his right thigh and he felt it sinking beneath him. He gasped, unable even to swear, and leaned to the left, lifting his other foot off the ground. The pain subsided slowly.

'*Jesús, Maria y Joseph*,' he croaked as his heart began to stop racing.

Baynes got up and helped Hanley back down on to his bed.

'I do not doubt your determination, only your capacity to see it through, William,' he said when Hanley was safely down. 'You cannot think of going anywhere, let alone a hard ride, perhaps dodging French patrols. It is impossible.'

The merchant patted him on the shoulder. 'Rest. You must tell me how it is to be done and I shall go. We need to know what the French are planning and Espinosa is best placed to tell us quickly.'

Hanley looked at the merchant, with his honest face and hard eyes. 'Take Williams,' he said. 'Send him here first and I shall tell him what he needs to know.'

Baynes looked at him oddly. 'You have a most suspicious nature.'

'I do believe that is meant as a compliment.'
'My dear boy, one of the highest.'

An hour later Williams found himself riding with
Baynes and a corporal's guard from the KGL
Hussars on the main road from Talavera to Madrid.
It was his first chance to try the Andalusian given
to him the day after the battle by General Cuesta,
and he could see that the animal far surpassed the
other horses. The mare was a little nervous, eyes
darting and ears flicking at each new sight or noise,
but when they had cleared the town and let their
mounts run she went smoothly into a gentle canter
that still threatened to leave the others behind.
Williams suspected that so good a horse required
a better rider than himself, but then he also
doubted his suitability – and indeed his taste – for
the task in hand.

Mr Baynes was as jovial as ever, talking away
even when Williams' replies were brief. Hanley
had chosen him, not the merchant, and it was his
friend who had explained the whole business and
what he must do. The cause was good, for the
general must learn what he could of the enemy's
intentions if the campaign was to be won. There
was nothing inherently dishonourable in the duty
itself. He was less sure about his companion.

'You have a fine steed, Mr Williams,' said Baynes,
as the redcoated officer pulled slightly on the reins
to slow his mount down. 'Very forward.'

'She is itching to run,' he replied, and let her go

for a moment so that he pulled ahead again and avoided more conversation. A few minutes later he slowed to a trot, and let the others catch up.

'I doubt more than a few of our staff officers are as well mounted.' Baynes was now even more red faced than usual.

Williams nodded. It was a thrill to own such a fine beast, but he doubted that he would be able to keep her. Fodder cost money, and as a lieutenant of a line regiment he was not entitled to receive this from the army.

'And to think when first we met you were on a borrowed mule! You must indulge us by slowing a little. I am sure that I can lead you to Rodriguez and his band, but to do that you are required to follow me!'

'Yes, sir, of course. I am not the most experienced of riders,' he explained. Silently he wondered why Hanley did not want to trust this man – indeed, would not trust anyone apart from him, since Pringle was still recovering from his wound. Some of what he had told Williams was intimate, not all to his credit, and it was understandable that he entrusted such matters only to a friend, but even so his caution was more than a little unnerving.

'I do not know what I truly think about Baynes,' Hanley had said when they were alone. 'He is probably square, or at least as far as anyone can be when they work for the government, but I cannot be certain any more about anyone. Not after the last few weeks. The Spanish have traitors, and perhaps . . .' Hanley had lapsed into silence again, but then he had smiled thinly. 'I may be starting at my own shadow. But I know I trust you. This is important, Bills, very important.'

Colonel Murray had come to see them off, and Williams wondered whether Baynes had brought the staff officer for his benefit. Murray was certainly a most soldierly individual, and it was easier to obey his orders than those of a spy. Williams wished it was the colonel and not the merchant who rode with him now. Even more he wished that Hanley had been well enough to deal with this murky business himself.

Baynes' voice pulled him back from his thoughts. 'The Third Battalion of Detachments performed most gallantly, but I know the cost was dear and must apologise for drawing you away from duties that were no doubt pressing.'

'Oh, they'll manage without me,' said Williams blithely. He began to wonder whether some of Hanley's talents for dissimulation were rubbing off on him. 'It is a pleasure to be of service.'

The merchant watched him for a moment, and then broke into a grin. 'I see you are the right man for the task.'

Williams hoped his face betrayed no reaction. The road was open ahead of them, so he gave the slightest nudge with his heels and felt the mare surge forward, hoofs pounding on the hard-packed earth. The noise almost covered Baynes' delighted chuckle.

CHAPTER 31

'She expected someone else,' translated Baynes.

The slim girl looked at them suspiciously. She was small and delicate, but moved with the grace of the dancer she once was. Her face was soft, the features pretty, and her brown eyes large and expressive. They suggested a quick wit, a great kindness and the profound sadness of one used to pain and expecting disappointment.

'Tell her I have something to say to her alone, and after that she can decide whether to trust us or not.' Williams was concentrating, going over in his mind the phrase Hanley had given him.

Maria Pilar looked doubtful as Baynes spoke to her. They had ridden to meet the irregulars. Hanley had told Williams that the captain would be able to send a messenger to one of Espinosa's agents in Madrid. Instead they found she was already waiting for them.

'Say that she is a lone star on a bleak winter's night, and that Guillermo is my friend.'

Baynes obeyed. Williams thought he saw a slight flush in Mapi's face as the merchant spoke the

words which Hanley had once said. He also understood something of what his friend had meant.
Mapi was beautiful and seemed so fragile that she
would break at the first touch.

The girl nodded. Williams looked at the merchant
until Baynes stepped back a few paces and joined
Captain Rodriguez standing at the door of the
little cottage. He walked slowly towards Mapi, and
then leaned to whisper in her ear.

The first phrases were in Spanish, and Hanley
had made him repeat them over and over again.
They were little pieces of lovers' talk, or the things
he said when he was young and believed himself
a great artist and thinker not bound by the rules
of society. The last words were the only English
he knew she understood. 'You are my life, my
inspiration.'

Williams was embarrassed to repeat the words,
and even more so because he knew that his friend
had tired of the girl and in the end deserted her.
'He will understand if you hate him,' he said in
Spanish, just as he had been coached. It was no
doubt an easy thing for Hanley to say.

Maria Pilar's eyes were moist. She stared up at
him and Williams was overwhelmed by her beauty
and her sorrow. He wanted to hold her close, to
comfort her like a child and claim that everything
would be all right, but he was afraid to do it.
Williams felt guilty because Hanley was his friend.

Mapi took his hand and squeezed it. He was not
sure what she meant and whether the touch was

really for him or Hanley. It still made him feel better. He called to Baynes and the girl told her story.

Espinosa was dead, hanged when he was denounced as a spy. Mapi did not know who his accuser was, but since then several of his servants, friends and agents had been arrested or killed. Espinosa might have told his interrogators a lot before they sent him to the gallows.

She carried the last report from him. Together with a dispatch captured by Captain Rodriguez and his men, it changed everything.

'We must ride immediately,' said Baynes, who had earlier spoken with anticipation of rest and a good meal.

'Tell her she must not return to Madrid,' said Williams. The merchant looked at him strangely.

Mapi simply stared at him, without any mark of emotion. 'I imagine she will do what she thinks best,' said Baynes. 'She deserves fame and glory, for she may well have saved us from utter disaster.'

Soult was not alone. Apart from his own corps, he commanded Ney and Mortier with all their regiments. Sir Arthur Wellesley was marching unawares to attack fifty thousand men who would crush him however bravely his men fought. So they rode hard, and Baynes could not keep up the pace set by the Andalusian mare, and so he gave the captured documents to Williams, who rode on with the best mounted trooper of the escorting hussars. They went to Cuesta first, and on from him to Wellesley.

The hopes of marching into Madrid died. Once again the British Army retreated.

'I must express my profound thanks for the kindness you showed,' said Williams stiffly. It was over a month since he had seen Baynes. 'Too many brave fellows were left behind to be captured.' Absent-mindedly the lieutenant tapped his pocket. There were two letters inside, part of a fresh packet of mail sent to the detachment which had been dropped in a river and ruined. One letter was wholly illegible, but his heart told him it was from Jane MacAndrews. Did she write in greeting, in friendship or to tell him bad news? The second letter was from his sister and the only words he could read were *dreadfully worried*. Fear gnawed at him.

A wind blew gently from the sea, taking the edge off the heat of the sun. Williams was still sweating all down his back. Much as he dreaded the motion of the ship, it would be good to settle in a cabin and cool down. He wanted to be home, even though he dreaded what might await him there.

'The kindness was chiefly the work of La Doña Margarita,' said Baynes modestly. 'I merely informed the lady of the plight of men who had done her good service in the past.'

When Marshal Victor advanced on Talavera, the outnumbered Spanish Army had withdrawn. Well over a thousand British wounded too weak to travel easily had been left behind. The French

471

reaped a rich harvest of prisoners, whom they treated with kindness. Hanley and Pringle, along with Dobson and his wife, had escaped in some style, riding in the carriage of La Doña Margarita. Wickham also got away – Williams suspected to the chagrin of the lady.

'Nevertheless you have my thanks.' Williams inclined his head in the gentlest of bows. 'Now, if you will excuse me, I should go aboard and ensure that the Grenadier Company is suitably accommodated.' The remnants of the 106th were sailing home to rejoin the main body of the regiment.

Williams turned, and marched away. Hanley was sure his stiffness of manner expressed distaste at the merchant and the dark world he inhabited. At the moment he was inclined to agree with his friend.

'It all seems such a waste,' he said when Williams was out of earshot.

'Could have been far worse,' said Baynes, 'far, far worse. Sir Arthur's – forgive me, but I am not yet used to the name – I mean Lord Wellington's army survives when it risked utter destruction.' Talavera was hailed as a great victory in England, prompting a grateful monarch and his ministers to give the victor a new title.

'We won a battle and lost the war.' Hanley's tone was bitter. 'My friend Pringle said much the same to me at Corunna.' His leg still ached, and he leaned on a cane as he stood on the harbour side, although this was now more through habit than necessity.

He felt worn out, drained of energy and every drop of enthusiasm.

'Not the war, dear boy, but one round. We shall be back in the mill soon enough. I am on my way to Cadiz to help things along. A happy chance, since it permits me to bid you farewell and wish for your speedy return. We shall need you.'

'Austria has surrendered. Surely Napoleon will now return to Spain with all his might.'

'All the more need for clever men to help us outwit the enemy here.' Baynes smiled, and even Hanley found it hard to see past the open, honest face, to the steel beneath. 'But it is late in the year, and unlikely that much will happen before next spring. Wellington is convinced he can hold on in Portugal.'

'For how long?'

'Until the wind changes. Austria is beaten for the moment, but has no cause to love Boney. The same is true of Russia and Prussia. We need to keep going to give them a chance to recover. Then one day, who knows – perhaps a Spanish army marching into Paris. Poor Don Gregorio would have loved such a day.' Cuesta, worn out by his injuries and disappointment, had suffered a stroke and resigned his command.

'You begin to sound like Brigadier Wilson,' said Hanley with a smile.

'Do I indeed? Well, I suspect good Sir Robert would be assuring us we could be there next week if only the fools in charge gave him a few thousand men. Do you know he is already writing up the rout of his soldiers as a great victory.' Wilson had unwisely chosen to fight Marshal Ney's entire corps. His position was strong, but the vastly more numerous French veterans had forced their way through anyway. 'By the time he gets to London no doubt many of his political friends will happily believe him.' Baynes' tone was more amused than weary. Sir Robert Wilson had left his Legion to the charge of others, vowing never to return to the Peninsula.

'The truth does appear a very malleable thing,' said Hanley. 'At least in some hands.'

'Well, I suspect the danger is when a man begins to believe his own lies.' Baynes' head leaned slightly to one side, but his eyes never left Hanley's and radiated apparent sincerity. 'I do not believe you are prone to such weakness.'

'Velarde,' said Hanley at last. He was sure the merchant wanted to discuss the Spaniard. So did he, for he was plagued by the thought that his own mistakes had led to so many deaths and could so easily have led to many more and a great disaster. 'Have you news of him?'

'None. That may mean many things.'

'Perhaps he died with the others,' said Hanley when the other man failed to continue.

'That is possible. It is most certainly one way of vanishing.'

'If not, then surely he was the one who betrayed Espinosa and his people. His reward would no doubt have been great, and if we were blinded for a while so that Sir Arthur marched off to destruction, then he would be well placed in the new regime.'

'He did what we wanted at Talavera,' said Baynes.

'When it probably seemed to his advantage to do so. After that we nearly walked into a trap. Perhaps that was the big lie for which Colonel Murray kept searching.'

Baynes smiled again. 'You need to come back, William, as soon as you are well.'

Hanley did not reply.

'I have news of your particular friend,' said the merchant, 'and given her role in all this – and indeed her undoubted charms – I am very pleased to say that she remains in good health.' Baynes no doubt knew that Mapi had been Hanley's lover, but chose not to say anything.

'I am glad of that. Thank you for telling me.' Since Williams had spoken of the meeting, Hanley both longed and feared to see the girl. He wondered whether he would ever be able to make amends, and then thought guiltily that he was still more troubled by his own feelings that hers. 'I believe it was Velarde. Whether he turned traitor on the opportunity or was always working for them I do not know.'

'Then come back, William, come back. You can find him and kill him.'

'I am not an assassin,' said Hanley, and was shocked to think that he must sound like Williams.

'I am a soldier.' He bowed – again the echo of his friend's manner was more than a little amusing – and walked away to board the ship.

'Are you indeed?' Baynes spoke the words softly, ignored by the group of dock workers carrying bales of rice past him. 'Then I dare say you will do as you are damned well told!'

HISTORICAL NOTE

Send Me Safely Back Again is a novel, but the story is firmly rooted in the real events of 1809. The 106th Regiment of Foot is an invention – the actual regiment with that number having a brief life in the 1790s. However, I have tried to make the behaviour of its officers and men reflect the real lives of the redcoats in this era.

The 3rd Battalion of Detachments is another invention. In reality, the 1st and 2nd Battalions of Detachments were formed at Lisbon in February 1809 and served throughout the year. Like the fictional 3rd Battalion, they were composed of men left behind by their corps before or during Sir John Moore's advance into Spain – the campaign described in *Beat the Drums Slowly*. Many of the soldiers were veterans, and Wellesley was satisfied with their conduct in battle. The story of men on the Medellín Hill calling out for someone to lead them comes from an eyewitness account, but in spite of initial confusion the men held their ground. On the march, these men tended to be prodigious looters, largely because they were no longer within the close family of their own regiment, and were often led by officers and NCOs who were strangers to them.

As in previous books, many of the episodes in the story are taken from real incidents in these campaigns. Readers may struggle to believe that a man could be hit on the backpack by a cannon shot and then flung several yards without being seriously hurt. Yet a memoir by a soldier in the 61st Foot describes this happening to a sergeant in his company at Talavera. Major General Hill did ride into a group of French light infantrymen on the Medellín Hill at Talavera. One of his staff was shot and killed, his own horse wounded, but remained strong enough to carry him away. Only the inclusion of Wickham is an invention. At the Battle of Medellín I have given Williams and Dobson credit for the bravery of others. Cuesta was knocked from his horse and trampled by his own cavalry as they fled. He was then rescued by a small group including his own nephew and Colonel D'Urban.

D'Urban, along with all of the generals and virtually all the other senior officers in the British, Spanish and French armies, is real. Lower down there are more inventions. Baynes, Velarde, Epsinosa and La Doña Margarita are all fictional. Sir Robert Wilson is too colourful a character to have invented. His father was the portrait artist Benjamin Wilson, who was made Sergeant Painter by King George III when Hogarth died in 1764. The royal connection helped Robert's career, and he was indeed knighted by the Austrian Emperor. I have tried to give a flavour of Wilson's restless, erratic talent. He was a highly productive author and unrelenting self-publicist. He certainly provided a charismatic leader for the Loyal Lusitanian Legion. Reluctant to accept any authority, he moved swiftly from Portugal across the Spanish border, gathering up Spanish troops as well as a force of redcoats cut off during the retreat to Corunna, who were indeed mounted on horses and mules.

Wilson's operations were certainly a great nuisance to the French, much larger in scale than any guerrilla activity in that region at such an early stage in the war. He achieved a lot with very scant resources, but sadly his actual achievements never quite equalled his own spectacular claims. Wellesley did his best to rein in Wilson to follow orders, but was soon moved to describe him as ' . . . a very slippery fellow . . . and he has not the talent of being able to speak the truth upon any subject'. After Talavera Wilson and the Legion engaged Marshal Ney unnecessarily at the Pass of Banos and were soundly defeated. In the months and years to come Wilson rewrote the battle and turned it into a great victory. He soon left the Peninsula, never to return, but would be attached to the Russian Army in 1812 and the subsequent campaigns in central Europe, and managed to get himself involved in intrigues against the Tsar. After the war he became a fervent advocate of Bonaparte.

A more flamboyant figure even than Wilson, and

certainly a better soldier, was Lasalle, who led the charge at Medellín and epitomised the *beau sabreur* of Napoleon's army. Gaudily dressed, brave to a fault, charismatic and charming, in 1806 Lasalle had bluffed a Prussian fortress into surrendering to his lightly equipped regiments of hussars – dubbed 'the infernal brigade'. His party piece of aiming in a mirror and firing over his shoulder at wine glasses is well attested, as is his claim that 'an hussar who isn't dead by thirty is a *jean-foutre*' – an expression impossible to translate and variously rendered as blackguard, scoundrel or a more modern expletive. In Napoleon's Italian campaigns there are stories of Lasalle sneaking through enemy lines to visit his mistress. On another occasion in central Europe his hussars unexpectedly fled from the enemy. As punishment Lasalle is supposed to have drawn them up in full view of Russian artillery and kept them there for hours, sitting on his horse at their head and calmly smoking his pipe as shot and shell struck home. Like many of the tales surrounding him, no doubt this one grew in the telling. Lasalle was prone to spells of melancholy, but his spectacular boldness masked considerable skill in understanding ground and an instinctive judgement of when to charge. A few months after he appears in *Send Me Safely Back Again*, Lasalle was shot dead leading the pursuit of the Austrians at Wagram. He was thirty-four.

King Joseph Bonaparte was reluctantly made

King of Spain by his brother. A man of literary and liberal inclinations, he did his best to win popularity. Some Spanish welcomed him, and many of the higher posts in his regime were filled by Spanish aristocrats. In the end his efforts to consolidate his rule were thwarted by Napoleon's belief that his wider empire was simply a resource to be exploited for the benefit of France and his own ambitions, and also because the military situation was never brought fully under his control. As long as Spanish armies continued to resist, supported by the guerrillas and the regular forces of Britain and Portugal, then King Joseph could not feel secure. Many civilians who wished only for a peaceful life to go about their business and raise their families might well have come to accept Joseph's rule if his victory seemed certain.

Yet somehow, in spite of repeated French successes such as Medellín, the Spanish and their allies kept fighting. Spanish armies were routed time and again, only to reform in a matter of months and once again take the field. In the Peninsula the French proved unable to join their battlefield successes together. One reason was the difficulty of communication between corps operating considerable distances apart in country where couriers were often intercepted and killed unless given a strong escort. This encouraged the already pronounced tendency for each marshal or general to act independently – something already inherent in a military system designed to emphasise the Emperor and prevent the emergence of a rival. None of the marshals or generals respected Joseph as a commander, since his military experience was limited. They were equally reluctant to subordinate themselves to any of the other marshals for any length of time. The situation was made worse by Napoleon's frequent interference, issuing a stream of orders from far away. The overall plan for the 1809 campaign was drawn up by the Emperor as he was fighting the Austrians on the Danube. It was based on long-out-of-date information, and then took weeks to reach Joseph and his generals in Spain.

The French faced many difficulties which hindered their operations. Even so, and in spite of the renewal of war with Austria, large numbers of French soldiers remained in the Peninsula. Most of these men were veterans by now – even if they began their military service as reluctant conscripts. They were led by experienced officers at all levels, and commanded by generals and marshals all of whom had earned their rank through past achievements.

The same was not true of the Spanish. Badly neglected in the period before the war, the Spanish Army suffered a long succession of defeats and only one major success, at Bailén in 1808. Spanish losses were heavy, and included many of the professional soldiers from the old regular army. In spite of the disasters, the armies kept reforming, and new conscripts answered the demand of the authorities to present themselves for military service. Everything was short – equipment, uniforms, food and most of all money. There was also never enough time for training. In some ways the situation resembles the early years of the Second World War, when Allied armies with inferior tactics and equipment met their highly motivated and more skilful opponents. Often their generals were blamed for systemic failings beyond their control.

Don Gregorio de la Cuesta was scarcely one of history's great captains, but we should feel some sympathy for the difficulties he faced. There was simply neither time nor resources to make his army a match for the French. Yet it was vital to keep fighting, and that he did. It really was a miracle that he was able to take the field and join an Allied offensive so soon after the slaughter at Medellín. His reluctance to attack Victor on 23rd July surely led to his missing a great opportunity to overwhelm a single French corps, while his subsequent burst of aggression risked leading his own army to another disaster. Yet against that we should set his willingness to co-operate with the British in the first place, and the readiness with which Spanish troops were sent to support the British centre and to occupy the ground north of the Medellín Hill at Talavera.

Some of Cuesta's unpredictable and erratic behaviour was due to the Byzantine politics of the Spanish patriot cause. With government effectively decapitated by the French invasion, it proved difficult to rebuild it and create an authority capable of prosecuting the war effort. Regional juntas clashed repeatedly with the Central Junta, and at all levels factionalism was intense. Different parties and ideologies competed to shape the new Spain that would emerge from victory, and all too often ignored the fact that victory had yet to be won. There was serious talk of a general becoming dictator. Men like Cuesta believed with some justice that many of their fellow generals and subordinates were real or potential rivals. He clearly also saw Wellesley in the same light. To a degree he was right, for Wellesley did write to the British representative at the Central Junta expressing a hope that Cuesta would be replaced.

There is a tendency to see Wellesley as always the 'Iron Duke', from the very start the skilled diplomat and consummate general at the head of a superb army. With hindsight, Talavera becomes one of an almost inevitable sequence of successes, which in time would drive the French back across the Pyrenees. Wellington – as he became – won all the battles he fought, culminating in Waterloo, where the French 'came on in the same old style' and were defeated by the thin red lines of British infantry.

As is usually the case, reality was a good deal more complicated and there was little inevitable about his victory. In so many ways Talavera does not fit with the other battles of the first years of the war. It is important to remember that it was fought just a few days' march from Madrid, and that the Spanish capital was the objective of the campaign. Wellesley was on the offensive, much deeper into Spain than he would dare to venture again until 1812. All the more striking is the fact that he attempted this operation less than six months after Sir John Moore had found himself stranded deep in Spain following the defeat of the Spanish armies, and had been forced to retreat through the mountains and evacuate his men by sea.

There is a boldness about Wellesley's lightning attack on Soult at Oporto and the subsequent advance into Spain reminiscent of his years in India and his eagerness to close with the French in Portugal in 1808. There are also signs of inexperience. In 1809 Wellesley's army was almost twice the size of the force he had commanded at Vimeiro, and bigger than anything he had led in India. Neither the commander-in-chief nor his generals and their staffs had any experience of directing so large a force – unlike the French, by whose standards this was no more than a modestly sized *corps d'armée*. The divisions were new, formed in the course of the campaign, and not yet accustomed to working together.

Most of the battalions considered most ready for active service had marched with Moore, and few had yet recovered sufficiently from the rigours of that campaign to return to the Peninsula. Wellesley's army consisted largely of units left behind or recently arrived, and in many cases not yet accustomed to the local climate and conditions. More than half were second battalions, whose main role was supposed to be to feed recruits to the First Battalion of the regiment. Their soldiers tended to be less experienced and younger than the men of the first battalions. Large numbers had recently transferred from the militia, and many were indeed still carrying their old packs or wearing their militia uniforms when they fought at Talavera.

Signs of inexperience are not hard to find. On 27th July the troops at Casa de Salinas failed to post a proper piquet line and, as described in the story, several battalions broke when the French suddenly appeared. That night the KGL brigades were sent to the wrong place following a staff error, and when the mistake was discovered faced an aggravating extra march when they were already tired. Although this may explain why they repeated the same mistake and did not post piquets, it still does not excuse such sloppiness. The Medellín Hill was the key feature at Talavera, and yet its occupation was haphazard and incomplete. Major General Hill is usually blamed for this since his Second Division was supposed to hold the top of the feature. By his own admission he dined in town and only then went to check that his men were in place, arriving in time to run into the French attack. Hill would become Wellington's most trusted subordinate in the Peninsula and had already served in 1808 and in Moore's campaign.

Almost captured or killed as he rode to find out what was going on, Hill quickly got control of the situation.

Hill probably should have been on the Medellín supervising the deployment, and never repeated the mistake. Yet in the end Wellesley was the commanding general, and it was ultimately his responsibility to ensure that his instructions were carried out. As far as we can tell he remained with the Spanish throughout the evening, supervising the reorganisation after the panicked flight of the soldiers frightened by the noise of their own volley. It is entirely understandable that he wanted to be certain that his right flank was securely held, but even if he could not go in person it was a mistake that almost had serious consequences. The French attack came close to seizing the Medellín, and might well have succeeded if two out of the three regiments taking part had not got lost. The inattention of the generals also reveals a lack of experience among their staffs. All would learn from the near-disaster, and incidents like this no doubt reinforced Wellesley's tendency to do as much as he could personally.

Wellesley complained repeatedly about the indiscipline of his soldiers. Like Moore, he found them brave as lions in battle, but all too ready to plunder and misbehave on other occasions. At Talavera, eight battalions surged forward in reckless pursuit of the first wave of attacking French columns and were promptly chased back by their supports. A new line was formed only just in time to halt the French, until enough of the retreating troops rallied behind them. It was a tight thing. A good deal of the credit must go to Wellesley, who sent men down from the Medellín to plug the gaping hole in his line. As important was General MacKenzie, who moved his own brigade of his Third Division to shore up the right of the line. MacKenzie was killed in the fighting, and this probably explains why a weary Wellesley made little mention of his actions in his dispatch after the battle. The fictional 3rd Battalion of Detachments takes the place of the real (2/24)th Foot from MacKenzie's brigade throughout the Battle of Talavera. MacKenzie seems to have moved them first, positioning them behind the Guards in case they were driven back, before he began to bring up other troops. The 24th held the vital end of the line, suffering heavily as a result, so that by the end of the battle they were formed in just a single rank instead of the usual two.

The French ought to have won at Talavera. The Allies' plan had always been to keep the French armies apart so that each could be overwhelmed separately. They did not want to fight the combined strength of Victor, Sebastiani and King Joseph's reserve, and yet that is precisely what happened at Talavera. The Spanish Army was well emplaced on the right, but Wellesley's position was not a strong one. Unlike in his famous defensive battles, there was no ridge offering a reverse slope position, apart from along a small section of the Medellín Hill. Instead his battalions formed in an open plain, within view of the especially powerful French artillery. For hours these were able to pound the position. Ordering the battalions to lie down gave some protection, but scarcely made them safe. Although the British suffered some five thousand casualties against more than seven thousand suffered by the French, the British lost a significantly larger number of dead. This was doubtless a reflection of the number of men hit by cannon fire rather than the less lethal musket balls.

Most of the British losses were suffered by the infantry, and many of the battalions lost well over a third of their strength, and some even greater losses. Anson's brigade of light cavalry launched an exceptionally aggressive charge in the valley to the north of the Medellín Hill and lost large numbers of men and horses. It was tempting to include this dramatic episode in the story, but really it did not fit and it would have been difficult to involve any of the characters in something happening at the far end of the battlefield. We will probably see more of the cavalry's war in future stories.

The divided command which hampered the French throughout the Peninsular War probably made their attacks at Talavera less co-ordinated than should have been the case. A stronger, earlier effort to advance into the valley north of the

Medellín Hill combined with a frontal attack might well have proved very hard to resist. In the end, after one of the bloodiest encounters of the war, the French were repulsed and withdrew.

Strategically the French could claim a measure of success. King Joseph protected his capital. Had Wellesley continued his advance to face Soult, unaware that Ney and Mortier were with him, then it is hard to see how he could have avoided defeat. Such a defeat, following so close on the evacuation of Moore's army, might well have led to Britain abandoning the Peninsula. The Emperor Napoleon had already rightly concluded that the British Army was the single greatest factor in keeping the war going.

Fortunately, Wellesley was warned of the danger he was facing and withdrew in time. The French could not remain concentrated for very long, and soon dispersed. Although Joseph's capital was safe, the manoeuvres of the year meant that the French armies were not completing the conquest of Spain and consolidating the gains already made. In the longer term this helped Spanish armies to reform once again, and guerrilla bands to grow stronger.

In later years Wellington was very well informed about French dispositions and intentions. This was not true in 1809, with the result that the armies blundered around blindly, with little idea of the location of either enemy or allies. Both sides missed opportunities and had lucky escapes. Considerable effort was being devoted to creating a system for gathering and processing intelligence and topographic information, and Colonel Murray was heavily involved in this. Yet these were early days, and it took a long time for the system to function well. Like the rest of the army, these men were learning how to wage war against a tough and determined enemy well used to fighting on a grand scale. Apart from the personal trials and triumphs, this is at the heart of the story, as Hanley begins to find his niche in the army.

He and the others may be on their way home, but Wellington remained unbeaten at the end of 1809, and that meant that Britain's involvement in the Peninsula would continue. There are more stories to be told.

CAST OF CHARACTERS

Names underlined are fictional characters
TSG = True Soldier Gentlemen
BTDS = Beat the Drums Slowly

The 106th Regiment of Foot in the Peninsula

<u>Captain Billy PRINGLE</u> – Born into a family with a long tradition of service in the Royal Navy, Pringle's short-sightedness and severe seasickness led his father to send him to Oxford with a view to becoming a parson. Instead Pringle persuaded his parents to secure him a commission in the army. Plump, easy going and overfond of both drink and women, Pringle has found active service easier to deal with than the quiet routine and temptations of garrison duty in Britain. Through the battles in Portugal (*TSG*), and the arduous campaign in Spain (*BTDS*), Billy Pringle has won promotion and found himself easing into his role as a leader.

<u>Lieutenant William HANLEY</u> – Illegitimate son of an actress and a banker, Hanley was raised

492

by his grandmother and spent years in Madrid as an aspiring artist. His father's death ended his allowance, and reluctantly Hanley took up a commission in the 106th purchased for him many years before. He served in Portugal in 1808, suffering a wound at Roliça. Since then his fluency in Spanish has led to periodic staff duties. Even so, he was with Pringle and the Grenadier Company throughout the retreat to Corunna (*BTDS*).

Ensign Hamish WILLIAMS – Williams joined the 106th as a Gentleman Volunteer, serving in the ranks and soon proving himself to be a natural soldier. He was commissioned as ensign following the Battle of Vimeiro (*TSG*). During the retreat to Corunna, he became cut off from the main army. Rallying a band of stragglers, he not only led them back to the main force, but thwarted a French column attempting to outflank the British Army. He was praised by Sir John Moore for his actions, and was beside the general when the latter was mortally wounded at Corunna (*BTDS*). Fervently in love with Jane MacAndrews, Williams seems to find his cause continually thwarted by her unpredictability and his clumsiness.

Captain TRUSCOTT – A close friend of Pringle, Hanley and Williams, the slightly stiff-mannered Truscott was wounded at Vimeiro and suffered the loss of his arm (*TSG*). A slow recovery kept him from participating in the Corunna campaign. Since then he has taken charge of a party of the 106th left behind in Lisbon.

Corporal DOBSON – Veteran soldier who was Williams' 'front rank man' and took the volunteer under his wing. The relationship between Dobson and the young officers remains quietly paternal. However, at Roliça he displayed a ruthless streak when he killed an ensign who was having an affair with his daughter Jenny (*TSG*). Repeatedly promoted and broken for drunken misbehaviour, he has reformed following the accidental death of his first wife and his remarriage to the prim Mrs Rawson (*BTDS*).

Jenny DOBSON – Elder daughter from Dobson's first marriage, Jenny has ambitions beyond following the drum and flirted with and let herself be seduced by several of the young officers (*TSG*). During the winter she abandoned her newborn son to the care of Williams and Miss MacAndrews and left in search of a better life (*BTDS*).

Mrs DOBSON – Herself the widow of a sergeant in the Grenadier Company, the very proper Annie Rawson carried her lapdog in a basket throughout the retreat to Corunna. The marriage to Dobson has done much to reform his conduct (*BTDS*).

Corporal MURPHY – A capable soldier, Murphy and his wife suffered a dreadful blow when their child died during the retreat (*BTDS*).

Ensign HATCH – Lover of Jenny Dobson, the frequently drunk Hatch was a close friend of Ensign Redman, the officer Dobson murdered at Roliça. Hatch falsely believes that Williams was the killer.

Lieutenant HOPWOOD – Like many officers, Hopwood transferred to a regular battalion from the militia.

Ensign CLARKE – Another of the young officers of the 106th who served throughout the Portuguese and Spanish campaigns.

The 106th Regiment of Foot in England

Major MACANDREWS – Well into his forties, Alastair MacAndrews first saw service as a young ensign in the American War of Independence. A gifted and experienced soldier, his lack of connections and wealth has hindered his career. Raised to major after decades spent as a captain, he took charge of the 106th at Roliça, and led the battalion throughout the retreat to Corunna.

Mrs Esther MACANDREWS – American wife

of Major MacAndrews, Esther MacAndrews is a bold, unconventional character who has followed him to garrisons around the world. More recently, she managed to sneak out to Portugal, bringing her daughter with her.

Miss Jane MACANDREWS – Their daughter and sole surviving child, the beautiful Jane has a complicated relationship with Williams.

Lieutenant Colonel FITZWILLIAM – The new commander of the 106th, fresh from the Guards.

The British

Colonel Benjamin D'URBAN – British staff officer attached to the army in Portugal, but currently acting as observer with Cuesta's Spanish Army of Estremadura.

Mr BAYNES – A merchant with long experience of the Peninsula, now serving as an adviser and agent of the government.

Colonel Sir Robert WILSON – Commander of the Loyal Lusitanian Legion raised in London and Portugal, Wilson prosecutes a partisan war against the French. Enthusiastic and bold, he convinced the French that they were facing significantly higher numbers.

Corporal GORMAN – Light dragoon serving as cover-man to Sir Robert.

Captain James CHARLES, RA – Wilson's ADC.

Corporal EVANS – Redcoat left behind during the retreat to Corunna and now part of Wilson's private army.

Lieutenant Colonel PRITCHARD JONES, 24th Foot – Commander of the 3rd Battalion of Detachments.

Colonel MURRAY – As quartermaster-general, Murray served Wellesley in 1808, Sir John Moore in 1808–09, and returned with Wellesley in the spring of 1809. He contributed a great deal to making the headquarters of the army function, and in particular developing a far more effective system for the collection and processing of intelligence.

Lieutenant General Sir Arthur WELLESLEY – After several highly successful campaigns in India, Wellesley returned to Britain and several years of frustrated ambition before being given command of the expedition to Portugal. He managed to win the battles of Roliça and Vimeiro before being superseded. Along with his superiors, Wellesley was then recalled to Britain following the outrage at the Convention of Cintra, which permitted the defeated French to return home in British ships. Cleared of responsibility, Wellesley was given command in Portugal. The victory at Talavera would see him elevated to a peerage and the name Wellington.

Major General STEWART – Younger brother of Lord Castlereagh, the Secretary of State for War, Stewart managed to secure an appointment as Wellesley's adjutant-general. A cavalryman fond of ordering unwise charges, he displayed little interest in and less talent for the staff duties his post entailed.

Major General Rowland HILL – Already an experienced commander, 'Daddy' Hill would prove to be one of Wellington's ablest subordinates, and the only man regularly trusted with independent commands.

Major General MACKENZIE – MacKenzie commanded the Third Division. Shortage of general officers meant that he also continued to run his own brigade. MacKenzie played a distinguished part in the battle, but was killed in the process.

Colonel DONKIN – Formerly deputy quartermaster-general, he was given command of a brigade formed of two Irish battalions, the 2/87th and the 1/88th. This brigade joined MacKenzie's in the Third Division.

Lieutenant Colonel DONELLAN, 48th Foot – Donellan commanded the 1/48th. When the crisis came at Talavera, Wellesley sent him down to form a new line covering the gap left by the KGL brigades.

Lord PAGET – Eldest son of the Marquis of Anglesey, Lord Paget commanded the cavalry of Sir John Moore's army. However, following his elopement with Wellesley's sister-in-law, scandal would prevent any further service in the Peninsula.

General Edward PAGET – Younger brother of the above, he commanded the Reserve Division which acted as rearguard (*BTDS*). Returning to the Peninsula, he lost an arm at Oporto and was unable to resume active service for several years.

Captain GRANT, 42nd Foot – Original commander of the company in which Williams serves in the 3rd Battalion of Detachments.

Sergeant McNAUGHT, 42nd Foot – The senior soldier of a group from the 42nd Royal Highlanders serving in the same company.

Private PATTERSON, 42nd Foot – Private soldier in the same company.

Private SKERRET, 42nd Foot – Private soldier in the same company.

Sergeant RUDDEN, 43rd Foot – Senior soldier in a group from the 43rd Light Infantry serving in the same company.

The Spanish

Captain General Don Gregorio de la CUESTA – Well into his sixties at the time of the French invasion, Cuesta suffered a series of defeats at their hands. Although his judgement was often questionable, it is only fair to say that the forces at his disposal were poorly prepared and lacked every important resource. He seems to have suffered a stroke shortly after Talavera and retired.

Duke of ALBURQUERQUE – An ambitious subordinate, Alburquerque was enthusiastic about the British alliance and also keen to replace Cuesta at the head of the army. He achieved this aim after Cuesta's retirement. Political intrigues later saw him sent as ambassador to London.

Major Luiz VELARDE – One of Hanley's artistic circle from Madrid, now serving with Cuesta's army.

José Maria ESPINOSA – Another of Hanley's artistic circle, now working for Joseph Napoleon's regime.

Duke of ASTORGA – President of the central Junta, Astorga is a physically small man with a great sense of pomp and ceremony. His many critics have nicknamed him *rey chico* – the 'little King'.

PALAFOX – the hero of the first successful defence of Saragossa, Palafox has considerable political ambition.

La DOÑA MARGARITA de Madrigal de las Altas Torres – A widow recently returned from the New World. Her late husband was the heir to one of the great houses of Old Castile. The lady herself won acclaim as a heroine of the siege of Saragossa.

RAMÓN – Her servant, and a former hussar in her husband's regiment in the New World.

The French

General LASALLE – Dashing leader of French light cavalry. Although of aristocratic birth, Lasalle won fame and promotion during the Revolution and has since become a favourite of Napoleon. In 1806 he bluffed the Prussian garrison of the fortress of Stettin into surrendering to his lightly armed hussars. Since then he has fought the Russians and more recently the Spanish.

Marshal VICTOR, Duke of Belluno – Victor originally served in the ranks of the artillery, and then won rapid promotion during the Revolutionary Wars so that within three years he led an entire division. He has fought and beaten the Austrians, Prussians, Russians and recently the Spanish and is a capable, if extremely aggressive, commander.

General LEVAL – Commander of a division in Sebastiani's IV Corps, Leval leads a Dutch contingent and regiments from four of the small principalities of Germany.

KING JOSEPH Bonaparte – As Napoleon's elder brother, Joseph has reluctantly been moved from the comfort of his Kingdom in Naples to Spain, where he finds himself less welcome. A man of strong literary and philosophical tastes, he has done his best to win popularity. Recently he has lifted a ban imposed on bullfighting by the chief minister of his Spanish predecessor.

Chasseur LEBEQUE – A young conscript serving in a light infantry regiment, Lebeque happily undertakes the light duty of guarding the captive Hanley.

SOTERO – Spanish lawyer working for King Joseph – A Spaniard working for King Joseph,

Sotero does his best to convince his countrymen of the attractions of siding with the new regime.

General LAPISSE – Commander of the Second Division in Marshal Victor's I Corps, Lapisse has recently returned from skirmishing with Sir Robert Wilson on the Spanish–Portuguese border.

Marshal JOURDAN – As a young soldier, Jourdan served against the British in the American War of Independence. Now somewhat elderly for active service, he has been appointed as an experienced chief of staff to the Emperor's brother.

General SEBASTIANI – Like Napoleon himself, Sebastiani hailed from Corsica, and became closely associated with the future Emperor early on. In his career he has mixed diplomatic with military posts, but has proved a capable if unexceptional soldier.

The Portuguese

MARIA – High-class courtesan. In the summer of 1808 she inveigled Pringle, Truscott, Hanley, Williams and Dobson into a dangerous encounter with a rogue Russian officer.